JAN 1 1 2019

To Trust a Rogue
Heart of a Duke Series

For more information about the author:
www.christicaldwellauthor.com
christicaldwellauthor@gmail.com
Twitter: @ChristiCaldwell
Or on Facebook at: Christi Caldwell Author

For first glimpse at covers, excerpts, and free bonus material, be sure to sign up for my monthly newsletter!
Printed in the USA.

Cover Design and Interior Format

To Trust a Rogue

Heart
of a
Duke

THE
SERIES

USA TODAY BESTSELLER
CHRISTI CALDWELL ©

OTHER TITLES BY
CHRISTI CALDWELL

THE HEART OF A SCANDAL
In Need of a Knight—Prequel Novella
Schooling the Duke
Heart of a Duke
In Need of a Duke—Prequel Novella
For Love of the Duke
More than a Duke
The Love of a Rogue
Loved by a Duke
To Love a Lord
The Heart of a Scoundrel
To Wed His Christmas Lady
To Trust a Rogue
The Lure of a Rake
To Woo a Widow

LORDS OF HONOR
Seduced by a Lady's Heart
Captivated by a Lady's Charm
Rescued by a Lady's Love
Tempted by a Lady's Smile

SCANDALOUS SEASONS
Forever Betrothed, Never the Bride
Never Courted, Suddenly Wed
Always Proper, Suddenly Scandalous
Always a Rogue, Forever Her Love
A Marquess for Christmas
Once a Wallflower, at Last His Love

SINFUL BRIDES
The Rogue's Wager
The Scoundrel's Honor

THE THEODOSIA SWORD
Only for His Lady

DANBY
A Season of Hope
Winning a Lady's Heart

BRETHREN OF THE LORDS
My Lady of Deception
Memoir: Non-Fiction
Uninterrupted Joy

DEDICATION

I did not always write stories with imperfect heroes and heroines. After my son's birth, after I learned of his diagnosis of Down syndrome, it shaped the way I looked at everything: who I was as a person, what the word 'perfect' truly means, and the strength that comes from the trials and tribulations presented by life.

This story is dedicated to every individual who has braved what life has thrown at you, and came out on the other side to find happiness and greater strength. And if you are still clawing for that 'other side'...believe you'll get there.

Eleanor and Marcus' story, is for you.

CHAPTER 1

London, England
Spring, 1818

MARCUS GRAY, THE VISCOUNT WESSEX, had been betrayed by his mother.

Oh, it was not the *first* time he'd been so horribly deceived by a woman. It was just the first time that the woman who'd given him life had been guilty of that crime.

Marcus skimmed the front page of *The Times*, where it appeared the most pressing, important news and gossip members of the *ton* now woke to this day, pertained to two nonconsecutive dances he'd danced with Lady Marianne Hamilton and what that indicated for his marital state. He glanced up from the page and found his mother at the opposite end of the breakfast table, smiling as she buttered a piece of bread.

"You did state your intentions," she said, not taking her gaze from that well-buttered piece.

Marcus narrowed his eyes. "To *you*. I suspected, as such, that information was, at the very least, safe from gossips."

He caught the eye of his sister Lizzie. She gave him a do-you-really-not-know-our-mother-look?

"Come, Marcus, you are thirty. It is hardly a shock to Society that you are in the market for a wife," his mother chided.

"I told you," his sister's whispered words reached his ears. She popped a bite of sausage into her mouth.

Their mother eyed her flaky bread in a studious manner, gave a pleased nod, and dismissively returned to eating her breakfast. As though she'd not chattered his plans to at last fulfill his obligations to Lady Jersey and, through that indiscretion, to *all* of Society.

Marcus tossed down the paper and it hit the table with a soft thump. "I assured you I would see to my marital responsibilities in the near future." Never had he indicated an immediacy to those intentions. "Did you fear I'd change my mind?"

Reaching for her cup of tea, his mother paused mid-movement and then gracefully picked up the delicate porcelain cup. "Yes, yes I did."

With a growl of annoyance, Marcus grabbed his cup of coffee. His empty cup. A servant rushed over and filled it to the brim with the steaming, black brew.

Interrupting his murmured thanks, his sister leaned over and spoke in hushed tones. "Am I a horribly disloyal sister for being grateful that Mother's intentions have been securely settled on your marital aspirations?"

"Yes, the worst." To temper that lie, he leaned over and ruffled the top of her head. He didn't bother to point out that he didn't truly have marital aspirations that existed beyond a coldly emotionless bride who'd be content with the title viscountess and a rogue for a husband. Such a woman would fail to rouse grand passions and drive him to a maddening inability to think of any other.

On the heel of that flitted in a face from his past; the first woman to betray him. He tightened his mouth. That particular lady had been anything but dull and polite. Mayhap the title of viscountess had never been enough for that one. Marcus stared within the contents of his cup. Then, all these years later, there was still no knowing. The lady hadn't felt leaving after those fleeting, but meaningful to him months, merited much of an explanation.

Lizzie smiled. "I am ever so happy that you've selected Marianne as your future viscountess."

Selected Marianne? His mind muddied from thoughts of the past, it took a moment for Lizzie's words to register. In an unlikely pairing, Lady Marianne Hamilton had attached herself to his marriage-avoidant, wallflower by choice, sister.

Lady Marianne, The Incomparable of the Season, was lush, with sultry smiles, and rumored to be in the market for a *wealthy* husband. A marriage to that one would be about lust, power, and not the dangerous emotion called love that had nearly destroyed Marcus eight years earlier. Yes, Lady Marianne fit the proverbial bill in terms of his future viscountess. Nonetheless, his palms grew moist at the prospect of forever binding himself to one woman. Even if that fate was inevitable. His mother and sister proceeded to casually indulge in their morning meals while they flippantly discussed his future. He gave a tug at his suddenly too-tight cravat. Lest his sister believe his intentions for her friend were already decided, he pointed out, "I've hardly *selected* Lady Marianne for my future bride." He'd indicated an interest in the lady, but he'd not selected her. Not yet.

Lizzie froze with the fork midway to her mouth. "You danced with her, Marcus." She set the silver utensil down and gave him a meaningful look. "Twice."

"They were nonconsecutive," he felt inclined to point out.

Then like the veriest determined matchmaker, Lizzie proceeded to tick off on her fingers. "She comes from a respectable family." It wouldn't do to point out to his innocent sister that Lady Marianne's brother was a letch in dun territory that no respectable mama would see their daughter wed—even with his marquisate as a prize. The man was now reliant upon his sister to make a match and save his finances. A flash of pity filled him at the lady's unfortunate connections. "She is kind and clever and exceedingly lovely." With midnight black hair and a generously curved figure, Lady Marianne was unlike most of the porcelain, golden-haired ladies of Society. The perfect counterpart to those blonde English misses.

Say, a Miss Eleanor Carlyle, that temptress from long ago with sun-kissed hair and too-full lips. The woman who'd won his heart, and broken it, in short order.

Yes, midnight hair would be preferable—

His sister clapped her hands once. "Do attend me."

Marcus thrust memories of Eleanor to the furthest recesses of his mind. "Forgive me." He inclined his head. "You were saying?"

Lizzie let out a beleaguered sigh, and continued. "You are in want of a wife. She is in need of a husband." Ah, so his sister *did* know of the dismal financial circumstances her friend's family faced. Lizzie beamed. "Isn't that how most wonderful, romantic tales begin?"

"I would not know," he said, droll humor creeping into his tone. "I'm not in the habit of reading your gothic tales of forbidden love." He'd tried love in real life once and that foray had proven a remarkable disaster.

Lizzie gave a roll of her eyes. "It is not *always* forbidden love." She brightened. "Why, more often, it is a wealthy duke and an impoverished young lady coming together and finding love. Why, what is a more romantic match than that?"

"Indeed," he drawled.

Lizzie swatted his arm.

Pointedly ignoring her daughter, Mother turned her attention to Marcus. She folded her hands primly before her and spoke like all the tutors she'd personally hired for him through the years. "I do not merely want my children to make a *suitable* match, though I do. I care for you to make a *love* match."

His sister was nothing if not tenacious. "Oh, he could very easily love Marianne."

He scrubbed his hands over his face. He'd not disabuse his romantic sister of her naïve notions. After Eleanor's betrayal, he'd learned the perils of trusting his heart to a woman. No, when he ultimately married, it would not be because any emotion was involved—which was why Lady Marianne represented the ideal match. Emotionally aloof, she seduced with her eyes, and revealed a jadedness that matched his own. He could easily imagine that temptress in his bed, but there was little risk of his heart being involved.

"Oh, do stop scowling, Marcus," his mother said patting her mouth with a crisp white napkin, bringing him back to the present. "You'll hardly catch any young lady with that terrible glower."

He sat back in his chair and propped his elbows on the arms. "Oh, and are there young ladies expected or hiding even now in this house who I need worry about at this given moment?" he drawled.

His mother promptly choked.

He narrowed his eyes. "Mother?"

"Do not be silly," she squawked and in an entirely un-viscountess like move, she shoveled a heaping pile of eggs into her mouth.

"She is lying," his sister said under her breath.

Marcus cast a glance over at his sister.

"But as long as she is parading ladies before you, I needn't worry of her parading prospective bridegrooms before me."

Temporarily distracted from his own impending dire situation, he gave Lizzie a wry grin. For the almost twelve years between them, they'd always been remarkably of like thought where their mother was concerned. It appeared those likenesses extended to the realm of marriage. "Never tell me you are the only lady in the kingdom to not want a husband," he said from the corner of his mouth.

"Very well, then I shan't tell you." Lizzie grinned.

"What are you two whispering about?"

Brother and sister spoke in unison. "Nothing."

His mother muttered something under her breath about the woes of being a poor mama to troublesome children. Fighting a grin, Marcus took another swallow of the contents of his glass. As annoyed as he was with her for sharing his marital plans with the whole of the *ton*, she was a good mother determined to see him happy. As such, it was hard to—

"All children require a bit of guidance on the path to marital bliss," the viscountess persisted.

Marcus promptly spit out his brew. At his side, Lizzie's slender frame shook with mirth and servants rushed forward with cloths to clean the mess. "M-marital bliss?" he sputtered. Good god, is that what she would call it?

"Marcus," his mother scolded. "Oh, do not look at me like that, Marcus. I daresay I prefer you charming to bitter."

Scolding, she was always scolding. Since he'd been a boy of three pilfering pastries from the kitchen to a man of thirty. "You know it is my expectation that you'll find a young woman who makes your heart happy."

He sighed. Even when he'd stated his intentions to wed. No, one could never please a mother. "I will tell you clearly what would make my heart happy," he mumbled.

His sister snorted and then at their mother's pointed stare, promptly buried the sound into her palm. Perhaps she would be suitably distracted by mention of Lizzie's unwed state.

"Must you be so cynical?" the viscountess scolded. Again.

Marcus swallowed back the bitter rejoinder on his lips. He'd not discuss the reasons for his cynicism before his mother, his sister, or anyone. No. No one knew the foolish mistakes of his past and the reasons he'd no intentions of trusting his heart to a headstrong, passionate lady—not again. "I am a rogue," he said instead, managing his patented half-grin. Yes, he'd been the rogue for so many years. So many that he no longer knew any other way, nor did he care to.

"You are hopeless," his mother sighed. "Surely you've a desire to know even a dash of the love your father and I knew."

He'd not so shatter her with the truth. The last thing he desired was love. "I've a desire to visit my clubs," he said with a wink.

Lizzie's lips twitched. "I do wish I had clubs to visit." She let out a beleaguered sigh. "Alas, there is no escape for an unwed, eighteen-year-old lady." From behind her wire-rimmed spectacles, a flash of regret lit her eyes.

A twinge of guilt needled him. He didn't need to read the gossip columns or attend all the *ton* functions to know his sister's Come Out had been a rather dismal showing. For her earlier protestations on marriage, he'd wager all his holdings as viscount that his painfully shy in public sister's viewpoint was a mere façade; a means to protect.

Then, weren't they all protecting themselves, one way or another?

"They're all a bunch of foolish arses," he said quietly. "You're better off without most of them."

Lizzie laughed. "Just most of them?"

"All of them," he replied with an automaticity born of truth.

Swatting his arm, Lizzie gave another roll of her eyes. "Oh, do not look at me. I would far rather be attending your marital prospects."

"Yes, Marcus," their mother called out, tapping the table. "Let us do attend your marital prospects."

He winced. Bloody infernal perfect hearing. She would have impressed a bat with that heightened sense.

"Sorry," his sister mouthed once more.

He waved off the apology, finished his drink and then set his cup down with a hard thunk. "I am attending my marital duties," he said matter-of-factly. "I have stated my intentions to wed and do right by the Wessex line. You will have your nursery of little future heirs and spares running about."

His sister gave him a pointed frown.

"And troublesome sisters to those heirs and spares," he added with a half-grin.

Lizzie laughed and shook her head. "No wonder you are the charmer throughout." Then with an implacable look in her eyes, she settled her elbows on the table and leaned forward. "As for Marianne…"

Oh, bloody hell. The last thing he cared for or required was Lizzie's interference. "I do not need—"

Their mother banged her fist on the table. "Lizzie, that will be all. Marcus," she turned to him. "I see you require my further help."

"Your further help?" Marcus winged an eyebrow up.

Lizzie scooped up the forgotten copy of *The Times* and waved it about. "I believe she references her sharing of your marital intentions."

Their mother nodded. "Indeed, Lizzie," she said with the same pride she might reserve a child who'd solved a complicated riddle. "For which you still haven't thanked me, Marcus."

Ah, yes. Of course. "Yes, well, there is no surer way to assure a love match than to bandy about my fifty thousand pound worth," he said dryly. He inclined his head. "Thank you." *For making every last lady in the realm know I'm in the market for a wife. For single-handedly shifting all the desperate matchmaking mamas' consideration to me.*

She fluffed her hair. "You are quite welcome."

He consulted his timepiece and gave silent thanks for his previously scheduled meeting with his longtime friend, the Duke of Crawford. Marcus shoved back his chair. "If you'll excuse me," he said, hopping to his feet.

The viscountess let out a startled shriek. "Wherever are you going?"

He stifled a shudder. Goodness, it was moments such as these that made him long for the bachelor suites at his clubs. "I am going to my clubs," he reminded her. As though following his unspoken thoughts, Lizzie gave him a don't-you-dare-abandon-me-with-her look. "I am meeting Crawford at White's." Any other moment, a meeting with the illustrious, powerful, and entirely proper Duke of Crawford would have appeased his mother.

"Today?"

Not on this day.

"But…"

Which could only indicate… "Surely not…"

She had prospective future brides assembled and ready for a morning visit.

"Surely," he said quickly. "Business to discuss. The estates. Investments." Anything. Everything. As long as it wasn't Marcus' impending marriage, to an as of yet unselected young lady.

"Do promise you'll attend The Duchess' dinner party next week."

Those words froze him mid-movement. Blast, damn, and bloody hell. He'd quite forgotten the Duchess of Devonshire's annual, intimate, dinner party. His mother's lifelong friend who also happened to be Eleanor Carlyle's aunt. "Er…"

His mother's mouth fell agape. "You forgot." She slapped an indignant hand to her chest.

"I…" Forgot. *Put it from my mind*, just as he did every year, all things and anything, including *anyone* connected with Eleanor.

"He forgot," his sister supplied unhelpfully for him.

Marcus yanked at his cravat. "I had other plans for that evening." Plans, which included avoiding that blasted garish, pink townhouse. Just as he did. Every year.

He made to go when his mother called out in a panicky voice, staying him.

"Marcus," she said with a smile he'd learned long ago to be leery of. She clasped her hands in front of her. "Promise me you'll be there."

He rolled his shoulders. God, she was more tenacious than she'd been in the past five years combined of his avoiding the infernal dinner event. "I will try," he hedged.

By the narrowing of his mother's eyes, she detected his deliberate attempt at evasion.

His sister whipped her head back and forth between them, taking in the volley-like quality of the exchange.

Mother pounced. "At the very least, stay for this morning's visit—"

"If you'll excuse me?" He paused. "Again." Ignoring his mother's sputtering, Marcus sketched a quick bow, gave his sister a commiserative wink, and then hurried from the room, with a speed the god, Hermes, would have been impressed with. He moved with a single-minded purpose through the halls, boot steps muted on the carpeted, corridor floors.

He'd convinced himself that in simply assuring his mother he'd see to his responsibilities as viscount that she would have been as appeased as any other proper English mama in the kingdom. He gave his head a wry shake. He should have known better where the lady was concerned. After thirty years of sorting through his mother's peculiarly blended romantic spirit with her English peer's sense of obligations, it was his mistake. He made a sound of disgust. A mistake, that by the front of *The Times* and every other gossip column, would prove a damaging one.

Marcus turned the corridor and collided with a voluptuous figure. The young lady stumbled back on a gasp and that abrupt movement sent several midnight curls spilling over her shoulder. He shot his hands out and steadied her. "Lady Marianne," he said politely. The lady whose Come Out had been delayed by the death of first her father and then her mother had taken Society by storm and for very obvious reasons. "Forgive me." She possessed a dark, wickedly suggestive smile that set her apart from the other debutantes.

"Lord Wessex." Lady Marianne spoke in beguiling tones better reserved for skilled courtesans and not just out on the market debutantes. She collected those two loose tresses and toyed with them. "I could forgive you anything."

Unbidden, he dropped his gaze lower, lower to the generous cream white mounds spilling over the top of her dress. Marcus swallowed hard. No respectable miss had a place wearing such a gown. And no respectable gentleman had a place studying her so. Yet, this woman who exuded sexuality and tempted with her lips and eyes, bore no traces to the long-ago innocent who'd betrayed him.

He hardened his heart and appreciated Lady Marianne with renewed interest; for with her seductive offer and veiled words, she was still more sincere than the last lady he'd ever trusted. Marcus picked his gaze up.

By the narrowing of her cat-like eyes and her suggestive smile, Lady Marianne thrilled at his notice.

"If you'll excuse me." He dropped a bow and made to leave.

"Lord Wessex," she called after him in sultry, inviting tones that brought him slowly around. The lady fingered the trim of her bodice. He gulped. "I have heard splendorous things of your secret garden and would very much welcome a tour about the grounds with you."

He'd not met another lady in a garden after Eleanor. Nor did he intend to. The memories of her were too potent in those floral havens. "Perhaps another time," he managed, his voice garbled. Spinning on his heel, he continued his retreat. As he entered the foyer, he shot a glance back to see if the determined seductress followed.

His butler, Williston, strode to meet him. "Your mount is readied." The ghost of a smile played on his wrinkled cheeks, indicating that word had, no doubt, traveled about the viscountess' impending visitors.

"I am doubling your wages, Williston," he muttered.

A footman rushed over with Marcus' hat and cloak. With murmured thanks, Marcus jammed the black Aylesbury hat atop his head. "Good man, Williston," he said, shooting a glance over his shoulder as he shrugged into his cloak. No doubt, the ladies lined up by his determined mother would be arriving…

"Any moment, Lady Elliot is to arrive." Williston paused and gave him a pointed look. "With her *daughter*, my lord."

Marcus inclined his head. The man was worth more than all the king's staff at the Home Office, in his ability to ferret out information. "Good day, Williston."

A twinkle glinted in the older servant's eyes. "The same to you, my lord." He sketched a bow and then walked to the door with an ease possessed of a butler thirty years younger and pulled it open.

Hurrying outside, Marcus bound down the steps. When presented with one's pestering mama, a gentleman had little choice but to retreat.

At one time, he'd been unable to glimpse the neighboring ridiculously pink façade of the townhouse adjoining his own. He accepted the reins from a waiting groom and then effortlessly mounted his horse. Somewhere along the way, on his path to becoming a rogue, that pink façade had tortured him less and less, so that all the old hurts and regrets and fury had faded enough that he could move through life with a practiced grin and not as the heartbroken, shattered fool he'd been in the immediate aftermath of Eleanor's parting. Marcus nudged his mount, Honor, onward through the crowded cobbled streets of London.

How easy it would have been to let her betrayal destroy him. Though he would never again be the trusting man of his youth, he'd carved a new existence for himself without Eleanor in it. As Marcus rode, he lifted his head in greeting to passersby. Aside from his mother and sister, he took care to not love, to trust few, and to always be the blithe charmer Society saw him as. Life was safer that way.

Marcus brought his horse to a stop outside the hallowed walls of White's. He quickly dismounted and tossed the reins to a waiting servant. As he strode up the handful of steps, the door was thrown open and he stepped inside. Lifting his head in greeting to the patrons who called out, Marcus hurried to his table. A servant immediately rushed over with a bottle of brandy and a snifter. With murmured thanks, Marcus waved him off and proceeded to pour his glass to the brim. He took a long swallow and swirled the contents of his drink.

Today was very nearly the anniversary of their first meeting. Is that why Eleanor Carlyle owned his thoughts this day?

His lips pulled in a grimace. What a pathetic moment of one's life to commemorate year after year. In a world in which he'd come to appreciate, expect, and demonstrate order, the nonsensical habit of marking the day he'd met Miss Eleanor Carlyle was perhaps the antithesis of everything he valued in terms of order. Their meeting, in the real scheme of life, had been nothing more than a mere two months...just sixty days, one-thousand four-hundred and forty hours. When a gentleman was approaching his thirty-first year, why, the span of time he'd known Eleanor was insignificant. Yet, there was no explaining the heart.

"With that scowl, are you sure you are desiring company?"

He stiffened and glanced up at his closest, only living friend in the world. Auric, the Duke of Crawford, stood impeccably cool and perfectly ducal, as he'd been since the day their friend, Lionel, had met his end. Marcus jerked his chin to the opposite chair.

Wordlessly, Crawford slid into the vacant seat, waving off the bottle Marcus held out as an offering. "No," he declined. Instead, he sat there and drummed his fingertips on the immaculate, smooth surface of the mahogany table. "A bit early for brandy."

"Is it?" Marcus took a sip to demonstrate his thoughts on Auric's opinion on drinking spirits in the morning. To stem the argument on the other man's proper lips, he used the best diversionary topic at hand. "How is Daisy?" Formerly Lady Daisy Meadows, now Duchess of Crawford, the young lady was also the only sister to their now dead friend, Lionel.

Just like that, the hard, austere lines of the other man's usually unflappable face softened, demonstrating a warmth he'd never imagined Crawford capable of. "She is well," he said quietly. He glanced about as though ascertaining their business was their own and then looked to Marcus. "She is expecting."

Marcus stared blankly at him. "Expecting what?"

A dull flush marred Crawford's cheeks. "A child. We will be retiring for the country within the next fortnight."

Another child? The couples' first babe, a girl, Lionella, was just one. Despite himself, a vicious envy cloyed at Marcus' insides; it ripped at him like a thousand rusty blades twisting inside. For, if life had proceeded along a different path, even now he'd be a father to some, no doubt, precocious child. And if he were honest to himself in this instance, with Crawford's revelation laid out before him, Marcus could acknowledge—he wanted to be a father. Not the aloof, distant noblemen who turned a son's care over to stern nursemaids and tutors, but rather the manner of sire his own father had been. A man who personally taught Marcus how to ride and shoot. A man who'd bloody senseless anyone who dared hurt his children and who loved them fiercely.

Crawford stared expectantly at him and Marcus cleared his throat. "Congratulations." He forced a smile. "I am happy for the both of you." He toasted Crawford with his glass.

His friend trained a familiar ducal frown on Marcus' nearly empty snifter.

Likely, his friend saw the same indolent, bored lord as the rest of Society, more interested in spirits and cards than in the happiness of his friend. In truth, Marcus would slice off his smallest fingers to have a family of his own and, through them, a purpose in the efforts he put into running his estates. Oh, he'd never begrudge Crawford and Daisy their deserved joy. With the heartache of loss they'd known in Daisy's brother, no people were more deserving of happiness. Marcus passed his glass back and forth between his hands, eying the still unfinished amber contents within the snifter.

Some of the tension ebbed from Crawford's shoulders. "I understand congratulations are in order." The ghost of a smile played on the other man's lips.

Marcus looked at him quizzically. What was he on about?

"*The Times*, and your," he winged an eyebrow up, "intentions toward a particular lady."

Of course the *ton* would remark upon his declarative interest in the ladies. "Bugger off," Marcus complained. "Two dances hardly constitute an offer of marriage." Rather, it constituted a desire to possibly pursue more with a lady. He proceeded to pour his snifter full and then took a sip.

"Ah, so it is merely gossip then," Crawford said, his tone more matter-of-fact, always the coolly analytical of their unlikely pair.

"It is certainly gossip," Marcus said with droll humor, taking another swallow. It just wasn't necessarily *untrue* gossip.

Crawford reclined in his chair and continued to study Marcus in that assessing manner. Unable to meet his friend's probing stare, he absently skimmed his gaze over the club. "Daisy wished me to inquire as to whether the gossip is true." Ah, Daisy, the consummate romantic. Was every blasted body in the whole of England a romantic spirit? Even Crawford, now?

Marcus chuckled at the other man's bluntness. Then, when one was a duke just a step shy of royalty, there really was no need to prevaricate. He gave his head a despairing shake. "I've no immediate plans." He smiled wryly. "Despite my mother's best machinations." After all, with a lifelong friendship and a bond built on unimaginable tragedy—the murder of their best friend—he at least owed Crawford *that* truth.

Crawford studied him across the table in that very ducal manner so that all he was missing was the monocle, and then he gave a slow nod. "My wife wants your assurance that you'll settle for nothing other than a love-match.

And Marcus, once more, promptly choked. By God, between his mother and his best friend's words this day, they were going to drown him. He lifted his glass in salute. "Assure our girl of the flowers that I am grateful for her concern." Marcus gave his shoulders a roll. "When I do wed, however, it will be for the same reason every young nobleman inevitably marries." *Or will it be when I've finally let go of the past?* He gave his drink another slow swirl. "I'll wed a proper lady," like Lady Marianne. "And produce the requisite heir and a spare, and then the Wessex line is secure, while I'm free to carry on as all the other peers present."

Silence met his response and he looked up to find Crawford's pitying stare on him. Marcus' neck heated and his fingers twitched with the urge to tug at his cravat. When Crawford at last spoke, he did so in hushed tones. "Surely you want more than that?"

"No," he said with an automaticity born of truth. "I surely do not." He flexed one of his hands. "I'm quite content just as I am." Marcus downed the contents of his glass. No, he'd tried love once before and the experience was as palatable as a plate of rancid kippers. "Though I applaud you and Daisy for finding that very special sentiment."

Alas, after Eleanor's deception, he'd never been able to fully erase the bitter tinge in his words when speaking of love and romance, and any other foolish sentiment that schemer had ultimately killed.

Marcus skimmed his gaze over the crowd. Several affirmed bachelors tipped their heads in a conciliatory manner. No doubt, they saw another member of their respected club prepared to willingly fall. He sighed. Except after years of visiting scandalous clubs and carrying on with paramours, courtesans, and widows, he was quite…tired of it all. Oh, he'd never admit as much. To do so would hopelessly ruin his name as rogue. But it had begun to feel as if he moved through life with a dull tedium, with a restlessness that dogged him.

Not that he expected a wife to cure him of that boredom. But that woman would serve a perfunctory purpose that went with his title.

Crawford's frown deepened and he shifted. No doubt his desire to make sense of Marcus' reasoning was born of years and years of being a duke beholden to no one. His friend's chair groaned in protest as he settled his arms on the table and leaned forward. "I do not doubt you will find a woman who will value you as you deserve." A woman like Lady Marianne who *valued* his fortune and title. How very empty such an existence would be and yet far better than this hell Eleanor Carlyle had left him in. Crawford cleared his throat. "A woman who will also help you…forget…" *Forget.*

Crawford spoke of a world of hurts that existed beyond Eleanor. For not a soul *truly* knew of the two fleeting months of madness and his subsequent broken heart following the lady's betrayal. Even his mother, who'd celebrated in their whirlwind courtship, didn't know the extent of the hole left in his heart with Eleanor's parting.

Unnerved by the fresh remembrance of Eleanor Carlyle, Marcus shoved lazily to his feet. "If you'll excuse me? I have matters of business to see to." It was quite enough having to deal with a mother spouting of love and dying devotion of a worthy lady, that he didn't really require it from his closest friend, too.

"Oh?" Crawford drawled and in a manner befitting the once grinning, mischievous youth he'd been before life and loss had shaped him, he tipped back on the heels of his chair. "The whole wife-hunting business?"

He made a crude gesture that roused a chuckle from his friend. Marcus tempered that rudeness with a grin and then started back through the clubs with his patented smile firmly in place.

It would seem when a nobleman demonstrated interest in a lady, it signaled his intentions to wed, and there really was no escaping that news anywhere.

CHAPTER 2

SHE'D VOWED TO NEVER RETURN.

Mrs. Eleanor Collins gazed out the carriage window at the passing streets. Her spectacles lay forgotten on her lap and she fiddled with the wire frames. The carriage hit another bump on the cobbled road and threw her against the side of the conveyance. The sudden movement sent her glasses tumbling to the floor. Eleanor quickly righted herself and, for now, left that small, but important-to-her disguise, piece forgotten at her feet.

She'd vowed she would die before setting foot in the cruel, cold, and hateful world of London. Nor had those words been the over-dramatic ones of a young, naïve miss. It had been a pledge she'd *taken* as a young, naïve miss who'd seen the malevolent side of that town and knew there was nothing worth reentering that darkness for. Not when the risk was having the remainder of her soul consumed by ugly memories.

Until life had ultimately shown her that there, indeed, was something worth braving anything and everything for.

"Mama, your glasses."

Eleanor turned her attention to the small, golden-curled girl who held her spectacles in her small, delicate fingers. At just seven, Marcia was that something. That person she'd sacrifice anything and everything for. Including her sanity. Managing her first real smile that day, Eleanor accepted the wire-rims and placed them on her face. "Why, thank you."

"Are we almost there?" Excitement tinged her daughter's words.

She'd once shared this same eagerness to leave the countryside and enter the glittering metropolis. What a naïve fool she'd been. Her smile fell. "We are, love." *Unfortunately.* "Almost, there," she murmured, throwing her arm around her daughter's small shoulders and bringing the girl close to her side. Eleanor dug deep for strength.

"Ouch, you are squishing me."

Tamping down the nervousness churning in her belly, Eleanor forced herself to lighten her grip. "It's because you're so very squishable."

Marcia giggled. "Is it because you are excited?"

The familiar stone in her belly, formed somewhere between her father's death, her aunt's missive, and the arrival of the Duchess of Devonshire's carriage, tightened. "Oh, indeed," she managed at last.

A spirited glimmer lit Marcia's eyes. "I am ever so excited, too, Mama."

Regret tightened in her chest. "Did you not wish to remain in Cornwall?" Hadn't Eleanor, with her late father's guidance, carved a life that her daughter found joy in?

Marcia pumped her little legs back and forth. "Not forever, silly."

With a sigh, she absently stroked the top of her daughter's soft crown of curls. Yes, there had been a time when the thrill of the unknown had taken hold of her. She'd been full of fairy tales and dreams of magic and mystery and intrigue. Her heart tightened. And for a brief, very brief, moment, she'd known the joy that came from that grand adventure. His grinning visage flashed to her mind's eye, as it sometimes did. Eleanor pressed her eyes closed and did not thrust the memory of him away, as she often did. This time, she accepted the memory of Marcus, the Viscount Wessex, and let it wash over her with a familiarity born of yesterday, even with the passage of time.

He'd been her dream. He'd been the joy and the excitement. And in one shattered evening, nothing more of him remained… but the memory. Unease churned in her belly. By the very nature of his family's connection to her aunt and his residence alone, the risk of meeting was great. As such, the reality of that brought thoughts of him back with a shocking frequency…and when the first missive had come from her aunt, Eleanor had allowed herself an infinitesimal moment of hope—the hope of seeing him.

Her gaze trained unseeingly upon the carriage bench opposite her, she let open the gates she'd constructed to keep him out. Since their parting, she'd become a woman who confronted life with frankness. So it was the honesty she insisted upon that she acknowledged the truth—she missed him. And she always would. Nor was it just the memory of innocence she'd known in their time together. She missed what could have been. His smile. His laugh. Who they'd been when in each other's company.

Marcia tugged at her fingers and she glanced down distractedly. "What is it, dear?"

"Are you thinking of Grandfather?" Wide brown eyes stared back at Eleanor.

Sadness stuck her hard for altogether different reasons. "I always think of Grandfather," she murmured noncommittally, and it was true. Gone just six months now, there was no better father, nor could there ever have been a better man than he was while living.

"Someday you'll meet again," Marcia said with entirely too much maturity for a child of seven. "He promised we would and he would never, ever lie, Mama. So don't be sad." She laid her head against Eleanor's arm. "And remember what he said. 'Goodbyes are not forever.'"

They are just temporary partings.

Marcus' visage flashed behind her eyes. Once more. Perhaps it was her return to London, a land they'd lived in together, back when she'd been innocent and smiling and he'd needed laughter, but she could not extricate the thoughts of him from her now. Nor had that goodbye been temporary. The day she'd boarded her aunt's carriage and made her return to Kent, unchaperoned, alone, and broken, she'd known with an absolute certainty, for all her father's beliefs on goodbyes, the final one between her and Marcus had, indeed, been a forever goodbye.

And she wagered for the love she carried of him still in her heart, he would feel no such fondness for the woman who'd broken his heart.

"We're here."

"Hmm?" She blinked and then glanced about before her daughter's words truly registered. Her heart dipped somewhere to her toes and she plastered a smile onto her face, fearing the forced grin would shatter and reveal her a charlatan once more.

Married war widow. Grand lie.

Smiling, oft-happy mother. Sometimes a lie.

Thrilled to return to London. Absolute lie.

Seeming unaware of the tumult raging through Eleanor, Marcia bounced up and down on her seat, clapping her hands together excitedly. "Oh, Mama, it is to be the grandest of adventures."

Regret pulled at her heart. For Marcia, it should be a magical experience. Yet, the sad truth was mother and daughter's presence here was no mere familial visit. Though Eleanor had exchanged nothing more than letters with Aunt Dorothea over the years, the woman had proven herself the same benevolent relative who'd taken Eleanor in for a London Season. Now, however, Eleanor would come to her as a poor relation, in desperate need of salvation.

The carriage door opened and one of the woman's liveried servants held a hand inside. He helped Marcia down; all the while a budding panic filled Eleanor, tightening her throat, and threatened to choke her. She could not stay here. Even with Father's passing and her aging aunt's need of her, this place was not for Eleanor. The secret scandal left in Eleanor's wake had confirmed with the absoluteness of death itself that there could never be anything for her here in London.

"Mrs. Collins?"

She started and stared blankly at the white-gloved fingertips. For anything and everything that could or would ever be said about her, no one could dare utter the word coward of her. Eleanor slipped her hand into the footman's and allowed him to hand her down. The spring breeze pulled at her modest brown cloak and she tilted her head back staring at the front, pink stucco façade of a home she'd never thought to see again—a home she'd never wanted to see again.

Drawing in a steadying breath, she slipped her hand into Marcia's and gripped those fingers hard, drawing strength from the only person left in her life who truly mattered.

"Mama?" the little girl's whisper was nearly swallowed by the busy street sounds of passing carriage wheels rattling by.

Eleanor dropped to a knee beside her daughter and settled her hands upon the girl's shoulders. "What is it, love?" she brushed an errant golden curl that tumbled low over Marcia's eye.

"It is so very beautiful." Awe coated the little girl's words.

Raising her head, Eleanor looked up at the front of the town-house seeing it now through a woman's eyes. There had been a time when she'd been so very captivated by the mere impressive sight of the pink stucco finish townhouse; far grander than the modest cottage she'd lived in with her father. She'd brimmed with excitement.

"Ouch," Marcia flinched. "You are squishing me again, Mama."

She dropped a kiss atop Marcia's brow, and shoved to her feet. "Sorry, poppet. Come along." Stealing another peek at Aunt Dorothea's home, Eleanor drew in a steadying breath. The wildly animated woman with her two beloved dogs that Eleanor remembered was kind. "Shall we go see your aunt?" But would that still be the case after Eleanor had stolen from her home, without a goodbye, and a subsequent hasty marriage in the country?

"Oh, yes." With an excited giggle, Marcia slipped her small hand, warm, slight, and yet strongly reassuring, into Eleanor's. Her daughter tugged Eleanor toward the handful of stairs leading up to their new home—a home where they'd be poor relations, taken in and saved by Aunt Dorothea. All it would require was Eleanor to set aside the horrors of her past, remain hidden from the present, and accept the uncertainty of her future. She raised her hand and rapped once. How very difficult could all those feats be?

Her skin pricked with the sensation of being studied and she stiffened, but remained with her gaze trained on the door. It had been eight years since she'd made her hasty flight from London. No one would recall anything of the eccentric Duchess of Devonshire's niece who'd come to London, a girl of eighteen, and left but two months later.

Marcia shifted back and forth on her feet. "Why isn't the door opening? Did Aunt Dorothea change her mind? Do we have the wrong townhouse?"

Choosing the safest question to respond to, Eleanor said, "No, we do not have the wrong townhouse." She'd forever recall the extravagant home in the most respectable part of Mayfair. This was the very street where they'd met—

Emotion lodged in her throat and she rapped the door once more. Why wasn't the servant opening the door? Why was she here, on display for bored lords and ladies passing, while she wondered after *him*? In the earlier days, when her world had crumpled beneath her, she'd read the scandal pages, by then weeks old when they'd made their way to the quiet removed countryside of her home. She knew the day he'd become viscount. Knew when he'd become a rogue, gossiped about for his scandalous escapades with unhappy widows.

It had been the day she'd balled the papers up, put them under her bed and accepted that they'd both changed. She drew in a slow, calming breath and raised her hand to knock once more—when the door was blessedly thrown open. Her shoulders sagged with the weight of her relief as a different butler from the older man she remembered stood there. He eyed her a moment, this young man of indeterminate years, with a bewigged head and powdered face. He stepped back and then allowed her entry. To the man's credit, he gave no outward reaction to the coarse cloak worn by the duchess' poor relation.

Eleanor shrugged out of the garment and it was passed off to a waiting footman, leaving her horribly exposed in her old, brown skirts.

"Ohhhhhhhh," her daughter's irreverent whisper carried through the high-ceilinged marble foyer.

Pinpricks of regret stuck her heart once again, as she was confronted with a world her daughter would never, nay, could never, belong to. There would be no lavish life or soaring ceilings. A young maid rushed over with a wide smile on her plump cheeks. "May I escort you to your rooms, Mrs. Collins?"

Swallowing back the trepidation threatening to choke her, with Marcia's hand held in her firm grip, she silently followed the young woman up the stairs.

She'd broken a vow she'd taken almost eight years to the day— she'd returned.

CHAPTER 3

FROM THE EDGE OF THE majestic floor-length windows, Eleanor gazed through the gap in the brocade fabric, down into the crowded London streets. A small, sad smile played on her lips, reflected in the crystal windowpane. How very much had changed in eight years. Innocence died. Funds faded. And security became—precarious, making her dependent on that beloved aunt who once took her in for that first, and only, London Season.

Eleanor pressed her forehead to the sun-warmed windowpane and the cold metal of her spectacles bit into her face. Ignoring the biting sting of the wires, she surveyed the people below. Lords and ladies moved arm in arm down the fashionable end of May-fair. A particular couple snared her notice. For the impeccably attired gentleman with golden curls and the blonde-haired lady on his arm might have been a moment frozen in time eight years earlier…of herself…with another, equally grinning, whispering, young lord.

The massively rounded, panting dog at her side scratched Eleanor's skirts. Distracted, Eleanor looked down and found the incongruous pair of her aunt's dogs—two pugs, one black, one fawn—now eying her.

They had been sniffing at her skirts for the better part of the morning. Eleanor sighed. And all because she'd made the mistake of giving one of the mischievous devils a biscuit from her breakfast tray the first morning meal she'd taken here, one week earlier.

That dratted biscuit. She stroked them both atop their silken heads and leaned close. "Now, go."

They sat, showing her precisely what they thought of her and her orders.

Secretly she'd admit only to herself, she rather loved their devotion.

"They don't listen well," her aunt called across the room. As though to accentuate that very point, she pounded the bottom of a silver cane, crafted in the shape of a serpent, upon the hardwood floor, calling them over.

The dogs sniffed again at Eleanor's skirts. "You settling in, gel?"

"Quite," she murmured, patting Devil and Satan on their backs. They really were quite atrocious names for such docile, bothersome creatures.

...You could charm the devil himself, Marcus Gray...

Unbidden, Eleanor slid her gaze over to the window and pulled the brocade curtain aside. No, it was not a hope of seeing him that called her notice, but rather the crisp, blue skies and abundant sunshine and—

"And your daughter?"

Eleanor released the edge of the curtain with alacrity. "Also, well, Your Grace. Thank you for asking."

"Your Grace?" Her aunt settled back in the sofa she occupied and gave an inelegant snort. "Who is this polite, proper gel and what has she done with the spirited, always giggling girl I remember?"

The operative word being girl. "She's grown up," Eleanor replied automatically, looking down at her aunt's loyal dogs. Then, life did that to a person. It jaded you and chipped and cracked away at the innocence you carried, so all that remained was a glimmer of who you had once been.

"I preferred you giggling."

Eleanor smiled.

"There, that's better. Now, look at me, gel." The gruff command brought Eleanor's gaze to her aunt. "Stop hovering at the edge of the window. You've hardly left the corner since you arrived five days ago."

"Seven," Eleanor swiftly amended. She'd returned *seven* days ago without so much as a glimpse or whisper of him beyond the gossip sheets. The muscles of her belly tightened. Gossip columns that happily reported on the gentleman's roguish pursuits; so much so that she dared wonder if there was, in fact, another Viscount Wessex. Then, the king would not have been in the habit of turning out *multiple* Viscount Wessexes.

Eleanor stole another glimpse. It was curiosity more than anything else that called her focus back to that cobbled road.

"You counting, gel?"

She whipped her head back around. "Counting?"

"Seven days and not five. Are you unhappy here? I didn't bring you here to be melancholy and sad."

"I'm sorry." Remorse filled her and Eleanor quickly released the curtain. Widowed almost a year now, the Duchess of Devonshire had demonstrated her first display of weakness in the form of a letter she'd sent to her only niece offering employment as her companion. Eleanor's fingers tightened reflexively into tight balls as anxiety swamped her chest, making it difficult to draw breath. She could not be sent away. The allowance given Eleanor was the stability she would rely on to care for her daughter and never have to be dependent upon the whims of a man through the uncertain fate of marriage. "I will strive to do better," she pledged.

Her aunt leaned forward and Eleanor stiffened as the other woman brandished the tip of her cane under her nose. "Do you think I'm one of those miserable ladies to send a girl away? My niece, no less?" The dogs shifted nervously under the suddenness of their mistress' movement.

"No," she said softly. "I…" Except, she allowed those words to trail off, unspoken. For she no longer knew what to believe of people's motives and intentions. The truth was, for all her silence on the matter, her aunt likely knew that there had never been a Mr. Collins, and that the golden-haired child belonging to Eleanor would never possess the lineage to gain her entry into the *ton*. Cool, smooth metal touched her chin as Aunt Dorothea used her cane to nudge Eleanor's attention upward.

"Look at me, gel." Attired in her usual round gown made of Italian muslin, with its high waistline, her aunt's dress was suited to styles at least twenty years ago. "The modiste sheds tears when I order my gowns made up." Eleanor's lips twitched. "I've two dogs that sleep in my bed and accompany me wherever I go. Do I strike you as a woman who gives a fig for Society's opinion?"

Eleanor took the older woman in for a moment; her father's sister who'd married well when no one had dared dream a merchant's daughter would ever make an estimable match. The older woman had always marched to the proverbial beat of her own drum. Oh, how Eleanor admired her that strength.

Noting her scrutiny, Aunt Dorothea wagged her eyebrows. "Because I don't care a jot about what anyone thinks or says." There was a wealth of meaning to those words. Words that conveyed the clear truth that Eleanor had already suspected—she knew. Or rather, the duchess likely thought she knew, but in actuality could never glean the full truths of Eleanor's sad, sordid past.

Agony squeezed her heart. "Appearances matter," Eleanor managed to say.

Her aunt snorted. "Only if you are stupid enough to care." With that, she sat back in her seat, signaling the discussion was at an end. Relieved to have the matter done, Eleanor looked at the two books resting before her aunt; Mrs. Wollstonecraft's *A Vindication of the Rights of Woman* and *The Tales of Lord Alistair's Great Love*. Eleanor scooped up the gothic novel she'd been reading from earlier that morn. Her lips twitched. The duchess was, and likely always would be, a great romantic, and yet, what an unlikely and remarkable diversity in her reading.

"You've a problem with my books, gel?"

"No," she said instantly. And she didn't. She admired her aunt's love for love. Eleanor found hope in knowing that at least some people still believed in those sentiments. Though the actuality was that Eleanor far preferred the practicality of Mrs. Wollstonecraft's work to the romantic drivel of those novels her aunt favored. She opened to the page she'd last left on when Aunt Dorothea held a hand up.

"Enough reading for the day. Your daughter needs a walk. Take the nursemaid and a footman and go."

Eleanor's pulse picked up, and she gave her head a quick shake. "Oh, no." She'd be a daft ninny to fail to recall a day eight years ago when she'd walked down her aunt's front steps and collided, literally collided, with Marcus, the future Viscount Wessex. "I have my responsibilities to attend here," she insisted. For in truth, even as she craved the blue skies and country air, she could not bring herself to go outside.

There were too many demons out that door.

The past.

Marcus.

Him. The blackheart who'd singlehandedly shattered her future.

To leave this townhouse, Eleanor risked losing the much-needed control she'd claimed in her life.

Her aunt scoffed. "Youth is wasted on you fools of young age when you'd hover at a window and consider it a *splendid* time. When I was your age, gel, I was dancing in fountains and traveling the Continent." Her aunt's dry words brought a smile to Eleanor's lips. In a staid and stilted world of London Society, there was something so very remarkable and admirable about this woman before her. Sensing Eleanor weakening, Aunt Dorothea waggled her white eyebrows. "The girl I remember loved trips to the park and visits to the museum. And she certainly didn't linger at the window like an old recluse surveying the streets below."

Yes, there had been a too-brief moment in time when she'd loved the thrilling excitement London represented. She'd seen the world through a girl's eyes—craving those visits to the museums, parks, and oddity shops. Until she'd quickly discovered, London was filled with unkind figures who looked at her with loathing. They'd quickly shattered that naiveté about what this place truly was until she'd ached to return home. Then, Marcus had stepped into her world and he made it bearable. A wistful smile danced on her lips. Nay, he'd made it more than that. Together, she and Marcus smiled and laughed and teased and explored. For them, polite Society had ceased to exist.

"Not anymore," Eleanor said at long last. "I am a grown woman now, Aunt Dorothea." Even if in the deepest corner of her soul she missed strolling the grounds of Hyde Park and studying the magnificent flowers in bloom.

"That may be." The duchess banged her cane. "But you are going outside. That is an order. Now, go. Take my boys and your daughter with you." The childless woman's dogs had become more children than canines to her over the years. As such, the lines between children and dogs had blurred somewhat, when the duchess spoke of Marcia.

Eleanor gave her head a jerky shake. *I can't.* And yet…she curled her hands so tightly her nails punctured the skin of her palms. To remain shut inside was to make herself a prisoner. It represented one more absolute loss of control—at the hands of a man. She shoved to her feet. "I will go."

Surprise lit her aunt's eyes and she gave a pleased nod. "Good girl."

Eleanor shoved to her feet and set the book on the table. With each step she took for the door, strength infused her spine. Yes, her aunt was, as usual, correct. Where was Eleanor's spirit? She steeled her jaw. She'd not let life shape her into that cowardly, cowering figure that hovered behind curtains.

So it was, a short while later, Eleanor and Marcia stepped outside the front doors. Eleanor didn't know what she expected. Thundering from the heavens above? Thick, dark storm clouds passing overhead to signify the folly of her venturing out, past the safe walls of Aunt Dorothea's home? Alas, the sun shone bright and she raised a hand to shield her eyes from the glaring rays.

"Oh, Mama! It is splendid out."

Her daughter's words spurred Eleanor into action. Mindful of Mrs. Plunkett and the footman assigned as their escorts hovering in the open doorway, she started down the steps. "Indeed," she said, smiling gently down at her daughter. For her cowardice, she'd not allowed herself to consider Marcia being closeted away in a new home. Her daughter had long been a child of the outdoors, sitting in the gardens with her dolls dancing at her feet. And just like a parakeet, caught for the world's pleasure, Eleanor had gone and trapped her within Aunt Dorothea's walls.

"Can we please go to Hyde Park?"

"No!" the denial exploded from Eleanor's lungs.

Marcia cocked her head at a funny angle, dislodging a golden curl.

Drawing in a deep breath, Eleanor ruffled the top of her daughter's blonde tresses. "How did you find out about Hyde Park?"

"Mrs. Plunkett." Mrs. Plunkett was the nursemaid brought on by Aunt Dorothea so Marcia could have proper lessons. The young woman shifted guiltily on her feet and Eleanor gave the young woman a reassuring smile.

"Please, Mama?" Marcia yanked at her hand. "Can we not go? She said they have magnificent gardens and fountains and lovely ladies in grand gowns walk with gentlemen and—"

She dropped to a knee and settled her hands upon Marcia's shoulders, and looked into her daughter's hopeful, excited eyes. "We will go one day, poppet, I promise." She promised. And lied. She'd no intention of risking seeing either Marcus or...*him*...as she'd taken to thinking of the other, nameless gentleman.

Little shoulders sank. "You're lying."

Odd, this child of seven should know her so well. "I'm not." She hopped to her feet, ending any further debates on the veracity of Eleanor's words. "Now, Aunt Dorothea has charged us the important task of walking Sat—Satin and Devlin," she quickly substituted different names for the horrid names affixed those poor creatures.

Marcia skipped over to the footman with the two dogs at the end of leads, looking more like a captain guiding a ship at sea than a man being tasked with the chore of walking his eccentric employer's frequently misbehaving pugs. "Can I hold one?"

A protest sprung to Eleanor's lips but then the servant wisely handed over the lead to the older, slower pug. Little snorting giggles escaped Marcia as she allowed herself to be led down the fashionable, blessedly quiet sidewalk. Mrs. Plunkett hurried after her charge.

As they made their way to the end of the street, Eleanor studied her daughter's jaunty steps. Guilt pulled at her. The foundation of Marcia's life was nothing more than a weakly constructed lie and the moment that unsteady base was kicked out from under her, Marcia's fate would be cast into the same shadowy, murky haze of Eleanor's herself. But perhaps the lie could persist. Her daughter could find and wed a polite, respectable gentleman of the gentry who might not care if he, nay, *when* he, discovered the truth of his wife's legitimacy.

Eleanor's heart wrenched. For that detail would matter. To any and all. It was why they belonged in the country, removed from polite Society where the people removed from the *ton* were less driven by cruel gossip and the woes of others.

A small cry split the quiet, cutting into Eleanor's musings and her heart paused a beat. She found Marcia with her gaze. Devlin wrestled his freedom from Marcia's small fingers. The miserable pup yapped and danced past Mrs. Plunkett's reaching hands. Then he spun about. His little legs worked hard and fast as he raced in

Eleanor's direction.

She narrowed her eyes on him and, for a moment, he froze. "Oh no you don't, you miserable bugger," she declared. His pink tongue lolled out the side of his mouth from the exertions of his efforts, and then responding to the challenge there, he tore around her and raced onward, back down the route they'd previously traveled.

Eleanor started after him and stuck her booted foot out, effectively trapping his leash. "Ha!" she exclaimed, triumphant. Her daughter clapped excitedly, hoisting her clenched hands aloft and waving them in victory.

Despite herself, Eleanor laughed…and then registered the curious stares trained on her. She flitted her gaze about. A handful of lords and ladies on the street gawked in return. Eleanor swallowed hard, as all her dratted efforts to remain invisible were quashed—by a fawn pug that just then took advantage of her distraction and pulled free.

Bloody hell.

"No, Mama," her daughter groaned, her expression crestfallen. The footman bounded after the blasted pup, sailing past Eleanor. Giving her head a shake, she set out in pursuit, gaze trained on the fawn ball of fur. For all her aunt had done for her and Marcia, she couldn't very well go and lose the lady's beloved dog.

A tall, broad-muscled gentleman stepped into Devlin's path. The dog collided with a gleaming black Hessian and then staggered back, dazed when the stranger bent and scooped up the leash. Relief swept through Eleanor as she lengthened her strides. "Thank you so much, sir," she panted, breathless, as she stopped before the gentleman and reached out to collect that leash. "I did not…" She glanced up and her heart tripled its beat.

The tall, golden-haired stranger turned a hard, unforgiving glare on her that froze her thoughts. It suspended movement and time, and held her trapped in this peculiar moment where the world carried on around her in a great whir of noise and motion. Her heart quickened. She'd, of course, known that there was a very strong likelihood that with her return to London in the role of companion to the Duchess of Devonshire, with the walls of his townhouse sharing her aunt's, their paths would again cross. But the tales she'd read of him long ago in the papers had filled her with a false hope that he'd be so busy with his clubs and mistresses that they'd never again meet.

From where he stood on the London street, Marcus Gray, Viscount Wessex, looked at her through thick, long lashes that did little to conceal the fury snapping in his eyes. The seething recognition there sent her staggering back a step.

"Miss Carlyle," he said with a hard edge of steel to his words.

Emotion stuck in her throat. Gone was the sweet, gentle, young man who'd teased her and clipped a lock of her hair to hold it forever close. In his place was this silent, terrifying, broad, powerful stranger. Then, a mask dropped in place, tamping out all previous fury so she was left to wonder if she'd merely imagined it. He tipped his lips up in a slow, wicked smile. An odd fluttering unfurled in her belly.

"We meet again."

Marcus.

CHAPTER 4

OF COURSE MISS ELEANOR CARLYLE would not stay buried. Of course she'd reemerge when a young lady unlike her in every way, had garnered his notice. The irony of this moment could not have been penned better, even from Shakespeare himself.

The lady now wore spectacles and the pale blonde hair he long remembered was tugged back in a tight chignon. But the severe hairstyle and wire-rimmed frames could not detract from Eleanor Carlyle's ethereal beauty.

A handful of gold curls popped free in protest of the hideous coiffure; those loose coils, the ones he remembered from his past. Marcus resisted the urge to jam the heels of his palm into his eyes and try to drive back the image, for he knew by the honeyed scent that clung to her skin, that she was, indeed, real. That tantalizing summer fragrance had haunted his waking and sleeping moments.

By God, the traitorous, deceitful minx had returned.

A hard, humorless laugh escaped him and her cheeks went waxen. After years of forgetting, or trying in vain to fully forget, and losing himself in empty entanglements with other, equally lonely women, Eleanor had returned.

By the manner in which she troubled her too-full lower lip, she was not happy about seeing him. *And why should she?* She'd pledged to meet him in Lady Wedermore's gardens and instead of meeting him, he'd found empty grounds. And when he'd paid call on her the next morning, nothing remained but a note handed him by one of the duchess' maids.

Eleanor was the first to break the silence. "My lord," she greeted. Her voice was a barely there whisper. The frames slipped down the bridge of her nose and she promptly shoved them back into place.

Good, the lady should be fearful. He folded his arms about his chest and winged an eyebrow up. "Is that all you'll say, Eleanor? After all these years." He made a tsking sound and she flinched, the movement nearly imperceptible. "I should expect a far warmer reception."

As bold as she'd been when they'd met, she a girl of just eighteen, she squared her small shoulders and tossed her head back. "My lord, thank you for rescuing my aunt's dog."

He bit back a curse. Of course. The eccentric, pug-loving Duchess of Devonshire would ultimately drag her niece from whatever country rock she'd disappeared under when she'd absconded with his heart and happiness. All the old fury, the hurt, and rage that he'd thought safely buried, rose to the surface, threatening to boil over and consume him in a flood of emotions he'd thought dead. He took a step toward her and she backed up. "Never tell me you fear me, Miss Carlyle?"

She gave her head a frantic shake but continued her retreat, proving her unspoken denial a lie and Marcus delighted in the lady's trepidation, for it spoke to her guilt, indicated she knew she was culpable of all the charges he could heap on her lying head. Then she came to an abrupt stop, forcing him to cease his forward movement or bowl her over. He stopped so close, a mere hairsbreadth separated them. Marcus registered the rapid rise and fall of her chest, her slightly parted lips and, God forgive him, he wanted her still—

"Hullo."

He blinked, searching about, and then dropped his gaze downward to the wide-eyed girl looking up at him. Seven or eight years of age, with a riot of golden curls, the child had cheeks a cherub would envy.

Something pulled in his heart and he knew, knew without any confirmation, knew by the kissed by sunshine hue of her tresses and freckles on her nose. In all his imaginings of where Eleanor had gone and who she'd become, he'd never, ever dared consider that in that time, she had become a mother. For that would have made the man she'd chosen real in ways where he'd only previously existed as a shapeless, shiftless imagining. A man whom she'd truly loved and not the mere flirtation that she'd practiced upon Marcus. "Hullo." His voice emerged garbled.

The golden-curled girl spoke, jerking him to the present. "What is your name?"

"That is not polite," Eleanor gently chided, settling an almost protective hand upon the child's small shoulders.

"Marcus," he said quietly, ignoring the reproach in Eleanor's tone, and then he thought to add, "The Viscount Wessex." He dimly registered the duchess' footman reaching for the leash. With numb fingers, Marcus turned the dog over, his attention reserved for the little stranger. "And who are you?"

The miniature version of Eleanor dropped a perfect curtsy. "I am Marcia Collins."

He paused, as a distant remembrance trickled in. *"Who needs a miserable son? I would have a daughter who looks like you…"* Eleanor's laugh, even after all this time, trilled around his memory. *"And would you name her Marcia…?"*

The little girl spoke, breaking into the memory from long ago. "Do you know my mama?" With those five words, he had confirmation of a question he'd already had an answer to and, yet, it still sucked the air from his lungs. The woman he'd given his heart to had fled and was even now wed to another. She was a mother to this small child while Marcus lived his own empty life, pursuing his own pleasures. God, how he despised her for that; despised her with the same hatred he'd managed to bury years ago. Only now to be proven a liar in the street before the lady herself.

"It is a pleasure to meet you, *Marcia.*" At the deliberate emphasis he placed on the child's name, Eleanor tipped her chin up at a defiant angle, all but daring him with her eyes to mention the memory between them.

"The viscount's mama is a friend of Aunt Dorothea," Eleanor said quietly, her voice surprisingly devoid of emotion.

When had the young lady of his past become this stoic creature?

Marcia craned her neck back and unabashedly stared at him. "You know my Aunt Dorothea, then?"

"I do," he said gruffly, schooling his tone around the child. After all, it wasn't the girl's fault that her mother had been a fickle, flighty creature.

Then those brown eyes went wide. "Did you know my papa, too?"

Jealousy, potent and fierce, filled him, threatening to consume him for the man who'd won Eleanor and given her a child. Then Marcia's words registered.

"We should be going," Eleanor said quickly, color rushing to her cheeks.

Did you know my papa?

Not: *Do* you know my papa?

And all the resentment and anger he'd borne toward Eleanor and the fleeting hatred he'd felt moments ago for the nameless, faceless stranger who'd taken her to wife, left Marcus, leaving in its place an aching regret for her loss.

Eleanor reached for her daughter and Marcus dropped to a knee, intercepting her efforts to spirit the girl away. "I did not know your father," he said quietly.

Some of the excitement dimmed from the girl's eyes. "Oh," she said, scuffing the cobbled road with the tip of her boot. "My papa was a hero." She raised her gaze to his. "He was a soldier."

"Was he?" his voice came as though down a long corridor, a terse utterance belonging to another. In this moment, Eleanor's hasty flight, at last, made sense. In the note she'd left for him, but a handful of sentences long, she'd spoken of her heart belonging to another. She'd, however, failed to mention the name of the man whose heart she'd missed with such intensity, she'd fled in the dark of night. Now with Marcia's revealing words, he knew Eleanor had wed a man in the King's Army. That important piece somehow made his dead rival all the more real.

"Oh, yes," Marcia said with a solemn nod. "He was very brave and I miss him greatly." She wrinkled her brow. "Even though we never—"

"Come, Marcia," her mother said sharply.

The little girl sighed and then sidled over to her mother. "Well, it was very nice meeting you, sir."

"My lord," her mother whispered. "He is a viscount."

"Marcus will suffice," he insisted, not taking his gaze from the small child who by rights should be his, and was near enough in age that she could have been his, if life had played out differently and Eleanor had not chosen another.

"That wouldn't be proper," Eleanor said, with a slight frown on her lips.

Once again, he wondered at what had turned the giggling, bright-eyed girl of his youth into this guarded, hesitant woman before him now. "I insist," he said, looking pointedly at Eleanor. "After all, your mother and I were once friends."

Eleanor's body jerked erect as though he'd struck her. Good, she should feel something, even if it was guilt for not having had, at the very least, the courage to confront him in more than a letter and admit her defection. She'd owed him that.

The little girl alternated her stare between them. "You were, Mama? So it would be fine to call him by his name, then, wouldn't it?" Marcia continued on over her mother's quick protest. "I do like your name." She captured her chin between her thumb and forefinger and eyed him contemplatively. "Not the Wessex part." His lips twitched with his first amusement since their entire exchange. "But the Marcus part." A wide smile wreathed her plump cheeks. "It reminds me of my name. Do you like my name?" Each question and admission from the child's lips jolted him, throwing his once well-ordered world into greater tumult. "I was named after a powerful, mythical queen who ruled Britain long ago."

He forcibly reined in his emotions and offered a bow. "I think it is a splendid name, Miss Collins," he said, spreading his arms wide in a way that made her giggle. Marcus returned his attention to an unmoving Eleanor. Tension poured off her slender frame in waves and he welcomed the further crack in the lady's veneer. "In fact," he confirmed, deliberately needling, "I once said if I were to have a daughter, I would name her Marcia."

The little girl's eyes went wide and she yanked at Eleanor's hand. "Did you hear that, Mama?" She raised wide, innocent eyes to his. "My mama told me the same thing. She said she'd always known she would have a little girl named Marcia."

The muscles of Eleanor's throat moved, the first crack in her otherwise remarkable composure. And suddenly with Marcia's innocent admissions, his deliberate attempt to rile Eleanor only jabbed at his own heart with regrets for the way her life had turned out and the way his had not.

A small yap jerked him to the moment. The duchess' liveried footman adjusted the leads in his hand. Marcus cleared his throat. "I will leave you ladies to your afternoon." He sketched another bow. "Miss Carl—" He cut his words short. For she was no longer Miss Carlyle and yet, that is who she would forever be.

"My lord," her whispery soft voice was nearly lost to the carriages rumbling by.

With that empty parting, Eleanor turned on her heel with her daughter's hand tucked in her own, and her small contingent of servants, and did what she did best—left.

"I LIKED HIM, MAMA."

Eleanor pretended not to hear her daughter's insistent words. To acknowledge them only opened the gates for regrets she'd rather not let in.

"Mama," Marcia sighed, tugging at her hand. "Did you hear me? I liked the viscount."

Everyone had always adored Marcus Gray, Viscount Wessex. He possessed an inordinate amount of charm that was safe to no lady, young or old; her own daughter, included. "You do not even know him," Eleanor said, her gaze trained forward on the pink façade of her aunt's townhouse, her feet desperately aching to take flight. She concentrated on each carefully taken step.

"Do *you* not like him?" Confusion underscored her daughter's relentless interrogation. "He said you were friends."

Emotion clogged Eleanor's throat and a sheen of useless tears coated her vision. No, she did not like him. She loved him. Eleanor drew to a stop and, despite herself and good sense which she'd demonstrated a remarkable lack of for the better part of her life, she glanced back to the him in question. Alas, he was gone. *Did you expect him to be standing there staring after you like a lovelorn youth?* "I like the viscount just fine, love. He—" Is a good man, honorable, charming. Or he had been. A shiver raced along her spine. The man she'd loved was no more. Instead, he'd been replaced with a cold, emotionless stranger she no longer recognized. Which was for the best. In that way, she could keep Marcus properly buried with her broken heart and hopes she could have for them.

"He is what?" Marcia asked impatiently.

"He is perfectly acceptable company," she settled for.

Eleanor's daughter scrunched her nose up, indicating just what she thought about that rather empty endorsement of the viscount.

"Now, come," she urged, tugging Marcia's hand toward the townhouse.

A pained groan escaped her little lips "But you promised we could spend the day at the park."

Eleanor bit the inside of her cheek to keep from saying that she'd in no way promised a day at the park or even a trip from Aunt Dorothea's townhouse. She ruffled the top of her curls. "Don't you wish to tell Aunt Dorothea of the excitement this afternoon?"

"No, I want to stay outside in the sunshine," Marcia said with such a child's blunt honesty that, for the tension of the morning, a real smiled pulled at her lips.

"Another day," she promised as they reached the front doors. They made their way up the handful of steps and the door was opened almost immediately, admitting them and their small collection of servants and dogs.

"Why are you here, gel?"

Eleanor winced as Aunt Dorothea's stern voice boomed off the cavernous foyer. She looked up the spiral, marble staircase to where the older woman stood, poised at the top. She thumped her cane, demanding an answer.

"Mama said we had to come and tell you of the excitement."

Some of the duchess' disapproval faded, to be replaced with a spark of interest. "Excitement?" she asked, her tone gruff.

Eleanor shrugged out of her cloak and with a murmur of thanks, handed it off to the butler, while her daughter filled the silence for them.

"Oh, yes. It was very exciting, Aunt Dorothea." She folded her arms across her chest and gave Eleanor a pointed frown. "Even if Mama insisted on ruining all our fun."

With a little grunt, Aunt Dorothea eyed them with renewed interest. "Well, come along you two." She gave a jerk of her chin.

No further urging required, Marcia sprinted up the stairs. Eleanor winced at the less than decorous display. Alas, the smile on the woman's aged cheeks hinted at approval for the girl's spirit. At a slower, more deliberate pace, Eleanor mounted the stairs while

Marcia's eager prattling occupied Aunt Dorothea. All the while, Eleanor welcomed the distraction, using it as an opportunity to try and right her tumultuous thoughts.

Of course, their meeting had been an inevitable one. His town-house was on the same strip as the one she would occupy...until Aunt Dorothea no longer required Eleanor's services. Yet, in all the possible exchanges she'd run through, those had been coolly polite passings between two people who'd once known each other, but were now nothing more than strangers. By the reports she'd last read of him in *The Times*, he had become a shell of the man she remembered and admired. And so, in the meeting she'd fashioned for them, he would have tipped his head, perhaps with an icy disdain for the country miss who'd returned to a world she didn't belong to. She would have dropped a curtsy and continued hurrying by with regrets for what might have been and that would have been the extent of their exchange.

Eleanor reached the top of the stairs and paused, resting her hand upon the bannister. Except, the flash of ire in Marcus' ice blue eyes and the set hardness of his mouth hinted at a rage that belonged to someone more than an indolent lord. She pressed her eyes closed a moment. His reaction had been that of a man who'd cared very much that she'd left. Of course, he'd not feel any of that vitriol toward her if he knew the truth, knew the shame and humiliation she'd spared him from.

"What is the matter with you, gel?" At the suspicious question barked from halfway down the hall, Eleanor snapped her eyes open. "Are you distracted?"

"No," she lied. A warm heat suffused her cheeks. Her aunt and daughter stood in matching poses; hands planted akimbo, and if she weren't so humiliated at being caught woolgathering, she'd have found her daughter's mimicking the older woman rather endearing and more than a bit comical.

"She is. She has been that way since the excitement."

"Humph," Aunt Dorothea grunted once again. She angled her head toward the hall. "I, of course, must hear more." Without waiting to see if they followed, she turned on her heel and started down the hall to one of her many parlors. Marcia skipped after her.

With far greater reluctance, Eleanor followed along. She would not think of him. They'd seen each other but once. Nearly to the date of their first meeting. An innocent, naïve young lady would see that meeting through romantic eyes and blame fate and fortune. Eleanor sighed. She, however, had come to see fate as a cool, fickle, mocking creature that took minutes and moments and manipulated them in a cruel way. And those glorious meetings were then fatefully transformed into horrific exchanges that forever altered the course of one's life.

"Get in here, gel."

She jumped at her aunt's booming voice and hurried into the pink parlor. From the velvet curtains to the upholstered sofas, every last piece, parcel, and scrap of this room were pink. As a girl of eighteen, she'd been in awe of the cheer of the room. Now, she found the shade a nauseating reminder of her naïve days. Her daughter sat perched on the edge of one of the pink sofas, swinging her legs back and forth as she was wont to do. Eleanor hurried over and sat beside her.

Aunt Dorothea gave a pleased nod and then claimed the sofa opposite them. Then, to draw out the moment, she leaned over and poured herself a cup of tea, added three lumps of sugar, a dash of milk, and then held it up. Eleanor waved off the offering with a murmur of thanks and, with a little nod, her aunt settled back in her seat. "Now what is this about excitement?"

"Devlin broke free," Eleanor cut in before her daughter could speak.

A rusty chuckle escaped the older woman's lips. "Your mother changed my dogs' names, has she?" Eleanor mustered a conciliatory smile. "Well, Satin and Devlin will do just as nicely," the duchess said with a wink. "They don't seem to mind, do they?"

"No, Aunt Dorothea." Marcia shook her head enthusiastically.

Of course, Eleanor should feel some compunction, and yet she could think of nothing other than foolish regrets at the roguish man Marcus had proven to be.

Her aunt looked back and forth between her two guests. "Never tell me, *that's* the excitement?" Her tone was the same as one who'd been told the intrigue of the day was attending Sunday sermons.

Without awaiting permission, Marcia plucked an apricot tart from the silver tray of confectionaries set out. "Oh, that is not all," she mumbled around a mouthful of sugared treat.

Eleanor touched a hand to her daughter's knee. "We do not

speak with our mouths full, dear."

Marcia brushed the back of her hand over her mouth and dusted away traces of sugar.

With a sigh, Eleanor retrieved a napkin and handed it over.

Where most matrons would have looked on with horror at the girl's manners, an appreciative light lit the unconventional duchess' eyes. "Tell me more about this excitement."

"Devlin ran away." The little girl proceeded to tick off on her little fingers. "He managed to slip by me, and then Mrs. Plunkett, and then the footman," she paused, scratching her brow. "I don't know his name." She gave her head a shake. "And then *Mama*," Eleanor winced at the heavy emphasis placed on that two syllable word, "went running after him."

Her skin went warm at the attention fixed on her by the duchess. "I did not *run*, per se," she muttered under her breath.

"In the end, a gentleman saved him." She took another bite of her treat. "A Mr. Marcus." Then around yet another mouthful of her tart she added, "A viscount."

Aunt Dorothea leaned forward in her seat. By the light in her eyes, she was suddenly very eager for the telling of the story. "Oh?" She had, of course, long ago hoped for, even urged, a match between her niece from the country, a mere merchant's daughter, and her godson, the Viscount Wessex.

Eleanor remained stoically silent.

"Yes." Marcia nodded excitedly. "A Viscount Wessex. Though I greatly prefer the Marcus part to the Wessex part and he did say I was permitted to call him Marcus." She beamed. "Because he and Mama were friends."

Tamping down a sigh, Eleanor, to give her fingers something to do, grabbed a tart.

"Marcus?" her aunt asked.

"The same," Eleanor managed.

A pleased smile formed on the woman's lips. "He's a good boy."

"He's no longer a boy," she felt compelled to add. Just as she was no longer a girl. The stranger in the street a short while ago had been broader, taller even, than the lean youth of her past. She'd once believed there was no one more handsome than Marcus Gray. Seeing the broad-shouldered, thickly-muscled gentleman he'd become, proved she'd been wrong. With his unfashionably long blond hair and raw strength, he harkened to thoughts of warriors of old.

"He's still not married, that one." Her aunt waggled her eyebrows in a conspiratorial way. All relief at those words was fleeting when reminded of the man Marcus had become.

No, a gentleman the paper purported to carry on with scandalous widows and lightskirts likely wouldn't be. Instead, he'd relish in his freedom. Pain lanced her heart. She was better off with the memories of the good boy her aunt spoke of than having remained in London to bear witness to the person Marcus, in fact, was.

Eleanor's heart raced under the knowingness in the other woman's expression. "Marcia," the older woman said, not taking her gaze from Eleanor. "Will you fetch Satan? My pup deserves some of the morning breakfast."

What could her aunt possibly wish to speak with her about? Under the shelter of the table, Eleanor balled her hands on her lap.

The little girl eagerly hopped to her feet. "Do you mean Satin? Of course. What of Devlin?"

Her aunt looked in her direction once more. "If you can get that stubborn dog to comply, then bring them both along." She said nothing further until Marcia had gone.

With the little girl easily dispatched, her aunt pressed ahead. "Do you expect I shouldn't have known you were more than half in love with my godson all those years ago?" At Eleanor's muted silence, she waggled her eyebrows. "Hmm?"

All these years, Marcus had existed in her mind and memory as her secret alone. There had been something protective in that; something that made him real to only her, and as such, more dream than man. She gave her head a hopeless shake. "I don't—"

The other woman scoffed. "I would have had to be a blind bat to fail to see the way you two smiled and winked at one another all those years ago."

Eleanor curled her hands so tightly her nails dug painful crescents into her palms. "I don't know what you are talking about," she said with forced calm. Under the woman's piercing scrutiny, she sat there, exposed in ways she'd never been. How casually her aunt ripped open those painful pieces of her past and spoke of them with the calm and ease she might discuss the morning weather or the daily fashion. Unnerved by her aunt's faintly accusatory stare, Eleanor shifted. There was something wrong in lying to this woman who'd only shown her kindness through the years. At the very least, she was deserving of a kernel of truth. Eleanor wet her lips and spoke quietly. "I was young." A child who thought all that mattered was love. "He was very young." And not this hardened rogue the papers gossiped about; a nobleman who graced the beds of some of the most scandalous widows in London. "Time changes a person, Aunt Dorothea," she said, the truest words she'd ever spoken. *Life* changed a person.

Her aunt eyed her for a long while. "He is a good man," she said at last.

I would battle armies for you, Eleanor Elaine...

And I would never ask that of you...

The whispered words of long ago danced through her mind.

Yes, he had been, and she preferred, even in the pain of losing him, to have him forever frozen as that honestly smiling young man. Eleanor forced her fists open and smoothed her skirts. "It matters not. Time goes on. People change."

"And my dear godson did, indeed, change," her aunt said wryly. "A rogue he is, that one."

Her heart tugged and Eleanor glanced down at her lap. At one time, she'd only seen him in her life. He had represented the dreams in her heart.

The duchess probed her with a stare, but did not press her. "And even rogues marry."

The matter-of-factness of those words cleaved her heart. And yet, in a bid to stifle any further talks of Marcus and some proper, innocent miss, Eleanor gave a droll smile. "Do they?" The hard, commanding gentleman in the street struck her more as a man to seek out his clubs and his pleasures, without any intentions of tying himself to respectability.

A twinkle lit her aunt's eyes. "Why, do not be silly, girl! Reformed rogues make the best husbands. Your uncle was proof of that." Some of the woman's earlier amusement died, misted over by a sheen of tears.

Emotion wadded in Eleanor's throat and she leaned over and covered Aunt Dorothea's hand with her own. "Oh, Aunt Dorothea."

The duchess cleared her throat. "None of that." She drew her hand back and dashed it discreetly over her cheeks. "And we were discussing my rapscallion godson. The boy will wed." She wrinkled her nose. "Now it is just a matter of determining who he'll wed." Muttering under her breath, she leaned over and rustled through the stack of gossip pages on the table before her. She shoved aside her barely touched plate that rested atop the cluttered collection.

Eleanor quickly shot her hands out and steadied the porcelain dish, preventing the buttered bread and sausage from toppling to the floor.

"Ah." She removed a particular sheet. "See," she said, tossing the copy to Eleanor who automatically caught it. "Read there," her aunt jabbed a finger at the page.

The Viscountess W shared with Lady J that a certain Viscount W, notorious rogue, has settled his sights upon the Incomparable Lady MH...

A vise tightened about her lungs squeezing off airflow. He'd found a lady. A lady no doubt deserving of him. Seeing those words written added a permanency of truth; a reminder that time had continued on and for the changes between them. Of course Marcus would wed and, by that accounting, it would be one day soon. He'd wed a woman who was proper and polite and innocent, and all things a nobleman required in a wife. The agony of that gutted her in ways she'd thought herself long past caring.

"Well, anything to say, gel?"

What was there to say? Eleanor picked her head up from the page. By the look in her aunt's clever eyes, she expected...hoped? That Eleanor would be that woman? Only Eleanor never could be that young lady. Marcus, as she remembered him, deserved more in his viscountess than a tarnished, dowerless merchant's daughter. With steady hands, she set the page on the table before them. "I am here as a companion to accompany you to *ton* events. Who," Marcus, "the Viscount Wessex courts is not my concern."

Her aunt gave her an assessing look. "Will you still feel that way when he attends my ball this week and you watch him dance attendance on those simpering, colorless debutantes?"

Oh, God. Agonizing pain lanced Eleanor's chest and made it impossible to draw breath. To read the reports of Marcus and all the scandalous ladies he'd been tied to through the years had been a special kind of torture. But she'd not had to witness him charm and woo the lady reported on those pages. In coming to London, she'd thought there could be nothing more horrid than attending the *ton* events with her aunt. So many of her worst nightmares harkened back to one of those proper, well-attended balls.

But to bear witness as Marcus courted his perfectly pure, proper miss would crush those foolish pieces of her soul that clung to the dream of what they'd shared. Aware of her aunt's probing gaze on her face, Eleanor dug around for a response. Any response.

And came up empty.

"I thought so," her aunt said with a pleased nod. The duchess, however, was not through with her daily torture. "I've the boy's mother coming over for dinner tonight. With the sister." Lizzie. When Eleanor had last seen Marcus, the plump, dark-haired girl was just ten. She'd be a woman now. Eighteen. The same age Eleanor had been when she'd had her world torn asunder.

Then her aunt's words registered. Her heart sped up. "Do you?" those two words emerged choked to her own ears.

Aunt Dorothea nodded once. "Yes."

Marcus would come here. She would be seated across a dining table from him.

Footsteps sounded in the hall, followed by the clip-clop of sharp nails on the hardwood floor, and Eleanor was promptly saved from formulating any further response.

Her daughter reentered the room with a wide smile and a snorting, heavily breathing pug in tow. "Who is coming to dinner?" With eager eyes, she looked back and forth between the two women seated at the table.

Eleanor winced. "Marcia," she chided. They'd resided in the quiet of the Cornwall countryside so long, there had been little need or time to practice her daughter's social graces. Now, Eleanor regretted the failure of not imparting those necessary lessons. "It is not polite to—"

Her aunt banged the table with a fist. "Ignore your mother's scolding. I like a young lady with spirit and boldness."

A warm blush heated Eleanor's cheeks at the pointed look the duchess shot her way. Yes, one time Eleanor had, indeed, been lively and spirited—and careless—and it had cost her nearly everything, including her sanity.

"My friend, Lady Isabelle."

"May I come?" Marcia piped in. She swiped a piece of bread

from the sideboard and offered it to Satin.

"Sweet, it isn't done," Eleanor said regretfully, wishing there was a similar rule for children *and* companions.

"Of course you will attend," her aunt said with a glower for Eleanor. Her daughter brightened under the older woman's defense. "Don't allow your mother to make you conform and do everything and anything Society wants. You hear?"

Eleanor winced as her daughter gave a firm nod. Eleanor had spent the better part of eight years seeing that she and Marcia blended as much as possible with ordinary Society. She'd gone out of her way to avoid notice and focus, content to be the quiet war widow who'd loved and lost and now lived with her father.

"But the boy will not be there," her aunt said with a huff of annoyance. "Gone out of his way to avoid my dinner parties."

Eleanor's heart started and she scrambled forward to the edge of her seat. Why would he avoid her aunt? Then she sank back in her seat. Likely, he blamed Aunt Dorothea for having brought her fickle niece from the country.

The duchess gave her an assessing look and, unnerved by the knowing in those wise eyes, Eleanor attended her forgotten strawberry tart. *Your lips remind me of a summer berry and I want to lose myself in the taste of you…*

The confectionary treat fell from her fingers and toppled to the floor, raining down bits of sugar and crumbs. It landed on the Aubusson carpet with a soft thump, a corner piece breaking off the tart. Eleanor jumped to her feet and the duchess looked at her askance. "Will you excuse me a moment? I—" Except she had no reason to account for this urge to run away. With her heart thumping hard in her chest, she fled.

Then, wasn't that what she'd always done best in life?

CHAPTER 5

MARCUS STOOD AT HIS OFFICE window and surveyed the darkened streets below. How very much had happened on this particular street. Of course, it was the townhouse he'd resided in as a boy. But the happiest memories he held were of the cobbled roads below.

…Surely I should know the identity of the lady who shares the townhouse beside mine…?

…I am Eleanor Carlyle…and surely I should know the name of the gentleman who'd so boldly wish to know the identity of the lady who shares the townhouse beside his…

She'd returned, risen from the ashes, and gone was the wide-eyed, smiling girl. That young woman who'd claimed his heart had been replaced by a guarded, wary woman with a woman's frame. Was the gentleman she'd thrown him over for responsible for that transformation?

Marcus raised his glass to his lips and took a sip of brandy. This time, he did not stop the flow of memories, but let them in. He'd met the lady in that very street by happenstance almost eight years ago as they'd reached the front steps of their neighboring homes. She'd been the unfamiliar lady who'd stolen the breath from his lungs and who, with her boldness and spirit at first greeting, had captivated him.

The crystal windowpane reflected his visage; the wry grin on his lips. How apropos that she should reemerge and crash into his world with the same intensity all these years later. And as glori-ous as she'd been as a girl just turned eighteen, the woman she'd grown into was the stuff of golden perfection artists toiled over at their canvases, trying in vain to catch even a shimmer of such golden beauty. The breasts he'd once cupped in his hands, and only through the fabric of her modest satin gowns, were fuller, her hips wider, but her waist still trim. And yet with all that had come to pass, his body still ached to know her in the ways he'd longed to, but never had.

Marcus swirled the contents of his snifter in a slow, deliberate circle. This hungering was based on nothing more than a mascu-line appreciation for her delectable form. At one time, he'd been hopelessly bewitched by her beauty and spirit. No longer. For he was no longer the boy he'd been; a young man ravaged with grief and despair over the death of his friend; riddled with guilt, who, amidst the blackened darkness of death and sorrow, had found a glimmer of light in an otherwise bleak world.

"The duchess is expecting us shortly, Marcus."

He stiffened and shot a look over his shoulder as his mother swept into the room in a whir of silver satin skirts. In a bid for nonchalance, he took a sip of his drink. "You did not mention we'd be joined by the duchess' guest."

"The duchess' guest?" His mother slowed, but did not break her forward stride. Then she widened her eyes. "Oh, yes," she exclaimed and clapped her hands. "Eleanor! How did I ever forget to mention, the duchess' niece has arrived?"

Then, why *should* she have noted it? All the stolen interludes in the gardens between Marcus and Eleanor had been their private secret, shared only with the fragile stars and moonlight.

His mother crossed over and stopped beside him. "Very sad, very sad, indeed," she said, making a tsking sound.

He frowned. Long ago he'd come to expect his mother's flare for the theatrics, which extended to her veiled words intended to elicit intrigue. Never before had it grated more than it did in this moment. "What is sad?"

She gave a wave of her hand. "Oh, Mrs. Collins' situation. Very different now than it was seven years ago."

Eight years. For his indifference toward the lady and the anger he'd carried for her all these years, the muscles of his stomach

knotted involuntarily at his mother's words. The lady's circumstances should not matter; she was not his concern, and yet...
"And just how is it different?" he asked infusing boredom into his
tone.

Ever the consummate gossip, his mother stole a look about and
then dropped her voice to a furtive whisper. "I do know Dorothea
has never minded her family's mercantile roots." She furrowed her
brow. "Quite the opposite. I've often jested that she finds a perverse pleasure in them—"

"Mother," he said impatiently.

"Oh, yes. Right, right," she said, lowering her voice once more.
"Mrs. Collins' husband died some years ago, leaving her destitute."

For all the years he'd spent hating Eleanor, he should find a
perverse glee in her recent circumstances. And yet, as his mother
prattled on about the heroic Lieutenant Collins' tragic death, a
pressure weighted on Marcus' chest. Eleanor had returned as a
poor relation. Only she'd not returned alone. She'd come with her
daughter.

"...and then there were some terrible investments on Mr. Carlyle's part," his mother said, yanking him to the present. She paused
and tapped a finger against her chin. "All bad form speaking of
trade, but let me think what it was..." Then with a far too casual
shrug she lifted her shoulders. "Regardless, Eleanor is here, as a
result."

There were many reasons a person would come to London and,
yet, a niggling settled in his thoughts. The lady was here, in the
heart of the Season...

He tightened his fingers hard about his glass. "The lady has
come husband-hunting, then?" Marcus could not tamp down the
acrid bitterness burning his tongue. He would have given her his
name and, yet, here she was, no doubt, in search of wealth...just
like any other grasping woman. Marcus took another swallow of
his brandy.

His mother gave a shake of her head. "But that is what is peculiar
about Mrs. Collins' arrival."

"Return," he corrected. Eleanor had *arrived* eight years ago. She'd
returned eight years later. A widow. And still as gloriously beautiful
in all her golden splendor as she'd been. The heart-shaped planes
of her face, while the sun glinted off curls more gold than the

riches unearthed by Cortez, flashed behind his mind. No, she was more breathtaking now than she'd ever been as that eager creature straddling girlhood and womanhood at the same time. It mattered not what, if anything, was curious about Eleanor's sudden appearance, and yet; "What is peculiar about her return?" he forced the question out past tight lips.

His mother waved a hand about. "Well, she is here as a hired companion."

"A companion?" he repeated blankly.

"A *hired* one," his mother clarified, as there was a vast difference between the two. "She's here as the duchess' companion."

Something wrenched inside at the idea that Eleanor found herself a poor relation dependent on the charity of a kindly, older woman. He balled one hand into a fist at his side, leaving fingernail marks upon the palms of his hand. That was the fate the man she'd wed had consigned her to. Marcus braced for the gleeful response to Eleanor's current circumstances, but found none. Had she been his, he would have draped her in the finest satins and silks and seen her dripping in diamonds. Then, those things hadn't mattered to Eleanor. It was one of the reasons he'd so fallen in love with her. The fact that she'd gone on to wed a soldier in the King's Army who'd left her uncared for, spoke to hers being a true love match—not the mere flirtation she'd practiced on Marcus.

How could he have known her so well and not known her enough to gather there had been another murky shadow of a man between them?

It's because I didn't truly know her.

Footsteps sounded in the hallway. Lizzie's plump frame filled the doorway. "Hullo." She looked to Marcus and her perpetual smile dipped.

He schooled his features. With her skill at reading a person, she could have trained the Bow Street Runners. She'd always seen too much.

"Oh, splendid," their mother said with a smile. "Shall we?"

"Of course," he said, his tone flat. The sooner he could have this evening over, the sooner he could carry on with his own life. By his mother's revelation this evening, there was no need for him and Eleanor to move in the same circles. She was here as a hired companion. He was in town to wed.

Wordlessly, he followed after his mother. For the first two years of attending this intimate dinner party hosted by the Duchess of Devonshire after Eleanor's absence, Marcus had sat through each course, smiling politely, all the while feeling as though he'd had his heart wrenched from his chest. By the third year, he'd given up on the hope of her and succeeded in becoming a rogue who no longer cared—about Eleanor Carlyle, what they'd shared, and her betrayal.

Eleanor might now grace that same table, but she may as well have been any other woman. His love for her had died somewhere between the parting note handed him by the duchess' servant and the eventual realization that Eleanor Carlyle was never coming back. After that, he'd pasted on a smile and worn a proverbial grin ever since.

His sister matched her stride to his. "It could be a good deal worse," she said from the corner of her mouth. "We could be attending a horrid soiree or ball." She tapped his arm. "And I do like the duchess."

He took a noncommittal approach. But for the occasional appearance at those dinner parties hosted by the duchess through the years, he'd taken care to avoid Eleanor's aunt. Oh, the pain of Eleanor's betrayal had receded, but neither was he a glutton for forcing himself to think of what he'd once dreamed of.

Lizzie stalked over, a frown on her lips. "You are not your usual affable, charming self."

Marcus mustered a grin. "Aren't young ladies supposed to enjoy balls and soirees?"

"I despise them." A twinkle lit her eyes. "And I'm clever enough to know that you're attempting to change the topic, big brother."

"Perhaps a bit," he conceded as they reached the foyer.

They were helped into their cloaks and then Williston pulled the door open. A few moments later, they were ushered inside the Duchess of Devonshire's townhouse. Marcus shrugged out of his cloak and turned it over to a waiting servant. As they were shown their way to the receiving room, he contemplated Mrs. Eleanor Collins; so coolly unaffected by him in the street.

He'd suffer through this dinner and then he could be free of her, at last.

He flattened his mouth into a hard line.

Then, would he ever truly be free of Eleanor Collins?

CHAPTER 6

FROM HER SPOT OVER THE by the windows in her aunt's parlor, Eleanor fiddled with her spectacles. According to Aunt Dorothea, Marcus hadn't come to her small dinner gathering in five years. Pain twisted in Eleanor's belly. By that small detail and the fury in his eyes just yesterday afternoon, she gathered he'd not forgiven her flight. In his mind, she was likely the traitorous, capricious creature who'd engaged in a mere flirtation and then tired of him. Then, isn't that what she'd hoped he'd believed of her? For neither of the alternatives she'd run through in her terrorized mind would have ever been good. Had Marcus discovered the truth of that night, the young gentleman she'd fallen in love with would have either risked his life on a field of honor, or worse, shunned her for the shame that had befallen her. Both prospects had shattered her inside.

It was best he did not come tonight. Or any night. Seeing him earlier today had only roused the dreams she'd once carried in her heart—of him, them. Happiness. Love—

"You're fidgeting, gel."

Startled to the moment, Eleanor quickly donned her glasses and followed her aunt's pointed gaze downward searching for Marcus. Unwittingly, she fisted and un-fisted the fabric of her skirts, hopelessly wrinkling the drab, brown muslin. With alacrity, she let them go. "I'm sorry," she responded. Following that horrific night almost eight years ago, she'd taken to the odd habit of scrabbling at her skirts.

"Don't apologize to me, girl," her aunt said with a snort. "Apologize to your dress."

"Mama always wrinkles her gowns," Marcia piped in from her spot at the windowseat.

"Humph. Well, you certainly can't do any more damage to *those* skirts." That was saying a good deal with her aunt in her out-of-mode wide satin gown, taking exception with Eleanor's attire.

"I like these skirts," she said, defensively.

"Girl, no person likes brown muslin." Her aunt spoke in a tone that considered the matter settled.

In this, too, her aunt was correct. Through the years, Eleanor had striven to avoid any kind of attention. People tended to see those in extravagant garments of bright satin fabrics and not ladies who sported severe hairstyles, and perched wire-rimmed frames on their noses. No notice was good notice, and only protected one from probing stares and in-depth inquiries.

"You need new gowns, Eleanor." The stomp-stomp-stomp of the cane upon the floor made that statement fact.

"No," she said quickly. Too quickly. Her aunt eyed her through suspicious, narrow slits. When Eleanor next spoke, she did so in steadier tones. "That is, thank you, but I've no need. I'm here as your companion." And one of the only reasons Eleanor had confronted the demons of her past by returning to London was to provide companionship to the widowed, childless woman. "There is no need for anything more than my current wardrobe."

Marcia tugged at her hand, forcing Eleanor's attention downward. "But, Mama, you would look ever so lovely in new dresses." She looked to Aunt Dorothea. "Wouldn't she, Aunt?"

"She certainly will not look any worse than she does now."

A laugh escaped Eleanor, earning a scowl from the duchess.

"I was not making a jest, gel."

"My apologies," Eleanor said with forced solemnity.

"It is settled. We shall take you to the modiste." Then she flicked her gaze over Marcia. "And we'll have a dress made for Marcia."

An excited squeal pealed in the room as Marcia hopped up from her seat and jumped up and down. "Oh, truly? Truly? Truly? That will be most splendid."

"There is no need for dresses," Eleanor put in. She'd not accept any more of her aunt's charity than she'd been forced to. "For either of us."

Her daughter's exuberance died a swift death. Any other child would have stomped her feet and begged in protest. Through the years, however, Marcia had demonstrated a stoic maturity better suited to a child of far older years. "Very well," she said on a dejected sigh and regret filled Eleanor at never having been able to provide the world she wished for her daughter.

"See what you've gone and done, gel?" Her aunt glowered. "You've made the girl sad."

"Perhaps one or two new dresses," Eleanor conceded and her daughter's head shot up.

Brightness illuminated her brown eyes and she hurled her arms around Eleanor's waist, squeezing hard. "Oh, thank you." Then she suddenly released her mother and sprinted over to Aunt Dorothea.

"Marcia," Eleanor called out, anticipating the girl's intentions too late.

Marcia launched herself into Aunt Dorothea's arms and knocked the old woman back in her seat. "Oh, thank you ever so much, Aunt."

Eleanor rushed over but the duchess frowned over the top of Marcia's head. "Do you think I'm made of sugar? A hug from a small girl isn't going to hurt me, I assure you."

She rocked to a stop and took in the affectionate tableau as the childless, notoriously gruff Duchess of Devonshire patted Marcia on her back. For the first time since the missive had arrived more than a month ago, it occurred to Eleanor, with the offer of companionship on behalf of Aunt Dorothea, that this relationship was not truly one-sided. Perhaps her eccentric aunt needed them just as much as they needed her.

Footsteps sounded in the hall and Eleanor's heart skittered a beat as the younger butler appeared and announced the guests. "The Viscount Wessex, the Viscountess Wessex, and Miss Lizzie Gray."

Marcus stepped into the room, resplendent in a black evening coat, black breeches, and his immaculate, snow white cravat. He moved with the confidence and grace of a man who may as well have owned the very room he now entered.

A loud humming filled Eleanor's ears and she welcomed the distraction presented by Aunt Dorothea, who stood and engaged in the necessary trivialities. "You came," Eleanor blurted.

All conversation ceased, leaving nothing more than the echo of her humiliating words and the attention of five sets of eyes.

Marcia broke the stilted silence…"Mama, your skirts."… in the most awkward way.

Eleanor released the fabric of her dress and let her arms fall back to her side, and then remembering herself, dropped a belated curtsy. "My lady," she offered lamely to the Viscountess Wessex.

The years had been kind to the smiling, always benevolent viscountess. "Eleanor," she greeted. "It is so very lovely to see you," and spoken in those warm tones, Eleanor believed the woman. Eleanor shifted her attention to the curious young lady with thick, brown ringlets—Marcus' sister, older, taller, more grown-up than she remembered. Weren't they all, then?

Her aunt jammed the tip of her cane into the hardwood floor. "There is a new person joining us." She motioned to Marcia and in that innocuous, if unconventional, introduction diverted attention away from Eleanor, for which she'd be forever grateful.

As the two women greeted Marcia, Eleanor stood to the side in silence. Most members of polite Society would be scandalized by the presence of a child at a formal dinner, but then her aunt had always drummed her own beat and danced to her entirely made up rhythm. Through the introductions, Eleanor's skin pricked as Marcus studied her through thick, hooded blond lashes. As she'd never been a coward, she met his gaze.

He strolled over, with long, languid movements better suited to a tiger tracking its prey. With her heart scrambling into her throat, she retreated and then caught herself before taking any further steps. This was Marcus. As much as he might resent her, nay, hate her, he would never hurt her. She'd stake all she owned on that fact. She rooted herself to the floor and caught her hands upon the back of the pink sofa.

"I gather by your exclamation, Eleanor, you're surprised to see me." A lazy grin turned his lips upward. Gone was all the warmth and gentleness she'd once known in that smile. From his thickly veiled lids to his slight grin, he'd perfected the role of rogue with an ease of one who'd been born to the position.

As bold and teasing as he'd always been, of course Marcus would not let her earlier outburst rest. Eleanor wetted her lips. "I am, was," she corrected, "*surprised* you've come."

He propped his hip on the edge of the back of the sofa. "Did you think I would stay away because of you?" He studied her and the heated intensity of that stare burned her skin.

She met his unrepentant stare. "No." The lie tumbled easily from her lips. His gaze fell downward and she followed his stare to her skirts. Eleanor immediately released the drab, brown fabric and yanked her head up. He shifted, angling his body in such a way that she was shielded from the small party conversing behind him. That subtle movement brought their bodies so close, she felt the tension dripping from his frame.

He dipped his head close. "Were you hoping I stayed away?" His brandy-scented breath fanned her lips, bringing her back to another night, another man.

Her stomach churned and she closed her eyes a moment, but the insidious memories had already crept in; the repulsive taste of spirits, the maniacal laugh, her own gasping cries. She stumbled back a step, and in her haste to get away, knocked against a small mahogany table. Her fingers shot out instinctively to capture the teetering porcelain shepherdess but Marcus easily caught the piece, righting it. He assessed her in that searching, bold way of his. Eleanor sought glimpses of the youth he'd been, but once again, found only this hard, powerful man instead. A man who smelled of brandy and studied her with coolly detached eyes.

Thankfully, a servant entered and announced dinner.

"Come along, boy," Aunt Dorothea called out. "After years of avoiding my dinners, you owe me an escort."

A smile played on Marcus' lips. In that moment, he was that man and Eleanor was that girl, but then his gaze snagged upon Eleanor once more, and that gentle grin died. "Indeed, my lady," he called out. "It has been too many years," he said. If Eleanor were the wagering sort, she'd bet the meager coins left by her papa that those words were intended for her. He came to a stop beside the assembled guests and paused to sketch a bow for Marcia. "Miss Collins."

Her daughter executed a perfect curtsy. "Marcus."

He held his arm out for Aunt Dorothea and then offered his fingers to Marcia. "I daresay you require an escort as well, my lady."

Marcia erupted into a fit of the giggles and then slipped her hand into Marcus'. The sight of them paired; her golden-curled daughter and the tall, equally blond Marcus dug with all the vicious ferocity of a rusty dagger being plunged into her stomach. Emotion raged in Eleanor's breast, threatening to choke her with the force of it, as she stared transfixed at the little girl who, by rights, should have been his, *would* have been his, had life continued along the predictable path it had started.

Only…

Eleanor dropped her gaze to her daughter's crown of golden curls. She stared after the party as they started for the door, leaving her with the chaos of her own thoughts. If there had been no horror, there would be no Marcia. There would have been another child, but not this little girl who'd claimed Eleanor's soul from the moment she'd first held the crying, plump, red-cheeked babe in her arms.

Odd, Eleanor had been forced to sacrifice one happiness only to find an altogether different joy.

Marcus paused in the doorway and cast a lingering glance over his shoulder. Gone was the animosity she'd detected since their reunion, replaced now by a concern better suited to the man he'd been. She mustered a smile and started after them. The mask he'd donned fell back into place and he was once again the Viscount Wessex—stranger.

THE TWO OLDER MATRONS FILLED the dining table with the appropriate discourse; politely engaging Eleanor's small daughter, allowing Marcus the luxury of his own musings. Since their meeting earlier that afternoon, Eleanor had owned every one of his thoughts.

He told himself not to stare and yet, to have searched for her and then ultimately given up on the dream of seeing her again, he could no sooner lob off his right hand than he could stop taking her in. Albeit, in furtive, sideways glances, while she shoved her fork about her untouched plate, the only indication of the lady's unease.

How very different she was than the girl he remembered. Those luxuriant, golden curls were once again drawn tightly against her scalp in a severe coiffure better suited to a woman ten years her senior or a governess bent on respectability. No longer giggling and garrulous, she'd instead become quiet. Somber. Solemn.

He took in her drab, brown skirts and again a loathing filled him for the man who'd wedded her and left her dependent upon the charity of relatives for her and Marcia's survival.

Tired of the stilted silence between them, he spoke. "Do you find your meal unsatisfactory?"

Eleanor's head shot up. At her prolonged silence, he arched an eyebrow. Once upon a lifetime ago, she would have given him a teasing wink and witty rejoinder. "No." As though to prove the contrary, she popped a bite into her mouth. Those long, elegant fingers that had once effortlessly twined with his, like naked lovers united as one, she reached for her wine glass. The tremble of her fingertips drew his notice.

He took in the delicious sight of her crimson lips upon the rim of that glass, hating himself for envying the crystal object as he did. The lady had left him, chosen another, wedded, and returned, giving no indication that he'd been anything more to her than a mere diversion—and yet he still hungered for her. "And are you enjoying the pigeon in white sauce?"

She passed a dubious stare over the contents of her plate, the wariness in her eyes suggested a fear that he'd tampered with her food. "Er, yes. Very much." Which was very much, a lie. The lady hadn't taken any more than one corner nibble until now.

Marcus settled back in his chair, making himself comfortable, taking an unholy delight in the manner in which she shifted under his focus. Good. With the effortless ease with which she'd shattered his heart and violated his trust, the lady should squirm. "Or tell me, Mrs. Collins? Do you find yourself enjoying the pigeon one moment, and then being so very...*enticed* by the lemon roast that you completely forget—the pigeon?"

Red color suffused her cheeks and she raised her eyes to his. The silver flecks danced with fury, a reminder of the passion that had once been so very strong between them. Then with slow, precise movements, she picked up her fork and knife and delicately carved a piece of pigeon. "I don't know, my lord." He narrowed his eyes. She'd "my lord" him, would she? "I find the sweet aspect of the pigeon infinitely more agreeable than the bitter taste of the pig."

By God, had she just called him a pig? With a pointed look and very deliberate movements, she popped a piece of pigeon into her mouth, confirming that very supposition. The audacity of her. And yet…despite the lady's thinly veiled insult, a smile pulled at his lips.

Marcus rested his arms on the sides of his chair and drummed his fingertips, all the while studying her in silence. A girl-like blush blossomed on her cheeks and she studiously avoided his gaze. Alas, he'd spent the past years charming lonely widows and courtesans. The defenses Eleanor sought to erect were flimsy ones at best. "Never tell me you're nervous to be alone with me?" he drawled. He examined her through thick lashes and her skin burned ten shades hotter.

She spoke quickly. "Don't be silly." Too quickly. Belatedly she lifted her gaze to his. "Nor are we alone." She looked pointedly to the guests engrossed in discourse about the table.

"But we could be," he promised on a whisper, and leaned close, so close his thigh pressed against hers.

The slight, audible intake of her breath met his ears and he relished the lady's flushed cheeks, the muscles of her throat moving rapidly. For Eleanor's quick flight from his life, her reaction revealed a woman who was not immune to him. Marcus continued his deliberate seduction. "What if I said I came tonight to see you?" He hooded his lashes. "That I was compelled by your presence?"

Eleanor looked about and then when she returned her attention to him, she spoke in hushed tones. "I would say I don't believe you. I would say you don't see me differently than any widow you've bedded." She gave him a long, sad look. "You are not a man *any* woman holds power over."

He stilled. Her faintly accusatory edge not lost on his jaded ears. Did she not realize the power she'd held over him all those years ago? He'd have brought down kingdoms to secure her love. He dropped his eyes downward to where she viciously scrabbled at the fabric of her dress and the carefree response on his lips died. Eleanor followed his stare and immediately released the fabric and yanked her head up. God, even in the hideous garment she'd the beauty to rival Aphrodite. Yes, she could feign indifference, but the lady was as aware of him, all these years later, as she'd been as a woman of just eighteen, and there was something empowering in that discovery.

A child's giggle ripped through the moment, promptly dousing all trace of desire. His gaze strayed to Marcia. The little girl sat beside his sister, her plump, white cheeks illuminated by the warm glow of the candelabra. Whatever she said at that precise moment roused his sister to laughter. Suddenly shame slapped at his conscience; shame for hungering after Eleanor still and attempting to seduce her before polite company, and before her young daughter, no less.

Self-disgust gripped him. Reluctantly, he looked to Eleanor and found her studying him warily and it gave him pause. Who had put the suspicion there in her expressive eyes? Was her husband responsible for that cynical mistrust? Marcus gripped the arms of his chair hard, not wanting to imagine Eleanor dependent upon a husband who'd treated her with anything but kindness. Even as she'd broken Marcus' heart, he did not want to believe she'd suffered in any way over the years. He attempted to thrust aside the lurking questions.

Except...now his mind had wandered down a path for which there was no irrevocable course. And the questions about Lieutenant Collins flooded his consciousness: What manner of father had he been to the girl? Had they been a happy family?

As though sensing his attention, Marcia glanced across the table and gave an eager little wave. A golden curl tumbled over her brow and she shoved it behind her ear. Emotion pulled at his heart. What did small girls with golden curls do with their days? All the little pieces he would have known had she been his. Marcus dropped his elbows on the table and called over to the little girl. "Tell me, Marcia, how does a young girl spend her days?"

Seeming to note the attention of all the guests shift her way, Marcia sat prouder in her chair and firmed her little shoulders. "I enjoy reading." Which did not surprise him. Eleanor had been a voracious reader. How many libraries had they snuck away to during *ton* events? "I like to sketch." *I'm an atrocious artist.* A skill the girl had likely acquired from the papa. His gut clenched. Then she dropped her voice to a conspiratorial whisper. "I also like to fence. My mama said my papa was a master fencer."

Marcus stiffened, grateful for the duchess' boisterous laugh that saved him from responding. "A girl who fences. You've raised a splendid child," the older woman said, hoisting her glass aloft in toast.

Mother and daughter locked stares and some unspoken, powerful communication passed between them. Then with a sigh, Marcia dropped an elbow onto the table and buried her head into it. His mind traveled the path of time back to a younger Eleanor and he locked in a fencing match with invisible swords. She, becoming tangled in her satin skirts and landing in an ignoble heap upon the floor. He coming over her... The stem of his wine glass snapped and a servant rushed forward to relieve him of the burden and right the mess.

And not for the first time since he'd found Eleanor and that silly dog on the street, he damned her for returning and throwing his world into tumult. Just then, with every fiber of his being, he hated her for the pain she'd wrought. Never again would he yield that control to any woman.

The duchess called Marcia's attention back and the remainder of the meal continued with no further exchange between him and Eleanor. For all intents and purposes, they may as well have been strangers, and as the meal concluded and Marcia was escorted abovestairs by her nursemaid, he briefly entertained the idea of making his excuses. He squared his jaw and stole a sideways glance at Eleanor. He'd not be the hurt and wounded pup, driven off.

And so, escorting his hostess and her small smattering of guests to the parlor, he took an unholy delight in the way Eleanor cast a glance back over her shoulder at him. She troubled the flesh of her lower lip as she'd done whenever she was worried or contemplative and then swiftly diverted her attention forward. That slight nuance so patently hers, that only he knew—

Pain lanced through him as they moved down the hall. For that wasn't true any longer. Another had known her and known her in ways Marcus hadn't, nor ever would.

"When did you become so serious?" The duchess charged as they turned down the corridor and continued on toward the hall.

"I've always been serious," he said with a too-charming smile.

The older woman rapped him on the arm with her fan. "And you've become a liar. I'm old, Marcus, I'm not blind. I read the papers. You've become a rogue in *your* old age." She waggled her thick eyebrows. "Though I've read Lady Marianne Hamilton has snared your notice. I expected better for you," she scolded.

Eleanor shot a quick peak over her shoulder. Their gazes collided and she hastily looked away, but not before he saw the spark of pain that lit in her fathomless blue eyes.

"Hmm?" The Duchess went on, demanding his attention. "Will you marry that one? Surely, as your godmother, I'm deserving of that information from more than the gossip columns."

In front of them, Eleanor stumbled and then quickly righted herself.

"What's the matter with you, gel?" her aunt snapped.

"I merely tripped," Eleanor said hurriedly, not deigning to glance back. The tension in her slender shoulders, however, hinted at the lady's discontent. Did she care that he'd turned his attention on other women, finding, if not love, then a physical surcease with another? And why did he want that to matter?

"And she's a horrid liar, that one," The Duchess said in a hushed whisper he strained to hear.

"Oh?"

The older duchess snorted. "I don't intend to say anything else on it. You want to know about the girl, you ask her yourself." He blinked several times. She lowered her eyebrows. "And I won't be swayed by a charmer such as you. Ah, here we are," she said, as they entered the room, filing in behind Eleanor and his sister and mother.

As the ladies stood conversing, he studied Eleanor. The words exchanged lost in the distance between them. Periodically, Eleanor nodded and smiled. She should have been his. This should be a close gathering of those linked by familial connections. Instead, there was nothing but cool disdain, icy barbs, and insolent my lords and madams between them.

He tightened his mouth. All these years, he'd sought to bury the hurt caused by Eleanor's defection. With her reemergence in his life, she'd pulled the carpet of control out from under his feet. He'd never forgotten her. He'd never moved on.

And he hated her for opening his eyes to that realization.

The Duchess of Devonshire stomped her cane on the floor. "You, Lizzie, play for us." With that terse command, she slid into a pale pink armchair and his mother sat in the chair opposite. Ever obedient, his sister dropped a curtsy and rushed over to the pianoforte. She claimed a seat and began to promptly play.

Eleanor, however, hovered and he strode over, extending his elbow. "Would you stroll with me about the room, Eleanor?" he issued the challenge, partially believing she'd deny his request, yet wholly wanting her to put her fingertips upon his sleeve.

"He doesn't bite, gel," the duchess snapped over Lizzie's playing. At the unexpected interruption, his sister, usually flawless upon the instrument, fumbled the keys and then immediately regained her footing.

Eleanor jumped and then hastily tucked her fingers into the crook of his elbow and allowed him to escort her to the perimeter of the expansive parlor. All the while, Lizzie's haunting playing of Dibdin's *Tom Bowling* echoed throughout the cavernous space.

"Did you not wish to join me, love?"

She eyed him with a wariness he'd not believed her capable of. "What do you want, Marcus?"

You. The word rushed forth, born of truth. For all that had come to pass, he desired her still and he would not be content until he had known her in his arms. It spoke to his own weakness and her allure. "What do I want?" He wrapped those words in a seductive whisper that brought her lips apart. His gaze lingered on her mouth. "How can you not know?" Eleanor's breath hitched loudly and he reveled in that slight audible intake that spoke of her awareness of him. "I want you to accompany me about the room."

She looked at him with the same crestfallen expression of a child who'd had her peppermints plucked from her fingers. "Oh."

"The woman I remembered enjoyed those stolen moments alone together." How many words of love had he whispered in her ear as they'd strolled about this very space?

What a fickle creature she'd proven herself to be.

"Girl."

Marcus cocked his head.

"I was a girl, Marcus. I was not a woman."

Under the weight of that reminder, he took in her flared hips, her fuller breasts, straining the fabric of her gown. Yes, she was a woman, and for her betrayal, he wanted her still. Desire raged inside him; a hungering to know Eleanor in the only way he never had.

And why shouldn't I? She is a widow. I'm no longer the infatuated boy. There were no dangers in them sharing the pleasure of each other's bodies. Perhaps after he'd taken her to his bed, then he could be free of this maddening sway she'd always had over him.

Marcus shifted, angling his body in such a way that Eleanor was shielded from the small party conversing at the opposite end of the room. That subtle movement brought their bodies close. Tension dripped from her slender frame. "And we are both adults now, aren't we?" he whispered close to her ear. "There are no rules of propriety." As adults not bound by the same strictures of Society, they could avail each other of the pleasure of one another's arms.

Eleanor's breath caught. "Are you attempting to seduce me?"

"Would you like that, Eleanor?" he asked softly. He brushed his hand over her fingers and she gasped. Her lids fluttered wildly and a surge of masculine triumph gripped him. She may have wed another, but she desired him, still. "I have missed your kiss, Eleanor." He reveled in her flushed cheeks, her quickened breath and damned the audience that prevented him from taking her in his arms and showing her just how much. "And I would wager you've missed my kiss, as well."

Her lids fluttered open and she passed stricken eyes over his face. Swiftly withdrawing her hand free of his sleeve, Eleanor stumbled away from him. Shocked hurt replaced her earlier desire and that hot emotion danced in the silver flecks of her blue eyes. "I have no interest in being seduced by you." Was it anger or desire that caused her voice to quiver so? "And you, my lord, are in the market for a wife. Are you not?"

"Ah," he discreetly captured the golden curl that had sprung loose of her chignon, relishing the satiny softness of that tress. He'd not tell her that supposition was based on gossip fueled by two nonconsecutive dances and his own mother's machinations. "But I am not yet married and neither are you." But she had been. The faceless paragon she'd wed danced around the edge of his musings and resentment trickled to the surface. He tamped it down, forcing his lips up in a half-grin and released the lock. "Never tell me you're interested in that role this time?"

It was the absolute wrong thing to say. That is, as far as seductions went.

Eleanor stood there, her chest heaving. If looks could burn, she'd have reduced him to a charred pile of ash at her feet.

From across the room his sister concluded playing her piece.

"Eleanor, girl, come along and regale us with a song," the duchess called out.

Eleanor jerked her head toward the ladies assembled at the opposite end of the parlor. She squared her shoulders. "If you will excuse me, Aunt Dorothea? I promised Marcia I would read to her." She made her polite goodbyes to his family and before the duchess could respond, Eleanor dropped a stiff curtsy, snatched her skirts away from Marcus, and fled. She paused in the doorway and cast a befuddled glance in his direction.

He winged an eyebrow upward and that slight movement propelled her forward.

The lady gone, Marcus gave his head a wry shake. These were sorry days indeed, when a young woman reacted so to his attempts at seduction. His smile slowly widened. Except, the blush on her cheeks and rapid breaths bespoke her desire. He was not through with his seduction of Eleanor Collins.

No, he'd only just begun.

CHAPTER 7

THAT NIGHT, WITH QUIET ECHOING through the duchess' townhouse, Eleanor sat perched on the edge of her bed. The moon's glow penetrated the break in the curtains and cast a silvery white light upon the hardwood floor.

He attempted to seduce me.

Well, not quite, as they'd been in the presence of company. But Marcus' husky words and thickly veiled eyes had spoken to his intentions for her. With a sigh, she withdrew her unneeded spectacles and tossed them onto the nearby night table. By the pages she'd read of him in the gossip columns—sought after, whispered about rogue—it should really come as no surprise.

And yet, for all her indignation and shock, standing with their bodies nearly flush, his breath tickling her skin, there had been something else…something more…

A gentle spiraling heat began in her belly that harkened back to the times she'd spent in Marcus' arms. After years loathing the thought of any man's touch, with but the brush of Marcus' hand and nearness of his body, he'd awakened her to the truth—she still felt. For him. It had only ever been him. As she'd stood there in her aunt's parlor, with the haunting strains of Dibdin echoing throughout the room, her heart had tripped a beat with the desire to know the promise of passion; when she'd long ago given up any thought of ever knowing, ever *wanting* to know anything in a man's arms. How could she when the nightmares still came and her flesh still burned from the shame of the attack?

She slid her eyes closed a moment. For in this instant, she did not think of her attacker or the terror in being used for a man's pleasure. She thought of the tantalizing promise Marcus had dangled that had not elicited fear or shame. There had been something so very heady, something invigorating in wanting to know the promises Marcus hinted at.

He would be a gentle lover. For the passion in his fathomless blue eyes, she'd no doubt that he would stroke her with the same tenderness he'd once shown.

Eleanor jumped up and the cool of the hardwood floor penetrated her feet. She began to pace. When she'd received her aunt's summons, calling her and Marcia to London, she'd wanted to ball it up and burn it. For London represented nothing more than the pain of loss: of a once pure love, a shattered innocence, and all the dreams she'd carried that would never come to be. When desperation drove Eleanor to accept the post of companion, she'd deliberately not allowed herself to think of Marcus.

After all, lords like Marcus did not pine for young ladies of their youth. No, those bored noblemen who took their pleasures where they would, lived for their own enjoyment. That wasn't the man he'd been, but by the gossip columns she'd carefully snipped from copies of *The Times*, it was the man he'd become.

She'd not truly allowed herself to think of Marcus beyond the agonizing thought of what might have been. As such, she'd never once considered a man such as he would set out to seduce a bespectacled widow, attired in hideous brown skirts.

Eleanor stopped midstride and the midnight quiet echoed around her. And though there was a triumph in her body's response to him…there was an excruciating pain at his interest, as well.

For she didn't want him to be one of those indolent lords. She wanted to have arrived in London and found the gossips proven wrong; to see him as a man driven by more than the pleasures of the flesh.

As though in mockery of that foolish wish, her gaze snagged upon the ormolu clock atop her fireplace mantel. Ten minutes past twelve.

At fifteen past the hour, I will always be there. And we shall always know where we two are.

Her throat worked painfully with the force of her swallow. Twelve fifteen had always been their hour; the special time reserved for them. Regardless of ball or soiree or a quiet, eventless evening, midnight in the gardens belonged to them. And he'd always been there. She captured her lower lip between her teeth so hard the metallic hint of blood flooded her senses. Except once. Once he had not come and from that, their precious hour had been stolen forevermore.

...Were you waiting for me, sweet...?

Her body jerked, as the taunting maniacal laugh worked about her brain. With a small moan, Eleanor dug the heels of her palms into her eyes in a desperate bid to shake free of his memory.

She'd not allow him that hold. Not tonight.

Turning on her heel, she marched over, and grabbed her spectacles. Eleanor placed them on, and then collected her modest night rail from the vanity chair. She shrugged into the white garment and then strode to the door. Pulling it open, she peeked out into the hall.

The lit sconces cast an eerie glow upon the thin, crimson carpet lining the corridor. Eleanor hesitated and then stepped outside the same rooms she'd occupied as a girl of eighteen. Drawing the door closed behind her, she made her way through the hauntingly quiet halls. The floorboards creaked and groaned in protest to her footsteps, and she quickened her stride. Eleanor came to a stop at the servant's entrance and, glancing about once more, she slipped into the narrow stairway. Grasping the rail, she felt her way down the stairs. Her ragged breaths filled the small space, and when she reached the base of the stairs, she sprinted down the corridor.

For the familiarity of this place, she may as well have been a girl of eighteen, once again. Eleanor skidded to a halt beside the arched oak door and with trembling fingers, pressed the handle and stepped outside.

Of course, time had proven that when the dark demon of her past stole into her thoughts, she could not so easily shake free of his hold. This moment was no exception.

The fragrant scent of roses slapped at her senses sucking her back to a different midnight hour. Her feet twitched with the urge to flee the walled-in grounds and keep running—away from this area, away from this townhouse, away from her past.

Eleanor willed her heart to resume its normal cadence.

You are not the same weak girl you once were, Eleanor Carlyle. She clenched and unclenched her jaw. She'd not allow him his hold to stretch here to these grounds. Not in these gardens that belonged to her and, at one time, Marcus. With trembling fingers, Eleanor yanked the door closed hard behind her. A cold chill raked along her spine, raising gooseflesh on her arms. In a bid for warmth, she scrubbed her hands back and forth over the chilled flesh and looked about. *Do not think of it. Do not think of that nameless stranger...* She willed herself to think of Marcus, instead. His gentle teasing and the lock of hair he'd snipped in these very gardens and her first kiss and...

Another mouth, a foreign one, forced its way into those beautiful musings.

With a shuddery gasp, Eleanor leaned against the wood and found makeshift support from the hard surface. She closed her eyes as the memories slid in like insidious poison of a different garden, on another moonlight night. A jeering laugh echoed around the chambers of her mind and her breath grew ragged, dulling the night sounds.

Enough!

Drawing in a deep, calming breath, she counted to three and forced her eyes open.

Demons laid to rest, she took in the darkened garden with a now clear gaze. The soft, sweet smell of freesia and chrysanthemums blended, mixing with the stale London air. How very similar this space was all these years later. Why, the hands of time may as well have frozen a moment from long ago and held it suspended forever in this private Eden.

She looked at the high brick walls built about the enclosure. The blood red stones kept the ugliness of London outside and, through that, crafted a façade of purity. Eleanor skimmed her gaze about sadly.

A hungering to abandon London once more and return to the obscurity of the Cornwall countryside gripped her. For then, she'd not have to relive the worst parts of her life or the deepest parts of her regret. She'd not have to muddle through Marcus' tempting promises and agonize over the bride he'd soon take.

Soon. She smoothed her palm over her nightgown. Soon, she

would return with Marcia and then she could relegate this brief period of her life where other broken dreams went to die.

THE LADY HADN'T BEEN IMMUNE to him.

For the flare of indignation and shock in Eleanor's eyes earlier that evening, the blooming blush on her cheeks and the shuddery gasp she'd emitted spoke of a woman who desired him still.

With a glass of whiskey in hand, Marcus made his way through the empty corridors of his townhouse. The gold sconces lining the wall were lit intermittently, casting a shadowy glow off the satin wallpaper.

He came to a stop at the back of the townhouse and stared at the thick oak door between him and the outside gardens. He'd not entered this portion of the house in years. Absently, he finished his drink and set the glass down on a nearby mahogany side table.

Which in the scheme of life, it was an altogether long time to not move freely about your own home, and yet he hadn't. So why, at fifteen minutes past midnight, did he now stand at the door of the very garden he'd avoided? Unbidden, his gaze went to the brick wall dividing the gardens next door. Because of her. For like a phoenix rising from the ashes, Eleanor Elaine Carlyle had reentered his life. And more, she'd stolen into his thoughts—whether he wished it or not.

He cast a glance over his shoulder and stepped outside into the cleverly walled-in space. Specifically crafted by his mother and the older duchess who lived next door more than thirty years earlier, when the two women easily convinced their husbands to purchase the adjoining homes.

The half-moon hung in the night sky casting a pale white glow upon the earth. With the green grass and the flowers interspersed with flawless boxwoods, he might as well have been in the English countryside. Except the thick London air bespoke the truth. He closed the door behind him and, hands clasped behind his back, wandered deeper into the grounds; his boot steps silent upon the thick grass.

This had been their place. This had been their tucked away sanctuary, where they always knew precisely when they would find one another. A quarter past twelve was their hour; shared by only them.

… At fifteen past the hour, I will always be there. And we shall always know where we two are…

Until Eleanor had gone and shattered that pledge. She'd not shown up.

A second night had come and gone and, once more, their spot remained empty…and it had been empty ever since, but for the gardener who tended this area.

A night bird called out. The sad, lonely cry filled the night sky.

Marcus stopped beside the high-backed, wrought iron bench. The white piece situated against the wall hadn't always been positioned here. Rather, it had been dragged over, many years earlier, and from there on it had remained. He rocked back on the heels of his feet and in one fluid moment, built on insanity, he leapt up onto the seat as he'd done so many times. Extending his arms, he pulled up onto the edge and hefted himself atop the dividing wall.

With his legs hanging over the bricks separating his property from his neighbor's, Marcus sat there surveying the Duchess of Devonshire's also immaculate gardens. Yes, time stood still here, as well. The expertly tended rose bushes with their blooms now curled tight from the night chill, the ivy that clung to the brick wall, denser all these years later, and the only indication of that passage of time.

Marcus gave his head a wry shake. If the *ton* could see him, a notorious rogue who lived for his own pleasures hanging over the edge of his garden wall reminiscing of the only woman he'd truly wanted: a woman who, in the end, had wanted nothing more than a light flirtation.

A faint click thundered in the quiet and he shot his gaze toward the entrance of the duchess' doorway. Of course she would be here. He remained motionless as Eleanor stepped outside with tentative footsteps. He should go. He should allow her the privacy she craved and carry on with his own life as he had after her deception. He turned to leave, and then looked to her once more. The sight of her froze him so that any and all movement became a feat only the gods were capable of. In her modest, white night wrapper, bathed in moonlight, the lady had the look of a fey creature about to dance in the quiet woodlands. His mouth went dry and he was unsure whom he hated more in that instant—her for the hold she still had over his senses or himself for that weakness. Marcus forced his gaze away from her gently curved, slender frame, up to her face, and he frowned.

He detected the lines drawn at the corner of her mouth, the ashen hue of her skin. Who did she think of in this moment? Her beloved, departed husband? He balled his hands. And why should it matter so much if she did?

Eleanor stiffened, and found Marcus with her gaze. Then, they two had always moved in a synchronistic harmony; aware of the other when no one else was.

He bowed his head. "Eleanor."

Eleanor wetted her lips and cast a frantic glance about. Where was the bold, smiling creature of her youth who would have had a witty repartee for his younger self? When she looked at him at last, the guarded caution in her eyes glinted in the moonlight. "My lord," she said quietly, her words carrying in the night silence. Eleanor turned on a jerky flourish and made to leave.

"Never tell me you're running away from me, sweet."

She stopped mid-movement and spun back around. Even with the distance between them, he'd have to be blind to fail and note the wariness that bled from her eyes.

...I do not want empty endearments, Marcus.

Then what should I call you?

Love...I only wish to be your love...

The muscles of his stomach clenched at the long-buried memory.

Eleanor smoothed her palms down the front of her modest nightshift. "You shouldn't be here, my lord."

No, he shouldn't. Nonetheless, Marcus lowered himself to the ground. "With the friendship between us, certain liberties are permitted." The heels of his boots sunk into the moist earth, muting his drop.

"No." Eleanor shook her head vigorously. "They are not. Nor would I say we are friends."

The young lady was correct in that regard. But they had been, and at a time when he'd desperately needed a friend; at a time when grief had ravaged him and, in her, he'd found the ability to smile again and laugh. *Goddamn you, Eleanor Elaine.*

Drawing on years of practice as the unaffected rogue, he strode over. "Very well." He stopped so only a hairsbreadth separated them. "Then liberties are surely permitted given the friendship between our *families*."

She troubled her lower lip between her teeth, drawing his gaze inexorably to the slight, seductive movement. That slightly crooked front tooth, which had once mesmerized. He grimaced. God, what a hopeless romantic he'd been. Thanks to her defection, life had taught him there was but one purpose for a beautiful mouth such as hers.

Eleanor held his stare. "Why are you here?" she asked with a directness uncharacteristic of the ladies of the *ton*. As such, it was one he appreciated.

Marcus folded his arms. "Why am I here?" His mind stalled. Why was he here? Why, when the last place he should care to be was with the lady who'd wrenched his heart out and left an empty void in its wake? She was a woman who'd ruined him for that emotion, forevermore. And in the absence of any justifiable reason built on logic, he turned her question on her. "Why are you here, Eleanor?"

She continued to worry the fabric of her skirts. "This is my aunt's garden. I enjoy—"

"Here, in London," he said gruffly. Why, when she'd disappeared into the country and remained an elusive phantom these years, was she here now? Yes, there was the role of companion she'd come to take on…and yet, he'd wager all his solvent holdings that the duchess would turn over a fortune if her beloved niece so much as asked for it. He ran his eyes over the stoic planes of her face. Then, Eleanor had the grace and dignity to never beg for assistance. "Are you here to capture a new husband?"

He didn't realize he held his breath until she snorted. "I've as much desire for another husband as I do a megrim at midnight."

Even as the tension in his chest eased, an odd sensation yanked at his heart. Her handful of casually tossed words were more telling than anything else she uttered about the man she'd wed. Had she, too, been deceived by one who professed love and then ultimately brought nothing more than betrayal and heartache? Only, there was no glee at that possibility. Regardless of her betrayal, she'd once been a friend to him when he'd very much needed one.

As though she'd followed the path his thoughts had traveled, Eleanor glanced down at her slippered feet. He brushed his knuckles along her jaw, bringing her gaze back to his. Eleanor wetted her lips and, as she'd always done, filled the voids of silence. "Y-you may be rest assured of my intentions here. For your suspicions of me, I am not here to torment you." How could the lady not know she'd haunted and tormented him for years now? First, in her absence and now, with her reemergence. "I'm merely here to serve as my aunt's companion. We will move in entirely different social circles and there will be little need for us to see one another."

Marcus stared hard at her. Did he imagine the regret tingeing that pledge? He thrust aside those foolish musings. "It is quarter past the midnight hour," he murmured.

Crimson bathed her cheeks in a telling blush.

At the revealing silence, he winged an eyebrow up.

"I-is it?" she squeaked. "I-I did not realize the hour."

Liar.

Marcus grazed the pad of his thumb over her lip and her full mouth trembled. A surge of desire gripped him; a need to draw her close and explore the taste of her.

Eleanor's long, golden lashes fluttered wildly and she jerked her face away, dislodging his touch. "Remember yourself, my lord." She retreated a step.

"How very proper you've become." He infused a silken thread to his words. "I liked you bold and secretly scandalous." As she'd been. The young woman who'd pulled herself up and peered over this same garden wall in search of him.

Crimson color splotched her cheeks and as he advanced, Eleanor layered her back against the doorway. "I was always proper, Marcus," she said tightly.

Another wave of desire assaulted him. Her husky contralto, that seductive timbre had once haunted the better part of his waking and sleeping moments. Even after all these years, he wanted her still. He wanted to know her in the one way he'd not; in his bed, in his arms, with her reaching for him, pleading. He propped his hand on the door at her back, skillfully preventing her escape. "Where is the fun in proper?" he whispered. They were both mature adults. Why should they not renew their acquaintance in the way his body still longed to?

Eleanor snapped her eyebrows together. "I would expect a gentleman who is in the market for a wife would not be out here speaking such words aloud."

His lips twitched. "And what words have I spoken, love? What words do you deem too scandalous too utter?" It did not escape his notice that this was now the second time she'd mentioned his marital state. "Do you know what I believe, Eleanor?" Not allowing her to reply, he lowered his head close to hers. "I believe, in your mind, you've conjured all imaginings of how it was between us and how it could be again."

The muscles of her long, graceful neck worked and male satisfaction slammed into him at the hint of her desiring.

Marcus lowered his mouth to hers and claimed her lips, just as he'd longed to for years after she'd left. Her body went stiff in his arms and she pressed her palms against his chest, as though to push him away, but then she clenched and unclenched her fingers in the fabric of his coat, pulling him close.

What had begun as a kiss meant to taunt and torture became something more, something that sucked away his self-control and logic. With a groan, he deepened the kiss. Her lips quivered under his and she kissed him with the hesitancy of youth before parting her lips and allowing him entry.

Their tongues met in an explosion of long-suppressed passion. She tasted of sweetness and innocence and everything he'd thought to never again know. He dragged his mouth down the corner of her lips and then he gently explored the place where her pulse pounded hard at her throat. He sucked and nipped at the flesh.

She whimpered and twisted her fingers in his hair, anchoring him close.

"I have wanted you in this way since I first met you, Eleanor Elaine," he rasped against the satiny softness of her skin.

"Oh, Marcus." His name emerged as a breathless entreaty and sent lust spiraling. He continued his quest, passing his lips lower. With sure movements, he parted the fabric of her nightshift and her entire body jerked. On a small cry, she stumbled sideways, dislodging her spectacles.

Her skin flush from desire, Eleanor stood there, her chest moving in time to his. She readjusted the wire rims on her face and, with shaking fingers, she pulled the fabric of her nightshift closed.

"I do not want you, Marcus." In the absence of conviction, those words rang hollow.

He turned his lips upward in a slow, unsteady grin. "Oh?"

By the deepening blush on her cheeks, the lady knew as much. She set her mouth with a brittleness better reserved for a cynical spinster. "I-I am not looking to be another one of your conquests."

He closed the distance between them and captured a loose golden curl between his thumb and forefinger and raised the strand to his nose. The scent of honeysuckle whispered about his senses blending with the natural garden scents, intoxicating as any potent aphrodisiac. "A pity," he whispered against her ear and her eyelids fluttered. "Your body tells a different tale." He lowered his head so their lips nearly brushed. Eleanor's breath caught on an audible intake and another rush of desire coursed through him. "Tell me, what do you know of my conquests?" He should be thrilled with the evidence of her passion for him, and yet it was her words that held him enthralled. Why should she care who he'd carried on with over the years? Why, when she'd chosen another?

Eleanor blinked wildly and then hooded her eyes. "I know enough."

Marcus folded his arms at his chest. "Have you been reading about me, love?"

She danced out of his reach. "No!" The denial burst from her with such ferocity it hinted at the lie there. "And cease calling me 'love'."

He stalked toward her. She boldly held her ground. "Ah, then how do you know about my…how did you phrase it? Conquests?" Marcus tweaked her nose. He'd always delighted in eliciting a reaction from the lady.

Eleanor glanced frantically about and then shocked him with the directness of the stare she trained on him. "Do you wish to know the truth, Marcus?"

He inclined his head.

"I may have lived in the country all these years, but even an unsophisticated widow from the country reads *The Times*. It did not take any searching to see the man you've become."

The man I've become.

Fury lanced through him, blotting out all desire and warmth for the woman who'd betrayed him. "The man I've become," he gritted out. "The man I've become was a product of your betrayal, madam. I gave my heart to you, confided," the hell of Lionel's murder when he'd let no one into the tortured hell of discovering his friend's body gutted by his murderer's hand, "everything and you simply vanished without a word."

"I wrote a letter." She tipped her chin up at a mutinous angle. "Did you not receive it?"

Her words fanned fury within him. He'd received her goddamn note; a missive he'd clung to for years, bringing it out when he wished to remind himself that he hated Eleanor Carlyle more than he'd ever loved her.

He narrowed his eyes and refused to allow her the satisfaction of knowing she still had the power to wound. "I received your blasted letter," he bit out through clenched teeth. The words he'd longed to hurl at her for the past eight years tumbled to the tip of his tongue and only the years of deportment and propriety drilled into him from the nursery, onward, quelled the words. He tempered his tone. "You owed me an explanation." After all, he'd given her the whole of his heart and she'd given him a vague, empty note about a faceless, nameless stranger who'd won her.

"Explanation?" her voice came out woodenly.

He fisted his hands. "Yes, an explanation. As in, answers as to," *How you could simply leave after all we'd shared and the manner in which I let you into my world.* "What happened," he finished lamely.

"You think you're deserving of answers?" Eleanor looked at him as though he'd sprouted a second head. "More than I've already given you," she said when he opened his mouth to speak.

"Yours was not an answer." It was a goodbye. Those were vastly different things.

Tension filled the air. At last, it was between them. The unspoken past that hovered and danced, finally breathed to existence.

He braced for her stinging, tart rebuttal. Instead, she passed her wide eyes over him, sadness emanating from within their endless depths. "I gave you all the words you needed." Then, with stiff movements, she turned and started toward the doorway.

He suppressed the hungering to call out to her. For staring at her retreating frame, he finally realized it would not matter what words she gave him. It would not matter whether she spoke with love and longing for the man who'd claimed her hand and heart.

It would not matter if she'd missed Marcus, even just a little in her absence. The dream of them was as dead and gone as the charred ashes in a dirtied hearth. And with that truth, he could embrace the freedom in that and hold on to the only safe sentiment where Eleanor was concerned.

Desire.

"I want you," he called out, staying her movements.

Eleanor froze. The delicate span of her back went taut as she turned slowly around.

"I stopped loving you long ago," he said, those words born of truth. In the years following her betrayal, he'd come to see that sentiment as an empty one, built on a child's fanciful dreams and imaginings. Desire was safe. It was the only honest emotion. Eleanor stood stoic, unmoving, and just then he hated her as much now as he had years ago when he'd received that goddamn note. He hated her for being coldly unemotional and unfeeling. He gave his head a sad, little shake. How little he'd known her. "But I want you, anyway."

She widened her eyes.

He took a step toward her. "I want to know you in my arms and in my bed. I want to know your cries as you find release and you want me, too." He hooded his eyes. "And I promise you, Eleanor Elaine, before you run off and leave London," again, "I will know those pleasures and more…*you* will know those pleasures." Then, Eleanor would remember Marcus forever, no matter who came after Marcus and he could, at last, purge himself of this insatiable need for her.

Eleanor scrabbled her hands about her neck and gripped the collar of her modest, frilled, white nightshift. "Don't you see, Marcus?" She lifted her palms up. "I am a widow, but that does not make me a whore. And I'll not play the role of whore for you."

Shame sent heat racing up his neck. He took a languid step toward her, even as a volatile tension thrummed inside him. "You speak of there being something wrong in renewing where we left off."

A sad, quiet laugh escaped her. "Is this where we left off?" She raked a disappointed stare up and down his person. "With you determined to bed me and then move on to wed some proper English lady with a title and a spotless reputation?"

The air crackled and hissed with her stinging accusation and a curtain of fury descended over his vision. How dare she paint any intention he had to marry as dishonorable? *She* had been the one who'd turned him over for another. "Let us be clear, I would have wed you. It is you who left, so do not make my intentions of the past the dishonorable sort." His harsh tone drained the color from her cheeks and, yet, she proved as courageous as she'd always been.

"What of now?" She quirked a golden eyebrow. "Are these intentions honorable?" Silence fell between them and Eleanor gave a sad shake of her head. "That is exactly what I thought, Marcus. Find some other willing woman to take to your bed, for that woman will not be me."

Why? Why could it not be her? And was she even now, all these years later, still so hopelessly in love with her husband that she could not even countenance even the thought of another man in her arms or in her life? He balled his hands into hard fists, despising that such a truth should even matter.

She stopped with her fingers on the door handle, and then wheeled to again face him. "You speak of the man you became." The moon cast a haunting glow on her pale cheeks. "But the truth is, I did not make you anything." She motioned to him and he went taut at that dismissive gesture. "This is who you would have become. You are such a part of this world I never truly belonged to. Perhaps you would have married me." *I would have. I would have filled your days with laughter and turned the world upside down if it dared chased away your smile.* Marcus curled his hands at the force of that empty dream. "But you would have become the rogue the world knows."

"And is that why you left?" As soon as the words left his terse lips, his body jerked erect. How pathetic, how desperate, those words were, for this woman who'd never been deserving of him.

"Oh, Marcus," she said softly. With an ethereal grace, Eleanor drifted over. "I left for the both of us. Neither of us could have ever been happy with one another. Not truly and not forever." Another night bird called its song, haunting and sweet. She clasped her hands together and stared briefly down at the interlocked digits. "I should leave."

Yes, she should. In fact, she should have never returned. Then he'd not feel any of the old hurt and pain of her betrayal. "Not at all," he said stiffly. "I will leave you to your company. But before I do, Eleanor, know that before you leave London, we'll know the pleasure to be had in each other's arms." A flash of fear sparked briefly in her eyes and then was quickly gone so that it might have been nothing more than a trick of the moonlit night.

Without another word, Marcus tipped his head and strode over to the wall. He hefted himself over the ledge, sliding down the side. He claimed a seat on the wrought iron bench.

His ears attuned to her every movement, he detected Eleanor's shuddery sigh and then the click of the door as she disappeared inside her aunt's townhouse.

CHAPTER 8

HER AUNT'S DINNER HAD BEEN a disaster. The interlude in the gardens with Marcus was an even greater one. But she'd survived.

That is, after all, what Eleanor had perfected over the years. The art of survival. Surviving when one's heart was being torn open from the agony of loss. Surviving when the only parent one remembered, who'd given up all to try and salvage a hopeless life, died. Surviving when the horrors visited upon her should have destroyed her.

Two nights after the duchess' intimate party, Marcus occupied every chamber of Eleanor's mind. For with his parting pledge, he'd forced her to contemplate both how it had once been between them and the hell that had come to her in a different garden at her attacker's hands. And in her musings, Marcus wrestled control away from that night of horror.

Seated on the pink sofa, she eyed the volume of Mary Wollstonecraft's work on her lap, studying the gold lettering upon the leather book. She trailed her fingertips over those letters, recalling Marcus as he'd been; tempting and charming, and yet...*cynical*. A shell of the man he'd been. A man who'd kissed her with the same passion of his youth, but with a new roguish experience. An experience that came from years of countless courtesans and widows he'd bedded. She closed her eyes a moment torn between hating him for that knowledge and loving him for awakening this yearning within her.

After her rape, she'd believed herself incapable of feeling anything but revulsion from a man's touch. The memory of Marcus' searing kisses, the burn of his questing hand as he'd explored her body, all those once beautiful acts, had been torn asunder by another so that she'd come to view them as vile, violent, and shameful.

Just as Marcus had introduced her to the hint of passion years earlier, now he'd awakened her to the beautiful, healing truth—she was still capable of feeling something in a man's arms—something beyond hurt and pain. Her heart caught. Nay, not just any man could stir this need inside her. It had only ever been and would forever only be Marcus who had the power to make her feel and celebrate the glorious wonder of desire.

And she loved Marcus all the more for it. Eleanor forced her eyes open and stared blankly down at the book. She loved him, even as his guarded eyes revealed a cynical man, mistrustful and jaded.

Is that because of me? Her heart wrenched. Surely a man who'd moved on to become a notorious rogue, taking his pleasure where he would, did not harbor ill-will for the young lady who'd set him free? *He would if he loved me and I broke his heart...* And he'd never given her reason to doubt his love. Yet, she'd somehow convinced herself that what he'd felt for her had merely been the romantic sentiments of a young man who didn't truly know his mind and certainly not his heart. That had made the agony of leaving him bearable.

"I believe you are the one in need of a companion, gel."

Her aunt's words brought Eleanor's head up so quickly the spectacles slipped down the bridge of her nose. She pushed them back into place. "I'm sorry," she murmured and hurriedly opened the tome, fanning the pages to the last chapter of Mrs. Wollstonecraft's work.

"Bah, I've had enough of Mrs. Wollstonecraft today." The older woman leaned over and plucked the volume from Eleanor's hands. "I wish to speak to you about why I had you come here to London."

Panic jumped in her chest. "I will strive to do better," she said quickly. When her aunt's missive had arrived she'd been conflicted with warring sentiments; fear of returning and gratitude for the salvation offered Eleanor and Marcia. "I know I've been distracted." A vast understatement. She'd been woolgathering worse than a debutante who'd just made her Come Out and found love. Eleanor would know. She'd been that girl.

"You think I'm aiming to send you away, Eleanor Elaine?" Aunt Dorothea never used her name. Except when displeased.

Eleanor buried her shaking fingers in her skirts. "No?"

Her aunt snorted. "I've no intention of sending you away." Relief sagged Eleanor's shoulders. "Entirely for selfish reasons," the duchess added, her cheeks flushed. The usually stoic woman likely didn't wish to shatter the image she'd established as gruff, stern matron. "I do not care to be alone."

Not unlike her aunt in that regard, Eleanor could certainly identify with those sentiments. After Father's passing, even with Marcia, she'd been besieged by the aching loss of his steady, reassuring presence. "I won't leave you alone," she said softly. Even if being in London would ever rouse terror in her belly and agony in her heart.

The woman's wrinkled throat worked. "Of course you won't," she said gruffly. She thumped her cane and the two pugs trotted over. With a bent and aged hand, she rubbed them on the tops of their heads. "I lied to you, though, gel."

Eleanor angled her head. "Aunt Dorothea?"

"I know you'd not have come otherwise."

She shook her head. "I don't under—"

"Your uncle left you ten thousand pounds." Her aunt continued to pat her two dogs.

At the duchess' matter-of-fact deliverance of those life-transforming words, Eleanor's heart picked up a frantic pounding born of hope. "What?" she whispered. All the greatest terror that had robbed her of rest over her and Marcia's fate dimmed and a lightness drove back the terror that had weighted her waking and sleeping thoughts since Father's passing.

A smile pulled at the woman's usually stern lips. "I'm the one with faulty hearing, gel, not you. Your uncle settled ten thousand pounds on you."

As the implications of her aunt's revelation sank into Eleanor's slow to comprehend mind, she slid her eyes closed. A fortune. He'd left her a fortune which would allow her to care for Marcia, and never worry about being dependent upon anyone, and more…she'd never have to marry for convenience. A sob escaped her throat and she buried her face in her hands.

"Don't do that, gel," her aunt said, her voice gruff with uncharacteristic emotion. She patted Eleanor's knee the way she did her beloved pups. "I loved your uncle, but it doesn't mean he was intelligent in all the ways that matter, and certainly not in matters of a lady's mind." She snapped her fingers and the two dogs ambled off to their corner of the room where they claimed a spot on the sofa. "But there you have it."

There she had what?

The old woman leaned forward in her seat, and the chair groaned its protest. "Men, they assume they know what is best for all." Her aunt made a sound of disgust and Eleanor desperately tried to follow along.

Her aunt gave her a meaningful look.

Warning bells blared in Eleanor's ears.

"He wants you to reenter Society, Eleanor."

A pall of silence fell over the room.

The duchess' words came as though down a long hall and Eleanor curled her hands into tight fists. *No.* She could not. "I cannot." Did that weak, breathless avowal belong to her?

"The ten thousand pounds are contingent upon that, gel," her aunt interrupted, settled her palms on the arms of her chair, like a king issuing a decree.

Nausea churned in Eleanor's belly at fate's cruel jest. So this is why she was here. It was not merely to serve as companion to her lonely aunt. Fear made her mouth go dry and with fingers that trembled, Eleanor grabbed the leather book from the seat next to her and pulled it close to her chest. After she'd made her hasty flight, she'd vowed to never return to the place where horror lived on in her memories. Only a need to see Marcia cared for had forced her to set aside those fears. She could not, however, have a Season. Not again. She was not so strong that she could dance with the threat of someday facing the man who'd shattered her world. That would destroy her in the ways he'd not already succeeded. Eleanor slowly lowered the book to the spot beside her on the sofa, proud of the steadiness of her fingers. "Aunt Dorothea, I am sure Uncle meant well, and I am grateful," she said on a hurry. "But I do not need," want "to take part in *ton* events," she settled for, proud of the steady deliverance of those calm words, when inside her mind clamored.

To have hope and happiness dangled so very close, and then yanked back with a vicious cruelty. Why, with the shattered dream, she might as well have been the wide-eyed, hopeful girl she'd been all those years ago. Eleanor shook her head. "I cannot," she repeated, this time those two words ringing with conviction.

"You do not have to wed in order to acquire the funds," her aunt said with a frown. She reached inside a pocket sewn into the front of her gown, and fished around. "Ah," she muttered. She withdrew a sheet of vellum.

The ormolu clock ticked away the passing moments as Eleanor eyed the page before finally accepting it with stiff fingers.

"Go on," the older woman urged, jerking her chin at it.

Eleanor unfolded the page and quickly scanned the perfunctory list.

Don a colorful satin gown
Allow a gentleman to escort you in a curricle ride through Hyde Park
Dance one waltz at midnight
Attend a ball hosted by your aunt
Partake in ices at Gunther's…with a gentleman
Attend a performance at the theatre

She furrowed her brow. *These* were the items comprising her late uncle's list?

"Your uncle was about happiness," her aunt said, bringing Eleanor's head up. "He loved life and lived it to the fullest. He would have seen you happy."

"I am happy," she said automatically, folding the page. And she was. She had her daughter's love and Marcia gave her life a purpose that had meaning.

The duchess scoffed. "This is you happy, Eleanor?"

Unable to meet the woman's all-knowing eyes, she momentarily looked away. For in truth, even as Marcia filled Eleanor's heart, she had not truly been happy since she'd left Marcus and crafted a falsified life for herself.

"You just need to see to those items and then at the end," her aunt said, calling her to the moment, "if no gentleman has earned your affections," None would. "Then the funds are yours to do with as you wish, for you—" She closed her eyes. She could not do this. "Or your girl."

Her girl. Marcia. The child she'd sacrificed all for. Numb, Eleanor climbed to her feet. She wandered over to the window and peeled back the curtain. She stared down into the very streets she'd met Marcus. When any other young lady would have gladly given up a babe forced upon them, Eleanor had known only love for her daughter. She'd devoted her life to Marcia, just as Father had given up the life he'd established as a respected merchant and spirited her away, fashioning a new life for them in the far-flung corners of Cornwall.

Then, that is what one did when one was a parent. You sacrificed all in the name of love. She dropped her gaze to the folded page. In the scheme of all she'd endured, these charges tasked by her late uncle were so very small and would see Marcia provided for in ways she'd never been. This list was about so much more than Eleanor. It was about her daughter's future and security and time had already proven, Eleanor would do anything and be anything she needed to be for her child. "Six items," she said, woodenly.

It was but six items; only three of them requiring her to allow a man near her.

"You always were a smart girl."

A hysterical breath bubbled past her lips. If she'd been a smart girl, she'd not have gone off on her own and allowed herself to be trapped by a vile blackguard.

"And perhaps you'll surprise yourself and find love." Again, the word dangled unfinished between them.

"I won't." The denial ripped ragged from her. She'd never find love. She'd found love and that love would forever remain in the past; a gift to a younger, smiling gentleman from a younger, unjaded girl. Marcus, the way he'd been at one time, would always have her heart. Not this dark, bitter stranger she didn't know.

"You and I both know you will, gel." Aunt Dorothea gestured with her cane, motioning to Eleanor's skirts. "And you'll be needing new gowns for your Season. But for now, go."

At any other moment she would have politely declined and remained to see to her responsibilities. "Thank you," she murmured and all but flew from the room, desperate for escape. She sprinted down the corridors until her breath came hard and fast, took the corner quickly and came to a stop under a row of her late uncle's distinguished relatives. Her chest heaved from the force of her emotion.

Closing her eyes, she placed her forehead against the hard plaster wall, finding a comfort in the hard, cool surface. Her aunt spoke so easily of Eleanor rejoining polite Society and yet she didn't know what had driven her niece away; didn't know that Eleanor ruined, with a monster's seed inside her belly, had fled and reinvented a life for herself based on flimsy lies that could be unveiled if anyone bothered with the young widow.

For nearly eight years, she'd given no one reason to wonder about Mrs. Collins, young mother, war widow, and that invisibility had brought her some semblance of security in her disordered world. She'd briefly mourned the loss of the innocent young lady she'd been in Miss Eleanor Carlyle, and then swore to never be her again and, more importantly, never to return. For to enter the glittering world of Society, she danced with fire and, worse, there was the possibility of seeing him. Eleanor sucked in a gasping breath and knocked her forehead against the wall to drive back his leering, grinning visage. Yet he'd slipped in, as he too often did, commandeering her thoughts. That unknown man, the tall, dark-eyed, black-hearted bastard who'd stolen what didn't belong to him and forever shattered her world.

Restless, Eleanor pushed away from the wall and rested her back against the surface. Slowly, she sank to the floor and drew her knees close to her chest. Her skin crawled in remembrance of a cruel, punishing touch, the taste of his lips, brandy. Bile rose up her throat and threatened to choke her. She desperately needed the funds her uncle's will provided for her. The vast sum would save her from any fears or uncertainties of her or Marcia's future and yet, she may as well have been selling her soul to the devil himself in returning.

Eleanor dropped her chin atop her knees and rubbed back and forth. In coming back, a young widow, she risked becoming prey to other lecherous lords. Her skin burned hot with shame of that long ago night with a nameless stranger. Then weren't all women, regardless of marital status, prey to those rakish, caddish *gentlemen*?

"Are you hiding?"

A startled shriek escaped her and she slapped a hand to her breast. Marcia stood a handful of steps away, scratching her brow. "Marcia," she said breathlessly. "I didn't hear you."

"Because you were hiding?" Her daughter skipped over and sat beside Eleanor; her little shoulder pressed against her side. "But, Mama?" she asked in a whisper that was really no whisper at all.

"What is it, poppet?"

"This is really a horrendous hiding place. If you need help hiding, I will help you."

She tossed her arm around Marcia's shoulders and hugged her close. "You will be the first person whose help I ask."

Pride lit her brown eyes, but then her smile dipped. "Why are you sad?"

"I'm not sad." To prove as much, she forced a smile.

"Then scared?"

"I'm—" She stopped at the displeased pout on Marcia's lips. They had been closer than any two people could ever be. With the exception of Eleanor's now departed father, there'd been only Eleanor and Marcia. In their isolation from Society they had forged a special bond, and even though she was a child, there seemed something inherently wrong in not sharing something. "Well, you see, I have to go somewhere I don't wish to go."

Marcia tipped her head back and peered at Eleanor. "Where?" Then worry filled her eyes. "Not leave as Grandfather did?"

"No!" she exclaimed, hugging Marcia all the tighter. "No, I would never leave like Papa. Not until you're an old, hopelessly wrinkled, gray lady." She made a show of studying Marcia's curls. "Is there any gray? Hmm. I think I see one," she tickled the top of her daughter's head until little, snorting laughs escaped her and she wiggled back and forth.

"S-stop, M-mama. I- s-stop."

Eleanor relented and then gave her the truth. "Uncle gave me a list of...tasks," she settled for. After all, wasn't that what it was?

Marcia wrinkled her nose. "Tasks?"

"I have to go to balls and soirees," she amended.

"Why, that sounds wonderful." Attending those events would be about as enjoyable as doffing her slippers and stockings and walking across hot embers. "I should love to attend balls and soirees." There was a wistful, faraway quality to those words that tugged at Eleanor.

"Someday," she promised. She closed her eyes and drew in the fragrant, citrusy scent of her daughter's hair. This is why she'd endure another Season and the threat posed to her heart when Marcus was near, and the threat to her sanity of one day seeing *him*.

"You needn't be worried, Mama." Marcia scrambled backward. Then she beamed. "You need a friend."

"A friend?" There was not a friend she had in the world. "There is Aunt Dorothea."

Her daughter giggled. "Not Aunt Dorothea. Why, your friend, Marcus. You should invite him to go with you so you are not alone and then you won't be afraid."

Marcus. Help her? Why, he'd more likely welcome a date with the devil than acquiesce to her request for help. For all her fears of men and their nefarious intentions, she did not believe Marcus capable of hurting anyone. Even with his sneers and his snarls, she never believed he would hurt her.

Marcia hopped to her feet and held out her hand to help Eleanor up. "Come along, Mama. We need to find a new hiding place."

With a little laugh, she took her daughter by the hand. "You, my dear, need to find your way back to your nursemaid and return to your lessons." A groan escaped her daughter as they walked hand in hand abovestairs. And perhaps it spoke to Eleanor's desperation, but as they made their way through the corridors, she rather thought there was merit to her daughter's suggestion. She certainly required a friend.

Unfortunately, however, she'd forfeited all rights to Marcus' friendship when she'd left him with nothing more than several empty lines dashed upon a piece of parchment.

CHAPTER 9

THROUGH THE YEARS, MARCUS HAD come to enjoy *ton* events. Where most gentlemen sought ways to avoid those crowded affairs, Marcus had moved with an ease and comfort. He presented a carefree smile which polite Society had come to expect. He'd filled his life with inanity and quite reveled in it. Polite events and even more impolite events had provided a diversion from the horrors that still lingered from his youth. A young man of twenty-one, he, the Duke of Crawford and Lionel, the future Marquess of Roxbury had reveled in the impolite—they'd taken their pleasures in the Dials and only two of them returned alive.

Yes. *Most* balls provided a diversion.

Most.

Seated at the breakfast table, with his copy of *The Times* up, Marcus fixed on one line.

…The Duchess of D hosting her first event since the passing of the Duke of D…

Which had certainly not proven newsworthy to Marcus when he'd accepted that particular invite weeks prior. It was, however, significant with the arrival of a certain lady who'd be acting as companion to the duchess. For Eleanor's assurance that evening past under the half-moon with stars as their witness, that they needn't see one another and that they would move within entirely different Social spheres, they both knew that to be just another lie she'd fed him.

His fingers tightened reflexively upon the pages. No, there was no escaping. From her. From her charges in the garden at quarter past midnight. As though the life he'd lived in her absence was one he should be shamed by. As though she had been the honorable one and he—

"Do stop growling, Marcus. It is impolite."

The paper slipped from his fingers and he found his mother frowning at him with stern-faced disapproval. Her orders were met with a flurry of giggles and he looked to Lizzie and Lady Marianne Hamilton. So the lady would now take breakfast with his sister, now. He inclined his head. "My apologies, ladies. It is…" Marcus blinked.

Lady Marianne settled her elbows on the table and leaned forward in a way that put her impressive décolletage on display. "Have you not found anything that pleases you…on those pages, my lord?" She parted her lips slightly in a wanton invitation. "Surely there must be something of interest."

Unbidden, his gaze went to the cream white mounds fairly spilling over the top of her gown. Yet, the Marquess of Atbrooke's sister, the most sought after Diamond that Season was nothing, if not an innocent. He fixed his attention on the young lady and her come hither stare. With her midnight black curls piled high atop her head and crimson, too-full lips, the lady was a lush beauty who at any other time would have commanded his notice; a young woman who recently *had* commanded his notice.

Lady Marianne turned her lips up in a slow, enticing smile.

So why could he not stop comparing her practiced smile to another young lady's? A woman purer in her golden beauty; with freckles on her nose, and honest, if now guarded, crystalline blue eyes framed by spectacles.

He jumped as his sister called out. "Come, Marcus, have you not heard Marianne's question? It is entirely rude of you to fail to respond. Isn't that right, Mama?"

Skin flushed, he looked to his mother, who thankfully remained engrossed in the contents of her plate. "Indeed, Marcus."

Marcus reached for his cup of coffee and took a sip. "The information on the pages is entertaining enough, Lady Marianne."

Belatedly realizing the unintended veiled innuendo to those words, Marcus silently cursed at Lady Marianne's widening smile.

Setting his cup down so hard the black brew spilled over the side, he grabbed his copy of *The Times* and buried his face behind it once more. With a beauty such as Lady Marianne seated across the table and making eyes at him, he should be fixed on that particular lady. After all, he was a hot-blooded, living, breathing male. Though he had no intention of wedding any time soon, despite his mother's machinations, this cool, beautiful ice princess would pose the perfectly safe match for him. At the very least, he should hold her form and figure in masculine appreciation. Except... While his sister and friend resumed their prattling, he fixed his stare on one name contained within the pages of *The Times*.

...The Duchess will be joined by her niece, Mrs. C. Not much is known of the lady beyond...

Instead, he sat fuming about the duchess' blasted niece.

"...Oh, do hush, Lizzie, you are absolutely splendid in any color you don."

And yet, how could he not mourn the loss of what she'd represented? When life was hell, she'd dragged him out from the mire of misery, guilt, and despair, teaching him it was all right to smile once more.

"...Why must I wear white? This is my second Season?" His sister's lamentations cut across his musings and he again lowered his paper.

His mother tapped a hand on the table. "It, at least, presents the idea of a just on the market miss, Lizzie."

His sister snorted and shoved her spectacles on her nose. "Anyone who pays attention to gossip columns knows precisely what I am."

Lady Marianne made a sound of protest and covered Lizzie's hand with her own.

Marcus' smile dipped. "And what is that?" he said, welcome for the diversion away from thoughts of Eleanor and Lionel's murder.

She rolled her eyes. "I'm a wallflower and one who wears spectacles, at that."

How could not a single gentleman have realized his sister's worth? Fools, the lot of them. "There is nothing wrong with spectacles," he said, his frown deepened.

"Of course there is, Marcus," his sister said slowly. "Gentlemen do not want to wed a woman with spectacles." Eleanor's bespectacled visage flitted across his mind. Even with her tresses pulled tight to her nape in a hideous chignon and the spectacles on her nose, they couldn't mute the lady's effervescent beauty still, all these years later.

Their mother and Lady Marianne made simultaneous sounds of protest.

"Oh, pish-posh," Mother said. "You are plenty beautiful to wed."

As she launched into a rapid defense of her daughter's beauty, Marcus leaned over and whispered in his sister's ear. "We shall get you colorful skirts."

Her eyes lit with happiness and she clapped her hands together.

"Marcus," his mother scolded. "She cannot..."

"She can and she shall," he promised and tugged on one of his sister's ringlets. He'd come to appreciate long ago that joy was fleeting, and it was best to steal it when and where one could. If a colorful gown would bring even a dash of happiness to his sister, then she'd have it. "Color is what makes life interesting, isn't that right?"

"How very fortunate you are to have such a loving brother, Lizzie," Lady Marianne said softly, dropping her chin atop her hand. "One who will take you even now to a modiste."

"Truly, Marcus?" He bit back a curse as his sister scrambled forward in her chair. "Will you accompany Marianne and me?"

Marcus looked past the troublesome minx, Lady Marianne, whose brown eyes even now sparked with mischief, to his mother.

She shook her head tightly. "I will not support the purchase of any non-white or ivory garments, Marcus."

Bloody hell. He searched his gaze about the room for escape.

Lizzie hugged his arm. "You are the very best brother," she said softly. Her plump face settled into a solemnity that erased all her earlier happiness. "Not because of the gown, but because you wish to see me happy. You will make some young lady a very wonderful husband." She tipped her head at an odd angle.

At that peculiar, less than subtle movement, he shook his head. Lizzie jerked her head once more and he followed her less than discreet nodding to where her friend sat smiling boldly at him. Marcus shifted. By the invitation in Lady Marianne's smile, she was welcoming the role of prospective future viscountess. "Shall we?" he asked, his voice coming out garbled as he hopped to his feet.

A short while later, Marcus strode down the fashionable end of North Bond Street, trailing behind his sister and Lady Marianne. He conceded the role of chaperone was one he could do without. His sister said something to the young lady accompanying her on her shopping expedition. Lady Marianne glanced back at him, a wicked promise in her eyes.

Before Eleanor had reemerged, Marcus would have been tempted by the promise in Lady Marianne's eyes. Now, as Lady Marianne trailed the tip of her tongue over the seam of her lips, there was somehow a wrongness in appreciating the lady's lush beauty. He silently strung together a stream of curses. Why could Eleanor not have stayed away? Why, so he could welcome the lust and lack of emotion he'd known with every other woman after her?

This time, when Lady Marianne peaked over her shoulder, Marcus deliberately looked away.

There had only been one, and would forever only be one, woman who'd held his heart, even if she'd not been deserving of that foolish organ. Except, Eleanor hadn't evinced the jaded, cynicism of the Lady Mariannes of the world. Fresh from the country and uninfluenced by the *ton*, she'd laughed and smiled with an abandon to captivate even the most broken of men—which he'd been.

The two ladies came to a stop beside a shop front and then filed inside like a row of ducks on their way to water. He lingered outside, reflecting not for the first time on his exchange with Eleanor several evenings ago in the gardens.

They'd both established that even with the shared street between them, there was little reason for them to see one another, and they assuredly would not be moving in the same Social spheres. Eleanor had undertaken the responsibilities as companion to the Duchess of Devonshire, and Marcus would visit ball after ball in the comfortable role of rogue he'd adopted these years. Those truths should bring relief and yet, there was none. Instead, he thought of Eleanor, in her drab, brown skirts and tightly drawn curls, impoverished, reliant on her aunt for survival, and he didn't want her relegated to that dark and dreary world, even if it did preserve his sanity. She should be attired in the finest satins and silks, only those gowns would not be the whites and ivories befitting the innocent she'd been. Now, she could and should be draped in those bold hues that conjured wicked thoughts. He fisted his hands, loathing the idea that her status as widow had earned her the right to those bold colors.

With a silent curse, he stomped up the handful of steps into the shop, determined to shake Eleanor's potent hold on his thoughts. He'd already ceded too much power to her years ago. He'd be damned if he allowed her any more of that control, just because he pitied the poor relation she'd become.

He closed the door of the shop, and hovered at the entrance, taking in his sister and Lady Marianne examining bolts of fabric. Marcus tugged at his cravat. Gentlemen didn't belong in a modiste's shop, and but for the visits he'd paid to the fashionable shops with his mistresses over the years, he'd studiously avoided them.

A sharp yap filled the establishment. He stiffened and looked about. A fawn pug came bounding toward him. The snorting ball of fur plopped at Marcus' feet and licked his boot. He narrowed his eyes. A very familiar snorting ball of fur. The dog's curled tongue lolled sideways out of his mouth. It was hardly the little bugger's fault for sharing walls with a certain temptress. Marcus bent down distractedly and patted the pug on his head.

From within the shop, a familiar, aged voice called out. "Pay attention, gel. What do you think of this fabric?" He stilled as the duchess' gruff tone echoed off the walls of the establishment.

Marcus straightened. Of course the lady would be here. The lady was everywhere.

Drawn forward, Marcus advanced deeper into the shop.

"You need a ball gown, gel. We cannot have you dancing in those drab, brown skirts." He and the duchess were of like opinion in this regard, but then the implications of that pronouncement sank into his mind; Eleanor properly attired in decadent silks and satins which conjured the most forbidden thoughts, all of which found the lady on her back, arms outstretched and her hair cascading in a golden waterfall about her. "If you'll not pick a swatch, I'll do it on my own. You can't have a Come Out in those brown skirts."

Eleanor's murmured response was lost to him.

Marcus fisted his hands at his sides. The lady had professed to being in London for no other reason than to serve as companion and, yet, by all intents and purposes was prepared to take the *ton* by storm as the young widow, returned to polite Society. His sister and her friend forgotten, he followed the duchess' clipped and commanding voice, and froze. He peered down the aisle to where the lady stood alongside Eleanor.

The older woman stood beside the modiste with two bolts of fabric in her hands—a pale yellow satin, better suited to a young debutante, and a garish orange muslin. Eleanor shook her head with such vigor she'd give herself a headache for her efforts. "… No need…"

Marcus stood as a silent observer, eying those fabrics, neither of which would suit Eleanor. Not anymore. At one time, yes. Now, she should be adorned in crimson reds and rich burgundies. He gripped the wood pillar. With her golden tresses, he'd have her in the softest, luxuriant, pink silk; a touch of innocence with a suggestive allure.

"There is always ivory," the duchess muttered something to herself as she moved her hands over various samples laid out.

"Ivory would be a perfect choice," the modiste exclaimed in a thick, outrageously embellished, and most definitely, false French accent.

"I am too old for ivory," Eleanor declared at her side.

An inelegant snort spilled past the older woman's lips. "*I'm* old, gel. You are young." She flicked the sleeve of Eleanor's brown dress. "Even if you insist on dressing yourself like a pinch-mouthed governess." Dismissing Eleanor's continued protestations, she turned her attention to the plump shopkeeper. "We need a ball gown and another swatch of fabric."

The duchess' words merely reminded him of the lie she'd uttered in the gardens. So the lady was here for a London Season, and no doubt to find another hus—Marcus growled.

From across the shop, Eleanor snapped her head up and their gazes collided. Color rushed her cheeks, and where Lady Marianne's blushes had held little appeal, the sight of Eleanor, as she'd once been, unrestrained and sincere, filled him with a potent wave of longing. He braced for the moment she jerked her attention away. "Hullo," she greeted, breaking the silence, and shattering his expectations.

"Mrs. Collins," he drawled, strolling the length of the aisle. The pug trotted along at his side.

The duchess looked at him. "What are you doing here, boy? Surely nothing appropriate can bring you here." She softened that recrimination with a sly wink.

The ghost of a frown marred Eleanor's lips.

"I've accompanied my sister and her friend," he put in, his gaze trained on Eleanor.

Some of the tension left Eleanor's frame. So the lady was bothered by the idea of him with another. What an inexplicable reaction from a woman who'd thrown him over for another.

The duchess patted his hand. "You've always been a good boy, Marcus." She spoke of him the way she might one of her prized, legendary dogs.

He and Eleanor shared a look and her lips slowly tilted up in a hesitant smile. How very guarded she was. She protected the smile the way the King's Army preserved peace.

"You'll help us, Marcus." The duchess thumped her cane. "Not that I require help," she said, waggling her eyebrows. "But this one," she gestured to Eleanor. "With her brown and gray gowns believes herself of a great fashion sense."

He quickly passed a gaze over Eleanor. The lady could don the coarsest, darkest fabric and still shine more resplendent than the sun. "Oh?" he asked noncommittally. Marcus winced as the duchess flipped her cane forward and jabbed him in the knee. "Being a rogue all these years, you've forgotten your manners, I see. You owed the girl a compliment."

"Aunt Dorothea," Eleanor protested, her expression as pained as her tone. She looked to Marcus and gave a pleading shake. "You really do n—"

"Ah, yes, indeed," he said softly. He claimed Eleanor's hand. Her fingertips trembled within his as he raised them to his mouth. "With your beauty, you could set a trend where ladies abandon their white skirts for the shades of gray and brown your aunt now disparages."

Eleanor's breath caught and her lips parted. The room fell away. The incessant chattering of his sister and her friend at the front of the establishment, the yapping of the two pugs running about the shop, the modiste standing beside the duchess lifting different bolts for the lady's examination. His gaze fell to Eleanor's mouth and he hungered for the feel of her lips beneath his once more.

Then the duchess' sharp bark of laughter cut across the moment and the world resumed spinning. "A hopeless rogue is what he's become in your absence, Eleanor."

With quick movements, Eleanor wrenched her hand free, disentangling their interconnected fingers, and he mourned the loss. He would have severed one of his hands years ago, just to know her touch once more. Now she was here and that caress should be so fleeting. Desperate to reclaim his footing upon a situation fast spiraling out of his control, he forced a smile. "I thought I'd always been a, how did you refer to it? Good boy?"

"Some rogues can be both. You're one of them. Isn't that right?" She turned the question to Eleanor.

Eleanor clasped her hands before her. "I daresay I've not much experience with rogues."

Which only raised questions as to what kind of man she'd wed. Had he been a quiet, stoic soldier who'd shared Eleanor's love of music and sonnets? If so, the man had quashed her spirit, and for that, had never been deserving of the effervescent girl she'd once been. With that demon between them, Marcus cleared his throat. "I've interrupted enough of your enjoyments. I should return to my sister. If you'll excuse me." He made to turn when the duchess stuck her cane out, blocking his escape.

"I'm not done with you, boy." She jerked her head toward the beleaguered-looking modiste with her arms loaded with swatches of fabric. "Settle the matter and then we're done with you. Eleanor needs a ball gown."

Despite the lady's protestations some evenings earlier, she'd reentered his world and had come to wreak havoc once more. He gave Eleanor a coolly mocking grin. "Does she?" he murmured, not taking his eyes off Eleanor. "And for what does the lady require a gown?"

Her cheeks flamed red. Instead of being cowed, however, Eleanor angled her chin back. "I daresay even you know what a lady requires a ball gown for."

Even he? Oh, the little termagant. He folded his arms at his chest. "I would assuredly say a lady would require such a purchase so she might attend a ball." He quirked a slow, deliberate eyebrow. "Except, by your adamancy several evenings prior, I know that can't be entirely true."

Eleanor snapped her lips into a tight line and refused to rise any more to his baiting. He tamped down disappointment, relishing the spirit sparked to life in her eyes. The duchess knocked her cane into the floor once more. "Are you two finished squabbling?"

Eleanor and Marcus responded in unison. "We're not squabbling."

"Are you calling me a liar?"

They were both wise enough to say nothing on that score.

She made a sound of disgust. "Between the two of you, you cannot put forth a single suggestion on a gown. Perhaps your sister might." The duchess glanced about. "Now where is your sister? I'd make my hellos." The duchess, in her usual boisterous manner, bellowed for Marcus' sister. Eleanor flinched and mouthed a silent apology.

Despite himself, he grinned at the eccentricity of the older woman.

From across the shop, Lizzie came hurrying down the aisle with Lady Marianne trailing close behind. The duo stopped and a wide smile wreathed his sister's cheeks. "Your Grace, Mrs. Collins," she dipped a curtsy. "It is ever so lovely to see you," she greeted with a sincerity that brought an honest smile to the older woman's wrinkled face.

"Come closer, girl." She motioned Lizzie forward. His sister, ever obedient and proper, complied. "I've need of your assistance as your brother has proven wholly useless." A little giggle escaped his sister and he frowned. "Regardless, you managed to have this one," she jerked her thumb at Marcus, "bring you and," she looked over her shoulder, wrinkling her nose in distaste at the lady hovering beyond Lizzie's shoulders. "Your friend?" The wry twist to those words gave every indication as to her opinion on Lizzie's choice in friends.

"Oh, yes. Marcus is the most wonderful of brothers. He is so very faithful."

At his sister's effusive praise, Marcus cleared his throat. "Allow me to perform introductions. Your Grace, Mrs. Collins, may I present Lady Marianne Hamilton?"

ℴWITH THE VITRIOLIC GLARE TRAINED on Eleanor, the tight-
mouthed beauty at Lizzie Gray's side spoke more with that look
than any words ever could—Marcus, Viscount Wessex, belonged
to her.

A vicious, cloying, and insidious envy snaked through her like
a slow-moving cancer. It destroyed reason and logic and years of
resolve in putting Marcus from her thoughts so that she stood,
humbled and jealous, before this collection of politely chatting
Society members.

Just then, Marcus said something that brought a blush to the
young lady's cheeks. The shop filled with answering laughs, and
Eleanor stood there, the worst kind of interloper in a world she'd
never belonged to. She slipped away from the exchange and
retreated within the shop. Passing her hands over the tables of
fabric, she absently studied the cheerful yellow and green pastels;
cheerful colors deserving a virginal, cheerful wearer. And more,
fabrics and gowns befitting the Lady Mariannes of the world.

Eleanor had never fit in this world. As a merchant's daughter, her
people were the makers and sellers of goods. She drew to a slow
stop as Marcus inserted himself at the end of the aisle she strolled.
Eleanor wetted her lips and glanced through the bolts of fabric
and ribbons dangling from the ceiling that provided an artificial
sense of privacy.

His sister and her friend remained conversing with Eleanor's
aunt.

As he strolled closer, Eleanor shot a trembling hand out and
rested it on the wide, white column in a search for support. After
their exchange in the gardens, she'd expected he'd abandoned his
intentions to attempt to seduce her. And yet, the hot flare of desire
in his eyes and the promise on his lips told an altogether different
tale. She eyed him warily.

"Have you thought on the offer I presented you?"

She rounded her eyes. Surely, even Marcus was not so bold as to
talk seduction in the midst of a shop with their families just steps
away?

"I see you have," he confirmed.

She concentrated on his cynical grin and hard eyes; welcoming
that fury and embracing her own, for it prevented her from splin-
tering to pieces before this man who owned her heart. Why, with

his bold words and suggestive tone, he may as well have requested crimson fabric from the modiste and declared Eleanor his mistress. A panicky giggle bubbled past her lips. Ice flecked the cool blue of his eyes. Yes, the hard, unflappable gentleman he'd become would not take to being laughed at, and he likely interpreted her reaction as response to him and his highhanded ways.

"Have I said something to amuse you, Eleanor?"

Amuse her? Hurt and humiliate, certainly, but there was nothing at all entertaining in the suggestive glint in his eyes or the improper words on his lips.

"Not at all, my lord." At his smugly condescending expression, she seethed, tempted to plant him a well-deserved facer. Refusing to let him see how his words affected her, she forced a smile. "I do appreciate that I now have certain freedoms. Not, however, the freedoms you speak of," she dropped her voice to a hushed whisper and his intent stare fell to her lips. All the horror visited upon her by another mouth reared its vile memory and she retreated a step. Then without a jot of concern for propriety or the young ladies chatting with her aunt, she wandered down the long, wood table covered in bolts of fabric, putting much needed distance between her and Marcus.

Relentless, he advanced. "Oh?" Marcus drawled so low his words barely reached her ears. Nonetheless, Eleanor stole a glance about to ascertain whether anyone had overheard the shocking words from the roguish viscount. Alas, a brown skirt wearing, bespectacled widow speaking to a nobleman of Marcus' caliber would never be cause for notice. "And what freedoms did I speak of?"

She closed her mouth so quickly, her teeth snapped loudly, radiating pain up along her jawline. "You—I, that is…"

In a move she'd wager every coin dangled by her late uncle was deliberate, Marcus shifted his body, shielding her from the other patrons and shrinking the space between them. Her body stirred in an old, unfamiliar way and, for a moment, she closed her eyes and embraced the purity and completeness of her body's awareness of him as a man; aware of him in a way devoid of the fear and horror to plague her. She never wanted to open her eyes. Instead, she wanted to prolong this moment that allowed her a sliver of the young woman she'd been before everything that mattered had been stolen—her heart, her happiness, her virtue, Marcus…

"Eleanor?" Concern underscored that single word utterance and brought her eyes reluctantly open.

He stood impossibly close, so close the scent of sandalwood and mint fanned her senses, enticing her with the dreams of what would never be. "My l—" her words ended on a breathless squeak, as he fluidly guided her around the white column. Her heart thumped madly as he dropped his hands on the pillar, effectively framing her body within the shelter of his. She braced for the maddening terror and horrors of the past, and yet her blood thickened with a surge of hot awareness. "This is not proper," she whispered in a last, futile bid for propriety.

"You don't care about proper or improper any more than I do." He spoke with an unerring accuracy in that supposition. "What hold do you have over me, Eleanor?"

The same hold he had over her. Even with the threat of scandal steps away, her body thrilled at his nearness…and then his words registered. Her heart thumped a funny little rhythm. "You do not strike me as a man any woman has control over."

"They do not." A half-grin quirked his lips up. "You, however, do, Eleanor."

Despite his recklessly bold actions and suggestive words, she leaned closer to him.

He lowered his brow to hers. "I thought you'd not have a London Season." There was no recrimination there; his words more curious than anything.

She lifted her shoulders in a slight shrug. "I am not." Eleanor paused. For what would one call the list of tasks charged her by her late uncle? He'd not force her to endure an entire Season, but there were parts of the Season she was to participate in.

"And you detest those events now as much as you did, then." Marcus passed a searching gaze over her face.

"And you love those events now as much as you did, then," she said with a sad smile.

Just one other way in which they'd been different. The only pleasure she'd found in the two months of tedious affairs was secreting off with Marcus, dancing with scandal, all to avoid those same events.

He brushed his knuckle down her cheek and she leaned in to his touch, craving that warmth and gentleness. When was the last time she'd been held so tenderly? Not for years. For this touch was different than the one shared between a mother and child, or father and daughter. This was the caress bestowed by a man who hungered for her, even still with all the years of betrayal and hurt between them. And there was something so very heady in being touched and looked at where shame and humiliation didn't exist.

Their gazes locked. Teeming from the depths of his pale blue eyes was a passion that threatened to burn her. "Why do we continue to deny each other the only true emotion that ever existed between us?"

...Do not deny it, slut. You know you want this...

Eleanor shoved Marcus with such force that his arms fell to his sides. Mouth dry with fear, she rushed by him. In her bid to escape, she knocked against the table at her back, upending the whispery soft contents on display. Satins and silk swatches tumbled to the floor. Heart racing wildly, she skittered a frantic gaze about the shop, searching for escape. Her palms went damp within her gloves and she balled them hard at her sides while her raggedly indrawn breaths flooded her ears, muting all sound.

The absolute silence and still of the shop echoed like gunfire. The ladies of the shop gaped and gawked with rabid curiosity. Satin and Devlin were the first to break the quiet. Their noisy barks restored the shop to motion. Unable to meet the curious looks trained on her, Eleanor glanced away. Her gaze collided with Marcus. He stood frozen, eying her with consternation. Unable to meet his piercing stare, Eleanor blinked madly and dropped to a knee. She proceeded to gather the fabrics.

"I-I have it," Eleanor whispered to the French shopkeeper who rushed forward. The same woman ignored her and proceeded to gather the bolts until Marcus waved her off. The young woman rose, dipped a curtsy, and left. Then, wasn't that the way of their world? Gentlemen could command the world with a single look, while women remained at the bend and mercy of those same men.

With her aunt still occupied by Lizzie and her friend, Eleanor remained on the floor, wanting the wooden slats to open up and draw her in their folds. Tears popped behind her lids and she blinked them back. Until the day she drew forth her last breath, the monster who'd stolen that great gift, to be cherished and treasured, would haunt her. He was the demon of her past, who haunted her present, and would hold on to her future.

She jumped as Marcus fell to a knee beside her—silent and assessing. "Th-thank you," she whispered. Eleanor stole a peek at him and found his gaze on her quaking fingers, which shook with such force she dropped the items she'd already gathered.

His frown deepened. "Here," he said on a gruff whisper.

"I do not need your help," she bit out from the side of her mouth. She wanted him gone; from this shop, from her life. Needed him gone so she needn't have to face daily reminders of all she'd lost and all she would never have.

Marcus settled his hand over hers and she stiffened, braced for the taunting ice underscoring his practiced words of seduction. "Let me," he comforted. Wordlessly, she sank back on her haunches and allowed him to place the bolts upon the table. Spirited and bold years past, she'd proudly glided ungracefully through the steps of quadrilles and country reels, uncaring of Society's disapproving stare. How low fate had brought her that she should wish to crawl underneath the modiste's table like a beaten animal. God, how she despised what she'd become.

Marcus stood and held a hand out to assist her to her feet. Eleanor eyed his fingers a long moment and then glanced once more down at the floor. "Take my fingers," he urged softly.

She hesitated, still hopelessly transfixed by his extended gloved hand and saw equally powerful, white-gloved fingers that belonged to another. Her body broke into a cold sweat. *Not here. Not now.* Except, the mundane shop sounds dissolved, coming as though down a long, empty corridor and the floodgates opened. His punishing palm covered her mouth, cutting off all airflow, stifling her pleas. She was suffocating, dying—

"What is it, Eleanor?"

The quiet concern in Marcus' tone sucked her back from memories that would never die.

Except, Marcus' was different. She blinked slowly. Where another man's had brought her pain and suffering, Marcus had only shown her gentleness and kindness. Even now, hating her as he did, he still held his palm extended to her. Emotion wadded her throat and she tried to swallow past it. "Eleanor," he urged with such tenderness, her heart wrenched. Willing her tumultuous thoughts into order, Eleanor placed her fingers in his, allowing him to help her up.

Reluctantly, she drew her fingers back and clasped them before her. She made to return to her aunt, but then froze. Her gaze lingered on Lady Marianne Hamilton; a perfect future viscountess if ever there was one. The young woman took in their exchange with icy fury.

A chill ran along Eleanor's spine at the barely contained loathing in Lady Marianne's eyes. Unable to hold that venomous stare, Eleanor returned her attention to Marcus. "I did not lie to you," she said quietly. "I am not here husband hunting, Marcus. I am here because I have no other choice. I am here even as I hate London with every fiber of my being." She tugged at the fabric of her skirts and when she caught his attention on that distracted little movement, abruptly stopped.

With that, she hurried back to her aunt's side, her skin burned with the intensity of Marcus' gaze upon her person. Her daughter in her childish naiveté hadn't understood that friendships could not survive all.

Finished conversing, the two ladies shuffled off to inspect another bolt of fabric and the duchess looked up. "Well?" She stared at a point beyond Eleanor's shoulder. "What is it to be, my dear boy," her aunt called. "Never tell me I cannot expect an answer from you. The gel needs a gown and isn't any help on the fabric."

Eleanor curled her hands into such tight balls her nails dug painfully into the fabric of her kidskin gloves. *Why is he still here?* Perhaps he was right and their paths, by sheer nature of their history, familial connections, and a cruel fate, were inextricably intertwined.

"Pink." His deep, mellifluous baritone washed over her. "The lady requires a pink ball gown." *The softest pink blush stains your cheeks and I know it is a desire for me, and it is a secret that is only ours, sweet Eleanor…*

"Pink it is," the duchess said with a pleased nod.

CHAPTER 10

𝕴N THE END, SHE WORE pink. Despite the bolder, deeper hues favored by, widows, the soft pink satin fabric clung to Eleanor's skin. As she stared back at her reflection in the bevel mirror, the woman with tired eyes and a tense mouth, she saw the mockery of the pale pink shade better reserved for an innocent debutante. The girl she'd been would have donned this magnificent creation and thrilled at presenting herself to Marcus in this very gown. There was no longer anything magnificent about her.

What was she doing? Even for ten thousand pounds, this move was folly. The muscles of her throat worked painfully as she confronted the truth. Her uncle, even from the grave, exerted his ducal influence. He would have her present herself before London Society. Unknowing the dark secret of her past, he'd have her confront both the dreams and demons she'd left behind, both of which would always live within her. Two very different men had stolen different pieces of her soul and she could never, would never, reclaim those pieces.

Panic twisted at her insides. She could not do this. The man who'd stolen her virtue in the cruelest, most vicious way possible lurked like a specter; with Eleanor but one ball or soiree away from confronting the ugliest part of her existence.

A slight tugging at her skirts brought Eleanor's attention down to her gape-mouthed daughter. "You are a princess." The awe-struck whisper drew Eleanor back from the edge of madness.

A tattered and torn princess. "How can I be a princess when you are one? There cannot be *two* princesses." She tickled her daughter at the sensitive spot behind her nape until snorting giggles escaped her small, bow-shaped lips.

"S-stop."

Eleanor relented.

"Then I shall be a princess and you shall be a queen." Her daughter had inherited Eleanor's romantic spirit; that same spirit that had drawn her into hidden alcoves and fragrant gardens and ultimately led to her ruin. Fear curled her belly. For what had Eleanor's whimsy brought her, except for a broken heart and ruined name? Marcia pulled at her hand. "And tonight you must find a king and I shall have a new papa."

Agony slashed across her heart. In all her thoughts of Marcia's happiness, not once had she thought her daughter had a need or desire for a man to call Papa. There had been Eleanor's father, who'd treated the child with the same tenderness and love he'd shown her, his only child, through the years. Eleanor sank to her knee in a fluttery dance of satin skirts. "Oh, love," she said when she trusted herself to speak. "We don't really need a new papa though, do we sweet?" She brushed a loose, blonde curl back behind her daughter's ear. "You have a mama."

Little brow furrowed, Marcia scuffed the tip of her slipper upon the floor "Of course we don't *need* a new papa." A smile lit her face. "But it would, of course, be nice to have another. It is always merrier with three."

Ah, her father's words echoed across time, spilled from her own daughter's lips. How many times had he said that precise phrase to Eleanor? "It is also just perfect with two, though, isn't it?" She ruffled the crown of curls until Marcia drew back with annoyance.

"Well, that isn't what Grandfather said? He said three."

Eleanor sank back on her haunches. "Yes, he did, didn't he?" she murmured to herself. Except that had been years ago, when he, a robust, powerful man of forty-nine years had viewed himself as invincible and his life unending. Foolishly, Eleanor had allowed herself to believe and hope in that very same thing. For what could her life be without the steadfast support of a father who by Society's dictates should have cast her and Marcia out, and had, instead, given up all and redefined their lives?

"What about Marcus?"

She blinked. "Who?"

"Marcus." Marcia pointed her eyes to the ceiling. "Your *friend*. I am sure he would be a splendid papa."

So this vicious, agonizing wrenching was what it was to have an already fractured heart broken all over again. Pain weighed on her chest, making it difficult to draw forth breath. "Oh, sweet, you do not even know the viscount." As soon as the words left her mouth, Eleanor recognized the lie in them. Marcus, with his steadfast devotion to his sister and the sweet tenderness reserved for those worthy of his affections, those fortunate ones were treated like the princesses and queens Marcia spoke of.

Marcia wrinkled her mouth. "Well, I still believe he would make a wonderful papa."

For some other child he would, but it would never be her daughter. A vise tightened about her heart, wrenching every pained regret and dream she'd had from the organ. "I am sure he will make someone a wonderful papa, but he is just a friend," she added one more lie to the mountain of falsities she'd constructed her life upon. She tucked another curl behind her daughter's ear. Yes, he would be a splendid papa for some fortunate little girl or boy, but it would not be Marcia. Viscounts did not marry ruined women who'd adopted a false name and given birth to a bastard daughter. "Now, off you go," she said climbing to her feet. "You should be abed and Aunt Dorothea is likely thumping her cane in annoyance at my delay."

"But surely I can watch Aunt Dorothea's guests as they arrive." Marcia clasped her hands at her heart. "I so wish to see the guests. No one will notice me, Mama. You know I am the very best hider—"

"Woah," Eleanor said on a laugh. She placed her lips close to Marcia's ears. "Just for a bit and where no one can see you."

The little girl clapped excitedly. "I cannot wait to have a Season." She skipped to the door and then froze at the entrance. "Someday, I will find a prince, Mama." With her child's faith, she gave a jaunty wave and after a slight struggle with the door handle, wrested it open, and fled.

Eleanor stared at the open door a long moment, and then drawing in a steadying breath, started for the door. Her fingers twitched with the urge to wrestle the fabric of her skirts. With each soft tread of her slippered feet down the corridor, through the halls of her aunt's extravagant home, panic built slowly and steadily in her breast. For the terror in reentering Society, there was something calming, something reassuring, in being in the safety of Aunt Dorothea's townhouse. With her knowledge of every secret corridor, and *carte blanch* of the entire home, she could escape from the noise and crush of guests present.

And she would not be entirely alone through the horrid ordeal. Marcus and his family would be there. Even as his earlier reaction to her in Madame Claremont's shop had hinted at a man not in the least interested in anything other than seduction. Yes, experienced women like Eleanor were suitable for a man's bed and not much more than that. Gentlemen like Marcus wed proper young ladies.

Lady Marianne Hamilton flitted to her mind. By the furious glare she'd favored Eleanor with at the modiste's, the lady had intentions for Marcus.

A little sob tore from her throat but she didn't break her stride. As much as she longed to shut herself away and hide from the past and the possibility of seeing *him*, she'd not give him any more control than she'd allowed him these years. Instead, she took ownership of her fear, drawing forth his vile visage which had too much control of her these years; her unknown attacker, with his brandy-scented breath and his cruel fingers and that mocking laugh.

Fear froze her mid-step and she pressed her palms against the wall and drew in a calming breath. Then another. And another. The repeated rhythm her father had coaxed her through the years when the nightmares had come with ferocity and a staggering frequency. When her breathing settled into a calming, even cadence, she carefully stepped away from the wall. Eleanor smoothed her palms over her skirts, composing herself, and made her way to the foyer. She paused at the top of the stairs, casting one last, longing glance at the path she'd just marched, longing for the innocence of Marcia who was free to avoid all these affairs.

Her aunt paced back and forth, her two dogs nipped wildly at her skirts. One of the pugs looked up to where Eleanor stood frozen and barked once. The duchess spun about. "At last." She passed a glance over Eleanor's person and then gave an approving nod. "I've been waiting. It's not done to be late to one's own ball."

The gentle reproach set Eleanor into motion. "Forgive me," she offered, hurrying down the stairs. As she reached the bottom, Satin abandoned his mistress and rushed to Eleanor. He jumped at her skirts. Oddly comforted by his presence, she stroked the silky, soft spot between his eyes and he nudged her hand in approval.

"Well, come along, gel," her aunt commanded.

Knowing how that famed queen of France had felt on the final march up the steps of the guillotine, Eleanor trailed behind her aunt, silent as they made their way to the ballroom.

"The boy was right," her aunt said from the corner of her mouth.

Marcus. He'd been referred to as a boy since he'd been a lean, charming youth with a ready smile and even years later, with a broadly powerful frame and hardened, cynical grin, he was still "the boy" to Aunt Dorothea.

"About your pink skirts. I fancied you'd look a deal better in the orange with a turban, of course."

For the first time since she'd woken that morning with the terror of the evening staring back at her, Eleanor felt the faintest stirrings of amusement. "Of course," she said with a smile. "Every young lady requires a turban." Not that she was truly a young lady anymore.

"Wipe that melancholy from your face. You're a young lady. Any gentleman would be glad to wed you." *Glad to wed me?* A never wed widow with a bastard child? Unlikely. "Not, mind you, that I'm advocating you to wed just any gentleman. Pompous prigs, the most of them are."

Her aunt startled a laugh from Eleanor. Oh, how she loved the enlightened woman.

"Do you know who is not a pompous prig?"

She fought back a groan at her aunt's none too subtle attempt at matchmaking. "Er..."

"Wessex." Not the boy, this time. "Oh, he's become a rogue, one of those charming gentleman."

Eleanor knew. She gripped the edge of her skirts, taking her aunt's words like a lash to her soul. She'd read the gossip pages from long ago and knew just what he'd become, abhorring every woman who'd entered his life and given him that gift Eleanor never had, nor ever could.

A twinkle lit the woman's eyes. "Remember what I said about reformed rogues."

She swallowed a groan. Not this again.

"They make the best husbands," her aunt said. "Did I ever mention that your uncle was a rogue?"

Eleanor smiled gently, allowing the older woman the happiness of her memory. Let one of them have happy memories to sustain them.

"Yes, he was a rogue, until he wed me." The duchess' expression took on a faraway quality that softened her otherwise gruff countenance.

The old, childless Duke and Duchess of Devonshire had been hopelessly and helplessly in love. Until now, Eleanor had never considered the people they'd been in their youth. Had they once snuck away to hidden alcoves and danced with ruin, so they might know a stolen kiss and the thrill of each other's company as Eleanor and Marcus had once done? The couple had found love and, yet, had never known the joy of being parents. Eleanor, on the other hand, had tasted love and lost, and would remain unwed, but *would* know the unadulterated joy of her daughter's love.

What a cruel game fate played.

They reached the ballroom and Eleanor blinked, jerked abruptly back into her late uncle's dratted list. Just five, nay *four*, items now, until freedom was hers in ways she had never allowed herself to dream of, or hope for.

"It is time."

As Eleanor stepped inside the ballroom awash in the chandelier's glow, an eerie sense of stepping back into a different time forced Eleanor's feet to a stop and she remained fixed to the spot, staring out at the grand space. There'd been a time when an eager excitement had filled her at the prospect of stepping through the front doors of the distinguished townhomes. That had been quickly quashed by the unkind *ton*—noblemen who had ultimately decided her worth among them. She closed her eyes a moment. Not all gentlemen. One had been so very different. He'd not minded that she was born of a modest background or a horrid dancer. He'd been her friend, and almost her lover, in every sense of that word.

Eleanor forced her feet into movement and, drawing a steadying breath, fell into the role of companion alongside her polished, ever-confident aunt.

"You appear as happy as I am about this event your uncle insisted on," Aunt Dorothea said in a none-too-subtle whisper, ringing a startled laugh from Eleanor.

They made their way to the front of the receiving line to greet the duchess' still arriving guests.

Guilt needled at her. Secretly she'd hoped her aunt would have seen to her responsibilities as hostess and Eleanor could have slipped belatedly into the ballroom, escaping any scrutiny. The crush of guests already milling about the crowded room spoke to just how late she'd been. "I am sorry to have made you tardy to your own affair."

"Your *uncle's* affair," she said, waggling her eyebrows. "Determined to have some ducal control even in his own grave." There was a wistful quality there, which softened those words. The duchess lifted her chin in a regal greeting to guests who dropped curtsies and bows. "Eleanor, my dear. I am a duchess. As such, I'm afforded certain privileges. Arriving late to my own ball is one of them." She leaned close and spoke in a less than conspiratorial whisper. "Though in truth, even if I wasn't a duchess, I wouldn't give a jot about missing the bloody thing."

The blunt admission brought a startled laugh from Eleanor, attracting stares. She quickly smoothed her features into a mask.

"Bah," her aunt rapped her on the arm with her fan. "I've said it before. I prefer you laughing and bold, Eleanor. Ah, here comes Isabelle." Sure enough Marcus' mother made her way through the crush of guests, toward the duchess. "Will you run and fetch me a glass of punch?"

"Of course." Eleanor bussed her aunt on the cheek and, squaring her shoulders, started her march down the length of the ballroom. With each step, an invigorating sense of control filled her. In this moment, braving the *ton* and tackling the items upon her uncle's list, she re-exerted a hold over her life.

A tall figure stepped into her path and a startled gasp escaped her. "Forgive m—" She glanced up at the gentleman and her body went hot and then cold. For years, she saw this man everywhere, saw him with such clarity that she'd often believed he stood before her real as the day he'd been in that moonlit night that had irrevocably changed her life. Eleanor pressed her eyes tightly closed and called on the coaxings her father had taught her long ago. *Wake up. One, two, three, wake up.* Only this time, there was no waking. The devil before her was as real as Satan in the flesh.

A slow, jeering smile formed on his lips. Though softer around the middle with the passage of time, the hawkish nose and cold brown eyes of the gentleman staring down at her marked him as her dark demon. "Miss Carlyle." It was that same slightly mocking tone that had echoed in Lady Wedermore's gardens. "Or is it *Mrs.* Collins, now, I believe?" Oh, God, how did he know that? What else did he know? Her body went cold.

In her sleepless nights, of which there were many, she would lay abed imagining the words she would hurl were she to ever again see the nameless stranger who'd fathered her child. She'd crafted lists upon lists of horrible, ugly words and curses that no lady had a right to. Yet, in this instance, every single one went out of her head.

A liveried footman came by with a silver tray and Eleanor stared blankly as the gentleman at her side rescued a glass of champagne, casual when her heart could never resume a normal beat. "Champagne, Mrs. Collins?" Anyone to hear that offer would see a gentleman before them.

Eleanor knew better. "Leave," she said quietly. How was that one word so very steady?

The servant looked askance and, with a bow of his head, rushed off. And coward that she was, Eleanor made to go, as well.

Her attacker blocked her escape. "I see you've resumed where you left off with Wessex."

A dull humming filled her ears. *I am going to be ill.* To keep from crumpling into a boneless heap on the sidelines of her aunt's ballroom, Eleanor pressed a hand against the smooth, white pillar. The cold of that stone penetrated her gloves and she welcomed the chill on her clammy flesh.

Then he lowered his head. "I cannot tell you, Mrs. Collins, how much I dislike that." He sipped from his flute. "You are to stay away from him, Eleanor."

What should her relationship with Marcus matter to this man? Or was this merely another attempt to dominate her? Well, she'd give him nothing more than he'd taken that night. He'd already stolen so very much. "You do not have leave to use my Christian name." The sharp retort burst from her lips. With all the power he'd claimed over her and her life, she would have this control.

He snapped his eyebrows into a single line, but otherwise ignored her command. "Consider this your warning to stay away from the viscount."

She flicked her gaze about the room. Lords and ladies laughed and chatted at every turn. Couples danced the intricate steps of a country reel. Through the inanity, Eleanor's world quaked under her feet. How was the earth, in fact, still moving when time stood still in this horrifying exchange?

Then from across the room, she caught sight of her aunt conversing with Marcus' mother and there was a stabilizing reassurance in the casualness of that exchange. Eleanor ratcheted her chin up several notches. "You, sir, can go to hell."

And though not the vitriolic diatribe she'd always planned for the man, Eleanor swept away, her skin burning from the look he trained on her.

MARCUS STUDIED THE CRUSH OF guests with a distracted boredom from over the rim of his crystal champagne glass. Marcus had resolved to forget Eleanor and all the broken promises between them. Except, given the evening's festivities and the close proximity of their residences, it was a near impossible feat.

Unbidden, his gaze sought, and found, Eleanor as she cut a path through the ballroom. With a glass of punch in hand, she marched with a single-minded purpose. A swirl of dancers swallowed his sight of her.

He cursed.

"Goodness, Marcus, never tell me you are woolgathering," the Duchess of Crawford's teasing voice drawled from beyond his shoulder.

Marcus whipped around, adopting one of his effortless grins. "Lady Daisy Meadows. My girl of the flowers."

Daisy stood alongside her husband, the Duke of Crawford, who, by his black scowl, appeared to take exception with Marcus' possessive endearment for their late friend Lionel's sister.

"She is no longer of the Flowers," Crawford said in that coolly austere tone he'd adopted over the years.

"Ah, yes," he said on a sigh. And knowing it would infuriate the other man, he leaned close to Daisy and said on a loud whisper, "She'll always be my girl of the flowers."

With an unrestrained laugh, Daisy swatted his arm, earning curious stares from the nearby lords and ladies. "You are a flirt, Marcus." At one time they would likely have turned up their noses at the young lady's display. Having wed Auric, the Duke of Crawford, two years ago, she was now permitted certain luxuries and freedoms.

"Oh, undoubtedly." He winked and she laughed all the more.

Of course, having known the lady since she was in leading strings, he'd come to know she'd dug her talons into the particular details surrounding his presence here and would not relent. "It has not failed to escape my notice that you've ignored my observation."

"Your observation?" He deliberately slid his gaze out to the ballroom floor, taking in the twirling couples. He knew very well what observation Daisy referred to.

"You know very well what observation I referred to." Then, having known the young lady most of his life, she'd developed a rather bothersome tendency of predicting his thoughts.

"I'm merely here as chaperone." It was a blatant lie. Crawford eyed him with a dogged intensity that indicated he knew as much, but was too loyal and proper to counter the claim. Yes, Marcus' mother and sister were hardly in need of his company. Yet night after night after night, and now, as Daisy had pointed out, a fourth night, he'd taken to attending exceedingly dull events he'd have normally avoided at all costs. Well, not all costs. Through the years, the tedium of those affairs had been broken by certain widows.

His gaze collided with one of those very women and he stared blankly at the top of her head. How many empty, meaningless entanglements had he become involved in through the years, all with the intent of driving out the remembrance of Eleanor? Only now, with her back in his life, he saw the lie he'd perpetuated against himself. He could never forget her. Would never. For with the empty ache her betrayal had left inside his heart, the damned useless organ did, and forever would, belong to her. "Fool."

"Marcus?"

He snapped his attention back to Daisy, who eyed him with a

blend of concern and consternation. "Er, I was…" Heat climbed his neck.

Both duke and duchess stared at him with matching expressions, silently pressing for answers.

He searched for a safe reply. "I was—"

His gaze traveled to Eleanor who carried a glass of punch to her aunt, and was promptly surrounded by a swarm of suitors. A visceral hatred unfurled, burning hot inside him.

Only, by the feral gleams in the gentlemen eying her with lascivious stares throughout the ballroom, he was no longer the only one who'd developed a keen awareness of Mrs. Eleanor Collins. With a curse, he downed the contents of his champagne in one long, slow swallow. He slammed the empty glass down upon the silver tray of a passing servant with such force it rattled the other crystal flutes sitting there.

From the corner of his eye, he spied Daisy and Crawford exchange a look. Damn them and their knowing stares, and worse, the damned intimacy they shared; a bond he'd once shared with the woman now being ogled like a confectionary treat prepared by the king's baker.

"I don't suppose this is the er, person who has you—"

"No."

"Distracted," Daisy finished for her husband. Then with her innocent, always-hopeful stare, she took in the woman Marcus had made the mistake of studying overly long. Gone was the clear-eyed young lady who'd stolen away with him in hidden alcoves and private gardens, sprinting down corridors, hand in hand, risking ruin for those stolen moments. In her place was this aloof ice princess, resplendent in the palest pink satin. With her squared shoulders and the tilt of her chin, her proud, regal bearing would make a queen envious. The Duchess of Devonshire said something at her side and Eleanor responded, never so much as averting her gaze, trained on the crowd.

Look at me. Look at me and want me as you did. For that would be the ultimate revenge upon the lady who'd so betrayed him. Taking her in his arms and showing her such pleasure that she regretted the fact that any man had come before him and after they knew mindless pleasure in each other's bodies, then Marcus would be the one to cast her from *his* life.

As though sensing his attention, she froze. The lady darted her gaze about the room, passing over the interested lords converging upon her. Then her eyes met his across the ballroom. Marcus wanted to manage a mocking grin, avert his eyes, and give her the cut direct. After all, their paths, as she'd succinctly pointed out, need never cross and the lady would be fine if they didn't. Instead, he continued staring like every other besotted fool present. God, how he despised himself for the hold she had over him, still.

"Close your mouth, Marcus." Daisy's teasing whisper jerked him thankfully back from his own self-recriminations.

She'd made a fool of him once and he'd allow her to do it again. He snapped his lips together so quickly, his teeth rattled.

"I daresay we've found what has enhanced your responsibilities as chaperone," she continued.

Crawford settled a hand at the small of her back, and a look so intimate, a connection that didn't require words passed between them, and Daisy's smile dipped. "Oh."

That piteous, soft exhalation knotted his stomach, as his weakness for Eleanor Carlyle, now Collins, exposed him before his sole friends in the world. "If you'll excuse me," he said with forced lightness. "I've devoted enough of my brotherly services this evening and intend to seek out my clubs." His was a desperate effort to preserve his dignity. Before Daisy could issue any further questions or comments, he sketched a quick bow and started for the entrance of the hall.

He intended to leave. He intended to march through the crowd, past the colorful peacocks and swaggering swains who now sought a certain widow's attention and, ultimately, her affection. He intended to do any number of things that didn't involve looking back at Eleanor. But he cast a single, impulsive glance over his shoulder and then he spun on his heel and stared openly at the cocksure swains clamoring for her dance card.

Marcus balled his hands at his sides. Didn't they know the lady detested dancing in crowded rooms? Didn't they know the only reason she'd tolerated those awkward steps of the quadrilles and country reels was for the fleeting moments when Marcus could hold her in his arms? But then, how could they know that? How, when she'd left and wed another? How, when those thoughts no longer held true?

He forced himself to stand a silent observer to her success as she garnered the attention of the *ton*. Her aunt stood a useless chaperone at Eleanor's side, appearing bored by the whole display of attention when, in actuality, if she were wise, she would be a good deal more cautious with her niece's reputation. Any number of gentlemen would gladly have Eleanor to wed or in his bed.

They were welcome to her; every last fawning, leering fop in the bunch.

Determined to set her from his thoughts once and for all, he turned to leave—and registered her waxen skin. Gone was the pink blush of her youth. The pinched set to her mouth and the panicked gaze that flitted about hinted at a woman who despised the attention now shown her just as much as Marcus himself did, but for altogether different reasons.

Had her love of her husband been so very great that the focus she'd earned felt like a betrayal of sorts to the hero Marcia had briefly mentioned? A fop in purple satin breeches and a sapphire blue coat reached for her dance card. Eleanor jerked her arm close to her side and gave her head a terse shake. The young dandy, who by the look of him was not much older than Marcus had been when he'd made the mistake of trusting his heart to her, looked crestfallen. Until Eleanor said something. Lord Herington nodded like a chicken pecking at feed and then spun on his heel. He sprinted through the crowd and made for the refreshment table.

Ah, so the lady was not interested in the attention being shown her and she'd become very adept at rejecting unwanted advances. On the heel of that was the niggling wonder of all the gentlemen who might have pressed their attentions on her after the honorable Lieutenant Collins had died. Marcus wanted to take each of those faceless, nameless men apart with his bare hands.

Marcus should leave. And yet, he remained. Just then, Eleanor's gaze collided with his once more. There was an almost pleading in her soft blue eyes that even across the room called out, beckoned him. She wanted him. Not in the ways that had anything to do with the flare of passion that had always existed between them, but rather in a way that drew on the friendship they'd once known.

If he were wise, he'd ignore that desperate look in her fathomless stare. But then, he'd never been wise where Eleanor was concerned. Silently cursing himself for his inherent weakness for her still, he strode across the ballroom, bypassing those who inclined their head in greeting, his gaze trained forward.

The faint stirrings of a waltz echoed around the ballroom. Did he imagine her shoulders sinking with relief as he cut a swath through the collection of gentlemen she'd amassed? "Mrs. Collins, I believe you promised the next set to me."

CHAPTER 11

SURROUNDED BY A SEA OF suitors, not a single one of the
gentlemen could hold sway over Eleanor's attentions or affections.
They pressed in on her, like flies on a confectionary treat left in
the summer sun, until she struggled to draw breath. As her aunt
performed introduction after introduction, the names of the leering men blurred together, the woman's words coming as though
down a long hall.

Eleanor's body trembled and she could not keep from searching the room for that monster. *Do not think of him.* Except, in her
mind, she saw his mouth moving as he'd warned her away from
Marcus. Those same lips that had crushed hers and cut off airflow.

She was going to faint.

"Lord Fitzroberts…"

Her aunt gave her a questioning look.

Eleanor nodded, forced a smile, and curtsied. As Lord Fitzroberts
or Fitzherbert proceeded to speak with her aunt, Eleanor looked
about for Marcus.

In all her most hellish days, the joyous memories of Marcus had
sucked her back from the vortex of despair and fear.

Then she found the viscount with her eyes and her breath caught
hard. Nay, Marcus. He would always be Marcus. The wry, cynical
man he'd become had stood off to the side, boldly watching her.
Had any other man studied her in that possessive, penetrating way,
she'd have fled the hall in terror. For all that had come to pass, and

the horror she'd known, her heart still thudded wildly with desire for him.

"Eleanor," her aunt snapped her back to the moment. Brandishing her cane, the duchess motioned to a tall, lanky gentleman. "This pup is the Earl of Primly. A good fellow." That earned a disapproving frown from the gentleman. Then, what gentleman would care to be so categorized by the eccentric duchess?

The lean gentleman flushed. "Th-thank you for the k-kind w—"

"I didn't mean it as a compliment," she stated with a bluntness that only deepened the color upon the earl's sharp cheeks. "I was merely stating fact. Not a thing wrong with Primly." She shifted the tip of her cane to one of the gentleman ogling Eleanor's décolletage. "You may continue on Westfield." Cheeks flushed, the young gentleman with thick Byron curls slunk off. Aunt Dorothea thumped her cane three times. "Ask for her dance card, Primly."

Obligingly, he reached for Eleanor's card.

The earl froze, mid-movement, his hand outstretched; those long fingers he'd put upon her person. The young man was harmless, or appeared to be so, but then there had been another with an easy grin who'd ultimately stank of brandy and sin. *Oh, God.* She could not do this. "No."

"Eleanor?" her aunt prodded.

Her feet twitched with the urge to shove past the lecherous lords and run as far and as fast as her legs could carry her and continue running all the way back to the far-flung corner of Cornwall. She searched about for escape when, through her crush of suitors, Eleanor's gaze collided with Marcus'.

He grinned. "Mrs. Collins, I believe you promised the next set to me."

Her heart caught and she stared transfixed as the assembled gentlemen parted. Marcus came to a stop and eyed her through thick, hooded, golden lashes.

His words were a blatant lie, and a poor one at that. Every gentleman here knew Marcus, the Viscount Wessex, had not spoken to her until this moment. And yet, for his steady, reassuring presence and his innate ability to know when she needed him, Eleanor loved him all the more.

"There you have it," her aunt said to the men lying in wait. "Mrs. Collins has pledged this set to Wessex."

Some of the cloying panic in the attention being thrust upon her eased and Eleanor shot out a hand and placed her fingertips along his coat sleeve and allowed him to guide her away from the crush of gentlemen. With an ease that made her heart ache, Marcus tucked her fingers into the crook of his elbow and led her on to the dance floor for the waltz. "Marcus, I—"

"Come," he said quietly as he moved her hand onto his shoulder and positioned his own at her waist. "You'll not make me a liar before your rather impressive collection of suitors."

She nodded. "Yes, I would." Her hand fell to her side and he quickly moved it back into place.

"I daresay a waltz would be a very small thank you for having separated you from those swains."

"It would." The orchestra launched into the full hum of the haunting melody of the waltz and couples moved about them in the slow one-two-three step. "But I do not know the waltz."

"You do not know how to waltz?" He gave his head a bemused shake. "I'd not considered the dance had not arrived from the Continent until you left."

In the time she'd been gone the inane details of life—the dances deemed appropriate and practiced within the distinguished ballrooms of London, the cut of a gown, the style of a cravat—had all changed. How very insignificant when compared with how her life had been altered. She did another search of the room and a chill raked her spine. He was here. Watching. Her. Her exchange with Marcus.

"Trust me," he said quietly, jerking her to the moment. She darted her gaze about. Lords and ladies twirled about them; trained rabidly curious stares on them. Yet as smoothly confident as he'd always been, unfazed by the *ton's* interest, Marcus positioned her arms once again and then settled his hand at her waist. Through the fabric of her gown, her skin burned from the heat of his touch, momentarily robbing her of breath, in a response that had nothing to do with terror or remembrances of the past and everything to do with her body's subtle awareness of him as a man.

"I do not know what I am doing, Marcus," she whispered, jolting awkwardly through the dance.

He winked. "You can lurch to and fro and still evince a grace any lady would admire." Those words were surely the same, effusive praise he reserved for all the ladies he took to his bed and yet a thrill went through her anyway.

Not wanting him to realize the hold he still held over her, she found her first real smile that evening. "And you're the rogue the papers purport you to be."

He quirked an eyebrow. "Ah, you and those gossip columns, again. We need to find you new reading material."

She silently cursed and immediately sidestepped that glaring admission. "There is a good deal to read about, Marcus, but I long ago stopped reading about your name." Eleanor stumbled and trampled all over his toes. "I'm sorry," she muttered. "I did warn you that you'd be better suited to find a different dance partner." A woman of grace and his equal in every way. Eleanor loathed the unsullied lady with every fiber of her being.

"Why?"

"For stepping on your toes. I didn't intentionally do so, though there have been times you've deserved it."

Marcus shifted her in his arms and, drawing her closer, he helped lead her through the set. "Why did you read of the pursuits of a man you ceased to love?"

"Oh," she blurted. Embarrassed heat singed her neck and warmed her cheeks. And when presented with his probing stare and a question she had no desire in answering for what it would reveal, Eleanor stumbled against him.

He repositioned her once more. "Eleanor?"

She sighed. He was as tenacious as he'd ever been. "I never stopped caring about you, Marcus." Loving him. She'd never stopped loving him. Until she drew her last breath, her heart would forever beat for him and only him.

"Caring." He spoke in a flat, emotionless tone that gave little indication of his thoughts. "Not loving." A sad smile played on his lips, erasing all the cynical bitterness he'd evinced since her return. "Since you returned, and I learned you'd wed, I told myself that I didn't care, Eleanor. A woman who left as you did, forsaking all we shared, and giving nothing more than a note was undeserving of my regard and assuredly undeserving of my love." With each word, he twisted the knife of pain deeper in her already broken heart. "But it was not your fault, Eleanor. Was it? You loved another and it would be wrong to resent you for having wed that man, even as

I wished it had been me."

Tears popped up behind her lids and she blinked furiously in a desperate bid to keep them from falling down her cheeks, in crystalline trails of agony. For it had been her fault. Had she not gone to those empty gardens, her life would have moved in an altogether different direction. And with the cynicism burning from within his eyes, she needed Marcus to know that she'd not been false in the words she'd given him. "What if I told you I loved you, once? Would that matter?"

Marcus considered her a long while. "At one time, yes." He gave his head a sad, slow shake. "No longer, Eleanor. I've since moved on from the pain I knew after your betrayal."

She snagged her lip between her teeth and bit down hard. Why did it matter that he'd abandoned the dream of them? Eleanor missed a step and Marcus righted her.

"It is a one-two-three count," he whispered close to her ear.

How could he be so casual and unaffected when his blunt admission had slit open the still unhealed wounds of losing him? "It is scandalous," she said in search of any words to give him.

Then, employing the skills he'd likely practiced as a careless rogue, he lowered his voice to a husky whisper. "You used to enjoy the time spent in my arms."

Hating that other woman before this moment and women after, who would be the recipient of his seductive charm, Eleanor stitched her golden eyebrows into a single line. "I'm not one of your lightskirts, Marcus. Do not employ your charms on me. I would have you as a friend and nothing more." She glanced to the gentlemen at the edge of the ballroom floor looking for the face of the demon, and unease tightened her belly. He stood on the fringe of the ballroom sipping from his champagne flute, intently studying her. At the chilling amusement in that cold-eyed stare, Eleanor stumbled. She wrenched her eyes to the front of Marcus' snowy cravat. Panic lapped at the corner of her senses, threatening to pull her under. *Think of skating on a frozen pond. Think of Marcia, laughing as you tickle her under her chin.*

As the numbing terror abated, she fixed on the tasks doled out by her uncle. She'd but six acts, really just four remaining, that her uncle demanded of her, and then she could be forever free; free of Marcus' resentment, free of her own useless wishing, and free from the real and imagined threats posed by that grinning lord in the corner of her aunt's ballroom.

Marcus applied a gentle pressure to her waist and snapped her attention back to him.

"What is it?"

Had he been coolly distant, she'd have said nothing that mattered to him. Had he been the slightly angry, bitter gentleman who'd splayed her heart open just moments ago, she'd have managed a smile and a noncommittal reply. Except, gruff concern coated his inquiry and he was restored to the man she'd known as a friend.

Before her courage deserted her, she blurted. "I would speak with you on a matter of privacy." Intrigue flared in his eyes, and by the interest she detected in the silver flecks of his gaze, she gathered the direct path his thoughts wandered. "Not that."

His lips twitched. "Not what, Eleanor?"

She removed her hand from his sleeve and fanned her flaming cheeks, and then promptly stumbled. With a chuckle, he caught her. "But you did think about it."

"I do not know what 'it' you refer to." Eleanor ground the heel of her slipper into his instep, this time with a deliberateness that had him wincing. "Do pay attention." As Marcus guided her in a smooth circle, she sought another glimpse of her attacker. He stood in the same spot, looking boldly back, still taunting her with his presence. Eleanor swallowed hard. She didn't have much time before the set concluded and he returned her to the beast prowling on the sidelines. "Will you meet me?" *Haven't you learned the folly in sneaking off before?* Dark, wicked deeds transpire when one danced on the edge of respectability.

She braced for his roguish rejoinder.

Instead, Marcus passed a searching look over her face and then gave a terse nod. "Where?"

He capitulated so easily. "My aunt's library, following the next set." No doubt, he still believed theirs to be a meeting between two lovers. Her insides twisted. How many women had he coordinated meaningless assignations with in the homes of London's lords? And how many of those meetings had he failed to honor...? *Or was it only me who was abandoned by him that night?*

The music drew to a halt and they stopped. Unease, an eerie sense of familiarity to another night, stirred within, made all the more real by that nameless nobleman who'd cornered her. "You will come, then?" Couples politely clapped for the orchestra's efforts about them. "You'll not promise to meet and then never show?"

Marcus raised her fingertips to his lips and placed his lips along the top of her hand. "In all our stolen exchanges, Eleanor, not once did I ever fail to meet you."

As he ushered her from the dance floor, she bit down on the inside of her cheek, hard enough to draw blood. She cast a look back for the man who'd fathered her child. How could Marcus be so wrong about the one night that had irrevocably changed them?

She looked toward the gentlemen who waited, hovering like bothersome gnats, awaiting her company, and drew to an abrupt stop. There was nothing polite or proper in their hot, lascivious stares. They eyed her no differently than they might study a light-skirt; a woman to be plucked, there to bring them pleasure. And for the folly in requesting a meeting with Marcus, away from the safe eyes of the crowded ballroom, Eleanor recognized she'd little choice.

Marcus cast a glance over his shoulder. "Eleanor?"

Long ago, Eleanor had learned fear and desperation drove a person to do many things. She'd appreciated the extent of it when she'd fled London and shortly thereafter fashioned herself the widow of a soldier. With her father's assistance, they'd moved away from all Eleanor had ever known in the hope for freedom and a new beginning.

With reluctance, she pulled her gaze away and diverted her attention back to Marcus. She had no right to ask him for anything and yet with her daughter's innocent suggestion rooting around her mind, and the horror of this night, the words tumbled from her lips. "I'd ask that you stay beside me." His eyes became dark, impenetrable slips. She drew in a slow breath. "Please."

"Why?"

As she owed him at least one truth, for all the lies she'd given, she said, "Because I do not care to be prey for rogues who'd only seek a place in my bed."

"By your admission, I am a rogue." And one who'd been quite clear in his amorous intentions toward her.

"Yes," she concurred. "But you're different than the others." He always had been and always would be.

She expected him to toss her request for help in her face and march off, relishing her discomfort while he himself sought the comforts of some other widow.

With a brusque nod, Marcus remained at her side. Together they stood, surveying the guests assembled by her aunt. They stood so close their bodies, their arms, brushed, and some of the terror roused by that monster who'd dared enter her aunt's home receded. A liveried footman approached with a silver tray of fine French champagne. Marcus retrieved two glasses and handed one over to Eleanor.

"I do not drink spirits," she held her palms up.

"Take the damned glass, Eleanor," he mumbled.

"I don't…" At his glower, she sighed and took an experimental sip. The bubbling spirits touched her tongue and slid down her throat, unexpectedly delicious. She took another sip and then another. For her twenty-six years, she'd never imbibed of anything so forbidden. Yet, with each sip, she had to admit on this score, Marcus had proven himself quite correct. "It is delicious."

His lips twitched as she drained the remainder of her drink. He motioned over a footman and plucked the crystal glass from Eleanor's fingers. Then he deposited the fragile piece upon the silver tray and rescued her another. "Slower," he cautioned as he held out the next.

"I really shouldn't." She'd learned the dangers of doing the opposite of what she should be doing. Yet she accepted it, anyway. Sipping French liquor beside Marcus, the man who owned her heart, was the height of folly. Alas, it appeared an inherent flaw of her person. This time, when she tasted the champagne, her tongue warmed under the familiarity of the sparkling brew and her throat worked reflexively as she continued to drink.

"I said slower, Eleanor." Concern glinted in Marcus' eyes.

He spoke with the same concern he might show his sister, Lizzie. She swallowed. Oh, how she despised his brotherly tone. The French spirit proved potent, continuing to work its hold over her; it warmed her from the inside out and, with that, all her earlier trepidations lifted, replaced with an absolute rightness in being precisely where she was. Beside Marcus. As she'd been once and should always be. It also reinforced the rightness in enlisting his aid. "This is splendid," she said on a sigh.

From the corner of her eye, his lips again twitched. Marcus angled his body closer to hers, shrinking the space between them. Eleanor braced for the slow-dawning horror; the terror of undying memories—but they didn't come. She rounded her eyes. "I'm not afraid," she whispered. A giddy sense of excitement invaded every corner of her being and she briefly closed her eyes at the thrill of that discovery. How long had she dreaded being near any man? She'd allowed her attacker that power and control over her and yet, in this moment, she'd reclaimed an elemental piece of her life.

The creases of his brow deepened. "Why should you be afraid?"

There were all number of reasons. None of which had anything to do with him and everything to do with another. She'd not have him believe she feared him. Never him. Eleanor patted him on the hand. "Not you," she assured him. "You are perfectly safe to be around."

"Thank you," he said with a dryness that made her smile. Or was she already smiling?

"You were already smiling."

"Oh," she blurted. "Did I say that aloud?"

He widened his grin. "You did."

A bold gentleman in pale blue satin knee breeches approached. One glower from Marcus sent the dandy scurrying away in the opposite direction. Her heart thumped wildly in her breast.

A black scowl marred Marcus' cheeks. Had he been anyone else, she'd have backed up in fear. But this was Marcus and she knew implicitly he never could, nor ever would, harm her. "Has Brantley given you a difficult time?"

"Brantley?" She followed his gaze to the rapidly retreating lord. "I don't even know Lord Brantley." Some of the tautness about Marcus' shoulders, lessened. Nor did Eleanor care to know Lord Brantley. Or anyone. It could only be Marcus. "Will you meet me in my aunt's library?" Urgency threaded that request. Without awaiting his reply, Eleanor pulled her fingers free of his arm. "Do not be late." And with that, she lost herself in the crush of guests.

A SHORT WHILE LATER, MARCUS STRODE down the duchess'
corridors. The tread of his footsteps silent as Eleanor's breathless
entreaty danced around his mind. The lady spoke of friendship
and requested a private meeting, rousing old memories and painful hurts. For an infinitesimal moment, he'd entertained the idea
of leaving her in that damned library as she'd once left him. But
no sooner had the thought fully taken shape, he'd killed it dead.
With her furrowed brow and troubled eyes, she'd boldly questioned whether he'd honor that meeting. Her fears were likely a
product of her own faithlessness years earlier. Marcus slowed his
steps. The lit sconces cast ominous shadows about the wall and he
stared at the dancing orange flame as he confronted his weakness
for Eleanor.

In the midst of a ballroom, with strangers as their witness, she'd
whispered her request for help and, for all that had come to pass
between them, he could not deny her entreaty. Perhaps hers was
an apology, an apology he now knew she needn't make. Perhaps
it was the goodbye she'd owed him, years too late. He'd never
again trust her, but neither could he cut her from his life. *I am a
damned fool…* With a silent curse, he strode the remaining distance,
counting doors, and then coming to a stop. He glanced down the
corridor and then quietly pressed the handle and slipped inside the
room. It took a moment for his eyes to adjust to the thick cloak
of darkness that hung over the room and he blinked several times.
His gaze locked on the flash of pale pink in the inky blackness.

Eleanor muttered to herself, wringing her skirts hopelessly. There
was something so achingly sweet and innocent in that gesture; this
new, unfamiliar habit she'd adopted in their time apart. He slowly
closed the door, using the lady's distraction as an opportunity to
study her.

"Madness."

Yes, they were of like opinion on that particular point.

What are you doing, Eleanor? Have you not learned your lesson? She
paused and squinted at the ormolu clock atop the fireplace mantle.
"Where are you?" she muttered under her breath.

"I am here. Or is there another who—"

A startled shriek rent the quiet and Eleanor spun so quickly she
lost her footing.

His amusement died and he took the room in five long strides.

"Eleanor." He dropped to a knee beside her. "Are you hurt?"

She sat sprawled with her skirts rucked and wrinkled, looking like the shepherdess who'd misbehaved. "Marcus. You startled me." She glowered at him. "And you are late."

"Am I?" He took in the sight of her, his gaze lingering on her trim legs, the muscles of her calves spoke of a woman who didn't rebuff physical exertions. Friendship be damned. He wanted her with an even greater intensity than he did eight years ago. Then, he'd been a boy and she an innocent young lady. "Are you hurt?" he repeated, his tone gruff. Now, she was a woman, and he was just as powerless to her enigmatic pull.

Eleanor followed his stare downward to where it rested on her exposed legs and a gasp escaped her. She tossed her skirts down. "I am not."

He mourned the delicious glimmer of her naked legs, those shapely limbs he'd never before seen—until this very moment. With a sigh of regret, he shoved to a stand and, in one movement, guided Eleanor to her feet.

Eleanor clasped her hands in front of her and drew in an audible breath. "The reason I've asked you here—" Her words trailed off as he touched a finger to her lips.

How very methodical she'd become. "Shh," he whispered. She put requests to him, coordinated meetings, reprimanded him for being tardy, and then wasted little time with whatever had brought them together.

"But—"

"A drink first, Eleanor," he murmured and strode over to the eccentric duchess' sideboard. Marcus eyed the older woman's collection of crystal decanters and selected a bottle of brandy. He held it aloft.

Her lips tightened, with what he'd wager his entire estate's holdings, was disapproval. "Must you do that?" she snapped.

Yes, disapproval, indeed. By the fire flashing in her eyes, the lady did not approve of his drinking spirits. With a crooked grin, he pulled out the stopper. "I must." He swiped a tumbler and turned it over. "We both must."

Eleanor gritted her teeth so hard that the snapping of those porcelain-white, perfect rows filled the room. "I do not care to indulge in any more spirits this evening. I've already had two glasses of champagne." Which *had* left her with a soothing warmth.

"You are not indulging," he agreed. "You are having a glass. It is one of the freedoms afforded you as a widow." Marcus resisted the urge to point out that there were any other number of wicked freedoms permitted now but the flash of fire in her eyes indicated that even one misstep on his part and she'd swiftly kill this meeting she'd called for. For some inexplicable reason—he needed to know. He tilted the bottle.

Eleanor sprinted across the room and knocked the glass from his hands, where it tumbled to the floor with a loud thunk. Fury emanated from within her eyes. "No brandy."

With a sigh, he set down the bottle. "Very well." Some of the tension seeped from her shoulders. "Sherry, then." Before she could formulate a protest, he swiped a bottle and set to work pouring two glasses of the amber spirit.

She hesitated and, with a narrow-eyed gaze, stared at the contents of her glass, and then took a slow, almost experimental, drink. Her lips pulled in a grimace. "It is horrid." But she took another sip anyway, and another, her attention trained wholly upon the glass clutched in her white-knuckled grip.

Studying her through hooded lashes, Marcus took a sip and looked at Eleanor over the rim of his glass. "You asked for a meeting? And now you have it." Glass in hand, Marcus held it aloft in mock salute. "So tell me, what is it that has called you away from your throng of suitors?"

CHAPTER 12

ELEANOR STARED AT THE PALE droplets on the edge of her glass, transfixed by the lone, oblong shape as it slid down the side of the crystal, a teardrop falling to the bottom. The amber tear called forth all the fears of reentering Society and the need for a friend. Perhaps it was liquid fortitude, but she drew on Marcia's suggestion from several days past. She drew in a slow breath. "My daughter said I require a friend." Silence met her pronouncement and she glanced up to see if Marcus had heard her. "I said—"

"I heard you."

"Oh." She glanced into the contents of her glass once more. "You didn't respond and so I believed you didn't—"

"I heard you." The hard edge to those words made her wince. This man was the same angry, bitter figure she'd crashed in to on the street days earlier. She could not put a favor to Marcus as he was now. She bit the inside of her lower lip remembering the stranger in the ballroom. Her palms grew moist and the glass trembled in her hand. Droplets of sherry splashed over the rim and she quickly finished the contents of her glass. Coupled with the previous champagne she'd drunk, it filled her with a warm, reassuring coziness—and fortitude. What choice did she have but to enlist Marcus' support? With him at her side, she could face anyone. Including the monster of her past.

Noting her stare, Marcus sighed. "Forgive me." He scrubbed a hand over his face. "The correct response is, in fact, *why* do you require a friend?" And once more, he was the gentle, patient gentleman who'd won her heart.

"Well, everyone needs a friend, Marcus." Apparently, by his silence, he was not of a like opinion. Did she expect him to declare his loyalty to her, affirming the bond they'd shared, greater than any she'd known since? The stilted quiet should be deterrent enough and yet, somehow, found the courage to press ahead. "I didn't want to come here, you know."

He stiffened.

"Not here, per se," she motioned to the library. "To London, that is."

"You enjoyed London at one time," he pointed out.

Only because you were here. How had he not known that? She would have danced happily within the fires of hell if it had been in his arms. She looked off to the cool, empty grate of the hearth. "Yes," she murmured. But that had been a time before monsters and broken dreams. Eleanor gave her head a clearing shake. "That is not the case any longer." Which was just one more reason nothing more could ever transpire between her and Marcus. A great chasm had formed between two people who, by birth alone, had already been cast into two very different worlds. Encouraged by his silence, Eleanor pressed ahead. "My uncle insisted I come."

Marcus furrowed his brow. "Your uncle passed a year ago."

With her rambling, she was making a muddle of this. "In his will," she clarified. "He stipulated I…" She searched her mind. "Experience certain *things.*"

He propped his hip on the back of the leather button sofa. "Things?" he repeated.

"Yes." She gave a wave of her hand. "He provided a list. There are six items on it, but I do not need your assistance with all of them," she said hurriedly as his frown deepened. The more she spoke, the more lucrative her daughter's plan sounded, and the less daunting her uncle's list seemed. She spoke quickly. "My uncle left me ten thousand pounds." Marcus choked on a strangled cough. "However, he requires I accomplish the tasks set out for me, and if I do—"

"The funds will be yours," he said more to himself.

Eleanor nodded. "The funds will be mine." And Marcia's. They would never have to worry again or live in fear of the day when

Eleanor was no longer able to serve as companion to Aunt Dorothea. Where would they go? Who would take a widow with a small child on to her household staff? She thrust aside the fears. There was no longer a worry as to that…as long as she saw to the list.

He eyed her warily. "And you do not wish to marry?"

"Oh, no. Not at all." She'd rather pluck out her eyelashes than turn both her and Marcia over to some man's control.

Marcus continued to study her in that perplexed, silent manner. Eleanor shifted back and forth. She really could use another glass of sherry.

"You most certainly do not require any additional spirits, Mrs. Collins."

"Who?" Who was this Mrs. Collins woman he spoke of? A wave of jealousy slapped at her for this faceless creature.

"And by your tone, I take it you did not want any part of your uncle's list."

She'd rather dance with the Devil on Sunday. "I don't," she said with a matter-of-factness that produced a frown to his lips. "I thought you might help me…accomplish them, some of them, that is," she amended. "As it requires the assistance of a gentleman."

He ran his fingers in circles over his temple. "And that idea is so repugnant to you?"

Eleanor gave an emphatic nod. "Oh, yes." She took another sip and then frowned at her empty tumbler. "Not you," she said on a rush. "It is not repugnant if you are the one to help me." She held out her glass and he hesitated a moment, then reached for the bottle and poured her another. "I'd rather not be bothered with gentlemen who have dishonorable intentions." Which only roused unwanted reminders of those dishonorable sorts and she quickly swallowed down the sherry. Setting her glass aside, she reached for the unfinished tumbler in Marcus' hands and took several long swallows.

He continued to study her with that inscrutable expression that gave no indication as to his thoughts. That expression really merited another sip of sherry. Eleanor tilted the glass back. "Eleanor," he warned.

She closed her eyes a moment as the last of her fears slipped away, replacing it with the most delicious warmth. How had she not known how very wonderful a glass of sherry could be? What other pleasures in life did she still not know of? "I waaant you to be the gentleman to help me." Eleanor blinked. Or was it Marcus who blinked?

Perhaps they were both blinking? No one had ever mentioned that sherry made one blink. A lot.

"You want me to what?" His words emerged strangled and Eleanor slogged through the thick haze upon her thoughts.

"I waaant what?"

His lips moved silently as though in prayer. When he spoke, his voice came out strangled. "You asked me to—"

"Help me complete myyy list," she nodded several times in rapid succession. With two, she peered into her half-empty glass, correction, with two, nearly *three,* glasses of sherry her plan appeared more and more salient. She wrinkled her brow. "Court me," she blurted. "Not court you. Ladies do not court gentlemen." Though the Mrs. Mary Wollstonecraft her aunt had introduced her to would applaud such boldness. "Though you needn't court me," she said quickly when he plucked his now empty glass from her fingers and deposited it on the table beside him.

She frowned up at him. "That really wasn't well-done of you, taking away my glass."

His lips pulled in a smile and this was the grin of his youth; unjaded and sincere and she sighed. So wholly captivating. "It was mine."

She sighed. "Was it?" Why, a smile such as his could drive back the very darkest nightmare.

He nodded once.

He'd always been a gentleman. Even one to let a lady steal his drink. "Charming. So charming."

He widened his smile. "You find me charming?"

"Oh, yes. Absolutely." She grabbed for the bottle of sherry but he easily moved it beyond her reach. *Humph.* "Raaather, tedious. I find you tedious."

He folded his arms at his broad chest. That slight movement stretching the fabric tight over his impressive biceps. "And yet you require the help of this tedious gentleman?"

And intelligent. He was clever to remember as much. "Indeed."

The ghost of a smile hovered on his lips.

She looked sheepishly up at him. "Did I say that part aloud, as well?"

Marcus lowered his head close to hers and spoke in a none-too-subtle whisper. "You did."

"Oh." Eleanor worried her lower lip. "Well, you are clever."

He touched a hand to his heart. "I am honored."

She peered at him. No, it did not seem as though he was making light of her. She gave a pleased nod. "Will you help me then?

WOULD HE HELP HER?

Marcus cast a dubious glance up and down Eleanor's charmingly flushed frame. Her cheeks were a tempting red from the heat of the room and the spirits she'd consumed. It was hard to deny her anything.

Or it would have been at one time.

Years later, her betrayal still fresh, he wanted to toss that request in her face. So why did he not? Why did he consider her plea?

She'd asked him to court her. In the light of a new day, with the sherry and champagne fog gone, she likely wouldn't recall her ramblings or her request. But he would still recall the sneer on her usually innocent lips which spoke volumes on her thoughts of noblemen. Or was it marriage in general? He studied the silent lady before him and gripped his hands into tight fists, his knuckles drained of blood. With her defenses down, she'd revealed more than had she spoken to him in lucid, clear terms. The sincerity of that response brought forth insidious thoughts about the lady's marriage; horrifying possibilities that she'd wed a bounder who'd made their marriage a miserable one. And yet none of it made sense. Not when she'd spoken of love.

"Will you do it?" Eleanor asked, pulling him back to the moment.

Marcus dragged a hand through his hair. "Come along." He held out his hand and she looked at his fingers as though he'd dangled a snake before her eyes.

"You aren't going to help me?" At her wide, stricken eyes, his heart tugged.

This was the lady's power. Her hold was as strong now as it had been then. "I will think on it." For the course of a moment before ultimately rejecting her request. "But you, Mrs. Collins, need to retire for the evening."

She dug her heels into the carpet and remained rooted to the floor. "But you will think on it?"

"I will." When she was sober and logical enough to realize precisely what she'd asked of him. And with that same sober morning logic, she would realize why he could not help her.

"Come along." Marcus took her by the shoulders and gently guided her to the door. "We shall talk on the morrow, Mrs. Collins."

Eleanor dug her heels in once more, slowing their path. She shot a perplexed look back over her shoulder. "Marcus, I do not care to be called by some other woman's name. It isn't what one does with a f-ffriend," she slurred. "Ahh've decided that y-you aren't to call me by that name, anymore."

"And I've decided you are no longer allowed to imbibe in any form of spirits," he muttered under his breath. He pulled the door open and looked out into the hall. Silence rang in the corridor with a distant clamor from the ballroom activity. Marcus stepped out and drew Eleanor out with him.

She glanced up and down the carpeted hall and then speaking on a loud whisper said, "Is there anyone here?" The lady sidled closer and her hip brushed his. His body leapt with awareness and he gritted his teeth.

"There is no one here," he said tersely. "Here," he urged, leading her to the back servants' corridors. He pointed up the stairs. "I will make your excuses to the duchess." He needed a mistress. Or an inventive actress. Someone who could distract him from Eleanor Collins' allure. As soon as the thought slipped in, he kicked ash over it. No one would ever dull this hungering for her, except if he, at last, knew the pleasures of her body. "You turned your ankle."

"I did?" A frown hovered on her full, bow-shaped lips. "That is dreadful."

Despite the madness of this entire exchange, Marcus chuckled. "I am making your excuses." A curl escaped her loose chignon and he tucked it behind her ear, lingering his touch on the satiny soft shell.

"Ahh, yes, of course." She smiled. "How could I forget my foot? Myyyy ankle," she weakly amended. Aren't they really rather the same?" Eleanor tapped a contemplative finger against her lips and then quickly yanked up her skirts, drawing his gaze downward and God help him…a dull humming filled his ears at the enticing place where her trim ankle met her foot. "I suppose not," she said answering her own question and he gave his head a disgusted shake. Lusting after a goddamn ankle. What manner of rogue was he? "A person can't very well go walking with an ankle in place of a foot." She lifted her arms up and her skirts settled noisily about her.

He briefly mourned the enticing display of flesh. "What are you doing?"

"If ah've fallen, shouldn't you carry me?"

And with her arms held out and the invitation on her lips, Eleanor's husky contralto conjured all the most wicked, wanton dreams he'd carried for her. Marcus slid his eyes closed and prayed for patience.

The soft tread of slippered steps brought his eyes flying open just as Eleanor wound her arms about his neck, clinging to him like tenacious ivy winding its way up a garden wall.

Take her. Take her in your arms and rid yourself of the lady's captivating pull…

Why couldn't he be one of those truly roguish sorts? He sighed. Alas, he wasn't a total bastard that he'd accept the offering of an inebriated Eleanor. Marcus quickly disentangled her hands from his person. "Tired," he gruffly amended. "I shall tell your aunt you were fatigued." He reeled backward, seeking an escape from her hold.

Eleanor wrinkled her nose. "Am I injured or tired?"

"Tired," he managed the hoarse utterance. "You are tired."

She sighed. "Very well." Without a parting greeting, Eleanor swept through the doorway to the servants' stairs.

He embraced the much-needed distance between them, when her voice slashed through the quiet. "Do you know, Marcus? For all the rogue business and sneers and snarls since I've returned, you really are a gentleman—a true gentleman with honor and integrity. Not like all the other bounders."

Which bounders? He scowled. No doubt, a woman with an ethereal beauty to rival Aphrodite would have been pursued by countless gentlemen who'd put to her an indecent offer. *Just as I've done…* Guilt needled at his conscience.

While he flagellated himself with guilt, Eleanor's eyes took on a dreamy, far-off quality that sent warning bells clamoring. "Y-you're the only man I'd let carry me, Marcus Gray. Are you certain you'll—"

He yanked at his cravat. "I am certain."

"Oh, very well." At the forlorn note to those two words, he bit back a smile. Eleanor took her leave. And this time, remained gone.

With the silence his only company and her request dancing around his thoughts, Marcus dashed a hand over his eyes.

With her eyes and words, the lady had been all but pleading in her request for help and, yet, if he assisted her in completing the remaining items on that list, he risked being destroyed by her in ways he'd never recover. For his disavowal of the lady and their love, he'd proven he was not, nor ever had been, strong where Eleanor was concerned. The greatest risk she represented was to his heart and reason.

The sound of footsteps brought him spinning around. His heart started. Eleanor's daughter stood several paces away, a wide smile on her lips. He stood there frozen, eying this tiny, miniature replica of her mother.

"Hello, Marcus."

He dropped a bow. "My lady."

A dimple filled her plump cheek as she skipped over. "Are you having the most splendid time?"

Words escaped him and he stared, unblinking. Had she observed his meeting with Eleanor? On the heels of that horrifying possibility, he racked his mind to think of any improper or scandalous words he tossed at her.

"I wish I was permitted to attend," she continued, filling the void of silence with her child's prattling.

Of course. Some of the tension went out of his shoulders. "Indeed, it is a splendid time."

With a long, exaggerated sigh, she rested her cheek in her palm. "I saw but some of the ladies in their gowns. I was not quite close enough to make out the types of fabric. I believe most were in satin, but some were silk, and then Mrs. Plunkett came along and ushered me back to the nursery."

"Mrs. Plunkett?" he asked slowly, in a bid to keep up with the girl's rambling.

She nodded. "My nursemaid."

"Ah, of course. I was quite skilled at evading my nursemaids and tutors, as well."

Marcia folded her arms. "Yes, well, anyway, Mrs. Plunkett rushed me off before I could see any of the dancers. Have you danced this evening?"

His arms throbbed with the memory of Eleanor's lithe frame. "I did," he said giving his throat a clear.

"You are so lucky."

Yes, he had been.

Marcia took another step closer. "Did you waltz?"

"But once. With your mama," he felt compelled to add.

Her eyes lit up. "Truly?"

He crossed his heart and then bowed deeply. "Will you honor me with the second set, my lady?"

Marcia stifled a giggle with her fingers. "You are silly, Marcus. I do not even know the steps." Nonetheless, she evinced her mother's unwavering courage and climbed atop his boots, laughing uproariously as he awkwardly guided them about the floor.

And as her childlike giggles peeled off the hallway walls, a vicious envy threatened to devour him; envy for the man who'd called her daughter and for the happiness they'd surely known as a family, and for the regret that Marcia was not, nor would ever be, his child. With reality rearing its ugly head, Marcus brought them to a stop. "You are a splendid dancer. Your father must have been a skilled partner." He wanted to call the words back as soon as they left his mouth.

Marcia shrugged. "I do not know. He died before I was born and Mama doesn't speak of him."

He opened and closed his mouth several times. Yes, she'd mentioned that she'd not known her father and he'd erroneously assumed she'd been a babe. His mind raced to do the calculations. The sadness in her eyes stymied all questions. "Your mother is a splendid dancer," he said, in a bid to drive back the girl's solemnity.

By the restoration of her gap-toothed smile, he'd succeeded in his endeavor. "You must like her very much because Aunt Dorothea said Mama is a rotten dancer."

His heart missed a beat. From the mouth of babes… "I should

return to the ballroom," he murmured.

Eleanor's daughter sighed and, once again, the gesture so very much her mother's brought forth another swell of regret for all that could have been, but would never be. "I expect you'll help her," Marcia called out as he started to leave.

He froze mid-step.

"With her list. I told her you would help her because she is afraid and you are her friend." At his silence, the little girl stitched her eyebrows together. "You will help her?" There was hesitancy in that inquiry.

He had resolved not to. He had decided when he'd sent her abovestairs to politely decline and move on from Eleanor Collins. Standing here, with her wide-eyed daughter before him, he could no sooner reject the offer to help than he could cleave off his own right hand. "I will," he said quietly.

She beamed. "I knew it. Thank you for making sure my mother is not scared." Then dropping a swift curtsy, Marcia fled down the corridor and raced up the servants' entrance Eleanor had disappeared through a short while ago.

And as he stood there, staring after Eleanor's daughter, the first niggling question crept in—what did Eleanor Collins have to be fearful of?

CHAPTER 13

THE FOLLOWING AFTERNOON, MARCUS SAT in his office and stared into the contents of his brandy glass. He swirled the snifter in several slow circles and took a sip. With a curse, he took a long swallow of his drink, grateful when a knock sounded at his office door. "Enter," he called out.

The door opened. "Oh, dear," his sister said from the entrance of the room. "You're ever so serious again." He stiffened and turned around.

Lizzie sailed into the room in a noisy flurry of skirts. Her faithful friend, Lady Marianne, trotted along behind her, attired in a low-cut, sapphire satin gown a mistress would have compunctions wearing at this hour.

Marcus could not help but compare this woman's jaded cynicism to Eleanor's reserved thoughtfulness and dignity. Years younger than Eleanor, Lady Marianne possessed a worldliness that had once appealed to Marcus. Now he found himself repelled by the brazen promise in her eyes.

Sensing his attention, Lady Marianne misinterpreted it as favorable and toyed with her décolletage. Marcus quickly shifted his attention away. He set aside his glass and sketched a bow. "Lizzie," he greeted wary of the mischievous glimmer in her revealing eyes. With her telling reactions, she would have been horrendous at the gaming tables.

"Marcus. I thought you might accompany me," she cleared her

throat. "That is, accompany us," she motioned to the young lady hovering at the edge of the door. "To Kensington Gardens."

He glanced over at the dark-haired young lady, Lord Atbrooke's sister. "Hello, Lady Marianne," he greeted, struck not for the first time by a flash of pity for the young woman linked to the notorious reprobate.

"My lord," she whispered. A suggestive smile danced on her lips and lest he encourage his sister's friend any more than he had with his two dances earlier that Season, he glanced away.

"The gardens, Marcus," his sister prodded calling him back to the real reason for their visit. "Will you accompany us?"

"I—" Two pairs of wide, hopeful eyes studied him intently and he sighed. The alternative to not joining them would be to remain here haunted by the memory of Eleanor, last evening…and every evening before. "I would be honored to accompany you ladies," he acquiesced, wincing as his sister emitted a loud squeal.

"I've already had the carriage ordered up."

Of course, she had. He'd been unable to deny his sister anything through the years, and she knew he was neatly wrapped about her smallest finger and had been since she was a blubbering babe with barely any hair atop her head.

Except a short carriage ride later, strolling behind Lizzie and Lady Marianne, Marcus found himself wishing he were just this once, a less devoted brother. The infernal prattling that had filled the confines of his barouche continued with an incessant force, as he longed for the sanctuary of his office. Or his clubs. A parlor. A stable. An empty church. Really, anywhere but here in the midst of Hyde Park during the fashionable hours.

Just then, another round of giggles erupted. "Come along, Marcus, we are to the private gardens," his sister cheerfully ordered. With a sigh, he followed after them, down the dirt path, to the less traveled, floral sanctuary completed not long ago by Queen Charlotte. Lady Marianne stole a peek over her shoulder at him. She hooded her smoky eyes in a sultry invitation. His sister said something to the dark-haired young woman, calling her attention back but not before he saw a spark of promise in her gaze. Lizzie tugged her friend into the thick maze of flowers.

He took a step to follow behind them, but then with the same dogged awareness that existed since Eleanor had first stepped outside her aunt's townhouse and into his life, he felt her there.

Lizzie and her friend glanced over their shoulders, back at him, and Marcus waved them on. As the pair rushed off, he trained his gaze on Eleanor's familiar sun-kissed curls tightly drawn back. She sat upon a blanket, beside a kaleidoscope of colored blooms. Seated as she was, she may as well have been a woodland sprite stealing a moment in the floral gardens. A book lay on her lap, while she stared down at those pages as though they contained the answer to life.

The breath left him on a slow exhale. It took a concerted effort, but he removed his gaze, and looked to where his sister and her companion strolled, and then turned once more to Eleanor. After last evening's sherry and champagne indulgence, he'd believed the lady would be shut away battling a wicked megrim. Then she closed her book, a small groan escaped her, as though the slight thump of pages meeting pages had ravaged her head.

She stilled and stretched her long, proud neck like a startled deer. How many times had he worshiped the wild, fluttery pulse that had beat with an awareness of him? Eleanor glanced about and her gaze locked on his.

For an instant, joy radiated from the crystalline blue depths of her eyes. Then, as quickly as it had come, it was gone, so he was left to wonder if the moment had merely been fleeting. He gave her a long practiced, wry smile. "Mrs. Collins," he greeted, sketching a bow.

Eleanor hesitated and then with obvious reluctance, stood. "My lord."

Someday, you shall be a viscountess… I don't care about that, Marcus… No, it hadn't mattered. In the end, she'd chosen love. Someone else's love. He should leave. Instead, he took a step toward her. Marcus stood before her feeling like an untried youth. He beat his palm against his thigh. "Are you here—"

"With my daughter," she finished for him.

Then, they'd always had an uncanny way of knowing what the other had been thinking. How could he have failed to realize the secrets she'd kept from him?

Eleanor motioned beyond his shoulder and he followed her point. "She is with Mrs. Plunkett."

The little girl allowed one of the duchess' pugs to pull her down the walking trail. Her nursemaid, struggling to hold onto the feistier dog, matched Marcia's pace. He returned his attention to Eleanor and searched for some hint that she remembered their dance with madness in the halls of her aunt's townhouse. Her face, however, remained peculiarly blank. He should be grateful that she didn't recall the favor she'd put to him and yet…disappointment filled him.

Eleanor fiddled with her brown skirts. In all her golden splendor, she should be in satin fabrics as she'd been last evening, of hues to rival the blooms they stood amongst.

"I trust you are well?" Eleanor put forth the tentative question, better reserved for a stranger.

"I am and what brings you to these parks you've long avoided?" A soft, spring breeze filled the air, pulling at her skirts and a gold curl tugged free of her chignon. He shot a hand out and tucked the strand behind her ear. Her breath caught on an audible inhalation. He let his hand fall uselessly to his side. "Forgive me," he said quietly. At one time that would have been his right. Not anymore. Marcus turned stiffly on his heel and made to search out his sister and her friend.

"Reading." Her whisper soft response brought him spinning back around. "Marcia wished to visit the park and I came to read." She gestured over to the blanket at their feet. How many sonnets had he read to her during their two-month romance? Countless poems of Wordsworth, Keats, Coleridge.

His gaze fell to the ground and he started. A smile pulled at his lips. "What is this, Eleanor?" He stooped to better examine the title. *A Vindication of the Rights of Women*? Marcus picked it up and fanned the pages of the scandalous words of Mary Wollstonecraft. "You've become political?"

She rushed down in a flurry of skirts and fell to a knee. "It is my aunt's."

"Ahh," he said, drawing out that one syllable, knowing her so very well to know she could never quell her curiosity.

"What?"

"It is your aunt's." He held the volume from her reach. "And yet *you* are reading it."

Eleanor compressed her lips into a tight line and abandoned efforts to retrieve the small, leather tome. "I'll not defend my reading selection to you."

"Nor would I expect you to," he replied, returning his attention
to the words within the book. A stray breeze stirred the air and
the pages danced, drawing his attention down. "But tell me," he
touched a finger to those words. "Do you believe, 'It is vain to
expect virtue from women till they are in some degree independ-
ent of men'?"

Her cheeks blazed crimson. "I believe it is vain to expect honor
from gentlemen." She snatched the book from his hands.

He lowered his eyes. "Are you questioning my honor and after
your words to the contrary last evening, no less?" No one in the
course of his life had questioned his honor and yet the woman
who'd deceived him and left, should have doubt? Except now,
the faintest of warning bells blared at the back of his mind as he
recalled the favor she'd put to him.

"Yes. No." She pulled Mrs. Wollstonecraft's work close. "Not just
you."

Ah, *all* men. The Eleanor of his youth had been filled with a
wide-eyed optimism, seeing good in everyone and everything,
even members of the peerage who'd turned their noses up at her
entry to Society. They'd had but two months together. Eight years
was an eternity and the time had transformed her. What accounted
for the death of those innocent sentiments? Nay, *someone* had
transformed her. "Was it Lieutenant Collins who has thrown all
gentlemen's honor into question?" At last he gave that question
life; the same one to plague him since last evening and it emerged
as a low growl, born of feelings that he would forever carry for
her. Thinking that the man she'd chosen had somehow wrought
this transformation where she should trade sonnets for sermons on
politics, made him want to drag the man from the dead and end
him, all over again.

"No," she said softly. "He was a good man." That quiet assurance
quelled all the furious questions that had turned through his head.

His chest throbbed with a dull pain and he resisted the urge to
rub his hand over the still wounded organ. Odd he should feel
equally but very different hurts in worrying that she'd not been
loved the way she deserved and knowing she'd been loved by the
honorable Lt. Collins. "Yes. A soldier you said." He cleared his
throat. "I am glad," he said, those words hollow to his own ears

and yet, he was happy that, at one point, she'd known happiness.

"Marcus, are you coming?" his sister called from somewhere deep within the garden maze.

He glanced back reluctantly to where her voice had traveled from. Lizzie stood with her hands planted akimbo and a disapproving frown on her lips with Lady Marianne glowering at her side.

"You should go," Eleanor acknowledged.

Yes, he should. In fact, he should have never come over and interrupted her reading, but the questions of last evening lingered and by the spark of disquiet in her eyes, Eleanor feared he'd raise the matter. He held out his arm.

She eyed his elbow as though he'd offered her the head of a serpent. "What is that?"

"It is my arm, Eleanor." He'd have his answers. "Walk with me." And know why she'd wished for him to court her.

With a guardedness in her gaze, she continued to peer at him; that damned volume close to her chest as though she used it as a shield to protect herself from his attention. She glanced about and then eyed the book.

"Surely such freedoms are permitted among friends." Nearly lovers and almost his wife. Why had he waited to put an offer to her? Perhaps she'd tired of waiting. He tugged the book free of her fingers and tossed it to the ground, settling the matter for her. "Will you say no?"

"Would you allow me to?" The mischievous glimmer in her eyes momentarily robbed him of thought, as she became that girl and he became that young man.

"No," he said with a forced smile.

Eleanor placed her fingertips along his sleeve and walked stiffly at his side. Tension fairly seeped from her lithe frame. He took in the tautness of her narrow shoulders and the pinched set to her mouth. He frowned. By God... she was nervous—Of him? Or the request she'd put to him last evening? "I'll not bite you, Eleanor." He paused and stole a sideways glance at her. "Unless you want me to."

Her skin went ashen.

Where had gone his girl who'd laughed and teased? "I was merely jesting," he said quietly.

"I know," she said weakly. They stepped onto the graveled dirt path. His sister and Lady Marianne just ahead, glanced at them.

Lizzie inclined her head. "Mrs. Collins, what a surprise to see you."

He scowled at his usually cheerful sister's frosty tone.

"Likewise," Eleanor called back. Her gaze lingered a moment upon the frowning Lady Marianne and then the two younger ladies resumed their stroll about the well-manicured grounds, leaving Marcus and Eleanor alone once more.

"Why are you here?"

He winged an eyebrow upward. "And where should I be?" He'd sought to protect his wounded heart through the years and had erected walls about that broken organ.

"Your clubs, seeing to your gentlemanly pursuits." As such, he well knew the attempt of another to protect oneself from hurt.

"My gentlemanly pursuits?" Despite himself, a chuckle rumbled up from his chest. "And what precisely does that entail, sweet Eleanor?" The endearment slipped out as effortlessly as it had eight years ago.

"I daresay you know a good deal more, as a gentleman." Her serene face giving no indication that she'd noted his use of that special endearment.

Regret pulled at him again, only this time for entirely different reasons. "Time has made you somber, Eleanor. I preferred you smiling," he said turning her own words back on her.

"I've told you, Marcus," Not "my lord" but Marcus. "Time changes us. You are certainly not the same man I remember."

"You know me not at all," he pointed out, chafing at the ill-opinion she expressed with her blue eyes that may as well have been a mirror into her soul. He stopped and she withdrew her fingers from his person. "Come, surely we'll not dance around it."

Eleanor clutched at her throat, giving her head a shake, pleading with her eyes.

He lowered his voice, speaking in hushed tones for her ears alone. "You'd have me ignore your request."

She let her hands fall to her sides. "M-my request?" A crimson blush blazed across her cheeks.

"Tsk, tsk. You'd feign forgetting your request?"

"I don't know what you're talking about, Marcus," she hissed.

"For me to court you," he continued over her.

"I'll not have this discussion," she whispered, glancing past his shoulder for interlopers to an exchange that should have occurred long ago. She made to leave.

"And you will do what you do best, then, won't you?" he snapped and she froze mid-step, her foot failing to complete that final step. "Leave." He closed the distance between them so just a hairsbreadth separated them. "Nothing to say, Eleanor?" He cursed the waxen hue of her cheeks and the hurt, wounded expression in her eyes. What had she to be hurt for? She had left.

She held her palms up. "I do not want to argue with you, Marcus."

The fight drained out of him. For the truth was, Eleanor was, indeed, correct. This sniping and snapping didn't serve to make him feel better; it didn't provide answers. He ran his gaze over her face. "What do you want of me, Eleanor?"

WHAT DID SHE WANT?

Security. For her and Marcia. Safety; an assurance that she'd never again experience the horror and loss she'd known. She wanted those intangible dreams with such ferocity that she'd humble herself before the only man she'd ever loved for the hope of them. The warning given to her by that dark devil slid around her mind. Unbidden, she skittered her gaze about. Was he here even now? Watching in silent disapproval? Forcibly tamping down the terror he sought to rouse, Eleanor looked down at her and Marcus' interlocked fingers. "I want—" *You.* Several lines creased his brow. "To be friends again," she finished lamely. But for her father, Marcus had been the only honorable, true gentleman she'd known. She needed him to not hate her and she knew it was selfish, as he was deserving of his feelings. But there it was.

"Friends?" he repeated incredulously. "Is that what you believed we were?"

"No," she'd not lie to him on that. "I l—" *Loved you.* "*Looked* at you with great fondness."

"You're mad," he said, more to himself. He turned to leave.

Panic pounded in her chest; an agonizing fear that he'd leave and she'd never again see him. That this parting would be forever. "Wait!" She placed herself in front of him, giving him the full truths, the unfinished truths from last evening. "I believe I mentioned my uncle has left me a substantial settlement in his will." In the light of day, her head throbbing from too much drink, she could not sort out all she'd confided in Marcus last evening.

"Ten thousand pounds," he said and she winced, wondering just how much else she'd revealed. Eleanor took a steadying breath and the flimsy plan she'd concocted following Aunt Dorothea's revelation showed its thin threads. Marcus brushed his knuckles along her jaw, bringing her gaze up to meet his. "And these funds are important to you."

She managed a jerky nod. The funds represented everything.

"Your husband did not leave you cared for, did he?"

"It was not his fault," she said. After all, a fictional gentleman, helpful in some ways, was in other ways useless. Not wanting to become tangled in the web of her lies with more talk of the war hero, Lieutenant Collins, she continued hurriedly. "I will receive the funds set out in the will, if I…"

"If you…?"

Eleanor fished around the front pocket sewn into her cloak and withdrew the well-read scrap of paper. She turned it over to him.

Wordlessly, he accepted it and scanned the page.

"If I complete those items, then I will attain the funds…" She wet her lips. "That is, I'd thought *you* might help me." Even as the words left her mouth she realized how very pathetic her request was; how grasping and self-serving. Her rapist's face as it had been last evening, taunting and triumphant, flashed to her mind and Eleanor's mouth went dry. To not face the threat of that monster alone, she would hand over what remained of her pride if Marcus so asked it.

He picked his head up from that damnable list and studied Eleanor with a dogged intensity.

She shifted on her feet. Of course, it had been wrong to ask him. This was not the Marcus of old. "Forgive me," she murmured, and snatched the paper back. She'd survived that long ago night, alone, and as much as terror threatened the very whole of her sanity, she could face a handful of not so very difficult tasks on her own. She had no choice. Eleanor stepped left. He matched her movements and she raised a perplexed gaze to his.

"You wish me to court you?" Had there been the cool, mocking edge to his words to match the tone he'd taken since their chance meeting on the street days earlier, it would have been easier on her heart than the gentleness she saw reflected in his eyes that proved he was still the man he'd always been, even as Eleanor would never be the girl she'd been.

She drew in a breath. "It would appear that way to Society, but I do not wish to wed," she assured him on a rush. That much was true. The whole truth she could not utter; she feared *all* men's attention, proper or improper. "I thought with you there, and our history, that I would be spared from any possible interest," she warmed. How very arrogant he must find her. "But now I realize how foolish," and wrong, "it is to ask for your help."

Through this, he watched her with his thick, hooded, gold lashes. "Why should I help you?"

He shouldn't. "You are correct, you shouldn't." She dropped a stiff curtsy.

Marcus blocked her escape once more. "I didn't say I shouldn't. I asked why I should."

By the hard glint in his eyes, he expected her to turn his words of love and the affection he'd held for her into tools to manipulate. She couldn't do that. Just as she'd fled and spared him the trial of turning her from his life, for the love she had of him, so now she would not use his emotions as a way to force his hand. Instead, she appealed to the person she knew him to be. "There is no reason you should help me," she said matter-of-factly. "I am neither your obligation nor your responsibility and yet, I require help." And there was no one else to trust and no one else to turn.

He captured his chin between his thumb and forefinger and scrutinized her. "You'd have me deter suitors and lovers?"

Heat climbed up her neck and set her face ablaze. "I would."

Marcus leaned down, so close his lips nearly brushed the shell of her ear. She sucked in a breath. The faintest stirring in her belly only Marcus could rouse reminded her again of the woman she'd once been. A woman who'd hungered for this man and had done so without fear. "What if you want to take a lover, madam?"

"Never," she vowed. There would never be another to take Marcus' place.

"Then you've not taken the right gentleman to your bed, Eleanor." There was a promise there; words, darkly seductive and forbidden and by the very nature of them, should have sent her heart thudding in terror, and yet the warmth in her belly, fanned out and grew the flames.

"I do not care to speak of my bed or a man's place in it," she managed to get those words out, steady and calm. "Will you help me?"

"Marcus?" Their gazes swung as one to the end of the walking trail where Lizzie stood beside her friend. Both young women shot glowers his way.

"I'll be but a moment," Marcus said to his sister.

All the while, the young lady with midnight black hair and cat-like eyes, glared at Eleanor the way she might one of the slithering snakes atop Medusa's head. A knot pebbled in her belly. With her venomous glances at Eleanor and the possessive stares turned on Marcus, the young lady cared for him, that much was clear.

The two women wandered off once more.

The foolishness in this scheme again reared its head when presented with the lovely, more importantly, innocent young lady with eyes for Marcus. "This was wrong," she said stiffly, for too many reasons. The threat he'd pose to her heart, her senses. With jerky movements, she spun about and strode back the path they'd traveled.

"I will help you."

His words brought her to such an abrupt halt she nearly pitched forward. She remained with her back presented to him.

"I will help you," he repeated, from just beyond her shoulder and she jumped, failing to have heard his approach. Her heart raced at his nearness. "A pretend courtship then," he whispered into her ear. She angled her head sideways to look at him and there, in his eyes, was all the passion of their youth, only restrained with a man's total and absolute control. God help her, for the fears she'd carried these years and terror of ever having to bear the vile touch of a man, she now longed for Marcus' kiss. Mayhap then, she could purge the ugly from her person.

"A pretend courtship," she said, detesting the breathless quality of her voice.

He turned his lips up in a slow, seductive grin. "But for the rest of the Season."

A protest sprung to her lips and he lowered his eyebrows. "My mother has unleashed every matchmaking mama and fortune-hunter upon me. My offer to help is not based on purely magnanimous reasons, Eleanor."

"Marcus!" Lizzie called out, her tone this time beleaguered.

She gave a slow nod of capitulation. "Very well. You should go."

"Will you miss me, sweet Eleanor?"

Until she drew her last breath. Eleanor forced a smile. "You're a hopeless flirt, Marcus."

He winked.

"Marcus!"

Their gazes swung together to the entrance of the gardens. Marcia sprinted past her nursemaid, not heeding the woman's quiet reminder on proper behavior. She staggered to a halt before them, her little chest heaving with the exertion of her efforts. "Marcus. Mama, look. It is Marcus."

"I see that, sweet, but you must refer to him as 'my lord'."

Alas, Marcus had always possessed a charm that could make a dowager forget the rules of decorum at Almack's. "Oh, you needn't do any such thing."

"Yes, she does," she said with a sharpness that brought her daughter's head up. Not born a lady, nor even legitimate for that matter, Marcia would have to conduct herself in a manner above reproach.

Marcus favored Eleanor with a crooked grin and then he lowered his voice to a conspiratorial whisper. "I wouldn't have you go about referring to me as Wessex. Rather dreary name."

And Marcia was as charmed as any of those dowagers at Almack's. She giggled into her hand. "I do prefer Marcus, but Mama has always said Wessex is a splendid name, too."

He met Eleanor's gaze and held it. "Has she?"

Even Marcia in all her girlish innocence detected the interest in his tone. "Oh, yes."

Oh, no. Eleanor gave her head a slight shake, but her daughter either failed to see or chose to ignore that subtle movement. "His Lordship must return to his—"

In one smooth, effortless movement, Marcus sank to a knee and smiled at the little girl before him. With gold heads bent together and matching mischievous glimmers in their eyes, they may as well have been father and daughter, sharing a treasured moment while the world watched on. Marcia glanced up with her brown-eyed stare—the eyes of her true father, a monster who'd shattered Eleanor's life, but also left her a gift.

"And has your mama spoken often of the name Wessex?" Amusement threaded his words, except under the nuances of that humor there was something deeper there; something that hinted at an urgency to know.

Seeming to delight in Marcus' undivided attention, Marcia nodded with a solemnity better reserved for a woman years older. "Oh, yes. Surely you've heard the fairytale?"

Settling her hands upon her daughter's shoulder, Eleanor made one more attempt at freedom from the humiliating agony of the exchange. "Marcia, it is time to return to see Aunt Dorothea."

"But you said Aunt Dorothea was resting."

At the knowing glint sparking in Marcus' eyes, Eleanor pressed her lips into a firm line. "Surely Marcia might first share the fairytale of Lord Wessex," he prompted.

"Is not about Lord Wessex, silly." A giggling laugh escaped Marcia. Then with an impropriety that would have shocked any lords or ladies who happened to pass by, Marcia placed her palms on Marcus' cheeks and spoke in very serious tones. "It is about King Orfeo."

With matched solemnity he whispered, "Tell me about this King Orfeo."

The world fell away as Eleanor stood transfixed, struck by the sight of Marcia's small, delicate fingers upon Marcus. Any other gentleman would have likely stiffened or shifted with discomfort at the attentions given him by a child.

"Mama, do you wish to tell Marcus?"

But this was Marcus and he'd never been like any other gentleman, nor would he ever be—even with this natural ease around children.

Marcus leveled a piercing stare on Eleanor, blue eyes seeing too much; more than could ever be safe.

"Mama?" Marcia pressed, her tone befuddled.

Eleanor managed a jerky nod.

"Come, Mrs. Collins, will you not tell me your stories?" She'd have to be deafer than a dowager with cotton in her ears to fail to detect the suggestive twist of his words that sought far more than stories of pretend and legend.

Eleanor opened her mouth to call Marcia to her side when, with her small hands, Marcia forced his head back around to face her. "*I will tell you, Marcus.*"

And Eleanor, whose heart had broken for the loss of him and the dream of them, now broke all over, for entirely different reasons. He was a father Marcia would have been deserving of. Her throat closed with an aching regret.

"Poor Sir Orfeo lost his wife." As her daughter launched into tales of make believe, Eleanor darted her gaze about, searching for intervention from a bolt of lightning, the ground opening, Marcus' sister and the lady who'd been making eyes at Marcus.

"Lost his wife, did he? How does one go about losing something as important as a wife?" he teased, tweaking Marcia's pert nose.

Well, mayhap not the friend making eyes, but Eleanor would settle for any other of the small miracles or interruptions.

Marcia giggled, her hands falling to her sides. "Mama said it's very easy to lose someone."

Tension jerked Eleanor erect and this time, with all traces of amusement gone, Marcus met her stare again with questions. "Did she?" he questioned.

Eleanor held his gaze. All the while, her heart thumped a hard, fast rhythm. She must have more care what she said to Marcia in the future. It would appear nothing was safe or private.

"Yes." Marcia tugged at his sleeve, forcing his attention back to her. "The horrible fairy king stole her away from under the cherry tree." Large, brown eyes formed moons as she became absorbed in her telling. "He brought her to the Otherworld where she could no longer see her king and poor Orfeo wandered and wandered searching for her."

"What happened to them?" At his quiet inquiry, Eleanor folded her arms close to her stomach and held tight. Did he see her own story in the legend? Unnerved by the sideways look he cast her way, she glanced about.

Marcia captured his face once again in her small palms. "Why, he finds her, of course, silly." Because in tales of fairies and make believe, love never died and hope lived on.

Silence met the innocent recounting. Eleanor was the first to break into the tense quiet. She cleared her throat. "Now, we really must be going, Marcia. His Lordship has been good enough to stop and speak with us, but he must rejoin his sister." And Eleanor desperately needed to place distance between her and Marcus. For with every sweet, gentle interaction with her daughter, he threw her world into greater tumult so that the offer she'd put to him proved just another dangerous folly made.

With a smooth grace, Marcus shoved himself to his feet and captured her gloved hand in his larger one. He brought her hand slowly to his mouth. Yesterday, before her aunt's ball, she would have seen this innocent, yet wholly seductive, gesture as a means of taunting her. "Mrs. Collins." That smooth, husky whisper washed over her. Some great shift had occurred between them and as he placed his lips along the fabric of her glove, her breath caught. Marcus reminded her that she was still a woman capable of desire; for a touch, a caress, a kiss—proof that for everything stolen by the nameless stranger long ago, he'd not completely robbed her of this innate part of her.

And there was something freeing in that truth, only just now realized.

CHAPTER 14

"THE BEGINNING IS ALWAYS TODAY"

The beginning is always today.

Seated on the nauseatingly pink sofa where she kept company with her Aunt Dorothea, Eleanor repeated those words in a quiet mantra, over and over. The black inked words of Mary Wollstonecraft stared up at her.

Following her meeting with Marcus yesterday afternoon, she'd arrived home and begged off attending the planned events for the evening. Instead, she'd reflected on this inherent weakness where Marcus, the Viscount Wessex, was concerned. Oh, she'd never ceased to love him. Not one day in eight years had passed where she'd not remembered at least one memory they'd shared.

However, the cool practicality of life had conditioned her to the cold, empty fact—there could never be anything between them. Not in the way she'd wished or dreamed of. That one night in Lady Wedermore's gardens had shattered their present and any hope of a future. Such a fact had been an easy one to resolve herself to as the war widow, in the far-flung corners of Cornwall. Then, she'd accepted that their lives had continued and they'd been forced down two very divergent paths.

Only, seeing him with Marcia, waltzing with him, knowing the brush of his lips upon her palm, she wanted down the other path with an intensity that she'd crawl, kick, or beg for a right to travel once more.

The beginning is always today.

But that wasn't always true. Not where Eleanor was concerned. *Or could it be true? Could her life begin anew—?*

"What is it, gel?"

Eleanor glanced up suddenly at the old duchess, who wore a questioning frown on her face. "Do you disagree with Mrs. Wollstonecraft?" The stern set to her mouth indicated Eleanor would be wise to not question the esteemed philosopher so revered by Aunt Dorothea.

Dropping her attention to the handful of words that had frozen her, Eleanor traced the tip of her fingernail over each small letter. The writer, with her progressive, if scandalous, beliefs, spoke with an unerring accuracy on the injustices known by women and touted a world where women were not dependent upon men for their survival and happiness. Words that usually resonated, in this instance did not. "Today cannot undo yesterday."

"Of course it can't."

Her aunt spoke with such a blunt matter-of-factness, a smile pulled at Eleanor's lips. Shoving aside her distracted amusement, she sought to make sense of the writer's words. "Yet, she speaks of each new day as a new beginning. By the sheer nature of yesterday, Mrs. Wollstonecraft's words of today can never hold truth." Even as Eleanor would have sold the only parts of her unsullied soul to make it so.

Aunt Dorothea leaned over and tapped Eleanor on the knee. "Those beliefs are not mutually exclusive, Eleanor. Yours and Mrs. Wollstonecraft's. I believe the lady would not have spoken fanciful thoughts about erasing time and changing fate. Those are impossibilities."

Eleanor knew that better than most. And yet... "But how can today represent a new beginning if yesterday—"

"It's not a matter of changing the past, Eleanor. It is a matter of setting the past aside and *seeing* today as a new beginning."

A knock sounded at the door and they looked up to where the butler, Thomas, stood at the entrance of the room.

The duchess spoke over him. "Never tell me it's another of the scoundrels here to court my niece?" The older woman had become an almost vigilant protector of Eleanor, since gentleman after gentleman had come calling that afternoon.

"Er, no my lady." The servant with his powdered hair scratched his brow. "Er, that is I don't believe so."

"Humph," Aunt Dorothea groused. "I'll decide if the bounder is worthy of Eleanor."

At that maternal protectiveness in her aunt's tone, some of the tension went out of Eleanor's frame replaced instead with warmth. Her mother died when Eleanor had been just one. She'd known only a father's unwavering love. Moved by her aunt's parent-like devotion, she captured the older woman's wrinkled hands and gave them a quick squeeze. "Thank you."

"Come, enough of that," the gruff woman patted her knee awkwardly in return. "Well," she called out to the servant hovering in the doorway. "Who is here this time?"

"The Viscount Wessex has arrived for Mrs. Collins." Eleanor scrambled forward on the edge of her seat, earning a sideways glance from the duchess. "I've taken the liberty of showing him to the drawing room, but I can very well explain Mrs. Collins is not receiving visitors."

"No!" The exclamation burst from her. The embarrassingly loud and revealing denial bounced off the soaring ceilings. "That is," she drew in a calming breath and resisted the urge to press her palms to her burning cheeks. Marcus' visit was merely a product of the request she'd put to him; a pretend courtship to save her from unwanted advances and still, her heart thumped a too-fast beat as it always had when Marcus had been near. Aunt Dorothea pierced her in that assessing duchess-like manner that had terrified Eleanor when she'd first arrived in London all those years ago. "I will see His Lordship." Eight years later it was no less terrifying.

The duchess said nothing for a moment and then she gave a slight nod. "You heard my niece, Thomas. That will be all."

The servant sketched a bow and backed out of the room.

The usual frown adopted by her aunt turned up in an uncharacteristic, if rusty, smile. She picked up her cane and jammed the gold tip into Eleanor's slippers.

Eleanor winced. "Ouch."

"Run along, gel. The boy is waiting." A wicked glimmer lit her eyes. "Not that I'm opposed to making a gentleman wait. But he's a good boy, that one."

He was. By station established at birth and then circumstances determined by a vile, black cad, Eleanor, however, had been placed firmly in an altogether different category than the one occupied by Marcus. She knew that. Eleanor pushed herself to her feet and silently handed the book over to her aunt. Forsaking gloves long ago as a sign of independence, she'd said, the older woman took the volume in her bent and wrinkled fingers. Eleanor started for the doorway. Aunt Dorothea had drawn the erroneous, but expected, conclusion about Marcus' presence. Acknowledging for the first time since she'd enlisted Marcus' support the deception she perpetuated against the woman who'd plucked her and Marcia from an uncertain fate, guilt sluiced through her.

"Eleanor?"

She paused at the front of the room and turned back around.

"Remember," Aunt Dorothea held a finger up, "the beginning is always today."

With those words echoing around her mind, Eleanor made her way through the long, narrow corridors of the lavish townhouse, onward to the drawing room. If she were still the hopeful sort who believed in the power of the fairytales that she now read to her daughter, perhaps she could allow herself the dream of Marcus. The woman she was now well knew that a powerful viscount with extensive landholdings, a man who was revered and admired, could never bind himself to a woman who'd been stripped of her virtue and left with a bastard child.

Nothing could exist for them, except for friendship; the only possible connection that could be was that of mistress. *I want more than that empty entanglement.* She wanted a life with Marcus, without the threat of her past lurking. But it would always be there. The jeering monster in her aunt's ballroom had been proof of that. Voices within the ivory parlor brought her up short and she lingered at the edge of the door.

"Are those for my mama?"

Eleanor peeked around the doorframe and her heart caught painfully.

Marcus knelt beside her daughter. "No," he said, his words carrying to the entrance of the room. With his back presented, the item in question Marcia and Marcus spoke of remained hidden from view. "Though I suppose I shall give one of them to your mama."

He shifted and dropped his arm to his side.

Eleanor's gaze fell to the bouquet of wildflowers clutched in his hand and a vise squeezed about her lungs making it impossible to draw forth breath. Her daughter had been deserving of a father who spoke with the reverent gentleness in Marcus' tone; a father who would carry her around on his shoulders and spoil her with laughter and love. She captured her lower lip between her teeth, hard. Marcus would have been that manner of father.

Nay, he will be. Just not to my child...

"They are not for my mama?" Disappointment coated Marcia's words bringing Eleanor back from her agonized musings.

"They are not."

He held out the collection of white and crimson blooms. "They are for you, Miss Collins."

Oh, God. Eleanor gripped the edge of the door and drank in the sight of his broad, powerful form, seduced not by Marcus' masculine perfection, but by the sight of such a man so beautifully aware and kind to a mere child—her child. Tears popped behind her eyelids and she blinked them back furiously.

"For me?" For all the awe in Marcia's tone, Marcus may as well have plucked a star from the sky and handed it over to her care.

"For you."

The muscles of Eleanor's throat worked under the weight of emotion and she pressed her cheek against the doorjamb. Why would he be so nice to her daughter? He didn't know, nor would he *ever* know, Eleanor's flight had been to protect him and save him from some irrational sense to do right by her anyway. All he knew was the betrayal of a hasty note and word of a marriage to another. Yet for all the pain she'd caused him, he would help Eleanor avoid the attentions of lascivious noblemen and also be so heartrendingly sweet to her daughter.

"Why?" Her daughter's perplexed question echoed Eleanor's very thoughts.

"Do you know why?"

Marcia shook her head.

"Your King Orfeo's love—"

"Lady Eurydice," Marcia supplied.

"Yes," he said with a nod. "All she wanted was to steal those happy moments in her field of flowers."

"Instead, she was taken away by the horrible fairy and brought to the Otherworld."

Eleanor frowned at the cynicism of her small daughter's recounting. In the telling, through the years, she'd told the story of a lady lost, stolen from her love, and then ultimately found. She'd intended to convey a story of hope and reunion for her daughter, when Eleanor herself had accepted a very different end to her own story.

"That is true," Marcus said solemnly. He took the bouquet from Marcia's fingers and slipped free a lone daisy, holding it close to her nose. Her daughter inhaled noisily. "She was lost to that dark world, but not at first. At first she danced and laughed amidst those flowers and then found her happiness after. That is what matters."

Oh God. A shuddery sob worked its way up her throat and Eleanor buried it in her fingertips. Marcus stiffened. Heart hammering, Eleanor leapt backwards. She pressed a hand against her chest. Perhaps he hadn't heard.

"What was that?" Marcia asked.

Drawing in several, slow calming breaths, Eleanor pasted a smile on and stepped into the room. The two occupants of the room stood side by side. Marcus moved his inscrutable stare over her person and then settled those fathomless blue eyes on her face.

"Mama, Marcus brought me flowers." Unceremoniously, Marcia tugged the bouquet from his long, powerful fingers and raced across the room to present the display to Eleanor.

"Did he?"

"Oh, yes." With her chubby little fingers, Marcia held the single daisy up toward Eleanor. "You should have a flower, too." She tossed a look back at Marcus. "Perhaps when you visit again, you'll bring Mama flowers, too?"

"Marcia," she chided, her cheeks warm at her daughter's boldness.

He inclined his head. "You are, indeed, correct, Miss Collins. I have been remiss."

"What is remiss?" Marcia asked, her little brow creased with confusion.

Eleanor bent down and brushed her lips over the crown of Marcia's curls. "It means you need to return abovestairs to your lessons so you might learn all those words you do not know."

With a very grown-up sigh, Marcia said, "If I must."

"You must."

She gave a jaunty wave and without making her proper good-byes, sprinted from the room. Leaving Eleanor and Marcus and absolute silence in her wake. Fiddling with the lone flower, Eleanor wandered over and came to a stop beside the ivory sofa. "Hullo."

"Eleanor," he murmured.

Wetting her lips, she glanced about. How very comfortable she'd once been around him. Now she was a mere shell of the innocent woman she'd been. "Would you care for refreshments?" But one more thing taken from her by a stranger under the star-filled sky.

"No." Other than that husky, one word utterance, Marcus said nothing.

To give her fingers something to do, Eleanor fidgeted with her skirts, crushing the fabric in her grip. "I-I wanted to thank you, Marcus."

"Thank me?" He took a step forward and she retreated.

"For agreeing to help with a pre—"

In three long strides he closed the space between them and touched a finger to her lips, silencing the remainder of those words. "Shh." He leaned down, shrinking the space between them.

Fear clamored in her breast and she battled through the fast growing panic. This was Marcus. He'd never hurt her and she'd wager her very life that he'd never harm her or another. Not a man who could speak so gently as he did to a child; the child of a woman he hated, no less. Marcus whispered against her ear. "Be careful, Eleanor. A wrong word uttered and a lurking servant, and your efforts will be for naught."

Yes, he was, indeed, correct. She should bury all hint of discourse on the favor she'd put to him and yet could not quell the questions she'd had since in the gardens of Kensington. He'd so very will-ingly offered his assistance. "Why?" she blurted.

He brushed his knuckles along her jaw in the way he'd once done, forcing her gaze up to his. "Why what, Eleanor?" Fear bat-tled with a soft wave of desire and she desperately clung to her body's awareness of his tall, well-muscled frame, hungering for the uncomplicated joy she'd known in his arms. "Why have I agreed to help you?" The corded muscles of his arms tightened the sleeves of his jacket, a reminder of his power—and the danger he could pose. Arms that could overpower, subdue, silence.

A shuddery sigh escaped her and she managed a jerky nod. "You hate me."

"Yes. I've hated you for a long time."

His casually spoken words were a lash upon her heart.

"I hated you for leaving." She'd left because she had no choice but escape. "I hated you for writing me a damned note, after all we'd shared." After the attack, she'd been bruised and sore and battered. How could she have ever faced Marcus after she'd been so used by another? How, when she'd not even been able to stomach her own visage in a mirror? "And I hate you for having chosen another."

She slid her gaze away from his. With her flight, she'd chosen only him. Chosen to save him from humiliation and shame. "It was for the best," she whispered. For in the end, she'd allowed him the freedom to find a woman deserving of him.

He stilled that soft, gentle caress of her jawline. "Is that what you believe?"

"That is what I know." Pieces of her story that would never be his to learn.

She braced for the stinging bite of mocking words she'd come to expect from him; words she'd also come to recognize as an attempt at self-preservation. Instead, his lips turned up in a sad smile. The roguish grin would have been easier, preferable to this achingly empty expression of mirth. "Do you want to know the truth?"

She told herself not to ask, and yet she could no sooner quell the words than she could slice off her own right hand. "What is the truth?"

"I do not hate you." Her heart lifted and took flight. That admission was more poignant than any declaration of love he could give. "For everything that has come to pass, I care about you." Not love. Her wildly beating heart sank. Still, caring for her was a good deal better than the dark feelings of hate. "I want to see you happy." Marcus cupped her cheek and he lowered his lips close to hers, so close they nearly brushed. Close enough to remind her of how beautiful it had once been between them. "And God help me, I still want you."

God help her, she wanted him, as well.

He claimed her mouth with his. For an infinitesimal moment, a spark of desire lit from the brush of his lips on hers and she turned herself over to the wonder of his embrace. Marcus groaned, and parting her lips, he slipped his tongue inside.

He tasted of brandy.

Eleanor gagged. She shoved away from him with a startled cry and punched him hard. Her fist connected solidly with his nose. The sickening sound of flesh meeting flesh flooded her buzzing ears.

CHAPTER 15

MARCUS HAD RECEIVED ALL MANNER of interesting responses to his kisses through the years. Breathy pleas for more, desperate moans of approval. Not once, however, had he been punched for his efforts.

He touched his nose and winced. By God, too many counts in a ring against Gentleman Jackson himself and he'd never had a bloodied nose, but then with one dangerously wicked right jab, the lady had managed it. The warm trickle of blood penetrated his glove and Marcus yanked his kerchief from his pocket and pressed it to his nose, staring at Eleanor over the rapidly staining fabric. The lady continued retreating, her pallor white. "Bloody hell." He flinched as pain radiated along his nose.

For all he *did* know about Eleanor Carlyle, now Collins, he'd never known she could plant a facer like Gentleman Jackson himself.

She backed into a rose-inlaid side table. The fragile piece of furniture shifted under the sudden movement and a porcelain shepherdess tumbled to the floor. It exploded in a spray of white and pink splintered glass.

"A simple no would have sufficed," he said drolly and experimentally tested the soundness of the bridge of his nose. He winced. Yes, very possibly broken. By a slip of a lady. "I will say I've never quite received that—" His words trailed off. Eleanor's chest heaved with the force of her rapidly drawn breaths. The pale white of her cheeks melded with the stark white of the plaster walls. By God, she was terrified. Granted, he was livid about the whole deuced painful nose business, but did she believe he'd harm her? Annoyance stirred in his belly. "Surely you don't believe I'd hurt you."

Her eyes stood out, vivid blue moons in her face; trapped within their depths was a gripping terror. She had the look of a woman battling tortured demons. A chill ran along his spine. Then, the fleeting moment passed. She blinked several times and then on a soft cry raced over. "My goodness, Marcus. I've hit you."

"Yes," he said with the first stirrings of amusement since that very violent rebuffing of his advances. Punched. Walloped him with a force Gentleman Jackson himself would have been hard-pressed to not admire. Marcus gave his head a wry shake.

"I am so sorry." She moved her hands up, as though to affirm a break but then she swiftly lowered her palms to her sides. His gaze fixed on the tremble to her long, graceful fingers. He frowned as the faintest warnings stirred at the back of his mind. Why would Eleanor react so? Her response, paired with her humbling request for his aid melded together and he curled his hand into a balled fist. "It is all right," he assured her. "It is not broken."

"I—you surprised me."

Mere surprise? Is that all there was to account for her panicked reaction? A niggling of unease settled in his belly and he blotted his nose once more. Marcus touched his free hand to her jaw. "I came to escort you for a ride in my curricle."

She captured her lower lip between her teeth. "We can't. Not with your nose—"

"It has nearly stopped bleeding," he interrupted, pressing the crimson-stained fabric to his injury.

Eleanor hesitated; indecision raging in her eyes. Then she gave a slight nod. He extended one elbow and she placed her fingertips along his sleeve, allowing him to lead her from the room. As they walked, he examined the top of her bent head. Her skin, still a grayish-white from when she'd walloped him, and the trembling fingers on his forearm hinted at her terror. What was the cause of that sentiment? Upset over hurting him? Or something more…?

The knot in his belly grew and he forcibly thrust it back.

They reached the foyer and servants rushed forward with their cloaks.

Eleanor removed her fingers from his person and with those quaking digits, she fiddled with the clasp, and then she accepted her bonnet; a straw piece with faded roses sewn along the brim.

A memory trickled in. Eleanor as she'd been, wearing the same bonnet, only the colors had been crisp and those blooms so very full they had appeared real. This was the life she'd lived. This was the state her husband had left her in; a woman required to fulfill those charges doled out by a late uncle, all so she could know security for her and their child.

"What is…?" Eleanor's words trailed off as she noted the direction of his scrutiny. She yanked the frayed ribbons into a neat bow. "Shall we?"

The butler rushed forward and pulled the door open. Sunlight streamed through the entrance and splashed off the white, Italian marble floor. Stuffing the stained handkerchief into his front pocket, Marcus motioned Eleanor outside and followed behind her.

No words were exchanged until he set the curricle into motion. "Have there been gentlemen who have forced their advances on you?" he asked without preamble. Because if there had been, he'd tear the bastards apart with his bare hands and feed them their own limbs for their evening meal.

From the corner of his eye, he caught the almost imperceptible tightening at the corners of her lips. She hesitated. "I am a widow."

I am a widow. That was, at best, an unspoken affirmation of his question and, at worst, a deliberately vague response.

"A widow who does not wish to take a gentleman to her bed." Unlike the countless widows he'd taken to his bed who'd relished the freedoms afforded them and more, the pleasure to be found in his arms. Pleasure he would show Eleanor, if she allowed it of him. Marcus shifted the reins to one hand and covered her fingers with his. The full, red flesh of her lips quivered under his ministrations, but she did not pull away and for that, he was encouraged. "You'd deny yourself the pleasures to be had in a man's arms?" A fact for which he was grateful. The idea of her wrapped in another gentleman's arms shattered him.

"How very arrogant you've become, Marcus. You *are* a rogue." Yes, he'd fashioned himself into the indolent, charming rogue as a means of protecting himself from ever being hurt at the hands of a woman. He'd never been ashamed of who he'd become—until now, with the disappointment and sadness reflecting in the soulful depths of her eyes. "You expect I should take a gentleman to my bed because I am a widow? You'd have me sacrifice my self-respect and honor for what? A fleeting union of two people in a shameful act that should not exist beyond the bonds of marriage?"

A shameful act? "Is that how you view the act of making love, Eleanor?" Had her husband been one of those coolly detached sorts who snuffed the candle and came to her with coverlets drawn and her nightshift between them? What a bloody fool.

"I don't view the act of making love in any way," she said between gritted teeth. She darted her gaze about, as though seeking escape. The rapidity of her movement sent a golden curl tumbling from her chignon. She tucked the tress back inside her bonnet.

"That is a shame," he murmured. "A lady such as you should think of it, Eleanor, and think of it often. You should celebrate the power of a man's touch and dream of taking that man," Preferably only him. "In your arms and—"

She yanked her hand free of his. "I do not want your empty words of passion and desire." That was all he had to give anymore since she'd stolen off with his heart.

"Ah, yes. You want my friendship, for however many tasks you have left on your uncle's list? And then what, Eleanor? Will you disappear and run off, leaving," me, "London behind?"

Eleanor nodded and he started at that honest response. "I do not want Marcia to grow up in this world."

"Where will you go?" he tossed back, desperately requiring that answer so this time, when she walked out of his life, he didn't spend every day wondering where she'd gone to, was she happy, and worrying he'd never again see her. When she remained silent, annoyance stirred in his belly. "No response? Even now, you'd not tell me where you made your home? That isn't a friend, Eleanor." Suddenly, it was very important he know who she'd been, what she'd done, and where she'd gone in these eight years. At the very least, she owed him that much.

For a long while, she said nothing, and he thought she intended to remain silent. "The north coast of Cornwall," she said, her faint voice so soft he thought he might have imagined it. But then she cleared her throat. "A small village called St. Just."

Cornwall. A bitter laugh escaped him. She'd traveled to the opposite end of England. The emotional and physical gulf between them had been equally great. "Did your husband hail from there?"

She gave her head a slight shake. The muscles of her throat moved and she directed her attention to her tightly clasped hands.

Then, he asked the most important question he'd had all these years, the answer mattering as much now as when she'd been a young lady of eighteen. "Were you happy?" For the hole she'd ripped in his heart with her leaving, he'd never wanted to imagine a world in which she'd not been the smiling, laughing girl she'd been.

"I had Marcia." She paused. "Of course, I should be happy."

How neatly she sidestepped his question; her evasion more telling than affirmation or denial. "Ah, but it's not a matter of should you have been or should you not have been, but rather, were you?" Marcus shifted the reins to his opposite hand, and caught one of her tensely held ones. He slid his fingers into hers, interlocking the digits. He studied them. How very effortlessly they fit together.

"I was," she said softly, her eyes on their joined hands.

Marcus braced for more words from her on the paragon who'd held her heart, but she remained stoically silent. How was it possible to feel both this lightened relief, melded with jealousy for what they had known together? He removed his hand from Eleanor's and once again shifted the reins so he might more easily guide the curricle through the gates of Hyde Park, down the path clogged with carriages. Eleanor loosened the strings of her bonnet and pulled the piece free. She set it down on the bench beside her and closing her eyes, she turned her face up to the sun.

A vise squeezed off all hint of airflow as he worshiped the sight of Eleanor bathed in the warm rays of the springtime sun. It kissed the honeyed blonde of her curls, casting an otherworldly glow upon her. She was perfection. She was unfettered and untainted in her beauty; pure, while the women about those polished beauties of Society were as false as their smiles.

Eleanor opened her eyes and their gazes collided. "What is it?" she asked, touching her hand to her mouth.

He shook his head. "It is..." Everything. "Nothing." Marcus guided them off the well-traveled path, away from the crowds of lords and ladies out for their excursions. He leapt from the curricle and motioned forward a boy hovering about. Marcus withdrew a sack of coins and tossed it to the child who easily caught it. "Care for my mount and there will be more." Gripping Eleanor at her narrow waist, he helped her to the ground. She looked at him askance. "Your uncle did not know you well enough to know you never enjoyed a curricle ride." She'd once likened rides in Hyde Park to being a creature on display at a museum for all to gawk and gape at.

Eleanor started. "You remember that?"

Marcus remembered all about Eleanor Elaine Carlyle. He winked. "The duke failed to stipulate a length or duration to that carriage ride, so I daresay this shall suffice?"

The muscles of Eleanor's throat moved and a sheen of tears dusted her eyes. She blinked them back and then allowed him to lead her down the walking trail.

He opened his mouth to speak, when his sister's voice slashed into their exchange. "Marcus!"

Their gazes swung as one to Lizzie who wound her way determinedly through lords and ladies. At her side, marched a very determined, and a boldly staring, Lady Marianne Hamilton. The duo came to a stop before him and Eleanor and he damned the unwanted intrusion.

"Mrs. Collins, Marcus, what a surprise it is to see you here," Lizzie said, breathless from her near sprint to reach them. She brushed a damp, loose curl behind her ear. "Then it is really no surprise. You do so love rides in Hyde Park, just as Marianne does. Don't you, Marianne?" Lizzie turned her attention on the lady at her side.

"I do love to ride, my lord." Lady Marianne peered at him through thick, smoky lashes. "Perhaps we might one day have the pleasure of riding…together."

He choked, but by his sister's wide, innocent smile, she'd failed to note the young woman's veiled innuendo. By the tense set to Eleanor's shoulders, however, the more experienced widow detected the other lady's interest—and if the fury spitting in her eyes was any indication, she was anything but pleased with the woman's attentions.

Why would Eleanor be jealous? Why, unless she still felt something for him? A lightness filled his chest at the evidence of

Eleanor's interest.

"Do you enjoy riding, Mrs. Collins?" Lady Marianne asked Eleanor.

She smoothed her palms over the front of her skirts. "I…" She was afraid of horses. Another piece that made Eleanor Elaine the woman she was. "Do not…" she finished.

Lizzie slipped her arm in Marcus'. "I would speak to you a moment, brother. There is a favor I would put to you."

He swallowed a curse as his sister steered him away. "Can it not wait, Lizzie?"

She planted her hands on her hips. "You've been unpardonably rude."

Marcus cocked his head.

Lizzie pointed her eyes at the sky. "To Mar…" At his narrowed eyes, his sister coughed into her hand. "That is, to *myself*."

Bloody hell. From over the top of her head, he caught Eleanor's gaze. She gave him a slight nod and smile, and then turned her focus to something Lady Marianne said.

"…the opera. And it would be so splendid. Don't you agree?"

He swung his attention back to Lizzie and blinked furiously. What was she on about?

Lizzie tapped a finger against his lapel. "The opera. I simply wish you to accompany me to the opera."

He'd learned long ago to be wary of statements from Lizzie that began with "I simply wish…" Marcus folded his arms and winged an eyebrow up. "What else?"

She forced a smile. "You are always so suspicious, Marcus." She trilled a laugh that made him wince. "That is all." In a weak attempt at nonchalance, she patted her curls. He turned and started back for Eleanor when Lizzie called out. "Oh, and Marianne will be joining us."

Marcus resisted the urge to drag his hands over his face. Who would have imagined his sister would have proven to be a more meddling matchmaker than his blasted mother?

"I DO NOT LIKE YOU, Mrs. Collins."

Eleanor started. She opened her mouth, but no words came out for the flawlessly perfect, exotic beauty. In fact, she may as well have imagined the virulent statement from the young lady in her elegant, pale blue, satin skirts. Lady Marianne stood silently staring after brother and sister in the near distance. But all doubts over the realness of that admission were shattered as the young woman spoke once more.

"I haven't liked you since you arrived in London and snared the viscount's attentions and I've not liked you since you began inserting yourself into his life."

Having battled countless sneers and unkind whispers when she'd made her Come Out years earlier, Eleanor could well handle a spiteful eighteen or nineteen-year-old brat. "You are nothing if not honest," she said dryly. She cast a hopeful look in Marcus' direction. Alas, salvation was not coming from that score. Marcus remained engrossed in discourse with his lively sister.

"Are you making light of me, Mrs. Collins?" the young lady hissed.

"I wouldn't dream of it."

At Eleanor's attempt at droll humor, Lady Marianne Hamilton pursed her lips. She opened her mouth as though to launch a stinging attack on Eleanor, but then proved that years of lessons on decorum and propriety could not be easily forgotten—even in the face of spiteful hatred for an interloper like Eleanor. "He is a splendid gentleman, isn't he?"

Eleanor choked. Surely, she'd heard the young lady wrong.

Lady Marianne Hamilton made a tsking sound. "Why, an experienced widow, you've no doubt appreciated His Lordship's physique."

Heat slapped Eleanor's cheeks as she was reminded once more how hopelessly out of place she'd always been amongst the vipers of polite Society. "It is hardly appropriate to speak about—"

"Oh, come, a woman such as you? Why, the least shocking thing you've surely done is pant after the viscount."

A woman such as her? A sudden cold stole through Eleanor and a panicky unease unfurled in her belly. She fought to calm her racing heart. There was no way this woman knew her past. No way…

Lady Marianne turned her lips up in a slow, knowing grin. "You see, Mrs. Collins, noblemen such as the viscount wed young ladies such as me. His sister even knows it, and it is why she'll match-make for me and interrupt whatever scandalous deeds you intend with Lord Wessex." She flicked a glance up and down Eleanor's frame and she drew her shoulders back under the insolence of that stare. The young lady peeled her lip back in a sneer. "The viscount will dally with a merchant's daughter, but ultimately, he'll wed a lady—" She preened. "Such as myself. So you may carry on with Lord Wessex, but I intend to wed him and his fifty thousand pounds."

Eleanor saw, breathed, and tasted fury. His fifty thousand pounds? "Is that all he is to you? A fat purse to catch?" She would sooner slice off her own fingers, one at a time, than see him wed a creature such as this.

"That is not all he is. I will enjoy stealing off to the gardens with him…" Another icy shiver raced along Eleanor's spine as the young woman flounced her dark curls. Lady Marianne leaned close, dropping her voice to a barely discernible whisper. "And you do know much about midnight meetings in the gardens, don't you?"

The earth shifted under her feet. Eleanor clutched her hands to her throat at the ugly, horrifying truth. *She could not know. She could not.* The young woman smiled through Eleanor's silent torment. "After all, you are a widow and widows do know of midnight meetings in gardens, do they not?"

Eleanor dropped her arms to her sides and blinked once, twice, and a third time. Of course, she could not know. How could she? She balled her hands at her sides, detesting Lady Marianne Hamilton with a seething hatred. These grasping, title-seeking women who knew nothing of love and warmth. Eleanor tipped her chin up a notch. "Some lofty noblemen you speak of will assuredly wed you. But that man will not be Lord Wessex. He is entirely too good and clever to wed a coldhearted creature such as you." She prayed her words to be true. For even as Eleanor with her tattered past no longer deserved him, this woman deserved him even less.

Lady Marianne gasped and Eleanor took advantage of the lady's momentary shock. She turned on her heel and marched away, back to the curricle. Fury burned in her veins and fueled her movements. Surely Marcus would never fall prey to that viper's charms? Surely he—She gasped as someone took her at her elbow. Drawing her arm back, she swung about, but Marcus easily clasped her wrist, catching the blow.

"Never tell me you intend to blacken my eye now?" Droll humor laced his question.

The tension drained to her feet and Eleanor loosened her arm. "Marcus," she said flatly. "I did not hear you approach."

"Because you were sprinting away." He peered at her. "Did Lady Marianne say something to upset you?"

"No." Yes. Nothing that wasn't the truth, however. "We've accomplished the item on the list, Marcus. There is no longer a need for us to be here."

A muscle jumped at the corner of his eye. "Of course," he said tersely. He lifted her up and easily handed her into the seat. "Let us return, then, and cross this item from your list. I have issued an invitation for you and your aunt to join my family at the theatre later this week." He tightened his mouth. "Another item to strike from your list."

As the curricle lurched forward, Eleanor bit her lower lip to keep from giving in to tears. She stared blankly out at the merry couples; unfettered in their happiness. Her gaze snagged upon a young blonde woman seated beside a golden-haired gentleman. Their eyes and faces demonstrated none of the mistrust that time had wrought upon Eleanor and Marcus. In fact, she might be looking at the couple, as they would have been if life had carried along its safer, happier trajectory.

But it hadn't. Life had intruded and they could never, ever be that couple. Even if he offered for her and she wanted to accept, which she did, she could never give him the heir and spare he required as viscount. For the passion he'd roused with his kisses, her panicked reaction that morning was proof that no matter how much she wished it or willed it to be different, her mind and body were equally broken.

Her heart spasmed and she rubbed her palm over her chest to dull the ache. Her efforts proved futile. That organ had been broken long ago and could never be healed. How was she going to survive the rest of the Season, loving him more and more each day, while the chasm between them grew wide?

She looked up at him; silent and stoic when he was only ever grinning and laughing. Mayhap Marcus would not hate her so. Mayhap he would understand if she let him into her world in ways she'd never let anyone other than her father in; and he'd taken the truths and secrets to his grave. The risks of confiding anything in anyone had been too great; for her, for Marcia, for their collective future. The world was unkind to unwed mothers. It was even more so to the bastard children of those shameful mothers. As much as Marcus despised her for shattering his heart, he would never jeopardize Marcia's safety or security. His gentleness with Marcia, his willingness to help Eleanor accomplish the tasks set out for her by her uncle, were proof that he was the same man he'd always been.

Yes, Marcus might be the affable, charming rogue to Society, but he was still the fiercely loyal, considerate gentleman who'd first and forevermore captured her heart. He was unlike any other man.

And that was why he was deserving of the truth. So he could be free to make the match required of him as a viscount and not be burdened with the tasks Eleanor had been assigned by the late duke.

"Meet me in the gardens at quarter past the hour."

For a long moment she suspected he'd not heard that barely there whisper, but then, with his gaze forward on the lines of curricles before them, he gave a tight nod.

CHAPTER 16

HE WAS LATE. AND ELEANOR only knew he was late because she herself had not exited her chambers until quarter past the hour. Seated on the wrought iron bench, amidst the roses and gardenias, she scanned the garden wall separating their homes for sign of him.

A night breeze stirred the bushes and the cool air penetrated the fabric of her modest gray muslin dress. Her spectacles slipped down her nose and she removed the unnecessary pair. For eight years she'd almost never been without the lenses. Since she'd arrived in London, they'd been more of an afterthought. An afterthought when of all places, *this* is where she needed them most. She dropped her gaze to the rims. She'd used them as a means of protection. There had been something falsely reassuring about the spectacles. They were a kind of mask she'd put on to be what she wished the world to see because…what if they saw the truth? What if they saw the woman who was used and dirty and who still bore the traces of ugliness on her body and soul? More, what if Marcus saw her in all those worst possible ways? Tears flooded her eyes and she blinked back the useless drops. One squeezed past her lid and slid down her cheek, followed by another and another.

Footsteps sounded on the other side of the garden wall and she hopped to her feet. Heart pounding hard, she quickly dashed her hands over her cheeks.

Marcus shoved his form to the top ledge of the wall and her

heart caught painfully as he turned that charming grin on her. "My la…" His flirtatious greeting ended as his gaze snagged on her cheeks and that smile dipped.

Eleanor quickly angled herself away and brushed her palms over her cheeks. "My lord, I thought you'd not come," she managed to infuse a steadiness and cheer to those handful of words.

Marcus hung by his hands over the wall and dropped to the earth. He landed with a soft thump in the earth below and paused. His gaze lingered on her eyes. She braced for a rash of probing questions.

Slipping his hands into his pockets, he strolled toward her. There was something so very sweet and endearing about the languidness of those movements. He evinced the same cocksure strength he had as a young man meeting the girl she'd been.

Eleanor reflexively tightened her hold on the wire rims, the useless, flimsy disguise she'd donned through the years. The rims snapped and the crack of metal echoed in the quiet. Startled, she looked down at the two pieces in her hand. Her heart caught. "My spectacles," she whispered.

"Come, Eleanor, you never truly needed them."

She lifted her unblinking gaze to Marcus, unable to sort out whether those words belonged to him or her. Wordlessly, she held them out and he collected the broken rims and tucked them into his front pocket.

…I shall hold it close to my heart, so a piece of you is always with me…

Eleanor captured her quivering lower lip hard between her teeth. He palmed her cheek and she leaned into his silken soft caress. Closing her eyes, she took in every delicate touch, every pure moment between them, because the moment she breathed the truth into the night air, she would forever shatter the sincerity in Marcus' words for her. Eleanor drew in a steadying breath and opening her eyes. She stepped back.

"What is it?"

Gone would be that enticing, subtly seductive baritone. She lifted her arms. "My waltz at midnight."

He froze. "Of course, your li—"

Eleanor pressed her fingertips to his lips, silencing the words there. "It is not about the list." She smiled softly up at him. "This is for me, Marcus. I would take this dance, in your arms, not because someone demanded it or requested it. I would take it because, in this moment, at quarter past the midnight hour, I would claim that time that once belonged to us."

Desire sparked within the depths of his eyes and threatened to burn her and, God help her, his was a conflagration she'd gladly turn herself over to; to know a touch born of love and tenderness and passion. Marcus swept his golden lashes down. Without a word, he settled his heavy palm at her waist and guided hers atop his shoulder, and then with their fingers joined as one, amidst the fragrant, springtime blooms, he waltzed her barefoot about the gardens.

Their breaths mingled and melded, and with the stars glittering overhead and the moon setting the ground aglow, they danced. She closed her eyes and turned herself over to the beauty of being in his arms. How many years had she ached for this stolen moment at midnight, with the darkness of demons slayed, so all they knew was joy?

"We are missing music, Eleanor," he murmured and she opened her eyes, locking her gaze on the harshly beautiful angular planes of his face; the noble Roman nose, the hard, square jaw softened by the faintest cleft.

"We do not need music, Marcus." They never had. Their bodies had long moved in a synchronistic harmony.

He curved his palm about her waist and she reveled in the thrill of his touch. "Ah, yes, but what waltz is complete without music?" Then, his breath tickling her skin, he began to sing.

"…Oft in the stilly night
Ere Slumber's chain has bound me,
Fond memory brings the light
Of other days around me…"

As his husky baritone filtered about them, in a slightly off-key, discordant tune, tears welled in her eyes and slid unchecked down her cheeks.

"The smiles, the tears,
Of boyhood's years,
The words of love then spoken;
The eyes that shone,
Now dimm'd and gone,
The cheerful hearts now broken

Fond Memory brings the light
Of other days around me…"

Her breath caught on a sob and she dug her heels into the earth, bringing their dance to a jarring, painful halt. But then, ultimately, all beautiful moments died.

"Eleanor?"

The aching gentleness of Marcus' tone gutted her and she hugged her arms at her waist. Why could he not be the coolly mocking cynic who'd come to hate her? Why must he now be this soft, tender man who sang songs of lost love?

Eleanor rubbed her arms in a bid to bring warmth into her trembling limbs. Unable to meet the intensity of his eyes, she wandered over to the cherry tree and ran her hand down the firm, broad trunk. The wind stirred and the pink-white blooms danced over her head, wafting the purity of their fragrant scent about her. She searched her raging mind for the truth he deserved. Odd, how the single most defining moment of her life had gripped her and consumed her for eight years and, yet, she stood before him silent and unknowing of where and how to begin her story. His feet ground up gravel as he strode down the path toward the shelter of the tree. Eleanor turned to face him and lifted a hand. The only place to begin was at the beginning "I was there."

Marcus stopped so abruptly his feet churned up dirt and pebbles. A golden curl fell over his eye giving him an endearing, boyish look. "I don't—?"

"You believe I did not show, but I was there, in Lady Wedermore's gardens," she clarified. And then a healing calm stole over Eleanor, driving back all the fear and reservations and horror of speaking of that night. There was freedom in it that lifted a weight from her burdened shoulders. "I was there." She raised regretful eyes to his. "*You* were not."

MARCUS STARED AT ELEANOR.

At last they would speak of it; the one night between them which had built an eight-year chasm. "Is that what you believed," he asked slowly. "That I would not come?" Surely in all they'd shared, she would have known he would always come to her. "Surely that is not what would drive you into the arms of another."

The full moon cast its pale white light through the branches of the cherry tree and the glow kissed Eleanor's pale cheeks so that her teardrop glistened like sad diamonds.

At her stricken silence, he said gruffly, "I was there."

"You came too late."

Her agonized whisper ran through him. "I…" He took in the tense white lines at the corners of her mouth, the suffering that now bled from her eyes, and distant warning bells went off. Marcus dug his fingertips against his temple and rubbed, trying to make sense, trying, and failing…

It is because I do not wish to make sense…

He dropped his arm to his side with alacrity and when he spoke, there was a peculiar flatness to his tone. "What does that mean I came too late?"

"Someone else arrived first." Eleanor curled her hands at her sides. "A…man."

A man—? A thousand questions boiled to the surface, and with them, the pebble of unease in his belly grew to the size of a boulder. Her words led him down a path he did not wish to travel. "Did he threaten you with ruin?" he asked slowly, silently pleading with the fates.

A strangled laugh burst from her lips and she buried it in her fingers.

His mouth went dry and his gaze caught on the white-knuckled fist pressed against her mouth. An icy chill raked his spine and ran a quick course through him, freezing him from the inside out and yet perspiration beaded his brow as he considered the new Eleanor who'd returned to London. A woman fearful of men; who'd punched him…

The earth tipped, swayed, and dipped. "Oh, God," the agonized whisper came from the place where horror and fear dwelt. Marcus concentrated on breathing. No. The imagination was an active, dangerous beast. As long as she did not utter the words, they remained untrue fabrications of an irrational thought based on a handful of incidences.

She pressed her palms to the uneven bark of the cherry tree, as though seeking support. "He didn't threaten me with ruin." Eleanor lifted her ravaged eyes to his and spoke in curiously deadened tones that sent a chill skittering around his insides. "He *did* ruin me."

His heart ceased to beat and he tried to make out Eleanor's raspy words as they ran together.

"He said no proper lady would be out meeting a lord in the gardens. He said as a poor merchant's daughter, I-I was begging for any man between my legs."

Insidious thoughts slipped into his consciousness of Eleanor on her back with the monster who'd stolen her innocence rutting between her thighs.

His stomach heaved and he closed his eyes a moment to keep from casting up the contents at her feet. With her strength and courage, she deserved more from Marcus than his frail weakness.

"I fought him," she said, staring at a point beyond his shoulder, to the demons of her past and with those three words, she invited him into the world where she'd scratched, kicked, and clawed.

To no avail.

"Who was he?" The strangled plea tore from his throat. Who, so Marcus could end him with his bare hands.

"I did not know." She avoided his gaze and a flash of terror lit her eyes, and then was gone so quickly he might have merely imagined it. "I knew nothing but his face and that he stank of brandy."

The gardens echoed with the memory of imagined cries and pleas of some faceless, nameless stranger. Insanity licked at Marcus' thoughts and cast a thick, dark curtain over his vision, as he imagined a hell in which the man who'd raped her was a gentleman he took drinks with or spoke to at Social events. Marcus tortured himself, imagining that bastard yanking her skirts up, shoving a knee between her legs, and—His breath came hard and fast in his ears, deafening. *Oh, God.*

"At first, when he came upon me," she said more to herself, yanking him back from the precipice of madness. "I continued looking at the door, silently begging you to come. And then, I lay through his attack, silently pleading with you to not come. Because I could not bear it if you saw me that w-way." The faint tremor to that word had the same effect as a blade being thrust into his belly and twisted.

His heart lurched. Where had he been? Whatever waylaid him

that night, whoever it had been, was so very insignificant that he could not recall the name or reason for his delay. And yet, that trivial meeting had upended her world, shattered their happiness. He wanted to toss his head back and rail at fate. "Oh, Eleanor," he whispered, and he, who'd charmed countless ladies in her absence, was so wholly useless in this moment. There were no pretty endearments or perfect words that could take away any of her suffering.

She hugged herself tight and he wanted to be the one to hold her in his arms, to take the nightmares and demons she battled and own them, so they belonged to him alone. But that could never be. This horrible thing had happened to her, and no matter how strong, powerful, or wealthy he was, it was an act that he could not undo.

Silence descended and yet the rustle of leaves and ragged, broken breaths deafened him. Marcus opened and closed his mouth several times. He shook his head. Once. Twice. A third time. As he worked through the horror of her revelation, no matter how much he shook his head, no matter how much he willed her words out of existence, they remained, and there they would stay.

No.

She nodded once. "Yes."

Had he spoken aloud? How was he capable of words when his entire world was crumbling about him like an ancient castle blasted by cannon fodder? "Oh, Eleanor," he managed to rasp. How many years he'd spent hating her, when all along he should have hated himself. Self-loathing unfurled inside him. He had failed her in the worst possible way; and for that, she had suffered the greatest pain and hurt.

He looked down at his chest. Where was the crimson stain upon the fabric if his heart was bleeding so?

She made a soft sound of protest. "Do not look at me like that. I knew you would look at me like that when I told you and I cannot bear it, Marcus." Tears welling anew in her eyes, she shook her head hard. "So stop. Please." At that desperate entreaty, a strangled groan stuck in his throat.

He covered his mouth with his hand, and stalked over, obliterating the remaining distance between them, and then stopped, at sea. He was like a child's toy, stuck in a vicious squall, and it was ratcheting his world down about him. "How can I look at you with anything but love?" For even as he'd hated her for an imagined betrayal, he'd loved her beyond thought.

"Do not say that." She closed her eyes and a little cry burst from her lips. "Do not. I don't want that from you. Not here."

Not now. She'd deserved that profession from him years earlier. She'd deserved it the moment she'd reentered his life. Instead, he'd given her nothing but his scorn, and…

Bile climbed up his throat and he nearly choked. Oh, God. He'd tried to seduce her. With his every word, his every promise and pledge, he'd offered her nothing more than a place in his bed. A sob escaped him. The weight of his shame brought his eyes closed. There was a special place in hell for men like him.

Her husband had been worthy of her, after all. Worthy in ways that Marcus never had been. Suddenly, his dead rival, the man he'd hated since discovering his existence, earned Marcus' unending gratitude. She'd deserved the honorable Lieutenant Collins, a man he was grateful to for having been what Marcus had not.

He scrubbed a hand over his face. "That is why you left," he said woodenly. Of course it was why she left.

Her slight nod dislodged a curl. "That is why I left," she said softly. "He took everything from me. I was powerless, in every way. If you hated me, I wanted it to be for reasons within my control. I wanted you to hate me for decisions I made and not for something that was forced on me by a man I did not even know."

Marcus dug his fingers into his palms with such ferocity, he ripped the flesh. The sticky warmth of his blood coated his hand, and he welcomed the pain. "Did you know me so little that you think I could have ever hated you for that?" His voice emerged broken. "That I could have ever held you to blame?"

A single tear trickled down Eleanor's cheek and she moved over in a flurry of gray skirts. She captured his hands and forced them open. "How could I know that? How, when I hate myself even still, all these years later?" she whispered. In the way a wife might care for her husband, she reached inside his pocket and withdrew his monogrammed kerchief. She brushed the white fabric over the jagged wound left by his nail, gentling cleaning away his blood. Eleanor turned the cloth over to him and incapable of words, he tucked it away. She broke the silence, proving herself, once again, stronger than he had ever been or ever would be. "It is because I thought so much of you that I left. I do not doubt you would have done the honorable thing. You would have never been free until you found him and then you would have dueled him." Eleanor lifted his hand to her cheek and leaned into his uninjured palm. "And I would never have allowed that for either of us."

"I would have married you," he gasped out. *I will marry you.*

Her shoulders shook from the force of her silent tears. "I know you would have, which is also why I left."

What if he'd arrived in time? What would life be for either of them, both of them, even now? "Yet you gave another man that right." A right that should have belonged to Marcus.

Except I failed her. I was late meeting her, and she was alone, unprotected, and raped for my tarrying. He groaned and the sound tore from deep inside where agony and regret dwelled.

The sadness glowing from within her eyes blended with surprise. The potent emotion there stuck in his chest twisting the dull blade of agony all the more. "Oh, Marcus, you still do not know?"

He no longer knew up from down or right from left. "Know what?"

"There never was a Mr. Collins."

A night bird sang. Crickets chirped. *No Mr. Collins?* "Marcia…?" And the air left him on a whispery hiss.

"Who needs a miserable son? I would have a daughter who looks like you…"

"…And would you name her Marcia…?"

Good God. He choked. That night of terror had brought her a child. All of Eleanor's life remained a fabricated truth built by a young, unmarried woman. He tried to imagine the fear she would have known as a girl of just eighteen years; bruised and suffering, and compounding the horror with a babe from the monster who'd raped her. Yet…Marcus' throat worked spasmodically…that babe was now the child, Marcia; a little girl who worried over her mother being afraid and who'd waltzed on the tops of his boots.

Eleanor drew a quavering breath. "My father was a miserable merchant, Marcus. But he was a wonderful father. He moved us to the corner of Cornwall and allowed us to carve a new life, for me, for Marcia." She ran her palms down the front of her skirts. "So now you know."

Now he knew.

How very calmly matter-of-fact those words were when she'd ripped his world asunder with the truth.

And he would be irrevocably altered, forevermore.

Eleanor lifted tear-filled eyes to his. "I never stopped loving you, Marcus. The memory of you sustained me when I prayed for death." Then, leaning up on tiptoe, she touched her lips to his in a fleeting kiss that tasted of sadness, regret, and eventual parting.

Marcus remained frozen. "Eleanor, I…" *Love you. Want to make you my wife and Marcia my daughter.* He killed the request he so desperately ached to put to her. She deserved his profession of love and a plea for marriage, but both had to come later. To give them to her now would seem obligatory; prompted by her revelation, and not for what they were—driven by the love he'd always carried for her.

"It is fine, Marcus," she said softly.

It could never be fine. No right could undo these wrongs.

Then, ducking her head with the same shyness of her youth, she turned and left him standing there staring after her.

With Eleanor gone, he sank to his haunches and buried his face in his hands. He let fly the ugly curses that burned his tongue; hating himself for having failed her, hating the stranger who'd stolen her innocence in the cruelest, most heinous, way and hating time for having marched on. How much they'd lost.

Filled with a restlessness, he surged to his feet.

A breeze stirred the branches overhead and pink-white petals rained about him, settling on his coat sleeve. Absently, he captured a fragile petal and ran the pad of his thumb over the delicate piece.

When Eleanor had left, he'd thought of nothing but his own hurts. He'd allowed the agony of her betrayal to shape him into the man he'd become…and with the stars twinkling mockingly overhead as silent witnesses, he was forced to confront the truth—he didn't much like himself. He didn't like the man he'd become, and more, he didn't like who he'd let himself become…all in the name of bitter cynicism. He'd taken countless widows and courtesans to his bed, seeking a physical surcease and protecting his heart.

Why should Eleanor want such a man?

… This is who you would have become. You are such a part of this world, I never truly belonged to. Perhaps you would have married me…

But you would have become the rogue, the world knows...

The memory of Eleanor's accusation burned more than any switch he'd taken to his back at his cruel tutor's hands years and years ago. For Eleanor had read about him in the gossip columns and returned to London knowing precisely what he was—a rogue.

And yet, he was a rogue who wanted to be a husband. *Her* husband. He balled his hands and ignoring the pain of his previous wound, crushed the satiny soft petal in his palm.

He wanted to marry Eleanor. Not because she'd been raped by some nameless stranger. Not to provide her security and a future for Marcia. Even though he did want all of those things. No, he wanted to marry her because she had always owned his heart and, until he drew his last breath, the unworthy organ would beat for her.

Marcus continued to stand in the duchess' gardens long after Eleanor had left, until the fingers of dawn pulled back the night sky. He'd lost Eleanor once and he'd little intention of losing her now.

The only question remained: how to earn her love and trust... again?

CHAPTER 17

THE NEXT MORNING, SEATED AT the breakfast table, Satin and Devlin vied for Eleanor's attention…and not for the first time since her arrival, she welcomed the pugs' distraction. It prevented her from focusing on all she'd shared with Marcus.

She curled her toes into the soles of her slippers. Nay, that wasn't true. One couldn't very well forget the ugly, humiliating parts she'd shared with him…the only person, other than her father, whom she'd let into the lie that was her life.

Satin yapped at Eleanor's feet and she looked down at the panting pug. "Oh, you are not content to let anyone else have attention, are you?" she murmured, favoring the dog with a gentle pat. She offered him a strip of bacon, which he grabbed between his crooked teeth.

Devlin growled.

"Do hush," she chided. "There is certainly enough for the both of you."

He shoved the top of his head against her chair, as though in canine agreement, and then bounded across the room to his mistress' side.

"How are you doing with your list, gel?" Her aunt thundered from the wide-backed King Louis chair she occupied, freezing Eleanor mid-movement.

Satin yapped once, nudging her again. "It is coming along," she answered, praying her aunt would find those words sufficient so

Eleanor wasn't forced to, in the light of a new day, think about the most intimate, personal pieces she'd shared with Marcus. Or his palpable grief and regret.

"What does that mean, 'it is coming along'?" her aunt barked.

She sighed. Of course, that assurance would have never sufficed. Marcia glanced up curiously from her plate of eggs and toast. Avoiding her gaze, Eleanor cleared her throat. "Just that. It is coming along."

"Do you believe I'll be content with your veiled non-answers?" The older woman mumbled something under her breath that sounded a good deal like didn't-have-the-sense-God-gave-a-goose. "You will be able to cross the theatre from your list, gel. We'll attend this evening."

At the prospect of visiting those noisy, vibrant gardens amongst the unkind *ton*, her heart sank. God how she missed the simplicity of the countryside quiet.

"The opera," Marcia breathed, clasping her hands to her chest. "It is so very grand in London. I never wish to leave."

A denial sprung to her lips and Eleanor forcibly tamped down the panic. Her daughter loved the glittering world of polite Society. Just as so many other young girls were surely wont to do, Marcia longed to take part in balls and attend operas and stroll through Hyde Park. She dreamed of one day finding a charming gentleman. Never knowing, that by the circumstances of her birthright and Eleanor's past, this world was closed to her. Sadness squeezed at her heart, and as though he'd sensed her sudden disquiet, Satin jumped at the side of her chair. The loyal pug licked at her hand with his coarse tongue. Eleanor stroked Satin once more. "What a good boy you are," she cooed.

"I'm not so weak that I'd be distracted, Eleanor," her aunt barked from the opposite end of the table. "Even if you are complimenting my babies."

Marcia giggled and the older woman favored her with a wink.

A smile pulling at her lips, Eleanor inclined her head. "And I would never be so foolish as to think a woman such as you is anything but strong."

The lady's cheeks filled with color and she shifted on her seat. "Never think to silence me with compliments, either," she muttered. Though the happy glint in the woman's rheumy eyes hinted at pleasure over that compliment.

"I wouldn't dare," she said solemnly marking an "X" on her chest.

Satin worked his two front legs furiously against the leg of the chair. Eleanor winced as his sharp nails worked a wear pattern into the once flawless mahogany.

"No worries about that," her aunt thumped her cane. "Material pleasures are to be enjoyed. By dogs, too." She favored the faithful dog on her lap with an affectionate stroke.

Footsteps sounded in the hall and the trio looked up as the butler entered.

"Lord Wessex has arrived."

At his unexpected announcement, the silver fork slipped from Eleanor's fingers and clattered noisily upon her largely untouched breakfast plate. Heart thumping wildly, she stared at the young servant. In the light of a new day with her ugliest secret laying open between them, Eleanor could not face him. Not when she was still feeling raw and exposed.

At the stretch of silence, the butler looked between his employer and Eleanor and cleared his throat. "That is, I have taken to showing the Viscount Wessex to the parlor where he awaits Mrs. Collins."

The duchess inclined her head and the servant took his cue. He sketched a bow and backed out of the room.

Marcia clapped her hands excitedly. "Oh, wonderful, Marcus is here," she mumbled around a mouthful of scone.

"We do not speak with our mouths full, love," Eleanor corrected, proud of the steadiness of her tone when inside she was a quaking, trembling mess. Perhaps she could feign a megrim. Or perhaps...

"You're not going to turn away my godson, Eleanor Elaine," the duchess boomed, thumping her cane on the floor.

"I did not say I was turning him away," Eleanor complained, but neither did she climb to her feet and rush to the parlor. She'd resolved to not seeing him today. Following their midnight meeting, and all she'd shared, how could she face him? Oh, ultimately, she'd have to see him again, but not now. Not so soon after. To give her fingers something to do, she dangled a piece of bread over the edge of the table. Satin and Devlin raced forward and vied for supremacy over the offering. She grabbed another and Satin snapped it up and carried it back to his mistress' feet.

"Why would Mama turn Marcus away?" Marcia asked, little wrinkles of confusion marring her brow.

"Because—" How could she explain herself in a way that would ever make sense to her small daughter who'd come to idolize him?

"Because she's not as clever as I'd credited," her aunt retorted.

Eleanor's cheeks warmed. "I am not turning him away."

"Then go," her aunt shot back.

"Well, I like him," Marcia said unhelpfully. "Even if Mama does not."

"I like him just fine." She pressed her fingertips against her temples. Goodness, she'd not have to feign a megrim, after all. The two ornery ladies before her now were causing one, all on their own.

"Marcus danced with me," Marcia piped in and then promptly took another bite of her scone.

Eleanor dropped her arms to her sides. Her heart danced a peculiar rhythm in her chest at that loving tableau presented with her daughter's innocent admission. "You…"

"Danced with him. A waltz," Marcia said happily around her full mouth.

Proper manners be damned, Eleanor bit the inside of her cheek to keep the countless questions from tumbling from her lips.

"Oh?" the duchess drawled.

And the astute seven-year-old girl registered the focus trained on her and preened. She gave a pleased nod. "Well, I was watching the ball, as Mama said I could, and was returning to my chambers, and ran into Marcus in the hall."

"The hall," her aunt parroted. "Whatever was the boy doing in my corridors during the ball?"

Eleanor's cheeks burned and she turned a prayer skyward. *Please do not look at me. Please do not…*

The Lord proved otherwise busy, as He invariably did. Her aunt narrowed her knowing gaze on Eleanor.

"Well, he was dancing with *meeee*," Marcia said with a roll of her eyes.

"Ah, of course," her aunt said wryly. "*That* was what he was doing in my corridors."

Marcia nodded. "He allowed me to waltz on his boots and I very much like him, Mama."

An image flitted through her mind of Marcus balancing Marcia on the tops of his shoes while he guided her laughingly about the floor; the dream so very real because of what her daughter had just painted. Her throat worked and she cursed the silent attention now trained on her.

Daughter and aunt stared expectantly back at her.

And in this instance, facing one Marcus to the two probing ladies before her was vastly preferable. She surged to her feet and started her march to the door. Because she really didn't care to be called a coward. And she cared even less to have her intelligence questioned. It was not a matter of intelligence or bravery. Well, mayhap it was a bit of bravery…but rather—self-preservation. She sought to protect what little remained of her dignity. "I will go see His Lordship."

"Marcus," Marcia called out.

The older woman fixed an equal part pleased, equal part triumphant, smile on her niece. "Run along, gel. Run along."

Eleanor exited the breakfast room, when her daughter's whispered words carried through the doorway. They froze Eleanor.

"…Do you think he will marry her…?"

There was such hope in her little girl's wonderings that pain lanced at her heart.

"I do." Her aunt's firm assurance jerked her back into movement and, with frantic steps, Eleanor rushed down the hall.

Her aunt and daughter spoke so casually of marriage. One was the hopes of a fatherless child, the other of an older woman, romantic by nature, who did not know all the darkest, ugliest secrets that made Eleanor an unsuitable match for anyone. She reached the White Parlor and paused at the entrance to the room. Marcus stood at the floor-length window with his hands clasped behind his back. The sight of him, with his broad shoulders tapering to a narrow waist and strong thighs, was the beautiful perfection of a man who deserved more than a woman who'd been used by another.

He stiffened. As he turned, she braced for the veiled disgust and hesitancy of a man who didn't know what to do with a woman who'd shared her secret shame, and the moment stretched into an eternity of her mourning Marcus as he'd been before; kissing her, touching her, and unguarded in his attentions. A half-grin marred those perfectly formed lips; a smile that reached his eyes, and for the sincerity there, all the way into her heart which beat for him. "Eleanor."

"M–Marcus," she greeted, running her palm over her skirts. She searched for a hint of repulsion but found nothing but the same, smiling man he'd been. Nay. Eleanor lingered on his eyes. Where the jaded glint of a man long ago brokenhearted and betrayed had once been, was now a tenderness she didn't know what to do with.

Then he spoke. "I have thought long about your list." Marcus rocked on his heels. "I will not hold you to our previous arrangement."

Her heart paused mid-beat. *No!* She smoothed her palms down the front of her skirts. "You will not?" she managed, proud of the steady deliverance of that useless question.

He shook his head. "I will not."

He'd likely realized the folly in courting a ruined woman. That truth gutted her. "I-I will see to the list on my own, Marcus. Thank you for helping me complete the items that you did."

"Tsk, tsk, love." With the husky timbre to his retort, he was the charming, practiced rogue, once more. "I didn't say I would not assist you." He strode slowly toward her, hopelessly elegant in his sleek, black attire. "I, however, will not hold you to the remainder of the Season."

Grief scissored through her. *What if I want you to?* She'd been such a coward these years that she could not bring herself to utter the humbling question hovering on her lips. She stiffened as he lowered his head and claimed her lips in a tender, gentle meeting. He tasted of love and truth and new beginnings and she wanted all of it, only with him.

Marcus raised his head. "I want you to remain here because you want it, Eleanor." His breath fanned her lips and brought her lids fluttering. "I want you to stay in London not because you require the role of companion to your aunt and not because your uncle or I willed it. I want you to be here because you wish to be." A familiar, errant, gold curl fell over his brow and he offered her a slow smile that met his eyes. "And because I'm a selfish bastard, I want you to *want* to be here because you wish to be with me."

Warmth flicked to life inside her heart…as the slow, gradual understanding of his offer crept in. He would not force her to do something. He'd allow her choice, when the most elemental one had been stolen from her before. And God help her, she fell in love with him all over again. Wished to be the woman he deserved. Wished to be a woman who could share his bed and give him children.

He offered her his elbow and, her world in tumult, she eyed it in abject confusion.

"What are you doing, Marcus?" she whispered.

He brushed his fingers down her cheek, and then tipped her chin up, forcing her eyes to his. "Why, I am escorting you to Gunther's."

Gunther's?

"Item five," he reminded, running the pad of his thumb over her lower lip as he was wont to do.

Item five? Her list. Yes, a gentleman of Marcus' honor would uphold the pledge he'd taken to help her. Nothing would prevent him from doing so. Not even midnight revelations of her dark past.

Marcus lifted one eyebrow. "You do remember item five?"

"Of course," she said dumbly. *Liar. You only recall what item was on the list because he just reminded you.* "Gunther's. Ices at Gunther's." *Foolish girl, what did you secretly hope? That he'd come to swear his undying love and to ask you to be his viscountess, as your aunt and daughter suspected?*

Then in a move better suited a brother with a younger sister, he chucked her under the chin. "Shall we?"

Eleanor placed her hand on his sleeve and allowed him to escort her on to item five, and the beginning of the end of her list.

IN ALL THE TIME HE'D known Eleanor, those two glorious months long ago, and now, again eight years later, the lady had never been silent. Oh, she'd never been one of the prattling ones determined to fill a void of silence…but she had been at ease and comfortable. Assured.

Now, as he guided his curricle down the quiet streets of London, the hushed figure at his side bore no resemblance to the woman he'd come to know. He stole a sideways glance at her. Eleanor maintained a white-knuckled grip on the edge of the seat while she trained her gaze forward on the road before them.

The moment she had entered her aunt's parlor, studying him with trepidation and fear emanating from within her eyes, it had taken all the strength he'd possessed to give her the smile she deserved.

Did she believe he would look at her differently for what she'd shared? Did she think he would find her anything but beautiful and strong for what she'd survived? She had more strength and courage than any grown man he knew; including his weaker self. When most women would have crumpled under the weight of life's cruelty, Eleanor had moved on, finding a smile, and love for the child who'd been forced upon her.

And there was no other woman he would have for his wife. Even if she deserved better than a bounder such as he. He was self-ish and self-serving because he could not live in a world in which she belonged to another.

"Did I ever tell you about my first tutor, Mr. Chapman?"

Eleanor blinked several times as though blinking back the fog of her own thoughts. She cast a quizzical look up at him.

"He was a miserable bugger," he said cheerfully, guiding his mounts right at the end of the street. "I was a boy of seven. Not unlike Marcia, I delighted in exploring and certainly didn't appreciate being shut away in the schoolrooms receiving lessons from miserable Mr. Chapman. I was a rotted student."

Eleanor's lips twitched. "I don't believe you are rotted at anything you do, Marcus Gray."

He'd been a rotted protector. That had been his greatest failing. He gripped the reins hard. "Have a care, love," he said with false brevity. "Or I might believe you're trying to charm a rogue."

She laughed. "I wouldn't even know how to try to accomplish such a feat."

There was no, nor had there ever been, trying where Eleanor Carlyle was concerned. She'd wooed and won his heart with her unfettered smile and bold spirit outside their London townhomes. He'd been hopelessly and helplessly hers, since.

"What of your Mr. Chapman?"

"Right, right," he continued, steering the curricle through a throng of conveyances. "Miserable Mr. Chapman was a miserable man. Stern, unbending, and—"

"Miserable?" she supplied with a little laugh.

"Yes, indeed. When I was a boy, I could not read. Two years of the bugger calling me a lackwit and lazy." Even all these years later, he recalled the frustration of staring at the pages unable to make sense of the words upon them. The frustration had been so great that when in the privacy of his own company, he'd hurled those small leather tomes across the room. "He had a switch." His skin still burned in remembrance of the lashes dealt. "He would ask me to read aloud and brought that switch down on me whenever I stumbled or struggled through those readings." Which had been every single, horrid lesson.

The teasing light went out of Eleanor's eyes. "Oh, Marcus," she said softly and laid her hand over his.

He stared, transfixed a moment by the sight of her glove-encased fingers upon his person, wanting to have the right to that hand; wanting it joined with his forever. Marcus drew on the reins and guided the curricle to a halt on the opposite side of Gunther's "For two years, I believed everything Chapman uttered. I believed I was a lackwit. Why couldn't I read when I stared at those damned words day after day, hour after hour? Then one morning, my father entered in the middle of my lessons. Chapman was bringing that switch down on my back and my father stormed the room. He ripped that blasted birch from Chapman's hands and snapped it in half." Marcus neatly omitted the violent part, which resulted in his father beating the man with his own stick before destroying it. Gone too soon of an apoplexy at not even forty-two years of age, his father had evinced strength, honor, and love. Marcus held Eleanor's gaze. "I, of course, learned to read. My father insisted on delivering every reading lesson until those words began to make sense." He held his palms up. "It was not my fault I couldn't read, Eleanor. Chapman made it a thing of terror and horror. It took my father to show me that words were things of joy and wonder."

A slow understanding lit her clever gaze. She slid her eyes away from his. Uncaring of the sea of polite Society about them, with his hand he gently guided her focus back to him. "Marcus," she said, on a forlorn whisper. "What happened to me, it cannot be undone. It cannot be fixed."

Her words implied she was flawed and broken, and yet in her imperfection, there was not a more perfect person. How had he lived these years without her? How empty and purposeless his life had been. "Oh, Eleanor." What if she'd allowed him in and shared this burden? He ran a gaze over her person. How could she still not know their happiness was inextricably connected? "If I could undo that moment for you…" Marcus pressed his eyes closed a moment. But then there would be no Marcia. "But I cannot. You are not broken or something in need of repair. You are a woman of courage and strength who was wronged, and that does not make you undeserving of happiness and love." He paused, willing her with his eyes to see the truth. "It makes you more deserving. And I would be the man to show you both."

Eleanor looked down at her clasped hands. "Marcus, I—"

"We have both lost years of joy, Eleanor. Do not let him take another moment. At least let the remaining items on your list belong to us." He brought her hand to his mouth and dropped a kiss atop her knuckles. Not even a fortnight ago, he'd have been horrified at the possibility of the *ton* seeing him and making something honorable of his intentions. Now, if Eleanor would have him, he'd invite every gawking passerby as a witness at their wedding. "Whatever you want Eleanor. Whatever you desire, tell me and I shall bring it to you." And if it was the stars she craved, he'd climb to the heavens and grab down the moon.

She raised her eyes to his and a slow smile spread on her lips. And the same fluttering in his chest, the one from years earlier when she'd stepped out of her aunt's townhouse and into his life, danced madly now. Yes, flavored ices and curricle rides through London were safe. There were no risks, no resurrected pains of the past. "A chocolate ice, Marcus. I would have a chocolate ice."

It was not the moon, but it was a fleeting pleasure he could give. With a smile, Marcus leapt down from the carriage. He paused. "Oh, Eleanor?"

"Yes?"

"I would have married you eight years ago. Not even an evil fairy would have stopped me." Her lips fell agape and she touched a hand to her chest. "And I intend to wed you now."

Her breath caught on a gasp as Marcus winked and rushed off to fetch her ice.

CHAPTER 18

ℰLEANOR HAD BUT ONE ITEM left on her list. This final item she would see to without Marcus at her side. And after this evening's performance, Eleanor would have fulfilled all the tasks presented her by her late uncle. She should be elated. This moment meant security for her and Marcia. Never again would she have to live in fear over their precarious situation. She could pack up, board a carriage tomorrow, and take Marcia far, far away from this place.

Yet, there was no elation. There was no thrill of triumph and only mild relief. Rather, there was an odd, aching emptiness. How long had she spent hating London? Yet, to leave this time would mean to leave Marcus' smile and promises of happiness. It would mean no more of the gruff, wry Aunt Dorothea's love and guidance. Even the garden, that special place shared with Marcus, would be lost to her forever.

Eleanor skimmed her gaze over the noisy hall of The English Opera House. Odd, how such a cavernous space, brimming with theatregoers, should feel so empty. The candlelight and Argand lamps illuminated the massive auditorium and sent shadows dancing on the walls. Unbidden, she sought him out. Oh, there would be nothing proper in her attending the opera on Marcus' arm. It was a luxury she would have been permitted had she been one of those shockingly scandalous widows, and yet she was not one of those. Instead, she ached with a need to be not special, not different, but rather…ordinary.

"You look about as excited to be here as that indulgent queen being marched up to the gallows."

At her aunt's quiet interruption, Eleanor jumped. She flushed guiltily. "I…"

But the lie would not come. None of this appealed to her; not the balls or lavish halls. Not the operas or the musicales. She hungered for the simplicity of the Cornwall country where she existed as simply Eleanor Collins; young widow and contented mother… and very soon, she would have the funds to do exactly that.

"…And because I am a selfish bastard, I want you to want to be here because you wish to be with me…"

Marcus' husky baritone echoed around her mind. For the truth of it was, she wished to be here because of him. She wanted to be wherever Marcus Gray was. From the corner of her eye, a flash of white caught her notice and she stared unabashedly at the bright-eyed debutante in frilly white skirts and perfectly curled tresses. Longing pulled at her; a desire to be that carefree young lady with hope in her eyes and a smile on her lips and a belief in the goodness of all around her. Virginal. Innocent.

In short, everything Eleanor no longer was.

Her aunt tapped the arm of Eleanor's shell-backed seat with her cane. "He's arrived."

Eleanor didn't even pretend to misunderstand. She searched for him in the crowd.

"His box is to the right, center."

And then her heart dipped.

"He is with that miserable Hamilton girl. I never liked her mother. I liked the father even less. The brother, the Marquess of Atbrooke, is a scoundrel and the girl is mean. Isabelle should know better than to let that one near her daughter."

In her denigration, the duchess spoke with a matter-of-factness, and yet that did little to dull the pain of seeing Marcus settle into his seat, and the determined, grasping lady insert herself shamefully between brother and sister.

"Never understood why my goddaughter would ever be friends with that one," her aunt said and Eleanor blinked, welcoming the distraction.

She smiled at the protective, albeit grumpy, duchess. "Oh, Aunt Dorothea."

The old woman waved her off. "Bah, I am not speaking those words for your benefit. The girl is shameful in a way that young ladies should not be shameful." The duchess tightened her mouth. "Pressing herself against my godson in that manner, and with Isabelle inside the box?" She made a sound of disgust.

Even across the wide expanse of the auditorium, Eleanor could easily see the manner in which Lady Marianne shoved her full breasts against Marcus' shoulder. Green jealousy raged within her. It twisted and turned like a vicious cancer growing in power until it spread through every corner of her being. Her feet twitched with the urge to storm the theatre and remove the tentacle-like grip the young woman had on Marcus. The lady smiled, displaying two perfect rows of even, pearl-white teeth. She leaned up and whispered something into Marcus' ear and Eleanor's breath caught hard and fast in her chest.

"...It is about more than his fifty thousand pounds. He has a remarkable figure..."

Nausea churned in her belly and she searched Marcus for some hint of interest in what the lady offered—sexual pleasures he craved, but ones Eleanor could never provide him. Alas, his face remained an immoveable mask that gave no indication of his thoughts, desires, or even the crowd of onlookers taking in the show being put on by Lady Marianne and the Viscount Wessex. Bitterness pulled Eleanor's lips up in a smile. Why, what more of a show was needed than the one before the *ton* now?

Her skin pricked hot under the intensity of the duchess' stare. Eleanor forced her attention down to the stage, praying for the performance to begin. Praying for the night to end. Praying, when she'd long ago learned the futility of prayers.

"That boy loves you."

Eleanor jerked.

"And you can go on carrying whatever secrets of your past that made you leave him, but he cannot wait forever for you, Eleanor. He waited eight years and, this time, if you leave, he will end up with another."

A lump formed in Eleanor's throat and she tried to swallow. Her aunt painted an agonizing image of Marcus; a devoted, charming husband with a delicate beauty on his arm. They would have flawless, breathtaking, golden-haired babes and he would be the manner of father who unfailingly protected and loved those children. She thrust back the vicious imaginings. But it was too late. Her aunt had presented Marcus' future, with Eleanor neatly omitted, and she could not un-see it.

Her aunt twisted the blade all the deeper. "It may not be Lady Marianne Hamilton." She gestured broadly to the room. "But it will be one of them. And you have to ask if that is something you can live the remainder of your life with."

I have no choice…

"We always have a choice, Eleanor Elaine."

Eleanor started, unaware she'd spoken aloud.

Just then, the chandeliers were lowered and dimmed, and the orchestra built steady into the Overture of *Torvaldo e Dorliska*. Knight Torvaldo launched into song and the refined tenor demanded notice, and yet…Eleanor flicked her gaze across the theatre and her breath caught.

Marcus stared boldly back; his lips curved in a smile, his concentration turned solely on her. Only Marcus could manage to make a woman feel as though she were the only lady in a hall brimming with people.

His words from yesterday came rushing back. His determined pledge to earn her love. So many years she'd believed herself damaged; her soul as scarred as her body, for what was taken from her. Yesterday, Marcus had looked inside and known the thoughts she'd denied even herself. She did believe herself undeserving of love. The shame she carried, so great that she'd been unable to countenance sharing that dishonor with anyone. Instead, she'd allowed a stranger who stank of brandy to steal not only her virtue, but her own sense of self-worth.

Until Marcus.

She looked to him once more and found his gaze still unwavering upon her.

He forced her to look at what her life was, and more, look toward the life she dreamed of for her…for Marcia.

Why can I not marry him?

The threat hovering in the corner of her mind danced to the surface. That bastard who'd stolen so much would reenter her life and warn her away from Marcus? She firmed her jaw. She'd not allow him that power. What more could he do to her that he hadn't already done? So what *was* keeping her from Marcus?

He knew all and loved her regardless.

Eleanor bit her inner cheek. There remained the whole marital bed business. Anxiety tightened the muscles of her stomach. Could she truly subject herself to that horror? Could she spread her legs and take a man inside without feeling the remembered horror and pain? Except…she'd not been repelled by Marcus' kiss. In his arms, she'd felt for the first time alive in ways she'd been long dead. She'd burned with passion and a hunger for more. And with his gentleness, Marcus would never bring her hurt.

Trust him… She stilled. Nay. *Trust yourself. Trust that you are deserving, trust that you are capable of giving and knowing love, in every form, and if he asks it, give yourself over to him…*

For too long, she'd given control of her thoughts, emotions, and happiness over to the demon who'd visited her in Lady Wedermore's gardens. Through her own sense of guilt in being in those expertly manicured grounds, she'd taken ownership of that night. If she had not left the ballroom and had, instead, been a proper, respectable lady, then even now she would be married…and more…happy. But she had, in a stolen moment of impropriety, placed herself in that monster's arms…and for that she was blameworthy.

Now, with the orchestra soaring, there was a cathartic healing, in the music, the soothing calm of the foreign Italian, and her own at last settled thoughts. Eleanor drew in a cleansing breath. The horror and fear of that night would never, ever go away; it would always be an indelible part of who she had been, but it did not have to be all that defined her. Her future, her daughter, her ability to laugh and love, those were the ultimate triumphs.

She looked across at Marcus. He stared down at the stage below, but then, as though he felt her gaze, glanced out across the sea of Society. And she wanted those moments with him.

Eleanor smiled.

TONIGHT ELEANOR WOULD COMPLETE THE items on her list. With those tasks now finished, she would be free to dance out of his life, this time, never to return.

In the dim concert hall, Marcus stared across to where Eleanor sat. He soaked in the sight of her in her pink satin skirts, traveling his gaze over her cherished face, wanting to remember every delicate plane from the shock of freckles on her nose to the pale blonde of her hair, ethereal in its shimmering beauty. He wanted to commit every part of her to memory so that when she inevitably left, there would be this moment to cling to.

As though feeling his stare, Eleanor straightened her long, graceful neck and found him with her eyes. Their gazes collided.

I love you, Eleanor Elaine Carlyle, and I will love you until I draw my last breath...

She smiled and he sucked in a sharp breath. Oh, she had smiled many times since her return to London almost a fortnight ago. But this tilt of her lips was so vastly different than the melancholy, almost pained expression she'd worn since their reunion. This was the smile of her youth, of unfettered joy and excitement, and it was an alluring grin that transformed her from haunting, ethereal beauty to this spirited nymph.

Marcus stared across the auditorium, ignoring the performance below and the loud whispers throughout the hall, transfixed by that smile.

"It is quite magnificent, isn't it, my lord?" That sultry purr cut jarringly into Marcus' musings. Lady Marianne stared at him, and then with an unabashed boldness, she ran her fingertips along the lace trim of her plunging décolletage and trailed a path with her hand down his thigh.

He stiffened and stole a glance at his mother and sister who were blessedly preoccupied with the performance. "My lady, remember yourself," he said tightly out the corner of his mouth.

She leaned closer, pressing her breasts against his arm. "But I *do* remember myself quite clearly when you are around. I remember that I want you," her breath tickled his ear. "And that you are in the market for a wife." Lady Marianne squeezed his thigh, shifting her hand higher, and he jumped.

At one time, the cool, emotionless entanglement this lady presented, one where he'd have a feisty minx in his bed and a proper viscountess on his arm would have been all he sought in a match. No longer. And, stealing another glance at Eleanor who looked at the stage below—not really ever. He'd only wanted Eleanor.

Marcus made to move Lady Marianne's hand from his person, when she slipped her fingers into his. Marcus gritted his teeth. Had he ever admired the young lady's form? Her blowsy, wantonness stood in stark contrast to the innocence he'd come to love in Eleanor. "I am," repelled. "Flattered by your attentions, however, my heart is otherwise engaged." He spoke without malice, giving the determined young lady the truth to quell her attempts at seduction.

A hard glint iced over her brown eyes and a chill went through him as that menacing glimmer transformed her into a woman whose ugly shown from within. It tamped out all traces of the midnight-haired Diamond who'd captivated the *ton*. "I see," she bit out and stiffly drew her fingers from his.

The soaring crescendo of the performers upon the stage came to an abrupt halt, signaling the end of the first act. Marcus leapt to his feet, earning questioning looks from his mother and sister. "If you will excuse me a moment," he said curtly. "I see someone I need to pay my respects to."

Leaving the young ladies in the care of his mother, Marcus shoved through the red velvet curtains and all but sprinted through the still empty corridor. He made his way with long, purposeful strides to the one box which had commanded his attention, when a figure stepped into his path.

Marcus cursed as he nearly collided with Lady Marianne Hamilton's brother, the Marquess of Atbrooke. Bloody hell.

"Wessex, you are in something of a rush," the other man drawled.

He sketched a quick bow. "Atbrooke, a pleasure."

It was a lie. The man was a notorious reprobate who even with his title of marquess could not entice a marriage-minded miss, or a desperate to make a match with her daughter, mama. He tried to step around him.

The marquess shifted and effectively blocked retreat. "I wished to thank you for allowing Marianne to accompany you and your sister this evening."

"It was my pleasure." Another lie. The lady was a viper with nothing more than aspirations for the role of viscountess.

Atbrooke held a hand out and grinned. "I am looking forward to your visit soon."

Marcus eyed the outstretched hand a long moment. His visit?

Marcus choked. Was the man mad? By God, he thought Marcus would offer for his grasping sister? Ignoring those proffered fingers, Marcus said, "Er, if you'll excuse me?" He strode past a frowning Atbrooke and continued on his earlier path.

Lords and ladies now spilled into the hall and he worked his way through the throng of people. He damned Atbrooke's blasted interruption and the crush of bodies that slowed his movement. At last, Marcus reached the Duchess of Devonshire's box and parted the curtains. Marcus narrowed his eyes.

A tall, slender gentleman in pale blue breeches smiled shyly at Eleanor and more…she smiled in return. That same smile Marcus had appreciated a short while ago; the one that belonged to him and only him. Except that wasn't altogether true. For now, it belonged to the Earl of Primly.

"Primly is a good boy, Eleanor," the duchess was just saying as the earl collected Eleanor's gloved fingertips.

"I–it is a p-pleasure to see you again, M–Mrs. Collins. I thought I might…that is…i–if you would be amenable, I would pay you a visit t-tomorrow. O–or it doesn't have to be t-tomorrow," the gentleman said on a rush, color flooding his cheeks. "It can be another day."

Never. It would be never. A growl rumbled from deep within Marcus' chest, alerting the trio to Marcus standing there, gaping at Primly with his goddamn fingers on Eleanor. "I am afraid that will not do, Primly," he said, not taking his eyes from Eleanor. From the corner of his eye, he detected the other man's sharp frown. "You see, if the lady will have me, I intend to marry her."

Odd how silence could rage even amidst a noisy auditorium.

Eleanor fluttered a hand to her chest and shook her head back and forth. Marcus took a step toward her. "Marry me, Eleanor," he said gruffly. The lady had deserved effusive words and a bouquet of flowers. Instead, he made his entreaty before the whole of London, the duchess, and goddamn Primly. Belatedly, he dropped to a knee beside her chair and collected her hand. "Marry me, please," he said softly, those hushed words for her ears. "Trust me to be the one to show you joy and wonder." His voice grew gruff with emotion. "I love you, Eleanor Elaine, and I have never, ever once stopped. Do not go. Stay." *With me. For me. For us.*

His neck grew hot from the weight of his admission, before a sea of observers, no less. And yet, he would humble himself before the whole of the British kingdom for her, because he was nothing without her, but more, he was everything with her.

As the moments ticked by, stretching seconds into what may as well have been hours and days, the lady said…nothing.

Her lips parted and she touched quaking fingers to her mouth. "Oh, Marcus," Eleanor whispered.

Oh, God. Dread pebbled in his belly. It grew and grew until it weighted his every movement. She was going to say n—

"Yes." He strained to make out the faint utterance. She nodded once. "Yes," she repeated, this time with strength in that affirmation. "I will marry you." And her lips curved up in that wide, unfettered smile that had frozen him at their first meeting.

And scandal be damned, Marcus pulled her into his arms.

"It is about bloody time," the duchess muttered.

CHAPTER 19

THE BEGINNING IS ALWAYS TODAY

Eleanor traced her fingertips over those familiar words. He was going to marry her. And all the terror of the wedding night and all that came with being a wife receded under this giddy lightness in her chest.

"You have a smile to rival the cat that caught the canary," her aunt called from her high-back upholstered seat. She stroked Devlin who sat atop her lap. "As you should. Marrying Wessex is the best decision you've made in eight years."

Eleanor bit back a smile. Her aunt had been more gracious and generous than Eleanor deserved through the years for her to go about pointing out that the duchess, in fairness, couldn't truly speak to eight years of decisions her niece had made. She made a clearing noise with her throat. "Shall I resume where we left off?

She fanned through the book to the last pages read from Mary Wollstonecraft's work.

Her aunt slammed the tip of her cane down on the open book. "Bah, do you think I care about my Mrs. Wollstonecraft today?" she scoffed. "Nor should you be with me. You should be with Wessex, or your daughter telling her the news."

"I am going to tell her," she said defensively. She simply wanted to wait for the precise moment.

Whatever retort her aunt would make was quelled by the sudden appearance of the butler. "A visitor for Mrs. Collins. I have taken the liberty of showing the gentleman to the White Parlor."

Eleanor's heart sped up and she leapt to her feet.

"Ah, it's about time the boy arrived." A happy smile hovered on the usually gruff duchess' lips. "That will be all, Thomas."

Eleanor leaned down to place a kiss on her weathered cheek. "Thank you for everything," she said softly. For if it hadn't been for the older woman's timely letter, and salvation to be had in the post of companion, Eleanor would still be the broken, fearful woman she'd been for too long.

A blush bloomed on the older woman's face and she made a dismissive sound. "Go." She waved Eleanor off. "Do not keep that boy waiting any longer than you have."

With a laugh, Eleanor all but raced from the room. She moved briskly through the corridors, her skirts fluttering noisily at her ankles, and she stopped outside the parlor. How to account for this giddy sensation dancing around her belly better reserved for a woman many years younger? Then, that was the effect Marcus had on her. Smoothing her palms over her flushed cheeks, she stepped inside the entrance of the room.

And froze.

Many years after she'd been raped, she would see her assailant in the unlikeliest of places. She would see his face on that of strangers, in both sleeping and waking thoughts, and would be instantly transported back to the hell of that night. Never, in all those worst hauntings, did she imagine him as he was now, on a knee beside her daughter. For she'd not ever entertained the horrific possibility that he would meet, greet, or know Marcia in any way.

A dull buzzing filled her ears and her body went hot and then cold. She struggled to draw forth breath past the vise squeezing off airflow. Eleanor scrabbled at her skirts, willing her legs to move, willing words to come.

"Mama!" Marcia exclaimed, her voice coming as though down a long, empty corridor. "You lied. You said you only had one friend, but the marquess says he was a very good friend years and years ago, and the marquess has a birthmark on his wrist." Her daughter held her fingers up and smiled. "Just like me."

Eleanor shook her head, trying to bring her daughter's words into focus through the thick haze of horror.

Then he looked at her. This marquess, whose name she still did not know, who'd sired her daughter and shattered Eleanor's life with one heinous deed. It was the face of her worst nightmares and her greatest shame. He rose and smiled a hard, evil grin. "*Mrs. Collins.*" The mocking edge there hinted at a man who knew very well she was no widow and reveled in the power of his knowledge.

"Marcia," she said tightly as she rushed across the room. "It is time to return to your lessons." She settled her hands on her daughter's shoulders and steered her away.

"Mama." Marcia dragged her heels, forcing Eleanor to stop. She whipped her head back and stared with accusatory eyes. Brown eyes. His eyes. Oh, God. Bile burned like acid in her throat and she tightened her grip reflexively. "You are hurting me."

All the while, he stood a silent, malicious observer. This man, tall and slender with chestnut brown hair and noble features, would be considered handsome by most. And yet, under the façade, there was a blackened soul that would one day burn in hell for his crimes.

"Return to the nursery for your lessons," Eleanor said, gentling her tone.

"Very well." Marcia sighed. "But I do think it is very exciting the Marquess of Atbrooke has a birthmark like my own and I do not know why I cannot visit as he is your friend. You allowed me to visit with Marcus."

Heat slapped her cheeks and her skin pricked with the probing stare trained on her by the marquess. Eleanor willed her daughter to silence. Then, with Marcia gone, her daughter's words registered.

The Marquess of Atbrooke.

Of course, even the devil himself had a name…and that name made this man all the more real which weakened his indomitable hold. Her rapist, the father of her child, was a powerful marquess. Her mind stalled, as a memory flickered to life.

…He is with that miserable Hamilton girl. I never liked her mother. I liked the father even less. The brother, the Marquess of Atbrooke, is a scoundrel and the girl is mean…

She gasped.

Lady Marianne Hamilton's brother bent a low, mocking bow. "A pleasure to meet you again, *Mrs.* Collins."

Eleanor pulled the door closed behind her with a firm click to provide a flimsy barrier between the marquess and her daughter.

Because that is what mothers ultimately did. They locked themselves away with monsters, all to protect.

She clasped her hands behind her and layered her back against the door. "What do you want?" Revulsion lent her words an artificial strength.

"Come, is that what you'll say to me, love?" He sauntered forward. "After all these years and all we shared?"

Those words, eerily reminiscent of the ones uttered by Marcus upon her arrival almost a fortnight ago, brought an acrid taste to her mouth. All they shared? Memories trickled in as he'd rammed himself inside, tearing past the thin wall of her virginity, as he'd swallowed her scream with his punishing mouth. Eleanor held up a staying hand, as he continued coming. "Stop," she commanded.

And surprisingly, he did. He continued to eye her in that predatory way that made her body run cold.

Silent screams echoed around her riotous memories; the taste of his leather glove as she'd bit on the hand he'd placed over her mouth, suffocating from the weight of it, praying for the bliss of unconsciousness and, ultimately, so many prayers failed that night.

Fear tightened about her heart, as with his taunting words and punishing shame, she was transported back to another time and she stood quaking before him the same scared girl she'd been. The marquess stood with a sly half-grin that snapped her from her private hell. "We shared nothing, my lord." Nothing like the pure love she'd known with Marcus. "Why don't we set aside false pleasantries and have you say whatever it is you would say," she spat.

"Tsk, tsk," he whispered, taking another step closer. He looked meaningfully past her shoulder. "We shared something very special." *Please, no. I beg you...* "You have a lovely daughter."

Her heart ceased beating and then picked up a hard, frantic pounding. What manner of game did he play with her where he'd use Marcia as his human pawn? Eleanor willed herself to calm. A man who'd thrilled in the struggles of a resisting young lady would only relish any hint of her weakness. "I have tired of your veiled threats." Eleanor tipped her chin up, finding courage and strength in the truth Marcus had awakened her to. Since that long ago night, she'd blamed herself, and yet it was this cad before her now to blame. He had stolen from her a gift he'd no right to. And she would not allow this cad another victory over her. He'd already claimed too many. "I would have you say what has brought you here and then be gone. My aunt, the duchess, will not welcome your being here." And for the secrets she'd kept from her aunt through the years, Eleanor had no doubt that if she revealed all to the duchess, the woman would singlehandedly see to the marquess' ruin.

He stalked toward her. "Will she be so forgiving of you if she were to discover you gave yourself to me in Lady Wedermore's gardens?"

An unholy bloodlust filled her veins. Eleanor flew the remaining distance between them and cracked him across the face with such ferocity his head whipped back. The satisfying echo of flesh meeting flesh bounced from the plastered walls. Her palm stung from the force of the blow she'd dealt him and she welcomed the throbbing that only fueled her fury. The marquess palmed his cheek and then peered at her through thickly veiled eyes. "I gave you nothing," she seethed.

Undeterred, the marquess peeled his lip back in a snarl. "But then, isn't that what you do, Eleanor? You meet men in the gardens? Me. Wessex. Tell me, how many others have there been? Hmm?" He waggled his chestnut eyebrows. "Do you not think the viscount will not see the similarities there?"

Uncertainty blossomed inside her chest. All the old insecurities about her self-worth, her ability to love and be loved, floated to the surface. People saw what was easiest to see. A young widow. A respectable mother. A whore who met her lovers. As soon as the fears slipped in, she thrust them back. She'd not doubt Marcus.

And certainly not because of this devil's attempt at weakening her.

"The viscount is good and honorable. Everything you are not. He will see the truth." Her voice rang with conviction. She thrust a finger toward the door. "Now, get out," she commanded.

He shot a hand around her wrist, squeezing the more delicate flesh in a punishing grip that flooded her eyes with tears.

"I warned you away from Wessex."

Her heart stopped as she recalled his warning at her aunt's ball. At that time she'd thought his was nothing more than another grasp at controlling her. The determined glint in his eyes spoke of a different tale. One that she'd not indulge with questions. "My relationship with the viscount is no matter to you," she spat. A healthy fury coursed through her, invigorating and healing. "You would make something torrid of what I share with Lord Wessex, but you are evil." She wrenched free of his grip. "I will not allow you to interfere in my relationship with the viscount." Not again. As it was, this monster had wrestled eight years from her and Marcus. "*You* represent ugliness and filth, and I'd gladly see you in hell." She again motioned to the door. "As it is, I will have to settle for showing you to the bloody door."

Her breath came hard and fast with the healthy triumph of standing tall in his presence. All these years, she'd built him up as a larger than life monster, inhuman and invincible for it. The mark of her palm on his cheek still and the fury lighting his eyes showed a very human figure…and weak humans such as he were capable of a great fall.

Before she could move, Lord Atbrooke grabbed her hand and crushed it all the harder. "Let me be clear, Mrs. Collins. I am not asking you to stay away from Wessex. I am telling you." At his punishing grip, tears popped up behind her lids. "The viscount has intentions toward my sister."

Eleanor blinked through the pain of his hold. "Toward your sister?" she repeated dumbly. Is that what this man believed? "How could he possibly have any intentions for Lady Marianne?" she drew those words out relishing that truth. "He's already offered for me."

Shock etched his face and he loosened his grip. Taking advantage of his fleeting distraction, Eleanor jerked free and danced away from him. One scream would send a servant rushing, and then what a scandal that would be. For her, for Marcia. For the beloved aunt who'd taken them in. She'd not allow this man that triumph, as well. "Offered for you?" he repeated blankly. "But my sister—"

"Is a foul, scheming, fortune hunter that Lord Wessex is too clever to turn his future over to," she cut in.

A flush mottled his cheeks. "He would have married her…until you arrived, Mrs. Collins. I have seen the way he looks at her."

The marquess' charges landed like a well-placed arrow in her heart. For the gossip columns had not lied in their linking Marcus' name to Lady Marianne, and if Eleanor had not returned, she'd no doubt the young beauty would have ultimately seduced the rogue he'd been in Eleanor's absence. And yet… "But I did arrive," she tossed back those jeering words finding some solace in the truth.

Lord Atbrooke growled and she retreated another step, placing the ivory upholstered sofa between them.

"And he knows the truth of what you did."

He snapped his eyebrows into a single, menacing line.

"If you think he'll toss me over for the crimes only you are guilty of, then you are wrong."

The marquess looked at her for a long moment and then chuckled. "Why, I am not so very foolish to believe Wessex wouldn't have you at any cost." His chest shook with the force of his laughter. "That gent has been itching to get between your legs since he was a boy."

Her body burned hot with words that would turn Marcus' love and attentions into something vile and ugly. Then, should she expect anything more from a man who'd violate an innocent woman?

In a fluidly elegant move, he folded his arms before him, once more at ease. She gritted her teeth at that remarkable composure. "But you have already proven yourself able to leave him once and I've no doubt you will do it again." Will. Not would.

Eleanor gripped the edges of her skirt, wrinkling the fabric. "I will not." Not again. She could no sooner leave Marcus again than she could cut out her own heart.

"Not even for your daughter's sake?"

She stilled.

"Ah, I see I have your attention now."

And he did. God help her, just like that, with the mere mention of her daughter he'd reclaimed ownership of this meeting.

"Tell me, how will Society feel about a fickle young woman who seduced me, stole my heart, and then made off with my child, only to foist that bastard off on a war soldier?" He tossed his head back and laughed. "Then, isn't that what makes this all so delicious? Why, when searching turns up that there never was a *Mr.* Collins and you lied…" It would only cast aspersions upon her character.

His threat sucked the air from the room. Eleanor remained

unmoving and he may as well have run her through with a dull rapier. Her entire body jerked from the shock and pain of his dangled threat. She shook her head furiously. "You would not…"

"I would," he said, flicking an imagined piece of lint from his sapphire coat sleeve. "Quite happily. The *ton* would find tales of a merchant's daughter who gave herself to me years ago and left with my heart when she found I had no wealth to my name quite scintillating, no? More so when that schemer returned and seduced the plump in the pockets viscount." He grinned that evil, empty smile. "Of course, you could not have simply married the viscount all those years ago when you were carrying my bastard, but now you returned to work your wiles." She recoiled. "Why, imagine the scandal." He tapped a finger against the side of his mouth. "Well, I expect Society will applaud me for taking my daughter back from such a woman."

Eleanor bit the inside of her cheek so hard she drew blood and the metallic taste of it nearly gagged her. "She is not your d–daugh-ter," she said, weakly.

The marquess' renewed laughter indicated he'd detected that pregnant pause. "Perhaps. Perhaps not. But the Hamilton birth-mark is a quite interesting piece to the girl's paternal puzzle." He quirked a dark brown eyebrow.

The same man who'd stolen her innocence would so easily shatter the carefully constructed world she'd built for her…for Marcia—for the two of them together. All the dreams breathed into possibility two evenings prior, flickered like the spark of a candle and then went out. Eleanor would sacrifice everything and anything to be with Marcus—everything, except her daughter. "What do you want?" she whispered.

"I want you to leave," he said bluntly, all traces of his earlier lev-ity now gone. "I want you to take your daughter and go wherever it is you've lived and allow my sister Lord Wessex and his fifty thousand pounds."

She gripped the edge of the sofa, seeking purchase in the soft fabric. "I have money." The words tore out of her, desperate and quaking. "Ten thousand pounds." Or she would.

"I need more than your paltry ten thousand pounds." Paltry? It was a fortune that would last her the course of her life. Then should anything surprise her where this reprobate was concerned?

He peeled his lip back. "Furthermore, I will acquire much more in a marriage settlement between my sister and the viscount."

There was a finality to that pronouncement that the marquess wanted her to break Marcus' heart once more. How could she walk out of his life again? What would her world be without him in it? A sheen of tears misted her eyes and she damned the useless signs of weakness. In this moment, she proved herself the ultimate selfish creature and the worst kind of mother. For she wanted to spit in the face of the marquess' threat and risk all for Marcus. She made another appeal. "He does not love her." The futility of pleading with a monster registered and, yet, surely there was a shred of something decent within him that would allow Eleanor this one piece of happiness.

"It does not matter if he loves her," Lord Atbrooke said with a sneer. "He desires her. And when you betray him again, my sister will serve as the perfect diversion."

Oh, God. Her stomach pitched with nausea. How could she give Marcus up, knowing that one day another would take her place? Mayhap it would be Lady Marianne or mayhap not. But it was, as her aunt said...if Eleanor left him...this time he would move on and find another.

She slid her gaze away from the man who'd robbed her of everything that was her right—her virtue, her happiness, Marcus, her future. How very crushing. To come so very close to the greatest joy she'd thought herself undeserving of for so long and to have it crushed within this man's cruel hands. Eleanor looked to the marquess. "I will leave." Did that flat, hollow assurance belong to her?

Lord Atbrooke yanked off his gloves and beat them together. "You may return to London, but only after the viscount has wed my sister." He inclined his head. "I am glad you see the wisdom in this course, Mrs. Collins." Then, touching his fingertips to the edge of an imagined hat, he took his leave, shattering her world once more.

Eleanor stood there long after he'd left. When nothing remained in the room but the sound of her own ragged breathing and her heartbeat filling her ears, she let loose the sob she'd kept buried.

"What did that one want?"

Eleanor shrieked and slammed her hand against her chest. "Aunt Dorothea," she managed on an exhalation of air. "I did not hear you."

The duchess entered the room with her pugs trailing faithfully at her heels. She pushed the door closed with the tip of her cane. "Well?" her aunt demanded gruffly.

Of course her aunt would know of Lord Atbrooke's visit. With her loyal staff, the woman knew of all of what went on. All except that which had sent Eleanor fleeing. Satin scratched at her skirts and, welcoming the diversion, she dropped into the nearest chair. She scooped Satin up onto her lap and welcomed the heavy reassurance of the snorting, panting dog. "Lord Atbrooke paid me a visit," she settled for when her aunt leveled her with a demanding stare.

Her aunt snorted. "I know. Your daughter came to see me. She isn't happy with you for sending her away when you were being visited. By a friend."

Oh, God. Marcia and her dratted tongue. Her mind raced. What else had her daughter shared? The birthmark upon her wrist that matched the marquess'?

The duchess blazed across the room and settled unceremoniously into the seat across from Eleanor. Devlin hopped atop her lap and her aunt stroked him between the ears. "I cannot tell, gel, whether you are being deliberately obtuse or whether you take me for a lackwit."

As neither were really a favorable option, Eleanor remained silent.

"Was it him?"

Eleanor stiffened.

Her aunt rapped her on the knuckles. "That sent you running all those years ago? Was it him?"

Her mouth went dry as the duchess tiptoed around the darkest secrets she'd kept from all. "I do not know what you mean." How were those words so casual and steady when she was quaking inside?

The duchess leaned close and peered at her. "So it was." Of course she'd always seen more than even Eleanor herself, sometimes.

"I have to leave," she said quietly.

The woman gaped. "Leave?"

"I have fulfilled the terms of Uncle's list and I wish to return to

Cornwall."

"No one wishes to return to Cornwall," her aunt barked.

Leaning forward, Eleanor covered her aunt's hand with her own. "I am going to miss you, Aunt Dorothea."

Tears filled the older woman's eyes and she swatted at them. "Bah, I am getting weak in my old age. You are driving me to these silly tears." She gave Eleanor a watery frown and then patted her cheeks. "Is it because of him?"

It was because of Marcia. And Eleanor. And her sanity. "It is because of me," she settled for.

Her aunt gave her a long, hard look. "You have spent your days running, Eleanor Elaine Carlyle. You have convinced yourself time and time again that it is safer to hide from your past."

Unable to meet the rebuke in the older woman's eyes, Eleanor glanced down at her lap. The duchess touched her wrinkled fingers to Eleanor's chin, forcing her attention up. "You may be safe. You may feel a sense of security in removing yourself from the living. But you will never be happy, Eleanor." Tears clogged Eleanor's throat. "I suspect you know that, gel, because you've not been truly happy these years." The duchess tightened her mouth. "And you won't be happy when you leave Marcus, again."

The pointed look she trained on her was full of such recrimination and disappointment that Eleanor slid her gaze away. "I must leave," she finally managed. She sucked in a shuddery breath. "If it was only about me…" Eleanor gave her head a shake. "But it is not."

It was about Marcia.

The truth hovered in the air between them. "Will you allow me your carriage?"

"Bah," her aunt slashed her hand through the air and the dog on her lap growled in protest. "Do you think I'd send you away on a mail coach?"

The meaning there brought heat to Eleanor's face. All those years ago, she'd taken herself off without even a goodbye. "I wanted to bid you farewell," she said when she trusted herself to speak. It was why she would give her loyal aunt, the proper farewell *now.* "I—"

"It does not matter, Eleanor." She squeezed Eleanor's hand in her old, wrinkled fingers. "All these years, you've worried about Society's whispers and opinions of you, when ultimately, you should realize all that matters is your own happiness. If you can find that, then the *ton* can all go hang." She released Eleanor's fingers. "Regardless, my carriage is yours. And whatever else you'd take."

Eleanor stroked Satin's back. Unfortunately, what her aunt could not realize is that this was not really about Eleanor. Not any longer.

This was about Marcia.

There was no choice but to leave.

CHAPTER 20

"I AM GETTING MARRIED."

Shocked silence met Marcus' pronouncement. He stared wryly at mother and daughter, perched on the leather button sofa with their mouths rounded and eyes flared.

Lizzie was the first to break the impasse. She surged to her feet and raced across the room. "Oh, Marcus!"

"Oomph." He staggered under the weight of her form knocking into him.

"Marianne will make you a splendid wife. She has loved you since your first waltz and after the broken heart you suffered years earlier, you deserve nothing but happiness and love."

Marianne? He set Lizzie away. "Er… I am not marrying Lady Marianne."

Marcus may as well have announced the sky was falling on London for the shock in Lizzie's eyes. "You aren't?"

He looked over her shoulder, to where his mother sat primly, hands folded on her lap, and a pleased smile on her lips. "I suspect Marcus intends to offer for Mrs. Collins." Then, catching his eye, she gave him a wink.

He started. How much had his mother seen through the years that he himself had failed to see?

Lizzie furrowed her brow. "Mrs. Collins?"

Marcus continued his earlier path over to the sideboard. "Indeed." A surge of warmth filled his heart. "I have already asked the lady and she has acquiesced."

His mother clasped her hands to her chest and, with an uncharacteristic zeal, surged to her feet. "Oh, Marcus!"

Lizzie whipped her head back and forth between mother and son. "What?"

The pleased tones of his mother, Viscountess Wessex, and the disappointed, shocked ones of his sister warred for supremacy. "I have offered for Mrs. Collins and she has said yes."

His sister emitted a plaintive wail. "Oh, Marcus, surely not." From where he stood at the sideboard, Marcus turned a frown on Lizzie.

"I love her," he said plainly.

"I once heard mother and the Duchess speaking about your broken heart. It was Mrs. Collins, wasn't it?"

He hooded his eyes. "Lizzie, not everything is always as clear as it seems."

His sister slammed the back of one hand against her palm. "That woman has hurt you, broken your heart, and you would give yourself to her?" She tightened her lips. Marcus halted, with his hand poised over the decanter. In all his imaginings of how Eleanor would be received by his family, he'd never dared consider his loyal, loving, and stubborn sister would hold Eleanor guilty of whispered tales from long ago.

"Lizzie," their mother scolded. She rushed past her daughter and took Marcus' hands. "I am so very happy for you, Marcus. You have loved her for so very long and you were not the same man when she left. When the duchess said she would return, I had hoped…" A blush filled her cheeks and she promptly closed her mouth.

The ghost of a smile played on his lips. Ah, both her doting aunt and his determined mama had carefully orchestrated so much of Eleanor's return.

In a temper, Lizzie stamped her foot. "He was not the same because she broke his heart."

Looking over his mother's shoulder, Marcus glowered at his sister. "I appreciate your loyalty, but you do not know anything of it." Just as he'd known nothing about anything over the years. While Lizzie saw the surface of what she believed to be the truth, there were layers to Eleanor's departure that could never be explained. Those secrets belonged to her, and him, and someday Marcia— but no other. He grabbed a decanter of fine French brandy—and froze.

...He stank of brandy...

The bottle slipped from his hands and clattered noisily to the smooth mahogany piece.

Lizzie stuck a finger out. "Marianne has held out hope that you would marry her because she loves you."

He winced. Good God, is that what his innocent sister believed? Lady Marianne, with her thinly veiled innuendos, had clear designs on him that were anything but proper and polite.

Their mother passed a look between her children. "I would not have either of my children wed where their hearts are not engaged."

Lizzie made a sound of impatience. "Well, I would not have him wed where his heart was already *broken*."

Grabbing for a bottle of whiskey, he poured himself a glass. His sister had always been blindly loyal—to her family, to the few friends she'd known...but it was that blindness and her youth that prevented her from seeing that there were often layers to a person that went far beneath the surface. "I am touched by your concern, Lizzie," he began patiently.

"Do not patronize me," she gritted out.

He sighed and took a long swallow of his drink. "But I am marrying her. She is a good woman and a wonderful mother. We were parted by..." He searched his mind, but that black, blinding rage slipped around his mind. "A misunderstanding," he settled for.

"I want you to be happy, Marcus," she began.

"Good, I am."

His sister turned her palms up. "But I cannot be happy for you. Not even in this." Her mouth tightened. "If you'll excuse me?" Without another word, Lizzie marched from the room and slammed the door in her wake.

Marcus dragged a hand over his face. Had he inadvertently allowed Lady Marianne to believe his intentions were something more?

"She is just disappointed, Marcus," his mother said to calm him, slashing into his contemplation. "She will come around when she knows Eleanor the way you and I do."

He nodded absently and carried his drink over to the window. The rub of it was if he could rid the world of hurts and bring

Eleanor nothing but joy, he would. And yet, he could not. There would invariably be whispers and unkind words and cruelties that he would be just as helpless to protect her from. Even from his own sister.

From within the windowpane, he detected his mother as she walked over. She paused just at his shoulder. "You have loved her for a very long time."

His gaze fell to the streets below. Since the moment she'd stepped out of her aunt's townhouse and he' been standing there, he had loved her. "I have," he said quietly. First, with the simplicity of youth. When his world had been darkened by the death of Lionel, she had represented light and happiness and purity. The young woman that she'd been had dragged him from the pit of despair and shown him that there were, indeed, reasons to again laugh and smile. The woman who'd reentered his life almost eight years later came with maturity and strength and courage that made him fall in love with her all over again. His heart would forever belong to her.

His mother settled a hand on his arm and he started. "Lizzie is young. In time, she will come to love Eleanor."

Marcus opened his mouth but the words froze on his lips. He squinted, trying to make sense of the visitor exiting the Duchess of Devonshire's townhouse.

"What is it?" his mother prodded.

He gave his head a shake, instead focusing on the Marquess of Atbrooke. What business did the man have there?

His mother peered around Marcus' shoulder. "What would Atbrooke be visiting Mrs. Collins for?"

Her befuddlement echoed his own. "I do not know," he muttered. For there was no doubt the man was paying a visit to Eleanor. No one paid the duchess a call unless they were summoned, or a lifelong friend, of which the older woman had one—Marcus' mother.

Lady Marianne's notoriously caddish brother was deep in dun territory. Did he think to find his fortune at the Duchess of Devonshire's doorstep?

"You do not suppose he is hunting Eleanor's fortune?" she asked, those words spoken more to herself, a mirror of his own thoughts.

"I do not know," he repeated. Then her words registered,

momentarily pulling his gaze away from the gentleman below.

"Oh, come, Marcus," his mother scoffed. "Do you truly believe with the friendship I have with Dorothea that I'd not be aware of the funds laid out for her niece?"

"I do not want Lizzie visiting Lady Marianne," he said, never taking his gaze from Atbrooke, who adjusted his hat, and then with a singular focus on the midnight black mount across the street, bounded for that creature. He stared after Atbrooke until he rode off. Turning on his heel, Marcus stepped adroitly around his mother.

"Do I even have to inquire as to where you are going?" she called, amusement coating her query.

Marcus did not break his stride. "You do not."

He'd appreciated the proximity of Eleanor's residence from the moment she'd stolen his heart. This moment, he welcomed it for entirely different reasons. Atbrooke's visit was, no doubt, a detail Marcus would have invariably missed if his townhouse had not shared the walls of her aunt's townhouse.

Marcus reached the foyer and his loyal butler rushed to meet him. "My lord."

"Williston." Not bothering with his cloak, Marcus marched to the door. The older man rushed to pull it open and Marcus stepped out. He made his way to the duchess' door, taking the handful of steps two at a time. He turned his gaze out to the street once more. Had the bastard been attempting to court her? Notorious scoundrel that he was, the man could not have honorable intentions. He started back around as the butler pulled the door open. Marcus stepped inside. "I am here to see Mrs. Collins."

The butler's expression grew shuttered. "Of course, my lord. I will see if she is receiving visitors," the man responded, as he closed the door behind him.

He frowned. If she was receiving visitors? Why in blazes would she be receiving the likes of Atbrooke and then turn him away? Schooling his features, Marcus murmured his thanks.

The servant rushed off, leaving Marcus in the foyer to wait. Impatient, Marcus yanked the special license from inside his coat pocket and skimmed the document. Granted, the butler could not know that Marcus carried a special license from his visit that morning with the archbishop. No, the man was, no doubt, simply

seeing to his responsibilities as the duchess' head servant and yet...
he cast a glance down the corridor the man had disappeared a
short while ago. And yet it rankled that he'd be kept waiting in
the foyer.

"Are you angry?"

Marcus spun about.

Marcia sat at the bottom of the stairs with her elbows propped
on her knees and her chin resting in her hands.

"Marcia," he said, approaching the girl. He dropped to a knee. "I
did not hear your arrival."

An impish grin played on her lips. "I am quite good at sneaking."

He frowned, imagining Marcia in ten years with that very deft
skill. He clenched his jaw. Marcus would have to take apart any
man who thought to go sneaking with her.

"Oh, dear, you are very angry," Marcia whispered, pulling him
back from the harrowing thoughts of the not-so-distant future
when some undeserving rogue or rake was making a nuisance of
himself around the girl.

"I was merely thinking," he substituted.

"What is that?" She motioned to the official page in his hands
and he followed her stare.

"It is a surprise for your mama." He tweaked her nose.

She brightened. "Splendid." Then her smile dipped and she
scuffed the tip of her slipper on the marble floor. "My mama is
angry and I worried for a moment that you were both angry." She
paused and probed him with her older-than-her-years eyes. "With
one another. You are not angry with each other, then, are you?"

"Never," he said so quickly, her little shoulders sagged.

"Thank goodness." A beleaguered sigh left the little girl's lips.
"It must be just me that Mama is cross with and she is never cross
with me."

Marcus shifted and settled onto the marble stair beside Eleanor's
daughter. "I daresay your mama could never be cross with you."

"She was today," she replied automatically. Marcia stole a glance
around and then scooted closer to him on the step. "She squeezed
my shoulders and then yelled at me."

He puzzled his brow. That did not sound at all like the manner
of mother he'd come to know Eleanor as. She'd demonstrated
patience and love toward this child who'd also ensnared Marcus'

heart. Only concern or some shockingly disobedient act on the little girl's part could result in a crack in Eleanor's composure. "Did she?" he asked deliberately.

"Well, not yelled at me," Marcia mumbled and dropped her eyes to the marble floor. She swung her gaze swiftly back to his. "But she was angry and she would not allow me to meet her friend."

Those last two words gave him pause. Marcus knew everything from the smell of Eleanor's skin to her unease in polite Society. Not once had she mentioned, however, a friend. "Her friend?" he urged.

Not taking her chin from her hands, her daughter gave an awkward nod. "He was very nice and he said he was a very good friend of Mama's." *He.* Unease churned in his gut. "But Mama was not at all nice to him," she went on. "Not the way she is nice to you."

"What was his name?" he asked, infusing a calm into those four words when inside the disquiet redoubled in his chest.

"The Marquess of Atbrooke." She tapped the tip of her finger against her lip contemplatively. "Though he did not allow me to use his first name the way you do."

"Atbrooke," he repeated, dazed from that unwitting revelation. Surely not. Horror unfurled slowly inside him. It lapped at his consciousness and robbed him of thought. Surely it hadn't been Lady Marianne's brother who'd raped Eleanor and gotten a child on her. This child.

Marcia lifted an excited gaze to his. "And he even had a birthmark on his wrist, like mine." She turned her hand up for his perusal.

Oh, God. Marcus' eyes went to that crescent moon-shaped brown mark at the inset of her wrist. All the while, a dull humming filled his ears.

"Lord Wessex."

The pair on the steps looked up as one. Thomas stood there. "Mrs. Collins will see you."

Marriage license in hand, he shoved to his feet, and then held his other hand out to Marcia, who trustingly placed her fingers in his. "You should return to your lessons," he said softly.

She sighed. "Yes. Mrs. Plunkett will be looking for me."

Marcus watched as the girl made the slow climb abovestairs and then fell into step behind the butler. With each step, Marcus struggled to rein in the volatile rage coursing through him. He wanted to toss his head back and rail like a beast. He wanted to stalk from the townhouse, hunt down Atbrooke and shred him to pieces so that no remnants remained of the bastard who'd pinned Eleanor to the ground and taken the gift of her innocence.

Thomas stopped outside the White Parlor and announced him. "The Viscount Wessex."

Eleanor stood at the empty hearth, staring down into the metal grate. At the introduction, she turned slowly to face him. "Marcus," she said softly, pulling the brown leather book in her arms close.

He took in the ashen hue of her skin, the tight lines drawn at the corner of her mouth, and he *knew*. A heavy weight settled on his chest, like a boulder cutting off his airflow and slowly destroying him. She did not intend to wed him. He saw it in her empty eyes and the trembling fingers now plucking at her skirts. "Eleanor," he murmured and closed the door behind them.

She stared at him with sad, guarded eyes, but said nothing.

He strode toward her, when she spoke without preamble. "I cannot marry you."

Marcus staggered to a halt. "Why?" he braced for the same veiled, vague lies she'd fed him in the form of a handwritten note years earlier.

Her soft, shuddery breath filled the tense quiet. "Because I was foolish to believe my past did not matter. I deluded myself into believing I might never again see him and that Marcia would be safe." She dropped her gaze to the book in her hands. "Of course it matters. It always will."

Like navigating on a pit of quicksand, where one wrong move would mean ruin, he picked carefully about his thoughts. "It matters," he said at last and that brought Eleanor's head snapping up.

Her lower lip trembled. "I—"

Marcus closed the space between them in four long strides. "It matters, but not in the way you believe, or in the way you even now are thinking I mean, Eleanor Elaine. It matters because of the wrong done you. It matters that you were robbed of choice and right, and that another's will was imposed on you." Emotion roughed his voice. Gently disentangling the book from her tight-knuckled grip, he tucked the folded document inside, and set the volume down on a nearby side table forgotten. "Tell me why." Because he needed the words to come from her, as much as she needed those words spoken.

WHEN ELEANOR HAD BEEN A girl of ten, her father had taught her an American game of Hide and Go Seek shared with him by a fellow merchant. The first time he'd taught her, she'd raced to the spot of safety with her quick, agile father close at her heels. Her chest had burned with the exertions until it had been nearly impossible to draw breath.

Eleanor pressed her eyes closed and her chest rose and fell hard and fast. This moment felt remarkably like that long ago day. Since the Marquess of Atbrooke had upended her world for a second, irrevocable time, she'd been the same scared girl trying to muddle through his threats and the inevitable parting it would mean for her and Marcus. Staring at Marcus now, with palpable rage pouring from his tautly held frame, she'd little doubt that he knew the reason. And even knowing as he did, he'd hear the words and truth from her.

"Eleanor," he urged with a gentle insistence.

A broken sigh slipped past her lips and she strode over to the window, putting much needed distance between Marcus and the dream she'd been so very close to attaining. And for that, she could no longer remain. "After I had been…after that night in Lady Wedermore's gardens," she substituted, for she was still too much a coward to lend words to that night. "There would be days I awoke in the morning. With the cloud of sleep, I would believe myself back in London and smile, filled with excitement of again seeing you." She pressed her forehead against the crystal windowpane warmed by the sun's rays. Marcus' visage reflected back in the surface and she turned her gaze to the busy streets below. "But then, something would creep in. It would begin with a niggling in my mind, something prodding me, reminding me that my world was no longer the same, and then it all would come rushing back."

She turned to face him. "The other night in the theatre, Marcus. That was my moment of waking with forgetfulness." Eleanor offered him a quivering smile. "Today was the awakening. The reminder that no matter how much we wish it, or how much we will it, the past remains."

"What are you saying?" There was a gruffness in his tone.

Emotion wadded in her throat. "I cannot marry you," she whispered. If there was no Marcia, then she could face the scandal and gossip. Not now. Not with her daughter being the person who would suffer most. Once again, Atbrooke had stolen the happiness she'd imagined for herself and Marcus.

Tense silence thrummed between them. His gaze grew shuttered, but not before she saw the flash of rage and hatred.

Eleanor winced as those sentiments from their reunion in the London street not even a fortnight earlier flared to life, and a sliver of her soul died at the palpable sign of his apathy.

"Who?" he asked quietly.

She tipped her head. Of all the vitriolic words spilling from his lips, the last she'd expected was—

"Tell me, who are you afraid of?"

His knowing question sucked the breath from her lungs. The need to turn this burden over to him gripped her with a physical intensity and yet to do so would endanger the person whose very life meant more to Eleanor than her own. "I cannot."

He firmed his jaw. "You *will* not, Eleanor. Those are two entirely different things."

"What would you have me say?" she cried softly.

"The truth." How very easy Marcus made it sound. She dropped her eyes to his cravat. How very simple and enticing and right, in giving him the answers to the questions he both craved and deserved. One faulty misstep, however, could threaten Marcia's security and happiness. She chewed at her lower lip.

"Was it Atbrooke?" His quietly spoken question brought her head shooting up.

How very surreal to have this man she loved utter the name of her attacker. It let Marcus into her world in ways she'd fought so hard to keep him out.

"He called on me." Did that faint whisper belong to her?

Marcus' body jerked erect.

Of course, he'd not know how to make sense of that admission. Unable to meet his gaze, she glanced at the tips of her slippers. "The gentleman who…" Her throat worked spasmodically. "The…"

Her words trailed off as Marcus closed the space between them.

With a tenderness that threatened to shatter her already fractured heart, he took her chin between his thumb and forefinger. Had he been demanding or inquiring, she'd not have found the courage to continue. There was, however, strength to be had in his patience. When so much had been forced upon her, Marcus once more offered her choice, and there was something heady and beautiful in that power he turned over to her care. "I will have your word. I will have your word when I tell you, you'll not call him out, because I would share this with you." She spoke on a rush. "But I'll not share it if you intend to face him at dawn."

For a long moment, Marcus remained silent. The grating ormolu clock ticked on so long she thought he'd ignore her request, but then a black curse burst from his lips. "You have my promise," he gritted out.

"It was the Marquess of Atbrooke." Her voice caught, under the weight of the mysteries she'd not herself known all these years until just a few short moments ago; about the man who'd raped her, and fathered her child. She buried her face in her hands and sucked in great big breaths at the freedom in sharing this with Marcus.

Marcus drew her against his chest and she buried her face in the fabric of his coat. The sandalwood scent clinging to him wafted about her senses and drove back the stench of brandy and evil. She turned her cheek against the white lawn of his shirt and absorbed his strength. "He has promised to allow me my," daughter "secret, if I leave."

Incredulity spilled from his tone. "And you trust him?"

For how could a dastard like the marquess ever be trusted to honor any pledges or promises he'd made? Eleanor curled her hands into tight balls. Ultimately, it was not her own future or security she wagered with, but rather Marcia's. And for that, the decision had been made for her. "No." She shook her head. "But it is no longer just my happiness I have to worry after."

He clenched and unclenched his jaw. "You are not alone. I will stand by you."

"And what of your sister?" she countered, taking a hasty step away. At his silence, she continued, relentless. "What match will she make when my past is revealed and Society learns there was never a Mr. Collins and Marcia is no more of legitimate parentage than

I am a lady born and bred?"

Marcus captured her hands in his and turned them over. He raised them to his lips, one at a time. "So you will run, again, to protect my sister and Marcia? But who will protect you?"

Her heart skittered a beat. "We are not—"

He growled. "If you say you are not my responsibility—"

"He wants me gone." She hesitated, recalling the marquess' intentions for Marcus. "Lord Atbrooke would have you marry his sister." She brushed an errant strand of hair from his forehead. "I have to leave, Marcus."

"I'll have no one as my wife, except you, Eleanor Elaine." A muscle jumped at the corner of his right eye. He worked his powerful gaze over her face, as though he sought to imprint all of her upon his memory. "And I know you feel you must leave," he said quietly, brushing his knuckles down her cheek. "Oh, Eleanor, I have wanted you from the moment I first saw you eight years ago. I will want you until the day I draw my last breath."

His words spoke to their parting and should fill her with a warm solace. He understood her need to leave and loved her still. Yet... agony shredded the already broken and bruised organ that was her heart. For the greedy, selfish part of her wanted him to want her to remain, regardless. She wanted him snapping and snarling at the prospect of her parting. What a horrible, contrary creature she was. Shamed by her own selfishness, Eleanor willed her lips up into a smile, and then held her hand out.

He eyed her outstretched fingers. "What the hell is that?"

She looked about and then followed his gaze to her trembling hand. "As it is goodbye," again. *Oh, God, how can I leave him? How, when he is the other half of my heart?* "I am shaking your hand."

Marcus captured her fingers and drew them close to his mouth. He placed a lingering kiss upon her hand. "Is that what you believe?" His breath caressed her skin and shivers of warmth radiated from the point of contact and spiraled rapidly through her being. "That this is goodbye?"

"Isn't it?" she managed on a faint whisper.

He trailed his thumb over her palm. "You misunderstand me. I am saying goodbye to you for now. But I am coming for you. I will deal with Atbrooke and we will be free of him, and then you, Marcia, and I can be together." He pierced her with his gaze. "And not even God Himself with an army of angels at his side could separate us."

She gasped and Marcus kissed her hand once more. He turned on his heel and stalked out of the parlor and out of her life.

CHAPTER 21

PANICKY RAGE LENT JERKINESS TO Marcus' movements. If he'd not left Eleanor when he did, the fury pounding away at his chest would have exploded from him. She'd entrusted him with the truth, the least he could give her was a calming response. So he pounded away at the unfamiliar front door.

Except, with the much-needed space between them, a torrent of emotions whirred inside him so that madness and sanity waged a war within. For now, he had the name from Eleanor's lips, which had confirmed the truth he'd already suspected. He growled and pounded all the harder. He had a goddamn name and she'd expect him to not kill the black-hearted cad at dawn for the crimes he was guilty of?

He renewed his knocking, uncaring of the sea of passersby taking in his frenetic movements, uncaring that with his unkempt hair, the world now saw a man hanging off a cliff with nothing more than his nails and if he let go he would be forever destroyed. Marcus let fly a black curse and pounded once more. "Goddamn bloody—"

The door opened. An old, wizened butler stood peering at him through rheumy eyes. "May I help you?"

Marcus fished around the front of his jacket and withdrew a card. "Lord Wessex to see the Marquess of Rutland."

The old servant eyed the card a moment and then accepted it in his gnarled, white-gloved fingers. He peered down at the name and seal emblazoned upon that card. "His Lordship is not—"

Marcus stuck his foot in the doorway and willed the other man to see with the ferocity of his stare that he was not leaving. "I would see Lord Rutland immediately."

The servant hesitated a long while, and with a sigh, he moved aside and motioned him forward.

Lest the man change his mind, Marcus strode into the soaring foyer, dimly registering a lavish opulence to the home of one of the darkest, most feared, reviled, and scandalous lords in the realm. He'd not known what he'd expected; crimson fabrics and shocking murals, perhaps. But certainly not the innocent cherubs dancing in clouds of pastel overhead.

"I cannot promise His Lordship will receive you." The older man's reluctant tones spoke volumes.

Marcus gave a tight nod and waited as the servant shuffled off. By the devil and all his spawn, Rutland would see him. He'd take apart each goddamn room until the evil bastard granted him an audience and gave Marcus the only gift he needed.

As the moments ticked by, he yanked out his watchfob and consulted the timepiece. With a growl of annoyance, he stuffed it back into his pocket.

"His Lordship will see you."

Marcus spun about and found the servant studying him. With a gruff murmur of thanks, he fell into step behind the ancient servant. The man moved with slow, shuffling footsteps. With the marquess' notoriously ruthless reputation, Marcus puzzled that he would keep a man who was anything but quick in his employ still. The inanity of that musing kept him from focusing on the thirst for Atbrooke's blood.

"Here we are," the servant said with a slight wheeze. He pulled out a crisp white kerchief and dusted his brow. The man opened the door. "The Viscount Wessex to see you, my lord."

Marcus did a sweep of the room and his gaze landed on the marquess. Seated behind a broad, immaculate, mahogany desk, the man with his head bent over a ledger evinced power. "You may go," he said, not taking his gaze from his task.

The servant sketched a bow and then took his leave, closing Marcus in with the most dreaded lord in Society.

Marcus stood there, the forgotten visitor, as the marquess scribbled away at the page before him. He fisted his hands into tight balls at the grating scratch of the pen meeting paper. Periodically the marquess would pause, dip his pen into a crystal inkwell, and then resume that frantic pace of jotting notes upon a page. How coolly arrogant the man was. How unaffected, and how he hated this man, more stranger, than anything for that freedom from caring when Marcus' world was in tumult.

A growl rattled in his chest, and the marquess froze mid-movement, scratched something else upon the page, and then tossed his pen down. Then with an aggravating meticulousness, Lord Rutland folded the page and affixed his seal. The message of his movements clear...he was in control and Marcus' presence here was merely being tolerated.

"Rutland," he bit out.

Lord Rutland leaned back in his chair. "Wessex." The hard, noble features set into an impenetrable mask gave no indication as to what the widely reputed scoundrel was thinking, feeling, or whether he was even capable of emotion. He spread his arms wide, inviting Marcus to sit. "To what do I owe the pleasure of your visit?"

With jerky movements, Marcus marched over and yanked out the leather winged-back chair at the foot of the desk. He settled into the seat. "I am here to request your assistance," he said without preamble. Neither of them were friends and they were barely acquaintances. As such, there was no need for false pleasantries or niceties.

Rutland lowered his brow, but otherwise gave no indication that he'd so much as heard Marcus' reluctant bid for help.

Marcus layered his arms on the sides of his chair and leaned forward. The leather groaned in protest. "You have a book." Members of the *ton*, both polite and impolite lords and ladies all knew of the famed book. Purported to document the weaknesses and debts owed by the most notorious reprobates and letches, such a catalogue had once earned Marcus' disgust and disdain. Now he needed words penned within those pages. Needed the book to be as real as it was rumored to be. "You have a book," Marcus went on when Lord Rutland said nothing. "And I am in need of the name of one of the gentlemen who is surely on the pages." He'd wager his very life ten times on Sunday that Atbrooke owed countless debts to the very man before Marcus now.

Rutland shuttered his gaze and then shoved to his feet. With a nonchalance that made Marcus grit his teeth, the marquess made his way to the well-stocked sideboard. He paused and looked at the crystal decanters, lingering over his decision, and then selected a bottle of brandy. He turned, bottle in hand, and hefted it in Marcus' direction. "Brandy?"

"No," he said tersely. The man was utterly mad. Marcus gripped the arms of his chair hard. But then, he was desperate enough that he'd appeal to the mercy of a madman stranger.

The clink of crystal touching crystal filled the quiet as did the stream of liquid as the marquess poured his snifter full. With the same casualness that had driven him to that sideboard, the marquess strolled back to his desk, and reclaimed his seat. He took a sip. All the while, he studied Marcus over the rim of his glass with an indecipherable stare.

"You were saying?"

Marcus swallowed back the impatient retort on his lips. It wouldn't do to lash out at the one man who could help him in this moment. "A book," he repeated impatiently. "You are rumored to keep a book of men indebted to you. There is one gentleman who is within those pages." Fury thrumming inside him, Marcus snapped. "And I would have that man's name. I would own his debt."

Lord Rutland took another sip of his brandy and then cradled the glass in his large hands. "What business do you have with this man?"

The sole reason for Marcus' happiness, Eleanor, was what would make Marcus humble himself this minute, and yet he could not share that with this ruthless stranger. "It is not your business." The marquess lowered his eyes and Marcus turned his palms up. "But I have funds and will pay you whatever amount you name for the transfer of this gentleman's weakness and debt."

Rutland took another sip. And then, "I cannot help you." There was a gruff quality to the man's tone that hinted at a man who spoke to few.

Marcus sprung from his chair. "Whatever amount you name," he rasped. He planted his palms on the surface of the desk and leaned across the impeccable surface, shrinking the space between them.

"Any amount," he repeated, forcing a calmness into that promise, when inside, his heart was thundering painfully in his chest.

The marquess stared at him for a long while, until Marcus reclaimed his seat. His skin flushed with embarrassment. But then, when a man loved a woman he would humble himself before a ruthless stranger.

Rutland rolled his snifter back and forth between his hands. "At one time, I would have gladly helped you, Wessex. I would have helped you because it would have strengthened my power and influence, and I reveled in that." He shook his head. "But I am no longer that man."

Marcus sank back in his chair. Married several months earlier, little was heard from the marquess, and now Marcus knew why. He swiped a hand over his face, a mirthless laugh lodged in his throat. The rogue, rake, and scoundrel had been reformed. Bloody hell. He let his hand fall to his side. "Do you love your wife?" he asked with a bluntness that earned him a lethal stare.

"Say what it is you'd say, Wessex, and get the hell out," the other man commanded on a silken whisper that promised retribution should Marcus in any way threaten those he loved.

Marcus gave his head a clearing shake. "I am bungling this," he muttered. "Do you love your wife?" he asked once more, his tone quiet and incessant.

Still, Rutland said nothing.

"I suspect your silence is your answer," Marcus predicted and the vein pulsing above his eye indicated Marcus was one wrong word away from the other man charging over and pummeling him with his powerful fists. "I suspect you love her and you would do any-thing for her." He spread his hands out. "There is a woman whom I am in love with." Lord Rutland went still. "I would do any-thing for her." He held the marquess' impregnable stare. "Including humbling myself before you, a stranger." Marcus dropped his gaze to the desk and his eyes collided with that half-empty brandy.

He stank of brandy...

For the knowing of Atbrooke's identity made Eleanor's agoniz-ing telling, all the more real. Bile climbed up his throat and he choked it down. He wrenched his gaze away from that glass and found the marquess staring at him.

"The Marquess of Atbrooke would hurt her." Hurt Eleanor

when he'd already stolen so much from her. Marcus' throat worked and, uncomfortable with that show of emotion, he coughed into his hand. "If I do not destroy the gentleman, he will destroy her, and she is all that is good and kind, and she is a mother, and…" He buried his head into his hands, helpless and unable to save her just as before. Suddenly, the futility in being here assaulted him and he jumped to his feet. "Forgive me for wasting your time with the affairs of those who do not concern you," he said stiffly. Dropping a bow, he started for the door.

"Wessex," Lord Rutland called out, bringing him back around. He motioned him forward. "Please," he said quietly, gone was all earlier vestige of frigid guardedness.

Marcus hesitated and then as hope mixed with wariness, he reclaimed his earlier seat.

"I do not have a book."

And with those words, Lord Rutland killed that hope. The marquess gave his entire focus to his glass. "Not any longer. Had you paid me a visit one year ago, I would have pulled out that tome, scratched your name inside, and handed over the information you wanted in return. I resolved to not be the man I had been and some of that," he grimaced and yanked at his cravat. "*All* of that is because of the woman I married."

By God, the speculative whispers about London proved true. The Marquess of Rutland truly loved his wife. Loved her enough that he wished to be more than the ruthless scoundrel he'd been. Then, wasn't that the power of a woman's hold? She made a man wish to be better than the person he was. "I am sorry I have wasted your time," he said tersely. "If you will forgive me?" He made to rise, when Lord Rutland held a finger up.

"I did not say I would not help you." His heart stilled. "I just will not help you in the way you believe. I want nothing from you," the marquess said, his tone gruff. "I've no need for money or power, and nothing of the material which you may give. Atbrooke is an evil bastard." A sardonic grin formed on the hard lips of Society's most dreaded scoundrel. "And it is, indeed, quite a day when I identify others as such." He smoothed his lips, killing all earlier hint of weakening. "I am not unfamiliar with his proclivities." Had the man's proclivities included forcing other young women as he'd done to Eleanor?

A blinding rage clouded his vision and he blinked it back, attending those words.

Lord Rutland pulled open his desk drawer. He shuffled through pages and then withdrew a single sheet. He slid it across the desk.

Marcus glanced down and then froze.

"You are wondering what I want from you? You're asking what debt I'd exact for this favor?" The marquess shook his head. "The answer is nothing. I want the Atbrookes and Brewers gone from my life. The vowels are yours to do with as you wish."

With numb fingers, Marcus picked up the sheet. He promptly choked. Eighteen thousand pounds the man was turning over. He eyed Rutland dubiously over the top of the page. "I don't understand."

A ghost of a smile hovered on the other man's lips. "You are in love with your lady. As such, you understand. I've pledged to live a life that is good and I will not prey on others. So Atbrooke is yours to deal with."

Marcus tightened his fingers reflexively upon the page. "Thank you," he said hoarsely, studying the sum inked on the ivory velum. "I can never repay you." Not for this kindness. Not for allowing Marcus to claim freedom from fear of this man's machinations.

"I do not expect you to repay me," Rutland replied automatically. "But, Wessex?"

He glanced up.

"You believe you will find solace in revenge. You will tell yourself that as long as you ruin him, you will find happiness, but that isn't true." The marquess jerked his chin at the sheet. "That thirst for revenge, it will only destroy you. The only thing that will heal you, or the lady that sent you here to me today, is love. Until you accept that, neither of you will be free." A dull flush mottled Rutland's cheeks, and as though embarrassed by those words, he picked up his brandy and downed the remaining contents of his glass.

Allowing him his dignity, Marcus returned his focus to the page. Atbrooke's name glared mockingly back. Another surge of rage ripped through him. "Perhaps you are right," he said when he trusted himself to speak. "But if anyone hurt your wife the way he hurt…" A spasm gripped his heart and he cleared his throat. Even the hint of a suggestion of the crime committed against

Eleanor would bring her undeserved scorn and additional agony. In coming here to obtain information from Rutland, Marcus had sought the far lesser of the two evils. By the marquess' frank candidness he'd no doubt Marcus' confidence would be kept. Still, he'd already said too much. "Thank you," he murmured. "I am in your debt." In every way, imaginable.

Rutland tossed his hands up. "I do not want you in my debt," he growled. "Bloody hell, Wessex, I am looking to be free of it all."

Then, weren't they all seeking to shake free the demons of their past? How futile their attempts were.

The marquess again drew open the front desk drawer and withdrew a peculiarly shaped velvet box. He hesitated and then pushed it across the table.

Marcus eyed it and then wordlessly accepted the package. He lifted the lid and peered down at the heart-shaped pendant. Puzzling his brow, he glanced up. "What—?"

"It was a gift given my wife by the Marchioness of Waverly. The wearer is fabled to land the heart of a duke."

Despite the hell of that morning, Marcus' lips twitched. "I'm rather hoping the lady is content with my mere title of viscount," he said dryly.

A chuckle rumbled from within the marquess' chest. "Yes, well, the real truth is that the wearer will earn the heart of their true love." He motioned to the necklace. "You are better entrusting yourself to that emotion, than the revenge that would destroy you both, Wessex."

Brought 'round to the very reason for his being here, Marcus closed the lid. "I thank you. But I cannot—"

"Take the necklace. I just ask when you are married and happy, that you see it returned."

Marcus looked down at the two gifts given, humbled by this stranger's kindness. This man feared by all had proven himself more human than Marcus could ever hope to be. "I don't—"

"There is nothing to say," the marquess murmured.

The door opened. "Edmund, where have you—oh."

Their gazes swung to the entrance of the room to where a lady with nondescript brown hair and blue eyes stood staring back at them. Marcus and Rutland rushed to their feet.

"Phoebe," the man murmured with a reverent tenderness. "I was meeting with the Viscount Wessex."

"Forgive me," she said softly. With her plainness, there was nothing extraordinary about the lady, and yet there was a kindness and warmth in her eyes, and as Marcus stole a glance at Lord Rutland, the man's transformation made sense.

"No, my apologies," Marcus said, tucking the marquess' offerings in his front pocket. His gaze went to her rounded middle and a wave of potent longing so strong hit him so completely that it robbed him of breath and thought. In the marchioness, he saw Eleanor as she'd been, with her belly full with child, and he ached for the need to be a true father to Marcia, and to have more children with Eleanor. Forcing his eyes back to Rutland, he held his hand out, much the way Eleanor had a short while ago. "I cannot thank you enough."

For the marquess' waving off what he'd done this day, he'd turned over a fortune when most men would have exploited Marcus' weakness.

"Remember what I said," he returned and accepted the offering.

Marcus bowed his head and then with a polite goodbye for the marchioness, he took his leave. The marquess' words reverberated around his mind; the warning clear. He would turn himself over to love—as soon as he could be sure that Atbrooke would never threaten Eleanor and her daughter again.

Taking his leave of the marquess, Marcus drew his hat on and bounded down the steps to where a boy waited with the reins of his mount. Withdrawing a small purse, he tossed it to the lad. "Thank you," he murmured and climbed astride.

He had but one more call to make this day…and then there could be, if not a total healing for Eleanor, at the very least some peace and assurance that she need never fear the Marquess of Atbrooke again.

CHAPTER 22

A SHORT WHILE LATER, THE MARQUESS of Atbrooke's butler ushered Marcus from the foyer and down the hall.

As he walked, a vitriolic hatred spun inside him. It filled every crevice of Marcus' person until he tasted his seething animosity for the man whose company he now sought. He took in the chipped and cracked plaster walls, the threadbare carpets lining the floors, and reveled in even the small material discomfort the man had known. When it should have been far greater suffering.

"Lord Wessex!" The faint breathless cry brought him to an abrupt stop.

He stiffened, and angled around. Lady Marianne smiled that sultry, enticing smile and he fought down apathy for this woman who shared the blood of a beast. How had he ever entertained anything more with this one? "Lady Marianne," he said brusquely. "If you will excuse me? I have a meeting with your brother."

"La," she pouted and flicked his sleeve. "Surely you can spare a moment for me."

The butler discreetly dropped his gaze and a shudder of revulsion went through Marcus.

"I am here on a matter of importance," he said curtly.

She flared her cat-like eyes and triumph glittered within their cold depths. "A matter of importance, do you say?" she breathed. With no regard for the servant at their side, the lady layered herself to him, and rubbed her breasts against his chest. "You will not be regretful in your decision, my lord. I promise you that."

"Indeed, I won't." Then disentangling himself from Atbrooke's sister, Marcus followed along after the butler.

They came to a stop outside the marquess' office door and Marcus curled his hands, staring at the wood panel, wanting to take the door down with his fingers and choke the life from him.

The servant pulled the door open and announced him.

Atbrooke stood at the center of the room, a wide grin on his small lips. "Wessex, a pleasure," he boomed, waving him in as his servant took his leave. "I suspect what has brought you here." The man's mouth moved as he spoke but Marcus remained frozen, rooted to the floor, staring at that mouth, torturing himself with the hell of imagining those lips on Eleanor's, silencing her cries. "Would you care to sit?"

The marquess' words came as though down a long, empty corridor. Marcus strode across the room and, without breaking stride, buried his fist in the other man's face knocking him on his arse. He relished the crack as he shattered Atbrooke's nose and the warmth of his blood cascading over his fingers as Atbrooke wailed.

"Wessex, by God—"

Marcus hauled him up by his lapels and, for good measure, planted him another facer that sent his head reeling. He jerked the other man to his feet and dragged him to his face. "If I did not give my word to not kill you, Atbrooke," he seethed. Then with a violent bloodlust raging inside, he clasped his hands around the man's throat and strangled off airflow. The man's face turned a splotched red, and shades of blue and purple. God help him, Marcus wanted to kill the man. His breath came hard and fast. He wanted to end this bastard's right to live. He released him suddenly and Atbrooke collapsed to the floor gasping for breath. "I would see you gladly at dawn and end your miserable, worthless life for what you did." He leveled his fist into the man's stomach and a sharp, guttural groan split Atbrooke's cracked and swollen lips. "And I promise you, if you threaten my family again," For that is what Eleanor and Marcia were. "Then I will finish what I started this day." Chest heaving from his exertions, Marcus stared at the man's prone form.

Yet, with the bastard's blood staining his fingers and the piteous moans spilling from his lips, there was no sense of satisfaction. There was no vindication or triumph. For nothing could right the wrongs done eight years earlier.

Atbrooke struggled to push himself onto his arse. "Sh-she wanted it."

Marcus buried the tip of his boot in the man's groin, relishing the high-pitched squeal as Atbrooke writhed and twisted on the floor. He waited until the man quieted and then leaned down, shoving his face into the bruised and battered visage of Eleanor's attacker. "You are not to go near Eleanor Collins or her daughter. If you so much as utter their names, I will make this morning appear a pleasant social call for what I'd do to you."

Atbrooke continued to shudder and gasp, all the while glaring up at Marcus. "I have a right to the lady."

By God, the man was relentless. No wonder Eleanor would rush off with her daughter to be rid of the man's threats. He jammed his heel into Atbrooke's soft belly and the air left him on a hiss. His breath coming fast, Marcus yanked the ivory sheet given him by Rutland and stuck it in Atbrooke's face.

The man's eyes went wide. "What is that?" he rasped.

Pasting a hard, unforgiving smile on his lips, Marcus elucidated. "It is your debt, Atbrooke, transferred from Lord Rutland to myself. I own you and I will see you in Marshalsea." The color leeched from the marquess' flushed cheeks and Marcus relished the tangible sight of his terror; the trembling lips, the chattering teeth. "You will end up in a cell with other worthless bastards like yourself, feeding with the rats, and pleading with your gaolers."

Atbrooke clasped his hands to his throat. "You cannot."

He widened his smile. "I can and I will. Or…." he paused, allowing that word to linger. "Or you can leave. You can take yourself off and get the hell out of England. If you ever return, I will meet you at dawn and I will gladly end you." There were, after all, other ways to ruin a man that went beyond the polite pistols at dawn Eleanor worried over. "Are we clear?" he infused a lethal edge to that whisper and earned a juddering nod.

Tears streamed down the cowardly bastard's cheeks. "But where will I go?"

"I don't give a goddamn where you go." Marcus spat on the marquess' boots and then stuffed the vowels back into his jacket front. "You have until tomorrow morning, and if you are not gone, I will see your debts called in. I will sully your name with the truth of who you are so not a single desperate mama would ever accept you now or ever. Are we clear?"

"A-abundantly," the marquess slurred, his lower lip trembling.

Without a backward glance, Marcus turned and marched out of the room. He strode down the hall, as rage spiraled through him.

"Lord Wessex."

He cursed as Lady Marianne stepped into his path, a saucy grin on her crimson lips. She ran her long fingers down the lapel of his jacket. "I take it you've spoken to my brother."

Marcus stiffened. "I did."

She leaned up on tiptoe and he turned his head so that her kiss grazed his cheek.

A husky laugh bubbled from her lips. "Come, we are permitted certain liberties now that we're betrothed."

He choked. "You misunderstand," he retreated, putting distance between the grasping lady and himself. By two dances more than three weeks ago, she had ascribed more meaning to his intentions...*but then, if Eleanor had not reappeared, I would have pursued more with this lady. I would have found myself a member of this nest of vipers.* Bile stung his throat as he imagined calling Eleanor's rapist, brother-in-law. "I am marrying Mrs. Collins."

That admission wrung a shocked gasp from the young woman. Disbelief flitted across her face and she at last looked to his blood-stained hands. Atbrooke's sister shook her head in a befuddled manner and then quickly yanked her gaze up to his. "Marrying her?" she squawked. "But I thought..." She veiled her lashes and drifted close. "Why would you marry her, when I can bring you so much pleasure?" Lady Marianne layered her palms against his chest. "More than you ever knew possible," she promised, wrapping her tone in a sultry, seductive whisper.

He disentangled her hands from his person. "I am sorry you believed there was more there, my lady, but my heart is otherwise engaged."

All warmth extinguished from her brown eyes. Fury glinted hard in the gold flecks, and the icy glare transformed her into a thing of ugliness. "She is a poor widow with nothing to offer you. Allow me to give you babes of noble birthright, and she can be your bit on the side."

His lips pulled back in a grimace of loathing for this grasping woman who was too much a fool to see that Eleanor, with her courage and strength, was far nobler and of more honor than all the peerage combined. "She can offer me her heart and that is all I require," he said quietly. "If you'll excuse me."

Her cry echoed off the walls. "I made friends with your pathetic sister," she hissed. "I was her friend when no one else gave a jot about her because of you."

He balled his hands. His innocent, friendless sister would know hurt at this woman's treachery. How many members of the Hamilton family had brought pain to those he loved? At last, however, they would be free of their evil. In time, Lizzie would come to know that.

Marcus continued walking, with the lady spewing vitriolic curses in his wake, away from this house of ugliness and toward his future.

CHAPTER 23

KNUCKLES BRUISED, SORE, AND SWOLLEN from the beating he'd dealt the Marquess of Atbrooke, Marcus carefully lifted his hand and rapped on the front door of the Duchess of Devonshire's door. His other hand lay at his side, clasping two branches; meager offerings, but ones he'd no doubt she would prefer above all others. He clasped his hands at his back and waited.

That had always been the manner of woman Eleanor had been. She'd never craved pretty compliments and fancy baubles the way the Marianne Hamiltons of Society had. Rather, she'd been content with the simplistic beauty to be found in the world around them.

Marcus pounded again at the door. And waited. He frowned. And continued waiting. What in blazes? With a quiet curse, he lifted his hand and knocked once more, ignoring the pain that radiated from his bruised knuckles.

Just then, the butler pulled the door open, and for the hell that had been that entire day, a smile split his lips. "My lord," he greeted, dropping his gaze to the ground. He motioned Marcus inside.

Marcus did a sweep of the foyer, seeking out the mischievous little girl so often hiding from her nursemaid. Disappointment filled him at finding Marcia absent. "I am here to see Mrs. Collins," he said while reaching for the fastening of his cloak.

His fingers froze involuntarily at the red color that filled the servant's cheeks. A niggling of unease pitted in Marcus' belly as this moment, merged with a long ago day.

"That will be all, Thomas."

Marcus whipped his gaze up and found the duchess at the top of the stairs. With the aid of her cane, she started slowly down. Her dogs raced ahead and danced excitedly about Marcus' feet. "Your Grace," he offered belatedly, dropping a bow.

She stopped at the bottom of the stairs and waved off the pleasantries. "You are too late, my boy. She is gone."

The ground shifted under his feet and his stomach lurched. "Gone?" The inquiry ripped from him.

Too late.

"Left but an hour ago." The duchess reached into the pocket sewn along the front of her silver satin dress and extracted a note. "She asked I give you this."

Another note.

He stared dazed at that folded sheet; the unerring similarities sucking all logical thought and filling him with a cold emptiness. The branches slipped from his fingers and sailed to the floor. Wordlessly, Marcus took the page. He unfolded it, knowing even as he did what would meet his eyes.

Years ago, upon discovering Eleanor's betrayal, those words hastily written on a page, Marcus had believed that more words from the lady would have wounded less. Staring at them now, with her delicate, slashing strokes filling the page, he now realized—nothing would have ever dulled that pain. In her leaving, the same vicious agony of loss slashed through him.

Marcus crushed the page in his hands. This time, she'd given him a goodbye, but he'd foolishly convinced himself he had more than a handful of hours. Once again, she'd left.

But by God, she didn't get to leave this time without him having a say in their future.

THE DUCHESS OF DEVONSHIRE'S BLACK barouche hit another hole in the old Roman Road and tossed Eleanor against the side of the carriage. The book given her by Aunt Dorothea tumbled to the carriage floor and lay forgotten. Eleanor steadied herself and then flung her arm around Marcia's shoulders. They'd been traveling for more than an hour now and, with each mile passed, put London further and further away. The agony of again leaving him did not go away.

Instead, she sat huddled in the corner of her aunt's barouche hating herself now, just as much as she'd hated herself eight years ago. She hated herself for running, again. She hated that she'd allowed herself to be a victim of the Marquess of Atbrooke's scheming machinations. If it was only herself who'd be affected by Atbrooke's threats, then she'd gladly face the devil at dawn. She'd been shamed in the most horrific ways a woman could be denigrated. And yet, there was, this time, others to consider; beyond even just Marcus. Now there was Marcia.

"I do not understand why we had to leave so quickly," Marcia groused, favoring Eleanor with an accusatory glare.

No, she would not. Not for many long years would she gather the details that had sent them fleeing. And in the absence of any suitable words that would mollify her daughter, she asked, "Don't you miss Cornwall?"

Marcia wiggled out from under her arm and scooted to the opposite bench. "No, I did not miss Cornwall." Her saucer-wide eyes glimmered with anger. The show of anything other than Marcia's usual cheer and joy gutted her. "I loved London and I loved Aunt Dorothea and I loved M-Marcus."

Another piece of her heart broke off. "Oh, love," she soothed, reaching across the carriage, but her daughter slapped her hand away.

"Weren't you happy?" Marcia cried and the tears that welled in her expressive eyes cleaved Eleanor's heart.

"Of course I was happy," she said softly. And she had been. But it had never been about London or the bustling activity of the city or the grand opulence of her aunt's lavish townhouse. It had always been about him. Her throat worked painfully. She'd been happy in ways she'd believed herself incapable. Marcus had once said, after Lionel's murder she had taught him to smile and laugh again. Yet the truth was, he had taught her to smile. He'd reminded her of her own self-worth and, through that, she'd laid some of the demons of her past to rest. "We have to go home, Marcia. It is time."

"Why?" Marcia cried and that desperate entreaty bounced off

the carriage walls.

Eleanor claimed her daughter's hands and gripped them tighter when she fought to tug them back. "I love Aunt Dorothea and I love Marcus," she said, giving Marcia the truth that she deserved.

The anger went out of her little frame. "You do?" she whispered reverently, but then an angry scowl marred her features. "If you love him, then why did we leave? Why can he not be my papa?" Her lower lip quivered. "Did he not want to be my papa?"

Oh, God. Her heart breaking all over again, Eleanor plucked her daughter from the bench and pulled the girl onto her lap. She brushed a flyaway blonde curl behind her ear and struggled to speak past the pain of regret. "Marcus would have liked that very much, poppet." Eleanor hugged her close, selfishly taking the warmth in her daughter's small frame. "And someday, when you are older, I will explain it all in a way that makes sense." Even as it would never be solace or comfort.

Marcia wiggled away and took Eleanor's face between her hands. "Will we return?"

How insistent Marcus had been in thinking they would again meet, but just as Eleanor hadn't deluded herself then, neither would she hold a foolish optimism now. It was as her aunt said; Marcus would wed another and they would each live their lives with a regret for what might have been.

"Mama?" her daughter prodded, tugging at her hand.

"Someday." Never. How many fabricated truths was her daughter's existence based on?

Marcia leaned close and peered into Eleanor's eyes, as though sensing a lie and seeking the truth. The carriage hit another jarring bump in the road and Eleanor tightened her grip on Marcia, hugging her close. "Mama," her daughter grumbled against her chest. "You are squishing me."

Tears welled in Eleanor's eyes at the eerie similarity to her arrival in London almost three weeks ago. "Well," she said, her voice hoarsened with emotion. "It is because you are ever so squishable."

Only this time, there was no giggle. Her daughter jutted her chin at a mutinous angle and glowered all the more. "All we do is hide. We have no friends. We have no f-family. You just keep us locked away from the world. And I like the world, Mama," her daughter spoke with a strident plea. "But you are afraid. Afraid of everything." With each word uttered, she slammed her hand against her opposite palm. "Going to the park, and talking to kind strangers, and having fun, and I hate it." Then, in a show of defiance, she shoved off Eleanor's lap and scooted over to her seat. "I am tired of hiding from the world." Turning her face away, Marcia directed her gaze out at the passing countryside.

Those stinging condemnations buffeted around the carriage and sucked the air from Eleanor's lungs. With her intuitive words, Marcia saw more than Eleanor had in eight long years—perhaps in the whole of her life. She gripped the edge of the bench.

Forced to look at her pitiable existence through a child's eyes, Eleanor saw a woman who was running. She stared blankly at the opposite wall. She'd been running for so long that she'd forgotten what it meant to stay or how to find the courage to even do so. With Atbrooke's threat against Marcia, Eleanor had thought of nothing but escape.

Except, with her mind still ringing from her daughter's accusations and her aunt's disappointed charges, Eleanor truly looked at herself. The person she was and the manner she lived her life served as an example for Marcia.

What meaningful lesson had she really given her daughter in hiding from the world? And worse, what lesson would she teach Marcia if she ran from Atbrooke's threats?

I cannot leave.

The marquess might make good on his threats or he might not. But Eleanor was not alone. There was Marcus, and her aunt, and Marcia. With them at her side, Eleanor could face the threats and hold her head with pride. *That* was the lesson she would give her daughter.

Scrambling onto the edge of her seat, Eleanor shot a hand up and knocked hard on the ceiling.

"Ma—?"

"Woah." The driver's thunderous shout ripped through Marcia's inquiry and Eleanor pitched wildly against the carriage. Her daughter's cry peeled off the walls as the barouche lurched, swayed, and then settled into an abrupt halt.

The forgotten book on the floor slid atop Eleanor's feet. Silence thundered, punctuated by the rapid beat of her heart.

Marcia broke the quiet, giving a tug at Eleanor's hand. "What happened?"

Shifting on the bench, Eleanor claimed her daughter's hands. "We are not leaving," she said firmly.

The girl's eyes formed round moons. "We aren't?" she whispered.

Eleanor shook her head. "We are going back to London." To Marcus and Aunt Dorothea. And whatever danger lurked in London, still, they would face it as a family.

An excited cry split Marcia's lips and Eleanor grunted as her daughter slammed into her side. The book tumbled off her foot and she glanced distractedly down. A scrap of ivory vellum caught her attention. Furrowing her brow, Eleanor retrieved it and unfolded the note. As she skimmed the page, her heart caught.

Oh, God.

"Mama, what is it?" Concern made that question come out hesitantly.

Eleanor managed to shake her head.

"Mama?"

"It is—"

And then thundering hooves registered in the silence. The rumble of the driver's voice split the quiet countryside and penetrated the lacquered carriage.

"Is it highwaymen?" Marcia whispered, as she scrambled over to the window.

"I'm sure it is not, sweet." Fingers shaking, she drew back the curtain and peered out the window—at Marcus. She gasped and the fabric slipped from her fingers. There was nothing else for it. She was seeing him everywhere. Even in the countryside, away from London.

"Who is out there, Mama?" Anxiety wreathed Marcia's face as she curled close against Eleanor's side.

"No one, sweet," she murmured and peeked around the curtain once more. Her heart started. His face shadowed with a day's growth of beard, his clothes rumpled and dusted, and his golden tresses gloriously tumbled, there was not a more magnificent specimen of a man in all the kingdom. She gulped. Even if he *did* wear a ferocious scowl.

Turning the reins of his mount over to the duchess' servant, Marcus strode the remaining distance to the carriage. "I have been looking for you, Eleanor," he called out. Those words echoed through the quiet countryside.

Marcia gasped and scrambled over Eleanor's lap. She yanked the curtains all the way open. "Marcus!" Excitement rang in her tone.

Such unabashed love and happiness lit her daughter's eyes, that tears blinded Eleanor's vision, blurring Marcus as he strode the remaining distance to their stopped carriage. Reaching past the driver, Marcus boldly drew the carriage door open. His muscle-hewn frame shrank the space in the carriage as he leaned inside and looked about. His gaze locked with Eleanor's and the breath stuck in her chest at the heated intensity of his stare. She desperately tried to make out the veiled emotions there. Did he despise her now as much as he had then for leaving? Even as he knew the reasons for her flight? Then he reluctantly moved his attention over to Marcia.

He sketched a bow. "Hullo, Miss—oomph."

Marcia flung herself into his arms and he lurched back under the unexpectedness of that assault. With the ease of any natural father, he closed his arms about the bundle in his arms, and a fluttering danced in her belly as Eleanor fell in love with him all over again. She fell in love with him not with the innocence of a young girl but rather with the heart of a woman who'd known pain and suffering and the power of love in healing.

"Are you here to save us from the highwaymen, Marcus?" Marcia chirped excitedly.

With his elegant white-gloved finger, he tweaked her nose. "Are there highwaymen about?"

She nodded seriously. "There must be." Marcia dropped her voice to a less than conspiratorial whisper. "Mama was so scared."

"There are no highwaymen," Eleanor said softly.

Emotion lit the blues of his eyes and his throat worked. At his protracted silence, Marcia took his face between her hands and squeezed. "Why are you here, Marcus?"

He is here for me… nay, for us… Her daughter's mouth formed a small moue. "You aren't a highwayman, are you?" she breathed, wonder and excitement which would surely one day be the death of Eleanor, sparkled in her expressive eyes.

When at last he spoke, there was a gruffness to his tone. "I am afraid to disappoint you but I am nothing more than a mere, dull viscount." There was nothing mere or dull about him. From the crooked half-grin to his ability to charm and cheer young girls to dowagers, he was a man who commanded notice. He looked over the top of Marcia's gold curls and their gazes caught and held. "I am here because your mama has something that belongs to me and I have something to give to her."

Setting Marcia on her feet outside the carriage, Marcus stared at Eleanor for a long moment. His gaze went to the page in her hands and she swallowed hard, pulling it close. "Wh-what is it?" What game did he play? And to what end?

"Surely you know." Marcus' voice was low and soft, thickened with gentle warmth that fanned her heart. "You left and you took my note from the archbishop."

She blinked several times and then dropped her gaze to the page. Wordlessly, she held it out, and the air left her on a swift exhale as he tugged her out of the carriage and into his arms. Lowering her to the ground so her body slid down his frame, he held her close. "You took my heart, and my happiness, and my very reason for being." Raw emotion roughened his tone and tears sprung to Eleanor's eyes. He reached inside his jacket and pulled out an oddly shaped velvet case. Eleanor watched as he withdrew a gold heart pendant with a filigree setting. "This was given to me," he murmured. "I was told the legend behind this necklace will earn the heart of a duke."

Did he believe she could ever want the heart of anyone but him?

"Are you giving my mama that pretty necklace so she can find a duke?" Marcia piped in.

He dropped to his knee beside her daughter. "Well, you see, there is more to this necklace. It doesn't truly win the wearer a duke's heart, but rather, it brings love to the woman who wears it." Marcus looked meaningfully up at Eleanor.

"Marcus, p-please," she whispered, that aching plea catching with the force of her desire for eternity with him.

"I would tell you a story," he said gruffly, shoving up to his feet. "It is the real reason I've come all this way, you know," he said to Marcia who giggled at the thought. "Once upon a time, there was a king who lost his wife."

"Orfeo!" Marcia exclaimed behind them.

He nodded, looking at Marcia. "This story is much like that one. You see, an evil man found the queen under a cherry tree and took her far, far away from the king who loved her so much. The king searched years and years for her. He never gave up hope that he would one day find her."

A tear trickled down her cheek. "But he hated her while she was gone." For that was the truth he'd not speak on, but that animosity and resentment had been there.

"He hated how empty his life was without her," he corrected. He dusted a hand over his mouth. "He hated that he'd once been happy and that she was gone. He hated himself for not being worthy enough to hold her at his side."

Another tear sailed down her cheek. Followed by another. And another. Is that what he'd believed all these years? He'd seen a flaw in himself as the reason for her departure. How many years had she spent protecting Marcus from the horrors of that night in Lady Wedermore's gardens? Just then, she hated herself for having ever filled a man so wholly honorable and devoted and good, with doubt in himself.

Marcia's perplexed voice slashed across Marcus' telling. "Why is there so much talk about hatred in the story? Isn't it a fairytale about love?"

Yes, because with a child's eyes, mind, and soul, the world was a fairytale where there was no hatred or darkness or sadness. There was only love and eternal happily-ever-afters.

Eleanor tried to force out a reply suitable for a child's ears.

"It is," Marcus supplied for Eleanor. "For you see, this king loved his queen so desperately, he battled all for her. Even the darkest demon who stole her away all those years ago."

A little sob caught in her throat. She shook her head. For it wasn't possible.

"It is possible," he spoke with a quiet insistence and his breath fanned her lips. How harmonious their thoughts had always been. "He slayed the demon of her past."

"How?" she whispered. How when Atbrooke would always be present, in the shadows, lurking in wait to shatter Marcia's existence and, with that, Eleanor's every happiness.

"Yes, how?" Marcia urged, giving another impatient yank of his fabric.

"The man who took the queen was very selfish and greedy. He lost all his money and wealth to the king. The king promised he could live, if he allowed the queen and king to live in happiness."

Her heart tripped a beat and Marcus gave a meaningful nod.

"So he sent him far away?" Marcia's excited question fed those on Eleanor's lips.

Marcus nodded. "He sent him away. But the queen still was sad and scared." Tears misted her vision and blurred his beloved visage at his thinly veiled words spoken of a fictional queen. "She'd been taken away once and feared her happiness would be stolen, again. Do you know what she did, Marcia?" With the backs of his knuckles, Marcus wiped the tears from her cheeks. The task proved futile as those warm, soft drops continued to fall.

"What did she do?" Marcia pleaded.

Marcus stilled that gentle stroke and she mourned the sudden loss of his soothing caress. "I don't know," he said sadly.

No! The silent cry ricocheted around her mind. She needed the end of that story, needed to know how the fate of those two once tragic figures ended, how their lives turned out.

Marcia stamped her foot. "You don't? Surely you *muust*." Disappointment stretched out that last word.

He shook his head regretfully. "I am afraid not. I am afraid only your mama knows the end of this story."

Warmth suffused her heart and the air left her on a slow exhalation. With her daughter staring on, and the driver as their witness shifting awkwardly on his feet, Marcus had put their future into Eleanor's hands. So long, she'd perceived herself as powerless; at the mercy of a cruel man in a cold world. Marcus, however, stood asking her to love, to trust. "What if he returns?" The ragged whisper danced about them.

"Then we will face him together," Marcus pledged softly, drawing first one hand and then the next to his lips.

With the gift and promise he dangled before her, she closed her eyes wanting to grasp it, wanting to hold it close, and face forever with him at her side. "I ordered the carriage stopped," she said at last, opening her eyes and bringing the fairytale back to the now. "I could not leave." If she had, she'd have spent the remainder of her days hating herself for her weakness, hating herself for not believing in Marcus. In believing in them, together.

"I know you did." Marcus palmed her cheek. "Just as I knew you would not leave me again."

"How does the story end, Mama?" her daughter asked with a girlish exasperation.

Forcing her eyes open, Eleanor held Marcus' endless blue gaze teeming with love. "Why, how all fairytales end, love," Eleanor said with a watery smile. "With a happily-ever-after."

Marcus grinned. Lowering his head, he claimed her mouth in a gentle meeting that promised forever.

EPILOGUE

Two nights later
Spring 1818

THE PROBLEM WITH WEDDINGS IS that they ended, as did wedding breakfasts, and when they were all concluded and the house empty of the handful of guests celebrating said wedding, all that remained—was the wedding night.

Eleanor made a show of reading the pages of Mrs. Wollstonecraft's work on her lap. With the fire crackling and snapping in the hearth and Marcus at her side, his head bent over the copy given him of King Orfeo by Marcia earlier that morning before she'd gone off with Aunt Dorothea, they presented quite a bucolic picture.

The words of the page blurred together. Perhaps this was how they'd spend their wedding night. Perhaps there would be no climbing abovestairs and seeking out their chambers, and undressing and—

"Would you care to go abovestairs?"

Eleanor shrieked and the book tumbled to the floor where it landed indignantly upon its spine. "N-now," she croaked. "H-have you finished reading for the night? S-surely you have more pages left about King Orfeo? Or are you not enjoying it?" she asked on a rush when he opened his mouth to speak. "Or perhaps you'd care for another book." She searched about the expansive library, which certainly offered many selections. Filled with a building panic, Eleanor jumped to her feet just as Marcus spoke.

"I would go abovestairs with my wife."

She swallowed at his husky, mellifluous baritone. It ran over her like a warm summer sun. And there was nothing terrifying in that tone. This was Marcus, whose kiss she'd craved and even now… whose kiss made her heartbeat wildly erratic. She closed her eyes. But then, it was never Marcus she'd feared.

He settled his hands on her shoulders and her eyes flew wide. She stiffened and braced for that kiss, praying for the wildly erratic beat and not the long ago memories that once haunted her. He touched his lips to the corner of her temple. The caress was so gentle, so soothing, that the tension drained out of her.

Eleanor leaned against his back. "I am scared," she conceded, taking the strength provided in his arms. And for the fear, there was something freeing in actually giving those words truth. It was her fear and it would always linger at the back of her mind, but she was no longer that scared, silent woman who'd been claimed by the darkness of that night.

"I know, love." He placed another kiss against her temple and then tucked an errant blonde curl behind her ear.

"I-I know it is s-silly," she whispered, as he trailed kisses down her cheek, worshiping her with his questing mouth, and settling his lips at the place where her pulse pounded madly from her need of him and her fear of what that would entail. "I-I am not a virgin," she prattled. She hadn't been a virgin for eight years. "I-I birthed a daughter." And yet her teeth chattered with a virgin-like fear of their inevitable coupling.

Marcus swung her into his arms and pulled her against the protective shelter of his chest. "It is not silly." His chest rumbled and she turned her cheek against the soft fabric of his lawn shirt. She inhaled deep of the purely masculine sandalwood that clung to him, finding a calming peace in the familiar scent that was his and no other's. It was a smell that did not belong to her terror and the nightmare of her past, but entirely to Marcus, and she breathed in the pureness of it, letting it fill her lungs, and blot out remnants of another.

Marcus captured her chin between his thumb and forefinger

and tipped it up. "You are as innocent now as you were eight years ago, Eleanor, and I would be the man to show you how beautiful lovemaking can be."

She caught the inside of her cheek, aching to cling to that offer he made, and tearing from the room in terror for what that might entail.

"Trust me." And the simplicity of his gentle urging drove back the fear.

As though he carried nothing more than a sack of Cook's flour, he made his way from the room and through the quiet, now darkened, corridors. The candle's glow flickered from the satin wallpaper and she swallowed. "Marcus, someone will see."

"The servants have been dismissed for the night."

Her heart thudded with panicked dread as he mounted the stairs. "But—"

"My mother and sister have departed for the country." He dropped his chin atop the crown of her head. They reached the top of the landing and his smooth, even breaths gave no indication of the burden in his arms. "It is only we two tonight, Eleanor."

She closed her eyes and counted her deliberately drawn breaths. That truth should calm her and yet… He stopped outside a closed door. Her palms dampened as she forced her eyes open. The door stared threateningly back at her. It was just a door. A wood panel, really. She shook. Yet, it was what stood on the other side of that panel that sent fear dancing in her belly. Eleanor shook her head. "I am bound to disappoint you, Marcus," she said on a rush. "You have been with so many women and they were experienced," and not afraid, "and brought you pleasure and I hate it, and—"

Marcus touched his fingertips to his lips, gently silencing her terrified ramblings. "This night belongs to you, Eleanor Gray."

Eleanor Gray.

Her heart skipped a beat. After years of taking a fictitious name and assuming it as her own, Marcus had conferred an honorable name, given in love.

He brushed his thumb over her lips now turned up in a smile. "That is better, love," he said. Reaching past her, he pressed the handle and stepped inside.

Eleanor's breath hitched as he closed the door behind them. The inviting fire glowing within the hearth cast a soft light upon the room. A pink rose-petal path stretched out the length of the room, leading to a wide, four-poster bed sprinkled with those gentle blooms. "Oh, Marcus," she whispered, palming his cheek.

Wordlessly, he carried her across the room and then, as though he handled a gift of the Queen's china, he lowered her upon the downy soft mattress. She pushed up on her elbows as he shrugged out of his jacket and tossed the elegant black garment. It sailed to the floor in a silent heap. She wetted her lips, her heart pounding in a frantic beat.

Except, this moment was not born of fear of the past or what was to come, but rather a breathless anticipation for what was now before her. Marcus lay beside her, propping himself on his elbow and slowly touched his lips to hers.

Eleanor's lids fluttered closed and she turned herself over to the slow growing warmth spiraling in her belly and spreading out. Then, as fleeting as a butterfly's caress, he broke that tender contact. He moved to the edge of the bed and knelt at her feet. "What...?"

Her heart caught as he delicately drew off first one slipper and then the next. He set them down beside each other at the side of the bed and then drew her foot to his mouth. Bowing his head over it, he placed a kiss upon the top and worked those gentle caresses up to the point where her ankle met her leg. He worshiped the deliciously sensitive skin at the inner portion of her foot until a breathy little moan escaped her.

For the ways she'd been violated, she'd not truly been touched, not in the questing way Marcus unfurled the now mythical secrets of her body, and not in the heat building like a slow conflagration within. Like unwrapping a carefully wrapped gift, Marcus drew her stockings down and laid them on the floor beside him. With the night air cool on her flushed skin, Marcus massaged the muscles of her calf until her eyes slid closed of their own volition at the luxuriousness of that tender touch.

She shot them open once more as he continued to move those questing kisses along the lower portion of her leg. His breath tickled and caressed her skin, and sent shivers of anticipation racing at the point of contact. Eleanor bit the inside of her lip and turned herself over to sensation. "Wh-who would have i-imagined that a l-leg could elicit s-such a response?" she gasped.

A golden curl tumbled over his brow and he paused in his ministrations to favor her with a half-grin that sent her heart skittering.

"W-well, I-I suppose it is not my leg eliciting the response, but rather your l-lips." Heat rushed to her cheeks. *Stop rambling, Eleanor Elaine. Stop rambling.* Then, "I-I suspect the ladies you usually take to your bed d-don't ramble in this manner." Which only conjured unwanted, insidious images of Marcus with another woman; beautiful and eager in the ways he'd hope, taking him in her arms. And Eleanor hated all those faceless, nameless creatures who'd earned him the reputation as rogue.

The floorboards shifted as Marcus stood. Eleanor lay on her back, staring up at the ceiling overhead, not taking her gaze from the pale blue plaster as Marcus came down beside her. They lay with their shoulders touching, staring up at that same blue paint.

"I love you." The deep rumble of his gentle baritone went through her. The bed dipped, as he levered himself onto his side. He stroked a hand over her cheek and she leaned into that soft caress. "I've only ever loved you," he continued with an earnestness that sent another round of butterflies dancing in her belly. He brought his lips to hers and she turned her mouth up to receive his kiss, when he froze. Their breaths danced and melded.

She looked questioningly at him.

"I will never hurt you, Eleanor. If you want me to stop, whenever that moment may be, you need just say the word. That control belongs to you and I would never violate that gift." He touched his nose to hers. "Do you understand what I am saying?"

Love suffused her heart, lifting the organ that had always belonged to him. He would not consummate the marriage unless she ordained that act. Rather, he would wait until she was ready to trust herself to him with this sacred gift. "Oh, Marcus," she whispered and kissed him.

His body jerked and then he met her mouth in a tender exploration. As he slid his tongue inside, there was no pain or ugliness, but all the glorious desire she'd always known with him. Heat pooled in her belly and spread lower, and an incessant ache built between her legs.

He drew back and she silently cried out at the loss of him but he only moved his mouth, tormenting and tantalizing so that her breath came hard and fast. He worked a path of teasing kisses from her neck, lower, and ever lower to the neckline of her gown.

Unhesitant, he placed his lips there and worshiped the skin so the fire grew within, spreading like a fast-building conflagration.

Eyes closed, Eleanor turned herself over to feeling. She breathed in the heady masculine scent that clung to his skin, fixed on his broad, powerful hands as he guided her upright, and then mourned the loss of his questing mouth.

"I want to feel the satiny softness of your skin, to worship you as you should be worshiped," he said, his whisper a promise.

Tension flickered to life, as he unfastened the pearl row of buttons that ran the back length of her gown. But he placed his hands upon her shoulders and caressed her neck with his lips and desire tamped out all fleeting doubt and fear. Shoving the sleeves of her pink dress down, he slid it past her hips, and Eleanor kicked it aside, exposed, as she'd never been, naked to his gaze.

He studied her through hooded lids and she shifted under the scrutiny. The veiled expression gave no indication of his thoughts and then he spoke in tortured tones. "You are so beautiful, Eleanor. I have longed to know you in this way, in every way, since the moment I saw you smiling on the sidewalk."

Marcus drew her into his arms and she melted into the hard wall of his chest. Her nipples pebbled against the front of his lawn shirt; the over-sensitized flesh stirred that burning ache between her legs. He cupped her breast in his large, naked hand and she drew in a shuddery breath.

Even in their youth, she'd never known the joy of his hand on her naked person. There was something wicked and wonderful and endlessly beautiful in the intimacy of his touch.

Marcus stilled and peered questioningly at her. He made to withdraw, but Eleanor placed her hand over his and held him close. Their chests moved fast to a matched harmonious beat. Then he leaned down and brushed a faint kiss over the erect nipple and Eleanor drew in a shuddery breath through her teeth.

"M-Marcus..." And lest he do something maddening and foolish like stop, she wound her fingers in the luxuriant, unfashionably long, golden tresses and held him in place, wanting him to continue, needing him to go on forever. And then God help her, he did. He drew the sensitive, swollen tip into his mouth and sucked. Desire mobbed her senses. She undulated against him, desperate to appease the agonizing ache between her thighs. And because Marcus had always known everything there was to know about her, he palmed the soft thatch of curls shielding her womanhood. A long, whimpering moan slipped from her lips, endless, as he delved a finger gently inside, teasing, and caressing so that her whole body was attuned to nothing more than the incessant ache that only Marcus could satisfy. "Marcus, I want…"

Except, she didn't know what she wanted. For years, she'd believed lovemaking an act of shame and pain, and yet there was only beauty and wonder in Marcus' touch. In the way he drew her erect nipple between his teeth and tortured that bud, all the while he slid another finger inside. Eleanor's hips shot off the bed and she cried out.

"That is it, love," desire hoarsened his voice and there was something heady in rousing that hunger in him.

Emboldened, she began working his shirt up his body.

He groaned and stayed her movements. "Eleanor, what are you doing?"

"It is only fair that I see your body and know you, too," she whispered, her body flush with desire and her own boldness.

He dropped his neck back and his lips moved silently as though in prayer. In one fluid movement he pulled the garment over his head and threw it to the floor. He shucked off his boots with an ease any valet would have been hard-pressed not to admire. Then his hands went to his breeches and he froze.

Her mouth went dry, as she battled an inner war where desire warred with the logic of a remembered horror. If she gave this moment over to Atbrooke, she would lose. She would lose something that was beautiful and joyous and something she only should have ever known in Marcus' arms. Eleanor gave a slight nod.

Unhurriedly, Marcus loosened the fastenings on his breeches, his movements exaggerated and deliberate, and his meaning clear. He was allowing her to stop him. But she did not want him to stop. She wanted to know all of him.

Eleanor gasped as he shoved his breeches down, revealing the thick shaft jutting out tall and bold from a sprig of golden curls. She closed her eyes and flopped back on the bed, staring at that pale blue ceiling once more. She could not do this. No wonder there was pain. It was a physical impossibility. The sheer size of him and the shape of her…Eleanor shook her head. No. No. No.

It could never work. She stiffened as Marcus lay on his side. He draped an arm over her middle and held her close. Eleanor pressed her eyes shut and absorbed his warmth and strength. "It won't work, you know," she said, opening her eyes. "You are too big and I am…" She waved her hand. "Different than you."

The ghost of a smile hovered on his lips and he grazed his lips across her temple.

"W-well, of course we have to be different in that way for it to work." Nervousness made the words tumble out, rolling together. "But it is still not pleasant…and…"

He kissed her and the fear receded. "It will be pleasant," he breathed against her lips.

"D-do you promise?"

Marcus raised her breast with the reverence of a commoner carrying the king's crown and drew the nipple into his mouth. He laved and worshiped that bud until desire settled heavy between her legs. Eleanor lifted her hips desperate for more, but seeking, searching, and then Marcus provided.

He delved his finger into her wet warmth, working the slick folds until all conscious thought receded. She pressed herself against his hand. Her rapid breathing matched the franticness of her undulating body, and yet there was no shame in her body's honest response to his touch. Marcus increased his strokes, moving his fingers in and out on a maddening glide that robbed her of breath. With a panting moan, she wrapped her arms around him and clung tight. It was as though he was lifting her up, higher and higher, and she wanted to continue that climb until she reached the pinnacle of whatever magic he now wove.

He positioned himself over her body, lying between her legs, and she froze as the remembered terror of another—

"Look at me," Marcus urged with a gentle insistence that carried her gaze to his. "It is me," he whispered, stroking her cheek. "It is me and you, as it was always meant to be and as it has always truly been." He dropped a kiss upon her lips and she savored the sweet warmth, meeting his tongue in that gentle union that blotted out all fear.

Eleanor splayed her legs, taking him between her thighs and he positioned himself at the juncture of her womanhood. She braced for his swift entry, but he reached between them and again found her slick center with his searching fingers. A moan stuck in her throat as he continued his earlier torture until she was shoving against his hand, pleading for more.

He drew back his torturous fingers and slipped inside her and Eleanor's head fell back at the beauty and perfectness of him filling her.

She reached up and caressed his tautly drawn cheeks. Perspiration beaded his brow and dampened his hair. She brushed the too-long tendrils behind his ear. Their gazes held. "I love you," she whispered.

"And I love you," he said, his words roughened by desire, then with an agonized groan, Marcus slid deep as though their bodies had been destined for unity and then he began to move. He rocked his hips slowly and she lifted her hips tentatively matching his rhythm.

And with each thrust, he drew her higher and higher up that great climb, to the edge of a precipice and then she stiffened as her body hurtled over the edge and she cried out, exploding into a prism of white light and ecstasy. She dimly registered Marcus' echoing shout, as with his thrust he touched her very core, and then poured his seed deep inside. He touched her in a way that there was no pain or remembrance of the past, there was just them, as it was always meant to be.

Marcus collapsed above her, capturing his weight on his elbows. He rolled to the side and drew her close. The movement sent rose petals fluttering and dancing about them. Eleanor curled against him, wrapping herself in his warmth. A shy smile turned her lips up. "You kept your promise, Marcus Gray." He'd shown her with his every touch, his body's every movement, that lovemaking was a thing of wonder and beauty. He'd awakened her to the truth that nothing had been stolen from her. She was still worthy and capable of desire and feeling.

Marcus studied her through heavy, lazy lids. "And will you make me a promise, love?" He stroked his hand down the small of her back.

A delicious shiver traveled from where his breath tickled her neck. "Oh, and what is that?" she asked, angling to better meet his gaze.

"Promise me forever."

Eleanor leaned up and received his kiss. "Forever," she whispered.

THE END

OTHER BOOKS BY CHRISTI CALDWELL

TO ENCHANT A WICKED DUKE
Book 13 in the "Heart of a Duke" Series by Christi Caldwell

A Devil in Disguise

Years ago, when Nick Tallings, the recent Duke of Huntly, watched his family destroyed at the hands of a merciless nobleman, he vowed revenge. But his efforts had been futile, as his enemy, Lord Rutland is without weakness.

Until now…

With his rival finally happily married, Nick is able to set his ruthless scheme into motion. His plot hinges upon Lord Rutland's innocent, empty-headed sister-in-law, Justina Barrett. Nick will ruin her, marry her, and then leave her brokenhearted.

A Lady Dreaming of Love

From the moment Justina Barrett makes her Come Out, she is labeled a Diamond. Even with her ruthless father determined to sell her off to the highest bidder, Justina never gives up on her hope for a good, honorable gentleman who values her wit more than her looks.

A Not-So-Chance Meeting

Nick's ploy to ensnare Justina falls neatly into place in the streets of London. With each carefully orchestrated encounter, he slips further and further inside the lady's heart, never anticipating that Justina, with her quick wit and strength, will break down his own defenses. As Nick's plans begins to unravel, he's left to determine which is more important—Justina's love or his vow for vengeance. But can Justina ever forgive the duke who deceived her?

ONE WINTER WITH A BARON
Book 12 in the "Heart of a Duke" Series by Christi Caldwell

A clever spinster:
Content with her spinster lifestyle, Miss Sybil Cunning wants to prove that a future as an unmarried woman is the only life for her. As a bluestocking who values hard, empirical data, Sybil needs help with her research. Nolan Pratt, Baron Webb, one of society's most scandalous rakes, is the perfect gentleman to help her. After all, he inspires fear in proper mothers and desire within their daughters.
A notorious rake:
Society may be aware of Nolan Pratt, Baron's Webb's wicked ways, but what he has carefully hidden is his miserable handling of his family's finances. When Sybil presents him the opportunity to earn much-needed funds, he can't refuse.
A winter to remember:
However, what begins as a business arrangement becomes something more and with every meeting, Sybil slips inside his heart. Can this clever woman look beneath the veneer of a coldhearted rake to see the man Nolan truly is?

TO REDEEM A RAKE
Book 11 in the "Heart of a Duke" Series by Christi Caldwell

He's spent years scandalizing society.
Now, this rake must change his ways.

Society's most infamous scoundrel, Daniel Winterbourne, the Earl of Montfort, has been promised a small fortune if he can relinquish his wayward, carousing lifestyle. And behaving means he must also help find a respectable companion for his youngest sister—someone who will guide her and whom she can emulate. However, Daniel knows no such woman. But when he encounters a childhood friend, Daniel believes she may just be the answer to all of his problems.

Having been secretly humiliated by an unscrupulous blackguard years earlier, Miss Daphne Smith dreams of finding work at Ladies of Hope, an institution that provides an education for disabled women. With her sordid past and a disfigured leg, few opportunities arise for a woman such as she. Knowing Daniel's history, she wishes to avoid him, but working for his sister is exactly the stepping stone she needs.

Their attraction intensifies as Daniel and Daphne grow closer, preparing his sister for the London Season. But Daniel must resist his desire for a woman tarnished by scandal while Daphne is reminded of the boy she once knew. Can society's most notorious rake redeem his reputation and become the man Daphne deserves?

TO WOO A WIDOW

Book 10 in the "Heart of a Duke" Series by Christi Caldwell

They see a brokenhearted widow.
She's far from shattered.

Lady Philippa Winston is never marrying again. After her late husband's cruelty that she kept so well hidden, she has no desire to search for love.

Years ago, Miles Brookfield, the Marquess of Guilford, made a frivolous vow he never thought would come to fruition—he promised to marry his mother's goddaughter if he was unwed by the age of thirty. Now, to his dismay, he's faced with honoring that pledge. But when he encounters the beautiful and intriguing Lady Philippa, Miles knows his true path in life. It's up to him to break down every belief Philippa carries about gentlemen, proving that not only is love real, but that he is the man deserving of her sheltered heart.

Will Philippa let down her guard and allow Miles to woo a widow in desperate need of his love?

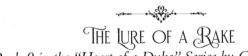

THE LURE OF A RAKE
Book 9 in the "Heart of a Duke" Series by Christi Caldwell

A Lady Dreaming of Love

Lady Genevieve Farendale has a scandalous past. Jilted at the altar years earlier and exiled by her family, she's now returned to London to prove she can be a proper lady. Even though she's not given up on the hope of marrying for love, she's wary of trusting again. Then she meets Cedric Falcot, the Marquess of St. Albans whose seductive ways set her heart aflutter. But with her sordid history, Genevieve knows a rake can also easily destroy her.

An Unlikely Pairing

What begins as a chance encounter between Cedric and Genevieve becomes something more. As they continue to meet, passions stir. But with Genevieve's hope for true love, she fears Cedric will be unable to give up his wayward lifestyle. After all, Cedric has spent years protecting his heart, and keeping everyone out. Slowly, she chips away at all the walls he's built, but when he falters, Genevieve can't offer him redemption. Now, it's up to Cedric to prove to Genevieve that the love of a man is far more powerful than the lure of a rake.

TO TRUST A ROGUE
Book 8 in the "Heart of a Duke" Series by Christi Caldwell

A rogue

Marcus, the Viscount Wessex has carefully crafted the image of rogue and charmer for Polite Society. Under that façade, however, dwells a man whose dreams were shattered almost eight years earlier by a young lady who captured his heart, pledged her love, and then left him, with nothing more than a curt note.

A widow

Eight years earlier, faced with no other choice, Mrs. Eleanor Collins, fled London and the only man she ever loved, Marcus, Viscount Wessex. She has now returned to serve as a companion for her elderly aunt with a daughter in tow. Even though they're next door neighbors, there is little reason for her to move in the same circles as Marcus, just in case, she vows to avoid him, for he reminds her of all she lost when she left.

Reunited

As their paths continue to cross, Marcus finds his desire for Eleanor just as strong, but he learned long ago she's not to be trusted. He will offer her a place in his bed, but not anything more. Only, Eleanor has no interest in this new, roguish man. The more time they spend together, the protective wall they've constructed to keep the other out, begin to break. With all the betrayals and secrets between them, Marcus has to open his heart again. And Eleanor must decide if it's ever safe to trust a rogue.

TO WED HIS CHRISTMAS LADY
Book 7 in the "Heart of a Duke" Series by Christi Caldwell

She's longing to be loved:

Lady Cara Falcot has only served one purpose to her loathsome father—to increase his power through a marriage to the future Duke of Billingsley. As such, she's built protective walls about her heart, and presents an icy facade to the world around her. Journeying home from her finishing school for the Christmas holidays, Cara's carriage is stranded during a winter storm. She's forced to tarry at a ramshackle inn, where she immediately antagonizes another patron—William.

He's avoiding his duty in favor of one last adventure:

William Hargrove, the Marquess of Grafton has wanted only one thing in life—to avoid the future match his parents would have him make to a cold, duke's daughter. He's returning home from a blissful eight years of traveling the world to see to his responsibilities. But when a winter storm interrupts his trip and lands him at a falling-down inn, he's forced to share company with a commanding Lady Cara who initially reminds him exactly of the woman he so desperately wants to avoid.

A Christmas snowstorm ushers in the spirit of the season:

At the holiday time, these two people who despise each other due to first perceptions are offered renewed beginnings and fresh starts. As this gruff stranger breaks down the walls she's built about herself, Cara has to determine whether she can truly open her heart to trusting that any man is capable of good and that she herself is capable of love. And William has to set aside all previous thoughts he's carried of the polished ladies like Cara, to be the man to show her that love.

THE HEART OF A SCOUNDREL
Book 6 in the "Heart of a Duke" Series by Christi Caldwell

Ruthless, wicked, and dark, the Marquess of Rutland rouses terror in the breast of ladies and nobleman alike. All Edmund wants in life is power. After he was publically humiliated by his one love Lady Margaret, he vowed vengeance, using Margaret's niece, as his pawn. Except, he's thwarted by another, more enticing target—Miss Phoebe Barrett.

Miss Phoebe Barrett knows precisely the shame she's been born to. Because her father is a shocking letch she's learned to form her own opinions on a person's worth. After a chance meeting with the Marquess of Rutland, she is captivated by the mysterious man. He, too, is a victim of society's scorn, but the more encounters she has with Edmund, the more she knows there is powerful depth and emotion to the jaded marquess.

The lady wreaks havoc on Edmund's plans for revenge and he finds he wants Phoebe, at all costs. As she's drawn into the darkness of his world, Phoebe risks being destroyed by Edmund's ruthlessness. And Phoebe who desires love at all costs, has to determine if she can ever truly trust the heart of a scoundrel.

TO LOVE A LORD
Book 5 in the "Heart of a Duke" Series by Christi Caldwell

All she wants is security:

The last place finishing school instructor Mrs. Jane Munroe belongs, is in polite Society. Vowing to never wed, she's been scuttled around from post to post. Now she finds herself in the Marquess of Waverly's household. She's never met a nobleman she liked, and when she meets the pompous, arrogant marquess, she remembers why. But soon, she discovers Gabriel is unlike any gentleman she's ever known.

All he wants is a companion for his sister:

What Gabriel finds himself with instead, is a fiery spirited, bespectacled woman who entices him at every corner and challenges his age-old vow to never trust his heart to a woman. But… there is something suspicious about his sister's companion. And he is determined to find out just what it is.

All they need is each other:

As Gabriel and Jane confront the truth of their feelings, the lies and secrets between them begin to unravel. And Jane is left to decide whether or not it is ever truly safe to love a lord.

LOVED BY A DUKE
Book 4 in the "Heart of a Duke" Series by Christi Caldwell

For ten years, Lady Daisy Meadows has been in love with Auric, the Duke of Crawford. Ever since his gallant rescue years earlier, Daisy knew she was destined to be his Duchess. Unfortunately, Auric sees her as his best friend's sister and nothing more. But perhaps, if she can manage to find the fabled heart of a duke pendant, she will win over the heart of her duke.

Auric, the Duke of Crawford enjoys Daisy's company. The last thing he is interested in however, is pursuing a romance with a woman he's known since she was in leading strings. This season, Daisy is turning up in the oddest places and he cannot help but notice that she is no longer a girl. But Auric wouldn't do something as foolhardy as to fall in love with Daisy. He couldn't. Not with the guilt he carries over his past sins... Not when he has no right to her heart...But perhaps, just perhaps, she can forgive the past and trust that he'd forever cherish her heart—but will she let him?

THE LOVE OF A ROGUE
Book 3 in the "Heart of a Duke" Series by Christi Caldwell

Lady Imogen Moore hasn't had an easy time of it since she made her Come Out. With her betrothed, a powerful duke breaking it off to wed her sister, she's become the *tons* favorite piece of gossip. Never again wanting to experience the pain of a broken heart, she's resolved to make a match with a polite, respectable gentleman. The last thing she wants is another reckless rogue.

Lord Alex Edgerton has a problem. His brother, tired of Alex's carousing has charged him with chaperoning their remaining, unwed sister about *ton* events. Shopping? No, thank you. Attending the theatre? He'd rather be at Forbidden Pleasures with a scantily clad beauty upon his lap. The task of *chaperone* becomes even more of a bother when his sister drags along her dearest friend, Lady Imogen to social functions. The last thing he wants in his life is a young, innocent English miss.

Except, as Alex and Imogen are thrown together, passions flare and Alex comes to find he not only wants Imogen in his bed, but also in his heart. Yet now he must convince Imogen to risk all, on the heart of a rogue.

More Than a Duke
Book 2 in the "Heart of a Duke" Series by Christi Caldwell

Polite Society doesn't take Lady Anne Adamson seriously. However, Anne isn't just another pretty young miss. When she discovers her father betrayed her mother's love and her family descended into poverty, Anne comes up with a plan to marry a respectable, powerful, and honorable gentleman—a man nothing like her philandering father.

Armed with the heart of a duke pendant, fabled to land the wearer a duke's heart, she decides to enlist the aid of the notorious Harry, 6th Earl of Stanhope. A scoundrel with a scandalous past, he is the last gentleman she'd ever wed…however, his reputation marks him the perfect man to school her in the art of seduction so she might ensnare the illustrious Duke of Crawford.

Harry, the Earl of Stanhope is a jaded, cynical rogue who lives for his own pleasures. Having been thrown over by the only woman he ever loved so she could wed a duke, he's not at all surprised when Lady Anne approaches him with her scheme to capture another duke's affection. He's come to appreciate that all women are in fact greedy, title-grasping, self-indulgent creatures. And with Anne's history of grating on his every last nerve, she is the last woman he'd ever agree to school in the art of seduction. Only his friendship with the lady's sister compels him to help.

What begins as a pretend courtship, born of lessons on seduction, becomes something more leaving Anne to decide if she can give her heart to a reckless rogue, and Harry must decide if he's willing to again trust in a lady's love.

FOR LOVE OF THE DUKE
First Full-Length Book in the "Heart of a Duke" Series
by Christi Caldwell

After the tragic death of his wife, Jasper, the 8th Duke of Bainbridge buried himself away in the dark cold walls of his home, Castle Blackwood. When he's coaxed out of his self-imposed exile to attend the amusements of the Frost Fair, his life is irrevocably changed by his fateful meeting with Lady Katherine Adamson.

With her tight brown ringlets and silly white-ruffled gowns, Lady Katherine Adamson has found her dance card empty for two Seasons. After her father's passing, Katherine learned the unreliability of men, and is determined to depend on no one, except herself. Until she meets Jasper…

In a desperate bid to avoid a match arranged by her family, Katherine makes the Duke of Bainbridge a shocking proposition—one that he accepts.

Only, as Katherine begins to love Jasper, she finds the arrangement agreed upon is not enough. And Jasper is left to decide if protecting his heart is more important than fighting for Katherine's love.

IN NEED OF A DUKE
A Prequel Novella to "The Heart of a Duke" Series
by Christi Caldwell

In Need of a Duke: (Author's Note: This is a prequel novella to "The Heart of a Duke" series by Christi Caldwell. It was originally available in "The Heart of a Duke" Collection and is now being published as an individual novella.

~★~

It features a new prologue and epilogue.

Years earlier, a gypsy woman passed to Lady Aldora Adamson and her friends a heart pendant that promised them each the heart of a duke.

Now, a young lady, with her family facing ruin and scandal, Lady Aldora doesn't have time for mythical stories about cheap baubles. She needs to save her sisters and brother by marrying a titled gentleman with wealth and power to his name. She sets her bespectacled sights upon the Marquess of St. James.

Turned out by his father after a tragic scandal, Lord Michael Knightly has grown into a powerful, but self-made man. With the whispers and stares that still follow him, he would rather be anywhere but London…

Until he meets Lady Aldora, a young woman who mistakes him for his brother, the Marquess of St. James. The connection between Aldora and Michael is immediate and as they come to know one another, Aldora's feelings for Michael war with her sisterly responsibilities. With her family's dire situation, a man of Michael's scandalous past will never do.

Ultimately, Aldora must choose between her responsibilities as a sister and her love for Michael.

ONCE A WALLFLOWER, AT LAST HIS LOVE
Book 6 in the Scandalous Seasons Series

Responsible, practical Miss Hermione Rogers, has been crafting stories as the notorious Mr. Michael Michaelmas and selling them for a meager wage to support her siblings. The only real way to ensure her family's ruinous debts are paid, however, is to marry. Tall, thin, and plain, she has no expectation of success. In London for her first Season she seizes the chance to write the tale of a brooding duke. In her research, she finds Sebastian Fitzhugh, the 5th Duke of Mallen, who unfortunately is perfectly affable, charming, and so nicely… configured… he takes her breath away. He lacks all the character traits she needs for her story, but alas, any duke will have to do.

Sebastian Fitzhugh, the 5th Duke of Mallen has been deceived so many times during the high-stakes game of courtship, he's lost faith in Society women. Yet, after a chance encounter with Hermione, he finds himself intrigued. Not a woman he'd normally consider beautiful, the young lady's practical bent, her forthright nature and her tendency to turn up in the oddest places has his interests… roused. He'd like to trust her, he'd like to do a whole lot more with her too, but should he?

A MARQUESS FOR CHRISTMAS
Book 5 in the Scandalous Seasons Series

Lady Patrina Tidemore gave up on the ridiculous notion of true love after having her heart shattered and her trust destroyed by a black-hearted cad. Used as a pawn in a game of revenge against her brother, Patrina returns to London from a failed elopement with a tattered reputation and little hope for a respectable match. The only peace she finds is in her solitude on the cold winter days at Hyde Park. And even that is yanked from her by two little hellions who just happen to have a devastatingly handsome, but coldly aloof father, the Marquess of Beaufort. Something about the lord stirs the dreams she'd once carried for an honorable gentleman's love.

Weston Aldridge, the 4th Marquess of Beaufort was deceived and betrayed by his late wife. In her faithlessness, he's come to view women as self-serving, indulgent creatures. Except, after a series of chance encounters with Patrina, he comes to appreciate how uniquely different she is than all women he's ever known.

At the Christmastide season, a time of hope and new beginnings, Patrina and Weston, unexpectedly learn true love in one another. However, as Patrina's scandalous past threatens their future and the happiness of his children, they are both left to determine if love is enough.

ALWAYS A ROGUE, FOREVER HER LOVE
Book 4 in the Scandalous Seasons Series

Miss Juliet Marshville is spitting mad. With one guardian missing, and the other singularly uninterested in her fate, she is at the mercy of her wastrel brother who loses her beloved childhood home to a man known as Sin. Determined to reclaim control of Rosecliff Cottage and her own fate, Juliet arranges a meeting with the notorious rogue and demands the return of her property.

Jonathan Tidemore, 5th Earl of Sinclair, known to the *ton* as Sin, is exceptionally lucky in life and at the gaming tables. He has just one problem. Well…four, really. His incorrigible sisters have driven off yet another governess. This time, however, his mother demands he find an appropriate replacement.

When Miss Juliet Marshville boldly demands the return of her precious cottage, he takes advantage of his sudden good fortune and puts an offer to her; turn his sisters into proper English ladies, and he'll return Rosecliff Cottage to Juliet's possession.

Jonathan comes to appreciate Juliet's spirit, courage, and clever wit, and decides to claim the fiery beauty as his mistress. Juliet, however, will be mistress for no man. Nor could she ever love a man who callously stole her home in a game of cards. As Jonathan begins to see Juliet as more than a spirited beauty to warm his bed, he realizes she could be a lady he could love the rest of his life, if only he can convince the proud Juliet that he's worthy of her hand and heart.

ALWAYS PROPER, SUDDENLY SCANDALOUS
Book 3 in the Scandalous Seasons Series

Geoffrey Winters, Viscount Redbrooke was not always the hard, unrelenting lord driven by propriety. After a tragic mistake, he resolved to honor his responsibility to the Redbrooke line and live a life, free of scandal. Knowing his duty is to wed a proper, respectable English miss, he selects Lady Beatrice Dennington, daughter of the Duke of Somerset, the perfect woman for him. Until he meets Miss Abigail Stone...

To distance herself from a personal scandal, Abigail Stone flees America to visit her uncle, the Duke of Somerset. Determined to never trust a man again, she is helplessly intrigued by the hard, too-proper Geoffrey. With his strict appreciation for decorum and order, he is nothing like the man' she's always dreamed of.

Abigail is everything Geoffrey does not need. She upends his carefully ordered world at every encounter. As they begin to care for one another, Abigail carefully guards the secret that resulted in her journey to England.

Only, if Geoffrey learns the truth about Abigail, he must decide which he holds most dear: his place in Society or Abigail's place in his heart.

Never Courted, Suddenly Wed
Book 2 in the Scandalous Seasons Series

Christopher Ansley, Earl of Waxham, has constructed a perfect image for the *ton*—the ladies love him and his company is desired by all. Only two people know the truth about Waxham's secret. Unfortunately, one of them is Miss Sophie Winters.

Sophie Winters has known Christopher since she was in leading strings. As children, they delighted in tormenting each other. Now at two and twenty, she still has a tendency to find herself in scrapes, and her marital prospects are slim.

When his father threatens to expose his shame to the *ton*, unless he weds Sophie for her dowry, Christopher concocts a plan to remain a bachelor. What he didn't plan on was falling in love with the lively, impetuous Sophie. As secrets are exposed, will Christopher's love be enough when she discovers his role in his father's scheme?

Forever Betrothed, Never the Bride
Book 1 in the Scandalous Seasons Series

Hopeless romantic Lady Emmaline Fitzhugh is tired of sitting with the wallflowers, waiting for her betrothed to come to his senses and marry her. When Emmaline reads one too many reports of his scandalous liaisons in the gossip rags, she takes matters into her own hands.

War-torn veteran Lord Drake devotes himself to forgetting his days on the Peninsula through an endless round of meaningless associations. He no longer wants to feel anything, but Lady Emmaline is making it hard to maintain a state of numbness. With her zest for life, she awakens his passion and desire for love.

The one woman Drake has spent the better part of his life avoiding is now the only woman he needs, but he is no longer a man worthy of his Emmaline. It is up to her to show him the healing power of love.

A Season of Hope
A Danby Novella

Five years ago when her love, Marcus Wheatley, failed to return from fighting Napoleon's forces, Lady Olivia Foster buried her heart. Unable to betray Marcus's memory, Olivia has gone out of her way to run off prospective suitors. At three and twenty she considers herself firmly on the shelf. Her father, however, disagrees and accepts an offer for Olivia's hand in marriage. Yet it's Christmas, when anything can happen…

Olivia receives a well-timed summons from her grandfather, the Duke of Danby, and eagerly embraces the reprieve from her betrothal.

Only, when Olivia arrives at Danby Castle she realizes the Christmas season represents hope, second chances, and even miracles.

"Winning a Lady's Heart"
A Danby Novella

Author's Note: This is a novella that was originally available in A Summons From The Castle (The Regency Christmas Summons Collection). It is being published as an individual novella.

~★~

For Lady Alexandra, being the source of a cold, calculated wager is bad enough…but when it is waged by Nathaniel Michael Winters, 5th Earl of Pembroke, the man she's in love with, it results in a broken heart, the scandal of the season, and a summons from her grandfather – the Duke of Danby.

To escape Society's gossip, she hurries to her meeting with the duke, determined to put memories of the earl far behind. Except the duke has other plans for Alexandra…plans which include the 5th Earl of Pembroke!

Tempted by a Lady's Smile
Book 4 in the "Lords of Honor" Series

Richard Jonas has loved but one woman—a woman who belongs to his brother. Refusing to suffer any longer, he evades his family in order to barricade his heart from unrequited love. While attending a friend's summer party, Richard's approach to love is changed after sharing a passionate and life-altering kiss with a vibrant and mysterious woman. Believing he was incapable of loving again, Richard finds himself tempted by a young lady determined to marry his best friend.

Gemma Reed has not been treated kindly by the *ton*. Often disregarded for her appearance and interests unlike those of a proper lady, Gemma heads to house party to win the heart of Lord Westfield, the man she's loved for years. But her plan is set off course by the tempting and intriguing, Richard Jonas.

A chance meeting creates a new path for Richard and Gemma to forage—but can two people, scorned and shunned by those they've loved from afar, let down their guards to find true happiness?

"RESCUED BY A LADY'S LOVE"
Book 3 in the "Lords of Honor" Series

Destitute and determined to finally be free of any man's shackles, Lily Benedict sets out to salvage her honor. With no choice but to commit a crime that will save her from her past, she enters the home of the recluse, Derek Winters, the new Duke of Blackthorne. But entering the "Beast of Blackthorne's" lair proves more threatening than she ever imagined.

With half a face and a mangled leg, Derek—once rugged and charming—only exists within the confines of his home. Shunned by society, Derek is leery of the hauntingly beautiful Lily Benedict. As time passes, she slips past his defenses, reminding him how to live again. But when Lily's sordid past comes back, threatening her life, it's up to Derek to find the strength to become the hero he once was. Can they overcome the darkness of their sins to find a life of love and redemption?

CAPTIVATED BY A LADY'S CHARM
Book 2 in the "Lords of Honor" Series

In need of a wife…
Christian Villiers, the Marquess of St. Cyr, despises the role he's been cast into as fortune hunter but requires the funds to keep his marquisate solvent. Yet, the sins of his past cloud his future, preventing him from seeing beyond his fateful actions at the Battle of Toulouse. For he knows inevitably it will catch up with him, and everyone will remember his actions on the battlefield that cost so many so much—particularly his best friend.

In want of a husband…

Lady Prudence Tidemore's life is plagued by familial scandals, which makes her own marital prospects rather grim. Surely there is one gentleman of the ton who can look past her family and see just her and all she has to offer?

When Prudence runs into Christian on a London street, the charming, roguish gentleman immediately captures her attention. But then a chance meeting becomes a waltz, and now…

A Perfect Match…

All she must do is convince Christian to forget the cold requirements he has for his future marchioness. But the demons in his past prevent him from turning himself over to love. One thing is certain—Prudence wants the marquess and is determined to have him in her life, now and forever. It's just a matter of convincing Christian he wants the same.

SEDUCED BY A LADY'S HEART
Book 1 in the "Lords of Honor" Series

You met Lieutenant Lucien Jones in "Forever Betrothed, Never the Bride" when he was a broken soldier returned from fighting Boney's forces. This is his story of triumph and happily-ever-after!

~★~

Lieutenant Lucien Jones, son of a viscount, returned from war, to find his wife and child dead. Blaming his father for the commission that sent him off to fight Boney's forces, he was content to languish at London Hospital… until offered employment on the Marquess of Drake's staff. Through his position, Lucien found purpose in life and is content to keep his past buried.

Lady Eloise Yardley has loved Lucien since they were children. Having long ago given up on the dream of him, she married another. Years later, she is a young, lonely widow who does not fit in with the ton. When Lucien's family enlists her aid to reunite father and son, she leaps at the opportunity to not only aid her former friend, but to also escape London.

Lucien doesn't know what scheme Eloise has concocted, but

knowing her as he does, when she pays a visit to his employer, he knows she's up to something. The last thing he wants is the temptation that this new, older, mature Eloise presents; a tantalizing reminder of happier times and peace.

Yet Eloise is determined to win Lucien's love once and for all… if only Lucien can set aside the pain of his past and risk all on a lady's heart.

ONLY FOR THEIR LOVE
Book 3 in the "The Theodosia Sword" Series

Miss Carol Cresswall bore witness to her parents' loveless union and is determined to avoid that same miserable fate. Her mother has altogether different plans—plans that include a match between Carol and Lord Gregory Renshaw. Despite his wealth and power, Carol has no interest in marrying a pompous man who goes out of his way to ignore her. Now, with their families coming together for the Christmastide season it's her mother's last-ditch effort to get them together. And Carol plans to avoid Gregory at all costs.

Lord Gregory Renshaw has no intentions of falling prey to his mother's schemes to marry him off to a proper debutante she's picked out. Over the years, he has carefully sidestepped all endeavors to be matched with any of the grasping ladies.

But a sudden Christmastide Scandal has the potential show Carol and Gregory that they've spent years running from the one thing they've always needed.

ONLY FOR HER HONOR
Book 2 in the "The Theodosia Sword" Series

A wounded soldier:

When Captain Lucas Rayne returned from fighting Boney's forces, he was a shell of a man. A recluse who doesn't leave his family's estate, he's content to shut himself away. Until he meets Eve...

A woman alone in the world:

Eve Ormond spent most of her life following the drum alongside her late father. When his shameful actions bring death and pain to English soldiers, Eve is forced back to England, an outcast. With no family or marital prospects she needs employment and finds it in Captain Lucas Rayne's home. A man whose life was ruined by her father, Eve has no place inside his household. With few options available, however, Eve takes the post. What she never anticipates is how with their every meeting, this honorable, hurting soldier slips inside her heart.

The Secrets Between Them:

The more time Lucas spends with Eve, he remembers what it is to be alive and he lets the walls protecting his heart down. When the secrets between them come to light will their love be enough? Or are they two destined for heartbreak?

ONLY FOR HIS LADY
Book 1 in the "The Theodosia Sword" Series

A curse. A sword. And the thief who stole her heart.

The Rayne family is trapped in a rut of bad luck. And now, it's up to Lady Theodosia Rayne to steal back the Theodosia sword, a gladius that was pilfered by the rival, loathed Renshaw family. Hopefully, recovering the stolen sword will break the cycle and reverse her family's fate.

Damian Renshaw, the Duke of Devlin, is feared by all—all, that is, except Lady Theodosia, the brazen spitfire who enters his home and wrestles an ancient relic from his wall. Intrigued by the vivacious woman, Devlin has no intentions of relinquishing the sword to her.

As Theodosia and Damian battle for ownership, passion ignites. Now, they are torn between their age-old feud and the fire that burns between them. Can two forbidden lovers find a way to make amends before their families' war tears them apart?

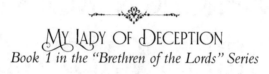

MY LADY OF DECEPTION
Book 1 in the "Brethren of the Lords" Series

This dark, sweeping Regency novel was previously only offered as part of the limited edition box sets: "From the Ballroom and Beyond", "Romancing the Rogue", and "Dark Deceptions". Now, available for the first time on its own, exclusively through Amazon is "My Lady of Deception".

Everybody has a secret. Some are more dangerous than others.

For Georgina Wilcox, only child of the notorious traitor known as "The Fox", there are too many secrets to count. However, after her interference results in great tragedy, she resolves to never help another… until she meets Adam Markham.

Lord Adam Markham is captured by The Fox. Imprisoned, Adam loses everything he holds dear. As his days in captivity grow, he finds himself fascinated by the young maid, Georgina, who cares for him.

When the carefully crafted lies she's built between them begin to crumble, Georgina realizes she will do anything to prove her love and loyalty to Adam—even it means at the expense of her own life.

NON-FICTION WORKS BY
CHRISTI CALDWELL

Uninterrupted Joy: Memoir: My Journey through Infertility, Pregnancy, and Special Needs

The following journey was never intended for publication. It was written from a mother, to her unborn child. The words detailed her struggle through infertility and the joy of finally being pregnant. A stunning revelation at her son's birth opened a world of both fear and discovery. This is the story of one mother's love and hope and…her quest for uninterrupted joy.

BIOGRAPHY

Christi Caldwell is the bestselling author of historical romance novels set in the Regency era. Christi blames Judith McNaught's "Whitney, My Love," for luring her into the world of historical romance. While sitting in her graduate school apartment at the University of Connecticut, Christi decided to set aside her notes and try her hand at writing romance. She believes the most perfect heroes and heroines have imperfections and rather enjoys tormenting them before crafting a well-deserved happily ever after!

When Christi isn't writing the stories of flawed heroes and heroines, she can be found in her Southern Connecticut home chasing around her eight-year-old son, and caring for twin princesses-in-training!

Visit *www.christicaldwellauthor.com* to learn more about what Christi is working on, or join her on Facebook at Christi Caldwell Author, and Twitter *@ChristiCaldwell*

CPSIA information can be obtained
at www.ICGtesting.com
Printed in the USA
LVHW012316040119
602857LV00008B/54/P